SUPER-DETECTIVE

JIM ANTHONY

THE COMPLETE SERIES

VOL. 3

SUPER-DETECTIVE
JIM ANTHONY
THE COMPLETE SERIES

VOL. 3

WRITTEN BY
VICTOR ROUSSEAU

ILLUSTRATIONS BY
JOSEPH SZOKOLI

ALTUS PRESS
2016

EDITED AND DESIGNED BY
Matthew Moring

ASSOCIATE EDITOR
Ray Riethmeier

PUBLISHING HISTORY
"Murder Syndicate" originally appeared in the April 1941 issue of *Super-Detective* (Volume 2, Number 1). Copyright © 1941 by Trojan Publishing Corporation.
"The Horrible Marionettes" originally appeared in the June 1941 issue of *Super-Detective* (Volume 2, Number 2). Copyright © 1941 by Trojan Publishing Corporation.
"Border Napoleon" originally appeared in the August 1941 issue of *Super-Detective* (Volume 2, Number 3). Copyright © 1941 by Trojan Publishing Corporation.

THANKS TO
Sheila Vanderbeek

Visit *altuspress.com* for more books like this.
Printed in the United States of America.

TABLE OF
CONTENTS

EPISODE VII

MURDER
SYNDICATE

A HUGE GAMBLING RING GOES IN FOR FIXING SPORTS...
AND FOR MURDER. IN MIXING WITH KILLERS, JIM
ANTHONY FINDS HIMSELF ON A SPOT—AND SO DO
SOME ASTONISHED CROOKS! THE MURDERED PRIZE-
FIGHTER, THE MISSING GANGSTER'S SWEETHEART,
AND THE RUTHLESSNESS OF HIS ENEMIES, ARE
CAUSE ENOUGH FOR JIM TO DECLARE WAR!

THE MAN WHO CALLED himself Anthony James—Tony, to his newly made friends—turned his head lazily and looked at the clock. It was half after five. He was sprawled flat on his back on a cheap daybed by windows that looked out on busy West End Avenue, near Seventy-fourth. His room—or apartment, as it was seriously named by Mrs. Zimmerman, who was janitress as well as rental agent—was designated as the Third Floor Front, and consisted of one room, quite large, and what had once, when the building was a private residence, been a sizeable closet. Now the closet sheltered a sink, a pantry, and a gas plate.

He arose then and stretched like a great cat, muscles tautening, bare feet gripping the floor, hands clasping at the back of his neck while a mighty chest expanded miraculously. He slipped a pair of unpressed, nondescript trousers over his yellow swimming trunks, lugged on a pair of wool socks and brown brogues with badly worn crepe soles. A moment later with a hastily donned blue shirt open at the throat, he stood before the cheap mirror of his dresser.

His skin was tanned, yet possessed that healthy athlete's glow for which a great many brokers would have traded a block of good stock. His hair was heavy and black, with a wave that usually angered him because of its stubbornness. His jaw, while hardly jutting, was wide, his chin firm, and his eyes black and bold, rather like those of a forest animal than of a man.

He grinned at his reflection, shook a handful of what appeared to be ordinary powder into his hands, then applied it to his firm cheeks. Immediately they took on a yellowish, sallow color, which he extended well down onto his neck. He buttoned the collar of the cheap blue shirt, tied a fifty cent tie in place and, using a small hand-mirror, noted that his sallow complexion went well below the collar level. From a trouser pocket he took a piece of sponge rubber, which fitted nicely beneath his upper lip, causing that lip to jut slightly, which in turn gave the jaw a sagging appearance because his mouth was constantly open. From another pocket came a small piece of copper wire, with a tiny suction disc attached to each end. This, too, went into his

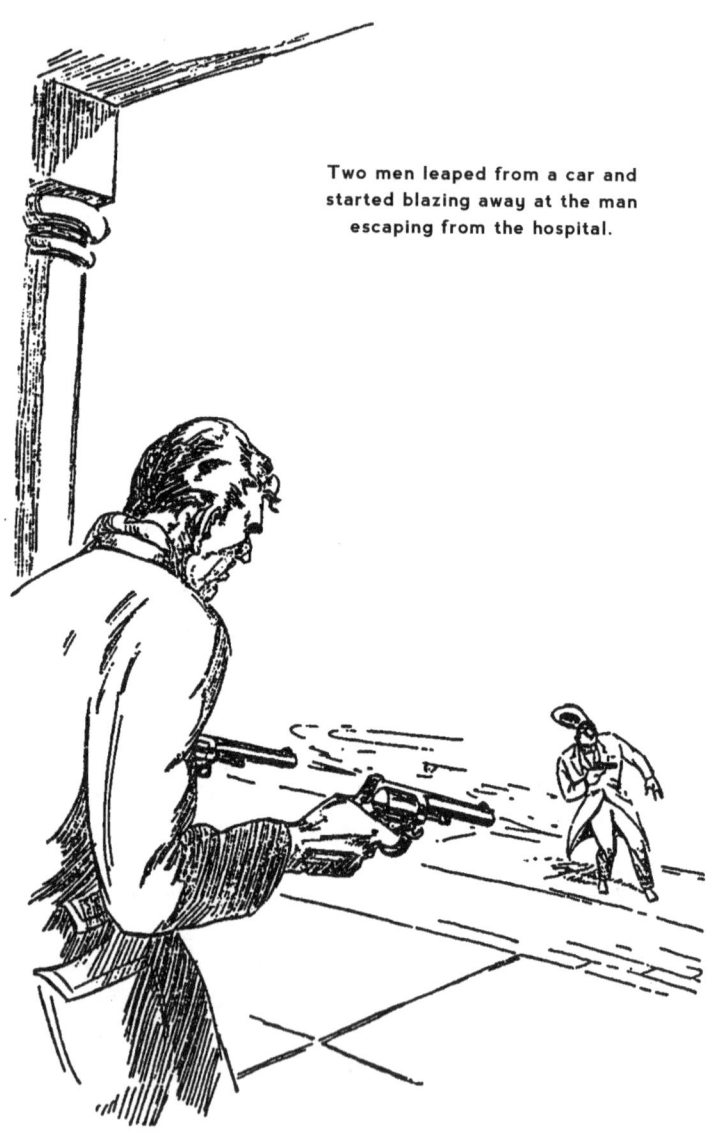

Two men leaped from a car and started blazing away at the man escaping from the hospital.

mouth, one cup attached to the inner surface of each cheek, the wire passing out of sight beneath his tongue. He muttered a few words and had to fight down the laughter that would have dislodged the gadget, for it caused both his cheeks to appear sunken—and the wire beneath his tongue not only altered his normal speech but gave the added artistry of a tongue-tied effect!

He slipped his arms into a coat that did not match the trousers, then sat down in a chair and pulled one pants leg high. From the coat pocket he took a piece of aluminum, with straps attached, which was in the shape of a wide mouthed V. Strapped to his leg, when he dropped his trousers and walked to the closet for his overcoat—a Walk-A-Flight-And-Save-Ten-Dollars model—his limp was more than pronounced; it was pitiful.

Now, with the exception of his broadbrimmed hat, his cane, and his glasses, Anthony James was ready for the street. The cane seemed an ordinary, stout stick, such as any crippled man might use. The glasses seemed of clear glass, but some trick of grinding made his eyes appear small, almost beady, as if viewed through the wrong end of a telescope.

AT THE HALL door he paused, and looked back searchingly to see if he was leaving anything which might cause questioning. For Tony James knew that twice, Mr. Zimmerman, who had taken a violent dislike to him, had searched his room. A man with ordinary powers of observation might not even have discovered the search at all. Mr. Tony James' powers of observation were very acute, indeed. And the fact that small, wizened Mr. Zimmerman had conducted such a scientific search proved to Tony James that the janitress' husband was not exactly what he pretended to be—an out-of-work longshoreman.

There was nothing on the long kitchen table against the far wall that might prove revelatory. Merely a few test tubes, a retort, a few bottles of various chemicals, some pieces of ordinary chemical apparatus. This was natural, for three weeks before, when Tony James had taken the room on West End, he had told the sympathetic Mrs. Zimmerman that he was a chemical engineer, crippled in an accident, living on a pension, and indulging in chemistry only for a hobby. The books lying about were ordinary books, nothing too heavy, the dishes in the sink, he thought, were a fine touch.

He closed the door and went out into the hall, limped to the head of the steps will his heavy cane doing yeoman duty. Going down the steps he remembered to breathe hard through his nose, as though exercise of any kind taxed his strength.

At the base of the final flight of steps, someone whispered in a scared, stricken voice, "Oh, Mr. James!"

He turned slowly, looking down the hall toward the rear. A woman stood before the closed door of First Floor Rear. Tony James had seen her before, and even in the faint light it was evident that she was a very comely young woman. Her hair was the color of high grade anthracite; she had eyes to match, though her skin was ivory rather than olive. Now she placed a forefinger to her red mouth, made a sssshhhhing sound and beckoned.

Tony James, walking with his shoulders well forward to conceal the depth of his chest, limped slowly toward her, his cane making scarcely any sound on the hall carpet. Even then his nostrils were twitching with the pungence of the scent she was using, and he noted that she was wearing an old and faded wrapper, meant strictly for the privacy of a dressing room.

She whispered, "Oh, Mr. James, I came out in the hall to see if I had any mail and my door blew shut! Will you see if your key works my lock?" He muttered something, fumbling in his pocket, and her fingers grasped his arm warmly. "Mrs. Zimmerman caught me in the hall like this and told me she'd make me move if I did it again, said she was running a respectable house!" She made a moue with her lips, flirted her head meaningfully. "Here, Mr. James, let me try, you're so nervous!"

He fell the touch of her warm fingers as she reached for the key, and started back nervously. The key clattered to the floor. She stooped quickly, with a breathless giggle, arose, put the key in the lock and twisted. The door swung wide. He stood peering into the intimacy of a woman's littered room. A pair of silk stockings hung on a hanger by the window. A bottle, a bowl of cracked ice, a siphon and a pair of glasses sat in plain view on the dresser.

"Oh, Mr. James, I can't tell you what a blessing this is! Won't you come in and have a drink to our luck?" She was inside now, holding the door open for him, smiling redly.

"Sorry," mumbled Mr. Tony James, "I have a very important appointment." He sounded exactly as a tongue-tied man would sound. He even extended his hand. She shrugged, laid the key in his palm, and he muttered, "Some other time, maybe."

He was only six or seven feet away when the door slammed viciously behind him. His grin almost tore the vacuum cups from his cheeks, and he caught himself barely in time, for the door of First Floor North opened and Mrs. Zimmerman's flushed face emerged. She peered at the front door, turned, saw Anthony James limping toward her. She brushed a lock of mouse colored hair from her face, smudging perspiration and soot on her forehead simultaneously. She smiled, stepped into the hall, all two hundred pounds of her.

"And good evening to you, Mr. James, out for your evening stroll, I see? I thought I heard the front door slamming!"

HE NODDED, SMILING politely, spoke as best he could in answer to her affable greeting. Over her ample shoulder he saw the suspicious eyes and leather-like face of Frank Zimmerman, her husband, pipe in one hand, newspaper in the other. He paused only a moment before going on out the front door and down the steps onto West End Avenue. He was grinning a bit wryly to himself, was Tony James, for his alert eyes had not failed to note the curtain at the window, slightly drawn back, so those suspicious eyes of Zimmerman could continue to follow him. He walked slowly, limping perceptibly, handling his cane with a shaking hand, and making his way into the hurrying traffic of the wide avenue, hoped he was giving a satisfactory performance.

Within the house, Mrs. Zimmerman was saying, "What you've got against that poor unfortunate young fellow is more than I can see, Frank Zimmerman. A fine man I say, always a day or two ahead of his rent day, which is more than I can say for some around here."

"And where does he get his money, I ask you?" growled Mr. Zimmerman. "Is it right he should lay on his back and mess around with those smelly chemicals all day? He'll blow us all up, mark my word!" He cleared his throat, hawking, hacking, looking around at his feet. Mrs. Zimmerman glared, bristled, he swallowed a bit hastily. "Nice young man, say you! I say we can't be too careful. You know what the papers say about the Fifth Column, and you'll admit he sounds like a foreigner!"

"His throat and tongue was hurt, poor lad!" snapped Mrs. Zimmerman. "He told me all about it. 'Twas an accident in a chemical plant!"

"Oh, Mr. James," she exclaimed. "I forgot
my key. Could you help me?

"Like a woman to believe what she wants to believe! Over three weeks he's been here, with no mail, no telephone calls, no visitors! Once a day he goes out of the house for an hour or so in the evening! Like he was hiding from someone!" The little man tried to look sly, knowing. He snapped his fingers. "And I, for one, wouldn't be at all surprised if that ain't it! He's hiding out in the Third Floor Front, hiding from someone or something!"

AS A MATTER of fact, Mr. Zimmerman was more nearly correct than even he believed in his suspicious little soul. For the man who called himself Anthony James, and spent some twenty-two of every twenty-four hours in the Third Floor Front, was, in reality, hiding from something. Jim Anthony was hiding from himself, hiding from his friends, hiding from his responsibilities as one of the world's most famous scientists, athletes and criminologists.

Here in this great metropolis there was a million dollar hotel named after him, a million dollar airport similarly designated. He was the owner of an immense metropolitan newspaper, and his other responsibilities were too numerous to mention. Being the son of a Comanche Indian princess and a world famous Irish adventurer and millionaire, he had inherited characteristics that made him a strange man indeed, a man who could never be entirely understood even by the most intimate of his friends.

Some three weeks ago, for example, he had found himself surly, tired, bored with his surroundings and his acquaintances. This had happened many times before, as usually is the case with mental workers who become engrossed in their tasks for months on end without real recreation. Often before, he had gone on an exploring trip, traveled to some little known part of the world. Or, if it had been a scientific study that had resulted in ennui and boredom, that burned out feeling, he had dropped it and switched with all his marvelous intensity to some athletic sport in which he had not previously engaged. On several occasions he had simply walked into police headquarters in New York, or FBI headquarters in Washington and volunteered his services for a period.

On this particular occasion, however, the circumstances were a bit different. He knew he had the finest and most loyal set of followers possible, including a beautiful fiancée, Dolores Colquitt. Yet on awakening, one morning, he found himself hating to see any of them! Boredom, but a different sort of boredom from any he had ever experienced before!

That morning, lying on his back on his own hard bed, he realized that his circle was too small, that there was one section of life which he really had never completely explored—the upper-lower class, as he called it. Consequently he had told Tom Gentry, his pal; Dolores; Mephito, his grandfather; and Dawkins, his valet, that he was flying alone to Mexico for a few weeks, absolutely incognito.

Instead of Mexico—he was on West End Avenue, as Anthony James. He used the disguise so that no one who had seen his picture so many times in papers and magazines, could possibly recognize him. Here, in the Zimmerman house, built over into apartments like a gigantic hive, he came to know the type of people in whom he was interested. The Zimmermans themselves; the black-headed girl, Miss

Martin; Colbert, who lived behind him and resembled a petty gangster; and all the others. And he enjoyed it immensely. His chemicals
were for his own amusement, and to further his established identity.
But had Jim Anthony but known it, he was mixing a strange concoc-
tion in his test tube of life! One of the strangest and most violent of
his career.

CHAPTER II

SPY-BRANDED

JAMES ANTHONY LIMPED SLOWLY along the short
block from West End to Broadway enjoying every step of it. The
fat and white aproned owner of the delicatessen store raised a plump
hand in greeting to that "Mr. James" who was such a good customer.
The Chinese laundryman, in his basement place of business, looked
up from his ironing board in time to see the heavy cane and the
limping legs go by his window. He reached behind him, snatched
something, trotted to his door and up the three steps that led to the
sidewalk.

"Hiiiiii, Mista James!"

Jim Anthony paused, peered into the moon-like countenance of
the oriental. "I findie handklerchef allee same belong you!" And as
Jim pocketed the cheap white handkerchief and thanked the laundryman, he was thinking of the beautiful honesty and friendship of the
gesture.

The Italian shoemaker waved, the clerk in the haberdashery nodded
and grinned. Across the street the doorman of an ornate apartment,
towering high above Seventy-fourth, chatted with a Western Union
messenger boy, while the pushcart delivery of a nearby grocery came
out of the alley with a fat negro pushing it. Life, decided Jim Anthony,
was very worth living, was very interesting and enervating among
these people who heretofore had been strangers to him.

At Broadway he peered south toward the subway station at Seventy-second, two short blocks away. While the street was teeming
with people, Jim decided the time had not yet arrived for which he
waited each evening. He liked to stand before the drugstore at Seventy-second, from around six o'clock in the evening until, perhaps,
seven, watching the subway vomit its masses of humanity to the street

Going down the steps
he knew they were
watching him closely.

surface, where they scuttled away like so many ants for home and fireside, or, at least, the privacy of their own four walls.

Now he entered the Federal Cigar Store on the corner of Seventy-fourth, and laboriously ordered a malted milk from the man behind the soda fountain.

The Federal Cigar Store had fascinated him for three weeks. The clerks were not the usual type that clerked behind cigar counters. There was a polished hardness about them that seemed out of place.

The store was well stocked with smoker's items, yet these hard clerks waited upon the customers silently, did not seem to care whether sales were large or small, and exhibited only the wares the customer asked for.

It was as if cigar selling and soda fountain business were not their real purpose in life at all.

The place was always busy. The flat box-newsstand outside was cluttered with all the metropolitan papers and punctuated with gaudy tipsheets, each proclaiming yesterday's successes. The Daily Racing Form however, was sold inside, with reverent hands.

Three phone booths, constantly in use, were against the rear wall. Next to them, in the corner itself, a blank door opened on Jim knew not what. Obviously there was a stock room of some sort back there, for clerks often disappeared to emerge with cartons of cigarettes or boxes of cigars.

But there was a constant flux of well dressed men going in and coming out, at practically any hour of the day, walking through the street door of the store, nodding at the clerks and heading directly for that mysterious room.

Jim drank his malted milk slowly, and decided a bookmaker must be holding forth in the rear of the store. Now the fat, well dressed man whom he knew to be boss of Federal came out of that rear room and walked to the cash register. Jim watched him with interest in the mirror. The fat man—whom he had heard called Dicey—always looked the same, as if he had just stepped out of a barber shop. His head was bald on top, his hair grey at the temples. His brows were shaggy over close-set and deep-set eyes, his nose fat and bulbous, covered with a tiny tracery of red and blue veins. Oddly enough, he was practically lipless, his mouth appearing as a slot through which gleamed a hint of gold teeth when he smiled, which was seldom.

DICEY RAISED THE cover of the cash register, lit a match and peered at the figure, grunting. He lowered the lid, locked the register, put the key in his pocket and came out from behind the counter to stand looking out at the busy street. Jim paid for his malted milk, hobbled toward the door, the sharp *ting* of the register following him. With his hand on the knob, he paused, for Mr. Frank Zimmerman scurried around the corner and hurried toward the subway kiosk. Grinning, Jim opened the door. The beady eyes of Dicey watched him through the glass as he picked up a tabloid, laid down a coin and made change meticulously. He turned and headed toward Seventy-second himself, breasting the surging crowd of homecomers like a swimmer fighting the current.

Jim stood before the chain drugstore at Seventy-second for a half hour, feeling at peace with the world as he watched this strange assortment of humans that came out of the subway shelter. The lights shone through the glass doors with yellow ferocity, and suddenly out of the shadows stepped Mr. Zimmerman, to peer impatiently at the steps leading to the subway. Jim was interested. Zimmerman was evidently waiting for someone and waiting impatiently. And almost immediately that someone appeared. It was Colbert, who lived directly behind Anthony James.

Colbert, Jim had decided long ago, was a character well worth study. He was one of those young-old men, whose body and features said he was in his late twenties but whose eyes were ageless. Those eyes were flat and black, and when Colbert watched anyone, be turned his whole body toward him; he seemed to have a stiff neck. He dressed well, conservatively, spoke but little, scarcely moving his lips. He never smiled. Somewhere, Jim knew, he had seen the man before; where, he could not say. There was merely that vague sense of having encountered him—or his picture—some time ago.

They came across the street now, toward the drugstore, the light shining on their features all the way. Jim Anthony's hearing was phenomenal; he could detect sounds the ordinary ear could never perceive, but in the rush and babble of traffic it was impossible. So he fell back on lip reading, at which he was also expert.

Zimmerman said, "I don't know a damned thing, I tell you, Colbert, but that's what the phone message said."

Colbert scarcely moved his lips; it was hard to get the import of what he said. "Repeat it, repeat it, the message I mean!"

"It was a woman's voice, and she said to tell you to watch your step because there was a spy planted right in the house. And I'll bet you I know who the guy is. It's that cripple, that guy with the glasses that hangs around all day in his room!"

Then they had passed Jim, where he stood in a shadowy doorway, leaving him grinning. What, he wondered, could that mean—that

Colbert should watch his step because there was a spy in the house? Why should anyone spy on Colbert? Jim had the curiosity of a monkey, as far as people were concerned, so when the two men turned into the bar halfway up the block he waited until they were at the bar, then limped in behind them. Passing them he saw Zimmerman nudge Colbert, saw Colbert stiffen, but Jim went on, far down the bar and slid laboriously up on a stool. There he ordered a small beer, took out his tabloid and shook it open, practically turning his back on Zimmerman and Colbert.

But, beneath his paper, set in such a way as to catch reflections in the bar mirror, was a tiny hand mirror, into which Jim could see. Also, it was fairly quiet in the bar, he could actually hear a few details of the conversation, and the rest he improvised with his mirror system.

Colbert said, "I don't know who the hell it could be that called. You sure they asked for me and left the message with you?"

Zimmerman nodded. He was peering in the mirror at Jim, his eyes truculent. "Sure. Colly, I don't like that guy, that James. What's he doing in here? I tell you, he's a phoney of some sort!"

Colbert shrugged.

Zimmerman whined, "Well, I don't like it. If the Big Boy finds out you're here and I've been holding you, hell won't be a foot away! I—"

"Shut up. When the Big Boy finds out anything it'll be too late. Come on!"

THEY WENT OUT the front door, Jim digesting the information he had garnered. Big Boy? The only Big Boy Jim knew of was Big Boy Moroni, successor to Dutch Schultz and the other once-big racketeers. Why would Big Boy Moroni raise hell about Colbert?

Jim arose, limped toward the door. At the curb Colbert was getting into a cab, Zimmerman had disappeared. Jim shifted his gaze and started for Seventy-fourth slowly, conscious that Colbert's dead eyes were peering through the back window of the cab at him. He raised his hand slowly as if to adjust his hat. Saw, in the mirror in his palm, that the cab wheeled into traffic, rolled slowly to Seventy-second and turned right. And the cab was distinctive, it bore a red top, evidently belonged to a private owner.

What was Jim's surprise, before he got to the corner of Seventy-fourth, to see that same cab wheel back into Broadway, to see Colbert alight and swagger into the Federal Cigar Store! Now why had Colbert taken a cab for that short distance? It was obvious that he wanted

someone in the cigar store to think he had come by cab rather than by subway, and because the cab awaited, the engine running, he knew Colbert desired, within all probability that whoever he saw should believe he lived elsewhere than a mere block away! Consequently, Jim, to whom it was a bit of a game, hailed the next cab around the corner, pulled to the curb and waited.

Now Colbert came out of the cigar store, accompanied by Dicey, the fat boss. Colbert was still thumbing through a thick sheaf of bills, and Dicey was saying, "It's too damned dangerous, Colly! The Big Boy will put the heat on me sure as hell!"

Colbert tucked the money into an inside pocket, stared at the fat man. "If you're more afraid of the Big Boy than me, the thing to do is turn me in."

Dicey shuddered. "You know I wouldn't do that. I'm just saying that you put me in the middle. I catch it if I do, I catch it if I don't!"

All the while Jim pretended
to read he was watching
them in his mirror.

Frank Zimmerman came out of the cigar store, to stand peering down at the papers on the newsstand. Conversation died, although he did not speak to Colbert. It was as though he did not want Dicey to know he was a friend of Colbert's.

Colbert said, "Be seeing you, Dicey, and don't do anything foolish!" He reached for a paper, and Dicey intercepted. He shoved Zimmerman aside, picked up a *Herald-Tribune*, folded it, and handed it to Colbert, who thrust it into his topcoat pocket, raised a hand in greeting and went to his cab.

Dicey watched him enter with set face, only his lips betraying him. The things he called Colbert were not nice. The red-topped cab pulled south on Broadway, and Jim's driver, prodded into action, followed. For some twenty minutes the red top cab seemed to scurry here and there like a water bug on a pond surface, and Jim, in his cab, knew Colbert was aware of being tailed, that he was trying to throw off his pursuer. Consequently he discontinued the chase, and had his cab head back for the West End address.

Traffic was bad, the driver was leisurely on the return trip; consequently it was a half hour before they reached Seventy-fourth, where Jim paid his driver and stepped out of the cab. Mr. Frank Zimmerman was standing beside the steps that led to the front door, the dark entrance of the garden apartment behind him. He swaggered out, cut

Jim off from the steps, and said, "There's a guy to see you, fellow, that way!" He pushed Jim toward the darker garden apartment entrance.

The man who was wailing was Colbert.

JIM ANTHONY HAD the strange, inherited ability to see in the dark, like a cat. He saw the hard, rocklike face of Colbert, saw the mean, intense look in his eyes, and also saw the pair of gleaming knucks on his gloved right hand.

"Look, guy," said Colbert, through the slot that was his mouth, "what's the idea of tailing me? From the sub to the bar to the cigar store and after that?" And, when it was evident that the man he knew as Tony James was not going to answer, he said, "Zimmy!" The word was a command. Zimmerman's hand shot forward, hit the center of Jim Anthony's back. He meant to shove him toward Colbert, who was already cocking his brass-knuckled fist.

Strangely enough the supposed cripple's back was as sturdy as a steel beam! His left arm shot backward; the elbow almost tore Zimmerman's head from his shoulders, sent him backward across the sidewalk to land on his shoulders and slide into the gutter—directly in the path of an oncoming car. The brakes screamed, the driver spun the wheels to the left, and was immediately crashed by a passing taxi, which in turn was hit from behind by a beer truck.

All this happened in seconds. Colbert could not stop his swing, but the knuckles swished harmlessly through the air, a good two feet from Jim's jaw, and the heavy cane cracked down sharply on Colbert's right wrist. Colbert stepped quickly backward, fumbled at his left-hand pocket. A piece of gleaming steel flew from the end of the cane; its rapier point came to rest but inches from Colbert's throat.

Police whistles were blowing now, pedestrians had helped Zimmerman to his feet; he was coming toward the dark scene. "Easy, easy," cautioned Jim, in his tongue-tied tones, I'll run you through!"

Colbert's hand came away; his brass knuckles had disappeared. Flatly, levelly, he said, "If you're here in an hour, stooly, I'll kill you!"

Jim Anthony laughed in his face. A cop arrived on the run. "What's happening here?"

Shaking with rage, Zimmerman pointed at Jim, snarled, "He hit me with his cane and damned near killed me! He—!"

Colbert, from the shadows, said, "I saw it all, officer. This poor cripple stumbled down the steps. That's all. He accidentally ran into this little fellow here."

And that was the way it stood when the cars straightened out and the crowd dispersed. Slowly Tony James entered the hall of the makeshift apartment house. There was Miss Lora Martin, fully dressed now, and seven or eight others, jabbering together. And Colbert seemed glancing over the mail on the table. As Tony James entered, he turned, muttered, "An hour, mister, one hour!"

A moment later Jim stood before his own door, the key in the lock. He twisted again—and again—and yet the lock didn't work! He withdrew the key and peered at it. And suddenly his jaw set grimly! He had a mind like a camera. Though he had never consciously looked directly at the key that opened the door to his apartment, he was certain this was not it, certain that the shape was slightly different. Besides, there were several bright new scratches on the key in his hand, where it had pressed unsuccessfully against the pins of the lock.

Where did he get this key? Where? And he knew. He recalled Lora Martin, scantily clad, before her own door, with a song and dance story concerning how she was locked out. He remembered how, in taking his key, she had dropped it. It had been very cleverly done, simply necessary to have a key palmed in her hand, and to give it to him, retaining the one to his room. But why should she want to get into his apartment?

GOING BACK DOWN the stairs he passed Colbert on the second floor. Colbert looked straight ahead, without giving any indication that he saw his late antagonist. A moment later, after Jim had beaten on the door of First Floor Rear several times, Mrs. Zimmerman came out of her own apartment to tell him that Miss Martin had gone out. When told of Jim's predicament, she gave him a passkey, and shortly afterward he let himself into his temporary home.

It was the work of a moment to get down to solid comfort again. Now he stood, the well known Jim Anthony, before his mirror, removing the sallow makeup. He wore absolutely nothing except the yellow swimming trunks. Himself once more, he went over his room meticulously with fingerprint powders. Strangely enough, he did not find a single fingerprint small enough to be a woman's! And yet he was almost positive that his solution of the key mystery was correct. The dresser drawer did not bear prints, nor did any of the instruments on his kitchen table. What had the woman wanted in that room? Why had she pulled the key gag?

He shrugged, sank down in a chair and reached for a detective book he had been reading for relaxation. As he opened it, something dropped out. Curiously he picked it up, sat staring at a snapshot. On first glimpse he was positive he knew neither of the people pictured. They were standing ankle deep in sand, before a big rock, evidently at a bathing beach. The man wore trunks. His body was not large, but it was finely muscled. His face—where had he seen that face? He shrugged, allowed his eyes to sweep over the scantily clad woman around whom the man had his arm. And again the same thought persisted—where?

At last a bit of recognition came to him. The woman was a blonde, evidently. And she was like a younger, softer edition of Miss Martin, herself! But the man? He turned the snap over. A few words were written on the back. They were, "Dale Shapiro and Myrna Karnes, November, 1939."

Just that, and nothing more.

Why, then, had the picture been placed in his book? And by whom? Lora Martin, whom the woman in the snap so greatly resembled, had the key to Jim's apartment—but the Zimmermans also had a passkey. He snapped his fingers, held the picture closer to the light. In doing so the book fell from the arm of the chair. A newspaper clipping fluttered down beside it. It, too, had been hidden in the pages. Almost absently he reached over and picked up both clipping and book. His eyes were intent on the photo. And understanding was coming to him. He knew now why Colbert's face was wooden, why he scarcely moved it when he talked!

For Colbert was Dale Shapiro! To a trained mind and eye the fact was inescapable. Studying the bony structures of Shapiro's face and closing his eyes to reconstruct Colbert's features in his mind, he saw clearly how a clever doctor could have altered Shapiro so that he became Colbert.

But why? And why had someone sneaked into his apartment and put the picture and the clipping in his book, Jim Anthony's book—or rather, the book of Tony James? It didn't make sense. He picked up the clipping. His eye read—MORONI LIEUTENANT MACHINE… and that was as far as he got.

THE BLAST WAS terrific! All the plaster on his south wall came down in a sheet. Sections of lath flew across the room. The concussion itself knocked him out of his chair. Behind him he was conscious of falling glass. The lights flickered—and went out. The chandelier, torn from its roots, shattered in the middle of the room.

He got shakily to his feet, the great roaring persisting in his ears. He shook his head viciously to clear it, sniffed, saw through the shattered wall that the apartment next to him—that of Colbert—was filled with smoke, lighted with flames. He took a forward step and fell on his face. When the blast had flung him from his chair he had twisted an ankle painfully. It was long and precious seconds before he managed to get to the hall door, only to find it hanging by a hinge.

Somehow he got into Colbert's apartment, and, by the light of the flickering flames, he saw in the corner what had once been a man. He leaped toward him, beat out the tiny flames that were burning the man's vest, his shirt and his trousers. Although Jim Anthony was accustomed to death, having looked upon it many times in the course of his adventures, this dead man sickened him. For literally the entire forepart of his face, as well as most of his chest had been blown away.

He fought his way into the hall with the man in his arms, was dimly conscious that several of the other lodgers were watching, horrified. Laying the body down, he returned, for *the man was not Colbert at all.* This time, when he came back into the hall he bore the unconscious Colbert in his arms.

Someone gasped, "So the cripple did blow his brains out! Say—who is *this* guy?"

Straightening, Jim Anthony heard the sounds of fire sirens outside the house. And again the accusation came through the smoke filled hall. "It must have been James, that cripple! He said he'd get Colbert, said he'd blow him up! Let's get out of here! There's a madman and he's nekkid as a jaybird!"

CHAPTER III

THE TRAPPER TRAPPED

WITH THE RUSH OF footsteps down the stairs, Jim Anthony smiled grimly to himself realizing his predicament. The noise from below told him that already members of the Fire Department were rushing into the house, and his own eyes told him that the fire

The supposed cripple came suddenly to life...

would be a joke to these well equipped fighters. Colbert was safe; the dead man would not be further harmed. And Tony James, supposed cripple and semi-invalid, stood revealed as Jim Anthony! He imagined the newspapers, saw what a Roman Holiday they would have with such a screwy story. For Jim Anthony's success was such that it inspired intense jealousy, the opposition press would ride him high, wide and handsome.

And who would believe that the multi-millionaire, James Anthony, would be living at such an apartment house for no reason at all? Because of his past exploits in the field of criminology, public opinion would be certain he had taken the apartment merely to keep tabs on someone; that his clever disguise was for that purpose alone.

...hurled the man
behind him into the
car at the curb.

So Jim Anthony shrugged, still grinning, and limped into the bath at the very end of the hall. Seconds later he was crouching on the narrow sill of the window. He knew these old houses, knew they were originally built as homes by people who took pride in their estates, knew they were built to last. Consequently he was not afraid to do as he did. Crouching for a moment only, his body expanded like a released steel spring as he shot through space. His strong fingers grasped the gutter pipe that ran down the corner of the old brick house. And in no time at all he was in the back yard of the apartment house.

New York taxicab drivers are accustomed to anything. So the driver of the cab who opened the door for the near nude young fellow who came out of an alley, said nothing at all. He merely opened his door wide, backed into the opposite alley and turned around, in order to miss the firewagon in front of the apartment. Not too long afterward he waited in the alley behind the Waldorf-Anthony Hotel while his fare disappeared into the garage beneath the gigantic black and chromium structure. A moment later a uniformed attendant came out with a bill for the fare.

The driver grinned. "Who was the Tarzan, pal?"

"That?" said the attendant in surprise. "Don't you know, don't you ever read the papers? That's Jim Anthony, just back from Mexico."

The cabbie scratched his head. "By Golly," he returned, "my geography book is all messed up then, for I sure picked the guy up around Seventy-fourth." But after all, he'd been paid, and well tipped, so he drove off.

UP IN THE penthouse, atop the roof of the forty-four story structure, Jim Anthony was already in the needle shower, the stinging water playing over his body. Dawkins, his valet, hovered about, his thin face beaming, fairly bursting with questions. When Jim turned off the shower and stepped onto the bath mat, Dawkins chuckled, "That Mephito, sir! W'at a joke h'on 'im! H'all day 'e Tinkers h'over them fire-sticks making a bad smell and saying you would get h'in bad trouble today! And 'ere you are, back from Mexico, safe h'and sound!"

Jim grimaced. Mephito, his Indian grandfather, of indeterminable age, had at one time been an honored shaman in his tribe. He was the possessor of nine magic fire-sticks. When these sticks were laid out in the proper pattern, along with such potent things as dried frogskins, live crickets and perhaps the mildew scraped from a long-buried skull, many wonderful things, portents and omens, could be read in the resulting smoke. Mephito relied on his own magic, rather than on that of his grandson, which included electronic tubes, black light and the like. And to Dawkins, the terrible part was that the old Indian, ninety times out of a hundred, was right in his prognostications! Now he welcomed the chance to laugh at the old medicine man.

Jim was no sooner in the bedroom slipping into clothing laid out by Dawkins, than the door burst open and his pal Tom Gentry rushed in, beaming and shouting his joy at Jim's "return." He asked a dozen and one questions concerning Mexico, all of which Jim merely sidestepped.

Then, smiling, Jim said, "And what happened to you, Tom, did you speak out of turn? That's a fine black eye you have there!"

Tom grinned, probed the black and discolored flesh tenderly. "That," he said, "is one of the damnedest things that ever happened to me. Listen, Jim, you know I always had a screwy idea I could beat the football games. You know these cards you pick up at the drugstores and cigar stores, with a list of ten football games on them? You can bet anything from a quarter on up and pick as many winners as you like. Four winners pay so much odds, five more, and all that."

Jim nodded. They were simply the usual football pool tickets found during the season throughout the United States.

"Well, Saturday evening, I took my card into Lacey's to collect. I'd had a swell day, picked seven winners and had quite a bit of jack coming. What, you don't know Lacey's? It's that bar on Fourteenth Street that has a gambling room in the rear. The payoff starts when all the games are finally in, around seven, and I guess there were forty or fifty of us in the back room waiting. The door opens and in comes Lacey, pale as a sheet, and a guy right behind him with a gun in his ribs. Right behind them comes a pair of thugs with sawed off shotguns. So the guy with the revolver on Lacey made us all step up and turn in our cards to *him*."

"And what was Lacey doing?"

"Trembling and shaking! This guy takes these cards and tears them all to pieces. And he told us cards like that were never any good from then on, and never to deal with anyone whose cards didn't read Seven-Eleven-Pool! Then he said in the future Mr. Lacey would handle the right cards. And Lacey said he would like hell, which was a mistake, because the guy conked him with the gun!

"They went out then and one of them threw a glass through the mirror and the riot was on! Everybody fought everybody else, and when the cops came the guys with the guns had disappeared, of course. Funny, wasn't it?"

Something clicked in Jim Anthony's mind like the snapping of a camera shutter. "The man with the gun, Tom, what did he look like?"

"Look like? Oh, not too big and not too little. Tough, sort of frozen faced, never moved it when he talked at all. And I remember he had the blackest eyes I ever saw. Why—?"

"And the card you bought originally at Lacey's? What name was on it?"

"B&B Pool, of course, Jim. That's Big Boy Moroni, you know. He controls everything like that, all the sports betting, the numbers, and

The whole wall suddenly blew in with a mighty explosion.

God knows what in this town. But I don't see—?" His voice died away, for he saw that Jim wasn't listening.

JIM WAS REMEMBERING the conversation he had overheard between Dicey, of the Federal Cigar Store, and Colbert. Something about "Big Boy" and how Dicey was caught in the middle no matter which way he turned.

He snapped, "You, Dawkins, change to street clothes and go up to Seventy-fourth and Broadway. Go in the Federal Cigar Store and try to get into the back room there, where I think there's a bookie. Play drunk, flash some money, anything to get an in, and watch a fat man who manages it all the time. They call him Dicey. I want to know all about this fellow named Dicey, *all about him!*"

If Dawkins was surprised his face didn't show it; he was too accustomed to Jim's apparent vagaries which afterward turned out to have an important meaning!

Already Jim was on the phone. "Hello, Dolores?"

"Jim, darling! Back from Mexico!"

It took him a few minutes to pass the amenities with his fiancée, but at last he got his message over. She, too, might have been puzzled, but she was, of course, willing.

She said, "The house is at Seventy-fourth and West End, and there's recently been a small fire there. I'm to go up there, find out everything I can about a woman named Lora Martin. If possible I'm to get acquainted with her. I'm to bring her to you. Is that right?"

It was right.

Jim turned to Tom. "Now, Tom, people named Zimmerman run this same house of which I just spoke. The woman is a big fine Irish woman. The man is a little wizened guy who is supposed to be an out-of-work longshoreman. I want you to find out everything there is to know about Frank Zimmerman. Get going!"

"And what are you going to do?" For, to Tom's amazement, Jim was donning street clothes, which he hated. His preference were all for loose slacks, sweat shirts and huaraches and the like, which were loose and unbinding. Yet here he was donning a soft collared shirt, throwing a necktie into place.

"Me? The first thing I'm going to do is go down and see Gibbons." Gibbons was managing editor of the *New York Star*, Jim's newspaper. "He ought to have some information I want. After that I'll probably go to police headquarters. However, it'll only take me a couple of hours altogether, so if you need me call me here after that time."

Tom grabbed his hat and left the room.

SEVENTY-FOURTH AND BROADWAY was an excited corner. A mere block away, on West End Avenue, the unusual had transpired. Something that touched in one way or another every chiseler and petty gambler was being discussed by everyone in the Federal Cigar Store. A cab driver came in, bought a package of cigarettes, and continued through the store and into the back room. He stood there for a moment scanning the various race results penciled on the blackboards, along with quoted odds on football games, hockey games, and prizefights.

Someone asked him how things were. He laughed, said all right, and shortly announced that people were sure crazy! A request for proof and further information revealed the fact that not an hour before, he had picked up a guy wearing a pair of yellow swimming trunks, a guy that came out of an alley right there in Seventy-fourth, just the other side of West End Avenue. He'd thought, of course, the guy was a dope or drunk, or some other sort of screwball. But by damn, he'd hauled him down to the Waldorf-Anthony garage and come to find out the guy was Jim Anthony himself!

A harsh voice said, "Now wait! What was that?"

The cabbie turned. He said, "Hiya, Dicey. I was just telling the boys that—" And he repeated his amusing story, concluding with, "Reckon if you got enough dough you can do as many crazy things as you want to do!" But Dicey hadn't heard that, he had turned and departed, hastily.

Nor was he the only one who left. One man with a belted overcoat and a white hat slid out like a shadow and entered a phone booth. Another, enough like him to be his brother, waited until the first was down the street at the bar before using the phone.

For some reason, the information that Jim Anthony, the famous criminologist who relied on science as well as physical prowess in the breaking of crimes, had been in the neighborhood, created consternation.

AT FIFTEEN MINUTES before eight o'clock Jim Anthony rode the elevator down to the lobby of the finest hotel in the city. He had a pleasant nod and a smile for all the help. He was intercepted a half dozen times by handshakers and well wishers before he made the door. A reporter, grinning at his own nerve because he worked for a rival paper, buttonholed him and asked for a statement on the Mexican situation.

At last he made the sidewalk, only to be grabbed by a pair of gushing schoolgirls, who wanted autographs. No sooner had he rid himself of these than a man stepped forward, a package in his hand. He simpered, "Pal, I ain't got a piece of paper, will you sign this package for me?"

Jim's eyes looked from the overdressed little man to the box. Printed in black letters on the box were the words, "There's a gun in here and my finger's on the trigger. Walk straight to the cab on the corner and get in."

Jim grinned at the man, saw that his eyes were unnaturally bright, knew that he was all hopped up.

"Well," snapped the little man, "you gonna sign up or not?"

Jim nodded pleasantly, answered, "Of course, of course. Let's walk down where the light is better."

With the little man beside him they made for the corner, some fifty feet distant. The door of the cab flew open, Jim saw a stocky Italian with a gun in his hand. The Italian flashed white teeth, said, "Welcome to our city, pushover."

Jim Anthony's reactions were a throwback to his mother's people, when constant alertness was the price of life itself. The moment the door swung wide, he sensed, rather than saw, that the gunman behind him relaxed. Evidently his part of the job was to get Jim Anthony into the cab, where the Italian was to take over. There was the tenth part of a second when neither gunman was really on his toes, and in that tenth part of a second, Jim Anthony acted.

His splendidly coordinated body accomplished two things simultaneously. He dove toward the Italian, and diving, kicked upward at the little man with the boxed gun. His hands closed on the Italian's gun, swept it upward against the man's jaw in a single motion. The Italian collapsed. Behind him, the boxed gun flew through the air for some six feet, hit the sidewalk and went off! The little man who had carried it turned and ran like a startled hare through the theatre crowds.

Jim snapped to the driver, "Easy, buddy, I'll do the talking!"

ALREADY THE POLICEMAN from the corner was coming on the run, fumbling at his buttoned holster. He roared, "What's going on here, what's—oh, it's you, Mr. Anthony!"

Jim grinned, "Sure is. My friend and I started to drive away when some fellow tried to stick us up, right here on Broadway." He chuckled, and the copper grinned at the ridiculousness of anyone even trying to stick up Jim Anthony, let alone on Broadway. "I kicked the gun out of his hand and he beat it."

He was safe in saying this because he knew the gun had fallen from the box, and hoped when the cop picked it up that the box would be accorded the brief glimpse usually given trash.

"But your friend—?"

"He has a weak heart, officer. Guess the poor fellow fainted. Better go on to his home with him, I guess."

He gave a short description of the little dope-head, and shortly afterward the sullen and frightened driver pulled away from the curb. Jim said softly, "Now turn right and go down the alley to the Waldorf-Anthony garage, my fine feathered friend."

The man turned right. He chattered over his shoulder, "Lookit, Mr. Anthony, I didn't know what was going to happen! These guys hire me cab, I swear it, and when the little guy leaves, the Italian shows me the rod and says to keep me mout' shut. I swear it, I'm a married man, I am, with six kids, and when the torpedo snaps out of it he'll tell you the same thing."

Which, oddly enough, he did. Though he refused to say anything further, he simply demanded that Jim Anthony call the law and have him arrested. Jim knew the meaning of that. Knew the man had faith in his own organization, his own gang, to spring him out of jail in a very short time.

Consequently Jim took him up to the penthouse and turned him over to Mephito, his wooden faced grandfather.

"Mephito," he said to his Italian prisoner, "is a pure blooded Indian. He knows lots of ways to make a man talk. Have a good time, Mephito."

CHAPTER IV

MYSTERY GIRL

HE WAS A TALL man, Gibbons, Editor of *The Star*, colorless, apparently, but the best editor in New York. He peered through horn rimmed glasses that gave him the appearance of a startled owl, and said, "By God, Jim Anthony, you beat hell! Would you mind repeating that again?"

"Not at all," smiled Jim across the desk. "I asked you for the files from the morgue concerning one Dale Shapiro and said I wanted to talk to the sports editor. Why does that startle you?"

Gibbons shrugged. "You probably saw the edition that just hit the street." And, when Jim shook his head, "Then why the interest in Shapiro? You mean to say you didn't know someone tried to knock him off with a bomb a couple of hours ago? Wait just a minute, I'll have the man that covered the story come in and give it to you." He rang a buzzer, gave an office boy the instructions and a few moments later the sports editor, a reporter and a man from the newspaper morgue, were in the office. The man from the morgue left a bulky envelope and departed. The others stayed.

The sports editor, in answer to Jim's questions, made a wry face. "These football pools," he snarled, "and these football bets, are going to ruin a swell game." He went into details concerning the pool bets, much as Tom Gentry had explained earlier in the evening. "The odds are all bad, they pick close games which may result in a tie, and the bettor loses all ties. They hire experts, sports writers like me, I'm sorry to say, who really know football. Their bets are unbeatable, for they usually give and take points. For example Notre Dame against Army and seven points would have looked swell, and did, to a thousand bettors. But the experts know the Army always plays like fiends against Notre Dame. But that isn't the worst. A man gets to betting a quarter or a buck, maybe two bucks, and the first thing you know he's betting important money. Northwestern plays Minnesota and it isn't a sport, it's something with an aggregate million dollars riding on it, Mr. Anthony."

Jim nodded. "These pools here, these cards, I understand Big Boy Moroni controls them?"

"He controls—or tries to control—everything east of the Alleghanies. I understand he's been having a little trouble lately, however."

"You mean someone muscling in? Who?"

"Nobody seemed to know the guy, except he was plenty tough. He—"

"All right," snapped Jim. "Now you."

The reporter began, "You want to hear about this Dale Shapiro, eh? Well, he was living at a house up on Seventy-fourth Street and—"

"Wait," put in Gibbons, "why not start at the beginning. Jim, according to the police, Dale Shapiro was machine-gunned to death in

March of this year. Seems he pulled a *faux pas,* and fell in love with his boss' girl friend, name of Myrna Karnes."

JIM REMEMBERED THE glossy little snapshot that someone had put into his book, the picture which was inscribed on the back, "Dale Shapiro and Myrna Karnes."

"Big Boy Moroni, according to the inside story, caught them together and it was too bad. Shapiro and the woman disappeared. Along in April his body bobbed up in the river, or what was left of it. Evidently the wire that held him to a weight of some kind busted and the guy came up."

"But," crowed the reporter, "it wasn't Shapiro at all! Let me—"

"But the body of the woman, this Myrna Karnes, was never found?"

"Nope. Never was, Mr. Anthony. Now here's what happened. There's an explosion at Seventy-fourth and West End in a converted apartment a little after six o'clock. A copper sees the flames resulting and calls the fire department. They get to the third floor and find two guys laying out in the hall. One of them is dead as hell, and they find afterward his name was Hymie Swartz, a dime a dozen gunman that was visiting the second guy. The landlady and her husband say this second guy—who's unconscious and maybe has a skull fracture—is named Colbert. But on account of Hymie having been killed in his room, the coppers fingerprint this monkey while he's still unconscious, and find out—what?" He paused triumphantly. "That he's Dale Shapiro with the damnedest face-lifting job you ever saw!"

Jim nodded. "Where is he now?"

"Medical and Surgery Hospital under police guard. But that ain't all!"

Jim smiled, "Go ahead."

"It's sort of mixed up, sounds like an Oppenheim novel, Mr. Anthony. It seems there was a crippled guy living in the front apartment on the third floor. A fellow named Zimmerman, that runs the house, says he was always suspicious of this cripple, on account of there was something phoney about him—"

Jim winced, grinned inwardly. And he'd thought his disguise was perfect!

"And Zimmerman says this cripple kept tailing Colbert-Shapiro all the time. So around six, just before they came in the house, Colbert-Shapiro jumped the guy, the cripple I mean!"

"And what happened?"

His body shot out like a
steel spring into space.

"The cripple threatened to blow his brains out. And by God he must have done it. For the folks on the same floor tell an odd story. When the smoke cleared away there was a nearly naked man coming out of Colbert-Shapiro's apartment with the guy, Shapiro, in his arms! And what do you suppose the cops found in the naked guy's apartment?"

Jim knew! He knew too damned well!

"They found a little brace attachment to tie behind a knee to create a limp. The guy wasn't crippled at all. And some other gadgets for disguise as well! Not only that but the cripple, or the fake cripple, was a chemist, he had apparatus and chemicals in his room, so that's where he made his bomb!"

"I don't get it," said Jim. "Why would he do that? Who was he?"

As Jim entered the cab, his foot shot back into his attacker's belly.

"Fellow named Tony James, but that's probably a phoney. I told you, Mr. Anthony, that according to Zimmerman, he spent a lot of time following Shapiro, and was always nosing around. Well, sir, in his apartment they found a snapshot of Shapiro and this girl, Myrna Karnes, with their names written across the back."

"Proving what?"

"That this James knew Shapiro in spite of his face-lifting! This Karnes girl came from a good upstate family, and she's never been seen or heard from. You can see what Shapiro probably did—he knew his number was up because he'd stolen the babe from Big Boy Moroni. So he gets a guy about his own size, dresses him up in his clothes, gives him identification and shoots hell out of him, wiring a weight to him and tossing him in the river. As a matter of fact, two witnesses saw Shapiro come out of his apartment and get the dose of lead from a parked car. Everybody thought it was odd then that the killers ran and got the body and tossed it in the car. Now we know why. But the Karnes girl never reappeared like Shapiro did tonight. This James must be connected with the Karnes family someway, he probably learned that Shapiro was Colbert and has been trailing him to find out something about the Karnes babe."

Jim nodded slowly, turned to the sports editor. "I think you'll find that Shapiro-Colbert was the man trying to muscle in on Big Boy Moroni's sports betting. About this James, I don't know. He—"

The reporter broke in, "He left prints all over his apartment. Like I say, James wasn't his real name, but if his prints are identified here or at Washington the police will soon find out something."

Jim grinned. His prints, he knew, were hardly on file anywhere.

The sports editor arose, snapped, "I wish to God it had been Moroni that got bombed instead of Shapiro and that screwy Swartz."

"Why?"

The sports editor shrugged. "I can't prove this, or I'd have printed it long ago. But Mr. Anthony, there's a sport gambling ring operating nationwide today. Fixed races, fixed fights, fixed games of all kinds! Any man can be bought, through reward or fear, you know, and that's what Big Boy is doing! And is he cleaning up! Well, if that's all—I have some work to do!"

Jim, too, arose. "So have I," he smiled, and thanked the other man. He would no longer need the envelope from the morgue that contained the clippings of the career of Dale Shapiro. Anthony was a sportsman, however, and the big editor's words created a feeling of revulsion within him.

The reporter shook hands, said, "Well, I'm going to follow the Shapiro story up, Mister Anthony. There may be some of it we can't print, but if you want any details, I'll have them. I got a hunch the police will find out the killer is fairly well known."

"The killer?"

"Sure, the guy that bombed Shapiro and killed Swartz; the fake cripple. Yeah, those boom-boom boys are all pretty well known, and the cops will hang this one high as a Christmas goose."

SO JIM BADE his own adieus and started out. He was passing the switchboard in the outer office when the girl looked up and saw him. "Just a minute, please," she said, "he's just leaving now." And, to Jim, "Mr. Anthony, there's a party for you. Will you take it in the booth?"

Jim nodded. Inside the booth he said, "James Anthony speaking."

A hoarse voice chuckled, "They said at the hotel you were there. Listen, James Anthony, or should I say Anthony James, are your prints on file anywhere?"

"Why?" Jim grasped the implications, naturally.

"Because if you don't want me to tell the coppers that the guy that bombed the Swartz laddy and Dale Shapiro now lives in a penthouse on top of the Waldorf-Anthony Hotel, you better listen close to me!"

No, his prints naturally were not on file. But should the police come to him, tipped off by this unknown informant, and take his prints, they'd check! Certainly it was ridiculous, but the very fact that Jim Anthony, under an assumed name and disguised, had stayed three weeks at that address would look bad.

"I'm listening. How much do you want?" He opened the door of the booth, gestured toward the switchboard. The girl stared for a moment, then understood and went to work.

"To begin with," growled the hoarse one, "about five grand will be enough. Can you get it tonight?"

"Not tonight," lied Jim, who could have raised a hundred times the amount in two hours time. "I can make it first thing tomorrow."

"All right, do it. Get it up to your hotel and have it ready. And you know what'll happen if you call copper?" The phone clicked.

Jim rushed from the booth. The girl shrugged expressively. "A pay station at Gray's."

IN A CAB headed for the M&S Hospital, Jim Anthony turned the thing over and over in his mind. It was clear that Shapiro, with his features altered, had returned to New York to muscle in on his former boss, Moroni. Yet he hadn't been recognized until his finger-prints were taken, and consequently how would Moroni have located Colbert in order to wipe him out? And if it were a gang killing, it would hardly be a bomb murder! Machine guns, or sawed off shotguns, perhaps. And where did Miss Lora Martin fit in? Where had he seen her before? And why had she obtained the key to his room, or apartment, and put a newspaper clipping and a picture in his detective novel?

"Mr. Anthony, will you help me open this package?"

Likewise, whose was the hoarse voice on the phone that wanted five grand for a beginning? He grinned, thinking he knew the answer to that one easily because of the smallness of the amount, and by the process of easy elimination.

Well, he'd soon find out a few things, he'd get them from this fellow Colbert or Shapiro. Either that or the police would already know all that Shapiro knew, and would willingly pass it on to Jim Anthony. And then there was his gang, all out working: Dawkins on an errand, and Dolores and Tom Gentry. And even Mephito doing a chore! That Eyetalian!

THEY HEARD THE shooting and the yelling while still two blocks from the M&S Hospital. Although his driver speeded up, a prowl car was at the hospital first and two policemen were leaning over a dead man on the curb. Another man with a bad wound in his chest was gasping out his life beneath an elm tree.

A copper rose from beside the dead man, mentioned a name, said, "One of Big Boy Moroni's torpedoes." Another policeman said, "So's this one beneath the tree! Looks like Moroni sent a few of the boys to watch the hospital and when Shapiro came out shooting, they got in the way and got bumped!"

Jim snapped, "Shapiro came out shooting? You mean—?"

A policeman said, "What's it to—oh, Mr. Anthony. Yeah, you know Dale Shapiro was here in the hospital? Well, a dame that said she was his sister came to see him. She brought him a couple of rods. He slugged the cop on duty and came out here and knocked off these boys, Moroni's boys, who evidently were sent by Big Boy to guard him—or maybe get him! And then Shapiro and the dame disappeared!"

"What did the woman look like?"

"They say she was swell looking, hair black as hell and black eyes, and very white skin. She dropped her purse and there was a letter in it. Here's the letter—the envelope, I mean. There wasn't no letter."

Jim took it from the policeman's hand. It bore a West End Avenue address. And the name written across it was, "Miss Lora Martin."

Now why, he mused, had the First Floor Rear risked her life to get a cold killer like Dale Shapiro out of the hospital?

CHAPTER V

BRAIN WAVES

BACK IN THE PENTHOUSE atop the Waldorf-Anthony Hotel, the squat Italian who had been kept prisoner by Mephito flashed a gold-toothed grin at Jim Anthony. "Chum," he said, "you ain't kiddin' nobody. There's no way in the world you can get any information out of me. I was told to do a job, and it went wrong, so what? Somebody else will do it. You lost your chance to turn me over to the cops. This here now is plain kidnaping!"

Jim returned the grin. As a matter of fact the man was right. Jim could hardly call in the police now. This Italian would simply deny the story, and the scared cabbie would probably claim to have seen and heard nothing. But, this part of the puzzle didn't fit in at all. Who would want to knock off Jim Anthony—and for what?

He said, "Maybe you're right. But you might be able to save yourself a bit of punching around by telling me where you and your hop-head friend were to take me." He took off his coat and started rolling up his sleeves.

"Gee, chum, you're killing me! Maybe another guy would punch me around a bit, but not Jim Anthony. I know all about you. As long as I wouldn't put my hands up to defend myself, you wouldn't take a sock at me at all. So, you might as well just let me go, because I ain't gonna tell you a thing. I will say this—me an' my friend wasn't to harm you none!"

Jim rolled his sleeves down again. The man was right. He, Jim Anthony, didn't have it in him to use third degree methods. But Jim had a plan.

He moved across the room to a liquor cabinet, his broad back cutting off the Italian's view. When he turned he had a drink in each hand. He shrugged, grinned wryly. "Let's have a drink on it, pal. I'm afraid you're way ahead of me." A hairy hand took one of the glasses, the liquor was thrown back into the gold toothed mouth, a pair of thick lips smacked.

"Now you're being a smart boy. As far as where me an' my friend was to take you—don't worry about that. You'll end up there soon enough, buddie. Do I go now?"

"Not till I come back. Help yourself to the liquor, I'll be about ten minutes. Come on, Mephito."

The old Indian grunted, pulled his red blanket over his stooped shoulders, and padded after his grandson. Jim locked the door behind them. Mephito said, "You fixem drink, me see."

Jim nodded. "Yep, Mephito. I did. In ten minutes time he'll be asleep. Maybe I'll find out something then, when his subconscious begins to function. Keep an eye on him and when he drops off, let me know." He turned and walked swiftly down the hall to his laboratory, while Mephito turned back into the room next to the one in which the Italian was already beginning to feel drowsy, like a well fed cat.

ONCE IN THE laboratory Jim swung his safe wide and spent some ten minutes picking out an assortment of bills to suit his purposes. When they totaled five thousand dollars, Jim closed the safe, took the bills across the room to a work table which bore a bunch of flasks. From several of these flasks he mixed an odd and evil smelling mixture in a test tube, and was painting the surfaces of the many bills with a camels hair brush dipped in the tube when Dawkins came back.

At the clearing of his valet's throat, Jim glanced over his shoulder. His eyes grew wide, very carefully he laid the camels hair brush on a porcelain tile, and began to roar with laughter. Dawkins shifted from one foot to the other, reddening slowly, a self conscious grin appearing on his Cockney face.

At last he managed to break in on Jim's laughter. "H'excuse h'it, sir, but you said the place was a bit of a bookie joint, and h'I thought to dress the part!"

He was carrying a shiny black derby in his right hand, and on the small finger of that same hand he wore a diamond as big as a small pea. His suit was the loudest plaid that Jim had ever seen and another diamond of similar size winked and blinked from the shrieking cravat tied neatly into the low collar of the striped shirt.

"Dawkins, I'll swear I don't know what I'd do without you, my lad! You certainly dressed the part! But what did you find out about this man Dicey?"

Dawkins came to the bench, raised his brows in surprise as Jim picked up the brush and went back to work. "Just a bit of preparation for an acquaintance of mine," said Jim. "Go along, tell me what you learned. But what's this?"

For Dawkins had laid a thick sheaf of bills at Jim's elbow. The little Cockney's thin chest swelled, he couldn't keep elation out of his voice. "Why, sir, you said h'it was a bookmaker's place so h'I h'extracted a bit of money for h'expenses from the fund." The fund was the money usually left around the penthouse for miscellaneous use of all the group. "H'It does seem h'I 'ad a bit of luck, sir, with the cards, so 'ere is 'alf the winnings!"

"Keep them," laughed Jim. "Now tell me about the place and about the man."

DAWKINS' ACCOUNT DIDN'T take long. He'd had no trouble whatsoever in entering the back room of the Federal Cigar Store. Indeed, it seemed to be quite open, for anyone who wished to enter—and bet. The place accepted horse bets, the walls being covered with quoted odds at all tracks, as well as bets on prizefights, football games, hockey games, and sports of a dozen different kinds. The card tables, according to Dawkins, were in a side room that opened into the main room, so that players could glance at the result boards as they whiled away their time with cards.

There had been five players in the poker game where Dawkins had won, and playing the part of an Englishman recently arrived, Dawkins had had little trouble eliciting the information he desired. Dicey's last name was Decker, and according to Dawkins' informants, Dicey was, indeed, quite a big gambler. He wasn't, of course, as big as Big Boy Moroni, but as a matter of fact was one of Moroni's lieutenants. Dicey

"How she slipped into the hospital and gave him that gun I don't know!"

owned four Federal Cigar Stores and two or three bars, all of which were gambling fronts.

Jim began to get some idea of the thoroughness of this gambling ring's organization when Dawkins, among the others, mentioned Lacey's as belonging to Dicey. For it was at Lacey's that Dale Shapiro, old Frozen Face, had started the riot in which Tom Gentry obtained his marks of battle.

Dicey wasn't exactly a gangster, according to the poker players. He was too brainy for that. Gambler, yes, and lieutenant to Big Boy Moroni in the gambling rackets, but hardly noted as a rough and tough boy.

"It didn't take you long," observed Jim.

Dawkins shrugged. "They closed the place h'early, sir. H'everybody was h'attending the fight." He mentioned the names of the two topnotch fighters who were even then meeting in Madison Square Garden, and Jim nodded, being a sports follower himself. "So h'I came on 'ome."

Mephito grunted, "Sleeps like baby."

So, Jim Anthony took the bills he had prepared and stacked them carefully, clutching each by its very edge only. Around them he snapped a rubber band, and returned the package to the safe from whence it came. "Dawkins," he said, "there's a sleeping beauty in the east living room. I want you and Mephito to bring him in here and place him on the couch." When the valet and the old Indian departed, Jim hurried to prepare his apparatus for the coming of the sleeping beauty.

The Italian did not move when he was borne into the laboratory. Jim leaned over him for long seconds, even rolled back an eyelid and observed the naked eyeball to see if the man had taken too much of the drug he had prepared for him. All pointed to success, for Jim was a master of the use of that drug, the ordinary truth serum combined with an East Indian drug that dulled conscious senses and sharpened subconscious perceptions and reactions.

NOW HE FITTED what appeared to be a double set of earphones over the sleeper's head, the small receivers clamping on the temples. From this headset ran a pair of wires to a small box-like object which sat on the table some feet away. While it closely resembled a portable radio set, and the tubes were electronic, instead of an amplifier it contained special graph paper and a small stylus which left a jagged green line in its wake as it traveled across the paper, thus recording thought waves of the man or woman who wore the headset.

Jim flipped a switch. The stylus traveled across the graph neatly, leaving a green line which was almost straight. Jim nodded. The man was receptive, he was absolutely blank. Now Jim turned away from the receiver and went back to his subject. He leaned close to the man's big ear, spoke aloud. "Jim Anthony, Jim Anthony, Jim Anthony." Slowly and distinctly he formed the words. He saw the eyelids twitch, saw the lips tremble slightly, and risked a glance at the graph. The stylus was traveling rapidly up and down, leaving a choppy green wave-like stroke.

"Lora Martin—Lora Martin...." His voice droned on and on, for long minutes. Over and over he repeated his own name, the name of Tony James, Lora Martin, Dicey Decker, Big Boy Moroni, Dale Shapiro, Colbert, Myrna Karnes, Zimmerman, the names of all those concerned with the bombing at the West End address. For Jim had more than a hunch that in some way or other this attempt to snatch him had something to do with the previous affair.

Ten minutes passed, fifteen. The door opened and Tom Gentry entered, his errand presumably finished. Dawkins held up a hand for quiet, and Tom nodded, seeing what Jim was doing, though his blue eyes expressed much curiosity at sight of the unfamiliar Italian on the couch. He sat down on the edge of the table, leaned back a bit too far and an odd thing occurred. A small radio stood on that table, a radio of the pushbutton type. Inadvertently he leaned against it, and so intent were all on the scene before them that none overheard the buzzing that denoted the warming up of the set.

Suddenly an announcer's excited voice filled the room, "...one of the wildest scenes of pandemonium the Garden has ever known! Not only was Kid Bolo clearly outpointed through the first six rounds, but in the seventh a terrific right sent him to the canvas for the count of nine. It was a matter of time then! And time only! So thought twenty-three thousand cheering fans who are usually for the under-dog, and the knockout of Kid Bolo would most certainly have been an upset, for he entered the ring a seven-to-two favorite. Bolo weathered the seventh, somehow. Between the seventh and the eighth someone, evidently a friend, slipped up the steps to Bolo's corner and whispered a few words. The Filipino fighter came out for the eighth like a madman, and in the first fifteen seconds battered his opponent all over the ring, knocking him out after some thirty seconds of the eighth round. The fans went wild, for most of the money was on Kid Bolo. An odd thing happened then, Kid Bolo swayed in the middle of the ring, and tears poured down his face! He shouted something about the bell, the bell, crossed himself and dropped on his knees, evidently praying...."

All in the room had paused to listen. Then Tom cut the story off, grinning, "Had a few bucks riding on Kid Bolo myself at that seven to two business." And, as he saw Jim slipping the miniature headset from the Italian on the couch, "Who's your fat pal, Jim?"

"Just an acquaintance, Tom. He'll sleep a little while. Let's go in the other room." But before leaving he pulled from the brain wave machine that part of the graph which bore the green marks of the stylus, and tucked it in his pocket.

BACK IN THE library he sank down on a deep divan and stared at Tom. Tom grinned, "Oh, yeah, that, Zimmerman! Well, sir, Jimmy boy, I'm afraid I overplayed my hand!" Jim cocked an inquiring eyebrow. "Well, he had no police record, at least under that name, and nobody in the neighborhood knew much about him except he was always about half lit, so that was my cue. I purchased a fine bottle and called at the Zimmerman house in person." His freckled face broke into a smile. "I told them I was a private dick sort of nosing around. That Zimmerman is quite a guy. He knew all that had happened there just like he'd seen it. Guess that was on account of talking to so many newspapermen."

"And what did happen?" Jim, of course, knew what had happened; he was merely getting a report on what various newspapers might think.

"Well, seems like Shapiro regained consciousness at the hospital and told the cops that this little friend of his that got killed came up to see him. Shapiro said he got excited about the fight tonight that we just heard the tail end of, and snatched the paper off the table to show him something. Then something went boom—and that was that. You know what Zimmerman thinks?"

Naturally he didn't.

"Zimmy thinks this fake cripple was sore at Shapiro, for he threatened to blow his head off in the hall. So he takes a little nitro and sits it on the edge of the table in Shapiro's rooms where the slightest jar will knock it off, and luck was running against Swartz instead of against Shapiro."

Jim laughed, but his laughter died at Tom's further revelations.

"As a matter of fact cops found a pan in this fake cripple's room that evidently had been used to boil off some dynamite. That's a way to get nitro, you know, skim it off stewing dynamite, for it comes to the top."

"What?"

"That's right, they found this pan in the front apartment, in a cubbyhole of a kitchen, and a little nitro was still clinging around the edges. But to get on with Zimmerman. I got him about half high—he'd been drinking already—and he claimed he already knew before the cops what caused the explosion—nitro. You know how some guys like to show off their knowledge when they get to drinking—so he gets to telling me all about different explosives and the way they work, everything from Cordeau-Bickford to ammonia gelatine dynamites. But about then he took one more snort to kill the bottle, and laid over as nice as you please and went to sleep! His wife walked in about that time and gave me the dickens for passing her old man out so I had to scram."

Jim arose with a bound. "Another errand, Tom. Get down to police headquarters and find out about that pan used to boil dynamite. Find out about prints on it, see if they agree with the prints of this Tony James found on the test tubes and stuff in his apartment."

"Heck, Jim, that's waste of time. They'd have to agree, naturally." But nevertheless, Tom went, for already Jim had turned his back and was examining the graph from the brain wave machine in the laboratory.

FOR MANY WEARY months Jim had studied such brain graphs, classifying them as to type. From his short conversation with the Italian he had been able to type him, and from these long months of study and practice he knew the exact length of mind-syllables on the graph, and thus was able to read them slowly but precisely. There on the chart before him, then, he had the Italian gangster's subconscious reactions to each name that Jim had intoned into his ear.

As luck would have it, he learned right at the very start who sent the man! For in response to the name, Jim Anthony, the Italian's thought waves read, "Big Boy'll take my scalp, Big Boy'll be sore as hell!"

Big Boy Moroni! From the Italian's conscious admission his purpose had been to take Jim somewhere. That somewhere, then was to Big Boy Moroni. Why? What did the gambling czar want with Jim Anthony, and if he merely wanted to see him, why didn't he either call in person, or by phone, or at least make an appointment. Jim Anthony wasn't a hard man to see! It didn't make much sense.

He read on down the strip. The name Lora Martin evoked no response at all, the Italian went right on with his worrying. Nor did the name Tony James wangle any erratic waves, nor that of Zimmerman. But there was a definite response to Dicey Decker, Moroni himself, Shapiro and Myrna Karnes. And one other, which aroused Jim more than any of the others. The Italian's subconscious mind reacted to the name Colbert, the alias under which Dale Shapiro had been living at the West End address. Which, of course, meant that the Italian knew him, for the response definitely read, "That guy! That guy! Just wait!"

The Italian belonged to the gambling king's mob. Consequently Big Boy Moroni had known about him. Did it follow then that Big Boy had somehow planted the bomb that killed the man, Swartz, in Colbert's room? A gangster didn't usually bomb out a victim!

But what was this—"The dirty rat, crossing the boss, that's his yellow neck…." At the very end of the graph. And suddenly Jim knew. It was the sleeping man's reaction to the fight news that had come over the radio, the news of the comeback victory of Kid Bolo!

"The dirty rat—crossing the boss—that's his yellow neck…."

Jim Anthony's blood boiled. For that strange sense of his that was not in ordinary men, was working. That animal sense that makes the sleeping deer awaken and spring to its feet, conscious that the wolf is nigh, though neither eyes, ears or nose tells him of its presence.

CHAPTER VI

KID BOLO'S LAST FIGHT

IT WAS A LITTLE after ten o'clock when Jim Anthony picked up the phone and called his paper, the *New York Star*. He knew that the sports editor would return to write his story of the fight just witnessed and hoped to catch him. The Italian's subconscious reaction to the news that Kid Bolo had won, picking an apparently hopeless cause out of the fire, so to speak, fell right in line with several things concerning crooked fights and sporting events that he had learned earlier in the evening. The sports editor was there, as Jim had known he would be, and in answer to Jim's questions, spoke slowly, as if a bit puzzled.

"Yeah, this Kid Bold is good, Mr. Anthony, right in line for a shot at the title. He was a big favorite tonight, six or seven to two was laid all around. His opponent punched him around considerable during the early rounds, dropped him in the seventh and, well, I tell you, Mr. Anthony, a funny thing happened."

"Go on, go on."

"Kid Bolo was sprawled out there on his stool, a badly beaten Filipino, just ripe for slaughter, and everybody was looking down their noses on account of their money seemed sure up the spout. Where this guy came from I don't know. First there was just Bolo's second working over him, then this guy went up the steps and whispered something in—"

"What did he look like?"

"Look like? Why, now that you've mentioned it, I don't know. He'd evidently caught a bust in the nose, his face was all taped up like they do for a busted schnozola, you know. Anyway, he whispered something, and then I don't even know where he went, for the bell rang and Kid Bolo went charging out there like a madman! You know the rest, how he knocked his opponent kicking and all."

"That's not the part I'm interested in. What happened after the knockout?"

"That was funny, too. Kid Bolo ran around the ring peering at the spectators yelling something about 'de bell, de bell' and I'll swear his eyes were like those of a madman, Mr. Anthony. Then he dropped on his knees and began praying in Spanish, and his seconds had to carry him out—like he'd passed out himself."

Jim's thoughts were way ahead of the man on the other end of the phone. "Was there any possibility of that fight having been fixed?"

The answer was a few seconds in coming, and that puzzled note was again obvious in the sports writer's voice. "Mr. Anthony, I'm going to tell you something and you mustn't ask me for my sources. A good sports writer has as many stool pigeons as a detective, you know. I spoke to you earlier in the evening about crooked sporting events lately. Well, I've been making an investigation in my own manner. Kid Bolo went into that ring a big favorite. Yet two days before the fight, one of my stoolies passed me word *not* to bet on him. Do you follow me?"

"I think I do. According to your sources, Kid Bolo was supposed to lose this fight. Which he did, up until the eighth round, up until a man with a bandaged face whispered something in his ear." Even as he spoke Jim was putting two and two together. The sports editor's tip-off dovetailed nicely with the Italian's subconscious reaction to the radio news that Kid Bolo had won the fight. And the fact that the man who whispered in the fighter's ear had a bandaged face meant one thing to Jim—disguise, not the result of a broken nose! "And try to tell me again what the Filipino did after the knockout."

Painstakingly the sports writer repealed the information concerning "de bell," and Jim interrupted with, "Who managed or owned this Kid Bolo?"

"A guy named Decker, Dicey Decker, that owns a chain of cigar stores."

A moment later Jim was talking to a friend of his whose club and pool hall was in a neighborhood where many of New York's Filipino's, Spaniards and Mexicans had settled. And this man told Jim that the prizefighter, Kid Bolo, spoke no English!

HE HUNG UP the phone with a creased brow, deep in thought. That sense of impending danger, that warning which he couldn't explain, was still throbbing through his body. He glanced at the clock, wished Dolores would return from her mission of investigating the Martin girl.

Back and forth, back and forth he paced. And he couldn't get the prizefighter, Kid-Bolo, out of his mind. Managed by Dicey Decker, who was a crafty gambler himself, slated to lose, according to his sports editor's inside information, yet knocking his opponent out in the eighth and apparently going hysterical. None of it made sense.

And where did it tie in with the bombing at the West End address? Considering that the bomb undoubtedly had been meant for Shapiro, it did tie in. Shapiro was trying to muscle in on Big Boy Moroni's gambling and betting rackets, the crooked sports fix.

Dawkins came in, the phone in his hand. "A gentleman, sir, h'insisting h'on speaking personally." He plugged the phone in.

Jim said, "Yes, yes, Anthony speaking."

The voice had a curious timbre, neither high nor low, but particularly vibratory. "Mr. Anthony, I'm very sorry to bother you at this time, but it is important to both of us that I see you tonight. Suppose I

Suddenly she had been
grabbed, tape slapped
on her mouth.

drop by in half an hour." And, as an afterthought, "This is Rodolfo Moroni, though sometimes I am called Big Boy."

Again that thought persisted—why did Big Boy Moroni wish to get in touch with Jim Anthony?

Jim said, "Oh, yes, a friend of yours, one of your henchmen, I believe, told me the same thing. You make your appointments oddly, Mr. Moroni."

Moroni chuckled silkily. "I suppose you'd look at it that way. I made a mistake, but look at my end of it. Why should the great Jim Anthony come to see me willingly? I sent the boys to bring you," he laughed again, "and now of course I see my mistake. Apologies, and all that. I may call at your place then in half an hour?"

"Certainly not, Mr. Moroni!" Some of Moroni's suavity was unconsciously reflected in Jim's voice. "The original plan was for me to call on you. So if you'll tell me where to get in touch with you say at midnight—?"

They fenced for a moment, with Alphonse-Gaston politeness, and at last Big Boy Moroni gave Jim an address and assured him that he was looking forward to midnight. Jim could not resist adding, "And Mr. Moroni, on tonight's fight, did your plans work out?"

His answer was that same silky chuckle, and the polite remark that Mr. Moroni hardly knew what Mr. Anthony was speaking about. Nevertheless, Jim noted the tightening of that voice, slight though it was, as though its owner had unconsciously hardened his jaw in a flare of anger at mention of the fight. To Jim Anthony, this was practical confirmation of his theory of a fix, and the theory given to the sporting editor of *The Star* by his stoolie.

MINUTES WENT ON and on. He gave Mephito instructions to load the Italian with coffee and send him downstairs—to free him. He paced the floor worrying about Dolores, remembering that Lora Martin had gone to the M&S Hospital and freed Dale Shapiro in a welter of blood. Why didn't Dolores come on? Could she have inadvertently gotten mixed in that escape and subsequent killings?

Tom returned to report that the pot in which a stick of dynamite had been cooked was devoid of fingerprints. And though Jim grinned at the information, knowing well now that it had been deliberately planted in the kitchenette he had used as Tony James, it was immediately cast from his mind. That persistent alarm bell, that siren shriek of nerve warnings was working overtime!

Who was in danger? Dolores? As a usual thing she was amply able to take care of herself. Who, then? Why did his nerves stay taut, like stretched wires, why did that unnamable something inside him keep shrieking for action.

He grabbed the phone, got *The Star* and found that the Continental Picture Corporation had photographed the fight. Shortly, much to Tom's amazement, the two of them were in a cab headed for the Bronx, where that company had its office. And soon Jim found the thing he wanted.

As usual, the Anthony name was an open sesame, and the company officials working on the fight film were glad to run it for him in the projection room. The fight went off just as Jim had heard, with the Filipino getting much the worst of the first few rounds, getting knocked down for a count of nine in the seventh.

During the seventh Jim leaned forward and watched keenly, asked for a rerun of the round. When it was over, he was convinced of one thing—the Filipino boy actually had been knocked down. To Jim's practiced eye it appeared, however that for just the fraction of a second he had lowered his left, so that a mighty right hook exploded against his jaw.

So far, he thought, exactly as arranged. Kid Bolo is losing like a master. He stiffened in his seat. Just as his sports editor had said, it was impossible to tell where the man with the bandaged face came from. Kid Bolo was resting on his stool, his arms along the lower ropes, utterly relaxed. Then the man with the bandaged face was whispering in his ear.

The Filipino had tensed, his gloves had gripped the ropes furiously. The ten second whistle had blown then, and the seconds couldn't pull the stool from beneath the Filipino. He rolled his head and looked at the bandaged faced man and his eyes were wild and white. The mouthpiece fell from his lips, and just then the bell rang. A second picked the stool from the ring and literally pushed Kid Bolo toward his opponent.

JIM WATCHED EAGERLY. But the action of the camera wheeled about to follow the fighters in the ring and he was unable to see what happened to the man with the bandaged face. The action in the ring was brief and terrific. The Filipino boy made short work of his opponent. And dropping him, with the referee counting over him, Kid Bolo staggered and reeled along the ropes like a madman, literally frothing at the mouth, his eyes rolling and fear-stricken, his voice shrill and near hysteria! What were those words, those words that were reported to concern "de bell, de bell!"?

Jim Anthony got them where others had missed, for two reasons. First, his hearing was as acute as that of a beast that staved off destruction by the sharpness of its senses, and second, Jim Anthony was a linguist. He knew Bolo spoke no English, his ear was attuned for a Spanish meaning in those hysterical rantings, and his ear found it.

"Devuélvanmela! Devuélvanmela!"

He could see how others evolved the bell theory, for, excited as it was, and spoken with the Spanish twist that gives a *v* a slight *b* sound, the word sounded, "day-bwell-ban-may-la, day-bwell-ban-may-la!"

And the literal translation of the expression was, "Return her to me! Return her to me!" Jim was out of his seat like a shot, headed up the dark aisle, calling back his thanks, Tom following at his heels in mystification. Jim knew that hunch of his, that extra sense, hadn't failed him now! From the time earlier in the evening that the sports editor had spoken so bitterly of crooked fights, it had done double duty! The Italian's brain wave reaction to the result of the fight should have told him how to solve his inner warning. And in the cab, speeding back into Manhattan Jim cursed himself.

The picture was clear now. Kid Bolo had gone into the ring a favorite, with a great deal of money riding on him. But, under instructions from Big Boy Moroni, he had been prepared to take a dive, in order that the bookies might clean up. It was the old familiar setup, a masterful dive by a man who knew how to make it look good.

Only something had gone wrong. After the seventh round the man with the bandaged face had told the Filipino something that made him change his mind! Told him something to inspire him to knock out his opponent, to cross Big Boy Moroni! And Jim had an idea what it was—the Filipino's hysterical words after the fight gave it to him. "Return her to me! Return her to me!"

Who? Who? That was what Jim Anthony was on his way to learn.

THEY PULLED UP before a well lighted place that bore the name, "Spanish Club" on its half painted windows. This was the place where Jim had called not long before to find out whether Bolo spoke English or not. The proprietor was beside himself at the appearance of his friend, Jeem, as he called him.

The place was strangely empty, which was queer, considering that a Filipino had just won a great fight. Surely his countrymen should be celebrating! As it was, three heavy-set men, Americans, shot pool idly on the front table.

"Es odd," agreed the proprietor. "Always before, when Kid Bolo ween, he come here after, to celebrate. Tonight these men come instead, and they tell me to get reed of all my customers. Thees I do not understand, but I do."

Jim nodded. He thought he understood. These men were waiting for Kid Bolo! These men worked for the gambling ring, the ring which

Kid Bolo had doublecrossed, according to their own warped standards. Quickly he asked where Bolo lived, then, "And Bolo is married?"

"*Si, Señor* Jeem. For two weeks he has been married, like the turtle dove! And such a beautiful wife he has *muy bonita*, little Maria!"

But Jim was gone, Tom again galloping after him to keep up. "Return her to me, return her to me!" *Her*, then, was Maria, Kid Bolo's bride of two weeks! No wonder, thought Jim grimly, he'd been willing to doublecross double-crossers, so to speak! Someone had stolen his bride, and holding the kidnaping over Bolo's head, had forced his hand, had forced him to win the fight, rather than take a dive as had been arranged.

The house was a duplex, on a singularly dark street, with three black sedans parked in front of it. One half of the place was dark, the lower floor, but the lights of all windows in the second story were gleaming brightly. Tom and Jim started for the duplex. Two men were leaning in the shadows of the entrance.

Viewing the picture and listening to the speech, Jim discovered something no one else had noticed.

Someone growled, "Where do you think you're going, chum?"

Jim recognized the voice, chuckled, "My fine Italian friend! You get around don't you? Take the other one, Tom!"

Already the Italian was snatching at his pocket, but his hand never succeeded in withdrawing the gun as he had planned. Instead, fingers of steel clamped down on that wrist. He found himself somehow spun around, found his hand and arm pulled behind him, and forced up between his shoulder blades.

"One sound and I'll break it off," snapped Jim. "Up the stairs!" He peered back over his shoulder just in time to see a gun spin through the air and land at his own feet. He grinned. Tom Gentry had disarmed his man—there could be no doubt of the outcome now, for Tom had few peers as a rough and tumble fighter.

ONCE IN THE hallway he heard a thudding and bumping. Up they went, until the door of the upper hall stopped them. At a word from Jim the Italian opened that door. In a split second Jim took in the scene. Two plug uglies were beating the little Filipino, Kid Bolo, literally to a pulp, with knucks. He was crouching in a corner, his arms crossed over his head, and when the door was flung open, a terrific blow had just caught him in the unprotected ribs and bounced him off the wall.

Against the far wall, the ever present cigar between his lips, his derby hat covering the shiny baldness of his head, was Dicey Decker! Kid Bolo's manager! All action ceased with Jim's rushing entry. There was time enough for Jim to say, "Funny, beating up your own fighter because he won a fight!" Then he hurled the Italian across the room where he crashed into Dicey, and together the pair of them went down in a tangled welter of bodies.

One of the plug uglies roared an oath, rushed at Jim. And Jim met that rush feet first, in a wrestler's flying dropkick. His snapping heels caught the man full in the chest. The man catapulted back as if shot from a gun, crashed against the wall with a thud that shook the house. A window shattered from the shock. The second plug ugly hesitated, and was lost, for Jim grasped the wrist that was extended to fend him off, wheeled, threw the man over his shoulder in a flying mare that crashed him into Dicey Decker and the Italian with another house-shaking thud.

When Tom Gentry bounded into the room a few seconds later, the captured gun in his hand, he found four men unconscious on the floor, and Jim Anthony leaning over ministering to a fifth, who was the Filipino fighter, Kid Bolo. Kid Bolo was out, beaten to a pulp by the cruel knucks. Jim picked him up tenderly and laid him on the couch, which was the only piece of furniture intact in the whole room.

PRESENTLY DICEY DECKER, the Italian and the two plug uglies were glowering at Jim Anthony from near the door. Jim's eyes sparked with his anger; his voice was like the crack of a whip. "…and you, Decker, remember this. If anything further happens to Bolo, I'm holding you directly responsible! I'll cripple you for life!"

Dicey spoke around his cigar. "You're a pretty big man, Anthony, but I think you'll find you're bucking a bigger one!"

Jim started toward him; the four of them gave way. Jim's fingers found the lapels of Dicey's overcoat, he lifted the fat man off his feet. "I know who you mean, of course. And I'm meeting Moroni myself at midnight. You can tell him for me I hate crooked sports, and that's the reason I'm seeing him. And so you won't forget—!" Crack! The back of his hand across Dicey's cheek was like a gun firing. The cigar flew out of the fat lips, the derby hat sailed across the room. Jim set him down with a thud. For a moment it seemed that Dicey would leap at him.

Someone picked up Dicey's hat and handed it to him. He gained control of himself, wiped the hat on the sleeve of his coat. His right cheek was a brilliant red from Jim's slap, his eyes were venomous. He said, "Don't worry—I won't forget!"

His three henchmen shambled and shuffled after him from the room. When the door closed downstairs, Jim turned to Tom, who was leaning over the fighter.

Tom's face was pale with anger; his freckles appeared black rather than their customary brown. "Damn them," he grated, "they busted his jaw, and his nose, and the Lord knows how many ribs! We should have—" But Jim was gone, headed for the bath and wet towels.

He never made it. For hurrying down the hall he peered into the last bedroom and saw the woman. Not woman, for even though her features were twisted despairingly it was evident that she was young. Maria? She lay there on the bed, motionless, and the prints of vicious fingers, killer's fingers were apparent on her throat. Her tongue still protruded, her eyes were white and wide and staring, bulging from their sockets. Her torn clothing revealed bruises and scratches.

FOR LONG MOMENTS he stared down at her with pity that extended to the young fighter himself. Why the killing? Bolo had done as bidden, he had refused to take the dive and had knocked his man out instead. Why was Maria killed, then? And did Decker and his men know the girl was back here in this rear bedroom? Had they, perhaps, killed the girl when she attempted to aid her husband?

This was a job for the police. Yet Jim felt implicated himself, because these gambling rings were behind this thing; and because as Tony James, at the West End address, he was supposedly tied in with the rings. Grimly he took an envelope and a nail file from his pocket, and a moment later had scrapings from beneath the Filipino girl's nails. He tucked it away in his pocket, set his jaw grimly and went into the bathroom. He wanted a hot towel, and the water refused for a minute to heat. Once he thought he heard a singular thud above the roar of the open faucet, but as nothing followed, he went on about his business.

Towel in hand Jim trotted down the hall toward the wrecked living room. At the door he paused, thunderstruck. Tom Gentry lay sprawled on his face, unconscious. Kid Bolo was as he had been left. Except for the knife, the hilt of which stood upright, where it had been thrust into his heart. The hall door was open.

LOOK FOR THE WOMAN

A **S JIM WORKED FRANTICALLY** over Tom, bathing the huge lump behind his right ear, he tried to piece the thing out. Had one of Dicey's men slipped back and knocked Tom out, and knifed the unconscious Kid Bolo? That didn't make sense. They might beat him up, but why kill him? It was more likely that Dicey and his crew hadn't even been aware of the dead woman in the back bedroom. Either that or one of them had taken the wife into that room, and killed her in the fight that followed.

And there was a counter to that thought, too. Jim had touched the body of the dead woman. He knew she had been dead at least an hour. He and Tom had arrived when the beating of Bolo had been in progress but a few minutes, for the Filipino was still taking it, and no man could take such a beating for nearly an hour and remain conscious.

No, it was obvious that Dicey and his crew had preceded Jim but a few moments, that they had left some of their members to watch the Spanish Club, in case Bolo wasn't home, and come on over here.

Tom groaned and stirred uneasily. Back down the hall went Jim to rewet the towel. Had Bolo killed his own wife? Not in such a manner as this, surely, for it was evident that she had fought terrifically. Why, two of her nails had been broken in the struggle. Besides, all indications were that he loved her madly. Loved her enough to doublecross his own manager and the belting ring behind him, enough to win a fight he had been supposed to lose!

The kidnaper then? The man who had forced Bolo's hand in the ring, between the seventh and eighth rounds? Why would he kill the woman after he attained his end? Jim turned the water on the towel, allowed it to run hot. Back he went, but this time paused to peer into the middle bedroom. Behind the door he found three cigarette butts, crushed beneath a careful heel. Someone had stood behind that door! Someone had stood there waiting, waiting—the killer?

It was a little plainer now. Jim was able to reconstruct what had happened. The killer perhaps had been caught by Kid Bolo before he could leave the house. He had ducked into this room and waited his opportunity. Kid Bolo had seen his dead wife—perhaps he had fainted, perhaps he had dropped down beside her to moan over his lost love.

The door of that rear bedroom commanded the hall in such a way that it would be practically impossible for the killer to have gotten out without Bolo having seen him. And, Jim decided, the killer wouldn't want to meet the Filipino gone amok! So he had wailed, waited.

Then Dicey's men had come, hammered on the door. Kid Bolo must have gone to open the door, and the beating must have started immediately, after a few minutes of which, Tom and Jim had arrived.

He hurried back the way he had come, leaned over Tom again with the towel. Again Tom moaned, and gradually his eyes opened; he winced, touched the swollen place with probing fingers. "What happened? Did the ceiling fall? Did—?"

He saw Kid Bolo, still in death, and his words died away. Quickly Jim explained about Maria, in the rear bedroom.

"Those guys," swore Tom, "and we had them whipped and let them get away!"

"I don't think those guys—if you mean Dicey's gang—were responsible. I don't think they even knew Bolo's wife was in there dead." He explained about the man who had waited so patiently behind the door of the middle bedroom. Tom's eyes widened.

"Then you figure this killer waited there until you were in the bathroom. He took a chance and tiptoed out, smacked me down and killed Kid Bolo? Why kill Bolo?"

It required a few brief moments to explain the setup for the fight, all that Jim had learned concerning the double-double-cross.

"Let's say theoretically that the kidnaper didn't mean to kill the Kid's wife. But she's beautiful, perhaps he got carried away. Follow me?" Tom nodded, grimacing at the wave of pain that shot through his head. "Then he killed Bolo because Bolo knew who it was that had murdered his wife! Do you see? One killing to cover an—come on, get to your feet!"

For the sound of approaching sirens could be plainly heard.

SOMEHOW TOM GOT to his feet with Jim's assistance. "We're going out the back way," snapped Jim, "because I don't want to waste a lot of time explaining just what has happened to the police. Come on, we can't give them a killer—yet! And some of this will be pretty embarrassing if we're caught! Hurry!"

They went down the shaking and rickety back steps into a small areaway, and over the back fence into the alley. A few moments later they emerged on a dark cross street and started walking toward Broadway. Tom was swearing. "That killer, whoever he is, is a fine guy. He kills Maria, he kills Kid Bolo, and he calls copper, thinking they'd catch us there. Where are we going?"

"We want to get in touch with Dolores, if possible. Here's a drugstore. Let's call up."

But Dolores Colquitt hadn't called the Waldorf-Anthony, nor had she returned to her own Park Avenue Apartment. And again that extra sense, call it hunch if you will, began raging and burning and fighting inside Jim's brain and body.

"Tom," he said, "you're going back to the penthouse to wait for word from her. She may be in trouble, and if she is, she'll naturally try her best to get in touch with me there."

"What are you going to do?"

"I've got a call to make. I'm a little early but I'm making it now anyway. Beat it, Tom. I'm going to call on Big Boy Moroni at the Hudson House."

AS A STRUCTURE, the Hudson House was unimposing, but for some years, since reaching power, Big Boy Moroni had made it an important building. There dwelled the Big Boy himself, with all his satellites, all his hired men. His offices were on the third floor, his apartment on the fourth. The fifth and sixth were rented to travelers

Dicey stood calmly by while his men beat Kid Bolo with brass knucks.

to give the place a front, and the top floor was given over to various members of the gang. The second floor was the recreation room, with pool and billiard tables, a long bar and several card tables along the far wall.

Directly past the registration desk a flight of wide stairs led upward to this game room. Jim approached the desk, said to the flat faced clerk, "I want to see Moroni, he's expecting me."

The clerk did not alter his expression. He merely said, "I'm not at all sure Mr. Moroni is in, but I'll have someone look for him. The name, please?"

"Jim Anthony."

The clerk struck a gong beside the register, a nondescript bellboy came forward and was dispatched on his errand. But Jim's keen ear had also caught the faraway vibration of a buzzer, and consequently was not at all surprised when two hard looking men drifted down the steps and eyed him curiously. He leaned against the desk and studied his fingernails.

One of the obvious gunmen took a position not twenty feet away from him, in a chair, his hand bulging in the side pocket of his topcoat. The other drifted past Jim to lean against the cigar stand, from which place of vantage he watched Jim with beady, suspicious eyes. The Hudson House, Jim decided wryly, would be a bad spot to start anything out of the way.

The bellboy shambled back to speak softly to the clerk. The clerk said, "Mr. Moroni is pretty busy right now. He wants you to go up to four, to his apartment, and wait, says he won't be long. The boy'll show you up."

Jim nodded, started toward the elevator. Both gunmen followed him. The door swung closed, the car started creaking upward. At four Jim stepped out. The bellboy and the two gunmen followed. One of them carried an automatic, dangling at his side. He said, "Sorry, bud, but it's a house rule." Jim grinned, nodded, and the second gunman went over him with practiced fingers.

"Clean," he announced laconically, and stepped back. His confederate did a disappearing act with the automatic, nodded. The bellboy came out and led the way down the hall. A moment later, after the knock, Jim Anthony was admitted to Moroni's luxurious apartment by a colored butler.

THE PLACE SURPRISED Jim, it was so luxurious and yet in such good taste, altogether out of keeping with his preconception of Big Boy Moroni. The living room, where he sank into a spacious divan of soft cushions, was massive, with velvet hangings, authentic furniture and several good pictures.

The butler said, "Mr. Moroni will be here directly, sir. Will you refresh yourself with a drink?"

"No, thanks. However, if you don't mind, I'll listen to the radio. There should be a newscast in a few moments."

The butler nodded, walked to a walnut cabinet that resembled a huge sideboard or buffet more than a radio, and soon had the dials adjusted. The soft and modulated rhythms of a society dance band filled the room. "I believe we are a bit early for the news," said the butler respectfully, and left Jim alone.

Not until he was gone did Jim's eyes revert to the picture above the marble mantel. A casual glance had simply told him that here was something authentic, something well done, by one of the better modern portrait painters. But now he actually started. He knew that woman!

He arose, went to stand before it for long moments. He knew her, not personally, but from a small snapshot that had been thrust into a book belonging to Tony James. For it was undoubtedly Myrna Karnes.

He turned away from the picture then, thinking of what had been told him at the office of *The Star*, that Myrna Karnes had been the cause of dissension between Big Boy Moroni and his erstwhile lieutenant in crime, Dale Shapiro. How Shapiro had stolen his boss' girl, this beautiful Karnes woman, and consequently had been marked for death. How he had prearranged his own demise, with a victim whom no one knew, only to bob up again with his face rebuilt and start bucking his old boss.

A recessed niche, only partially covered by a velvet hanging, drew him. It was across the room. He drew aside the curtain curiously, saw that the niche was guarded from desecrating fingers by heavy plate glass. Behind the glass, the light was dim, but he could make out several objects; a miniature picture; a small bust; and what might have been a statuette of Diana, the Goddess of the Chase. He leaned forward to see better.

A soft, suave voice said, "The small switch at the right illuminates it, Mr. Anthony."

He knew who it was at once, for he had heard the voice on the phone not much more than an hour previously. And in spite of himself he flushed, felt like a schoolboy caught at the cookie jar or the jam pot. He held himself, forced himself to refrain from whirling toward that voice, reached out and touched the switch. The diffused light flooded the niche. He saw then that the miniature, on porcelain, was

also of the woman Myrna Karnes, as was the bust. There was a small silver slipper, also on the top shelf, and the statue which appeared to be Diana, with the chaste lines of her body unobscured, was in reality a statuette of—Myrna Karnes.

He turned then, said, "Very beautiful, Mr. Moroni."

Moroni nodded.

"Another move and I'll break it off!" snapped Jim.

THIS WAS THE first time Jim had ever actually seen the famous gambler and gang leader. Pictures of Moroni were rare, and many photographers had felt his wrath and power when trying to snatch a candid shot in night clubs, or at some of the various race tracks he frequented. Jim had known vaguely that the "Big Boy" appellation had been attached to him because of his smallness, knew that Moroni had once been a jockey; but the slightness of the man startled him.

He could hardly have topped five feet, and shoulders, head, hands and feet were in accordance with his height. His olive skin and liquid brown eyes were those of the Southern Italian. His teeth gleamed whitely when he smiled, his black hair was greying at the temples. He wore a well fitting dinner jacket.

"Won't you sit down, Mr. Anthony. Drink?" Jim sat down and shook his head.

The butler appeared and mixed his master a tall drink. He raised it politely at Jim, sipped daintily. Here, thought Jim, is a man of steel and sinew, utterly without conscience. A man who fought his way to power the hard way, who has faced murder charges three separate times, and yet who seems like a small, tired businessman.

Moroni said, "You know the woman—Miss Karnes?"

"Unfortunately, no."

Hardly were the words out of his mouth than Moroni's answer cut the air like a knife blade. "Then what was a snap of Myrna and Shapiro doing in the book you were reading at Seventy-fourth and West End?"

Jim smiled, and waited. There was nothing else to do.

Moroni snapped, "I don't understand why you were in such a place with your name twisted to Tony James. I don't understand why you made an attempt on Shapiro's life, and I don't particularly care. But I want to know what you know, all you know, about Myrna!"

Jim arose slowly. Anyone who knew him would have been aware of the danger signs, the narrowing of the eyes, the bulge of muscle in the jaws. "I came here," he said slowly, "because I find you can learn more about a man, sometimes, from his natural surroundings than from the man himself. However, I believe you are a bit too accustomed to demanding rather than asking. So I'll bid you good night."

The little man was on his feet immediately, his face flushed, uttering protests that he did not mean to become dictatorial, but that he was merely excited.

"Why?" demanded Jim. But he knew why.

"Because," said Moroni slowly, "for the past few months I've moved Heaven and earth trying to find her." Now he leaned forward in his chair with clenched fists, glaring at Jim as if daring him to grin. "Tough and hard they call me, Anthony, a relentless killer, a hard leader. But I'm human!" He slapped his shirt bosom dramatically. "I've got a heart and a soul, I loved her, damn it, loved her as I've never loved anything in the world! Then Shapiro took her! It wasn't her fault; she was young, and heady with beauty; she fell for his lies!"

Now he was up, absurdly small, pacing back and forth in front of Jim.

"He disappeared with her, then faked his own killing, his own murder, the rat! But what happened to her? What happened to Myrna?"

THEN, AS IF exhausted by his outburst he sat down again and picked up his drink with shaking hands, drained it with a single gulp.

"I don't know, Moroni," said Jim. "This is going to be hard to believe, but I never saw her picture until some two minutes before the explosion, and if her name hadn't have been written on the back of the snap, I wouldn't even have known who she was. I wish I could help you, but I can't. Now there are a few things I'd like to—"

Moroni broke in, "You don't know the Karnes family, of Boston?" Jim shook his head. Morosely Moroni went on, "Hell, I figured you were a family friend or something and was trying to find her for them. Thought maybe you were giving it up, or had found she was—was—dead—and bombed Shapiro to even the score."

Dryly Jim answered, "Oddly enough, I never bombed him. There isn't any use to beat around the bush, Moroni. It's very obvious that I was Tony James, and equally my reasons for playing the role are my own. I think I know how you received the report of my being seen fleeing the—ah—scene of the crime, but we'll pass it up. My prints were in the room as those of Tony James, and I'd rather hate for them to be identified by the police as mine. You must have a price."

Moroni shrugged. "I don't go in for blackmail, Mr. Anthony, not the small amount you'd be willing to pay to keep out of it. I know your ability as a detective, know that in spite of all the circumstantial evidence to the contrary you could probably prove your innocence."

His shoulders drooped, all the life seemed to have gone out of him. "I'd sort of hoped you knew something about Myrna. And I'll admit I would have held this bomb thing over your head to make you give me the information."

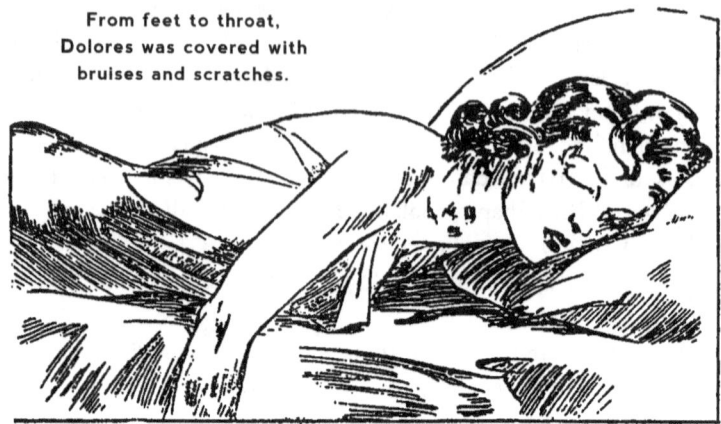

From feet to throat, Dolores was covered with bruises and scratches.

He arose, as a signal that the interview was over.

Jim too arose. Softly he said, "Would you like to tell me anything about Kid Bolo and his wife? Or shall I find out for myself?"

The eyes turned toward him were bright and alert now, not quite so liquid. "Don't worry about Kid Bolo, Anthony. He'll learn a lesson. Something went wrong and I'll find out what it is. Right now it looks like he sold me out. Some of these foreign pugs are hard to train."

"Bolo was to dive, and the books—meaning Big Boy Moroni—would clean up. Pretty foul, Moroni, rigging the boxing racket."

Moroni shrugged. "The stock market is often rigged," he said dryly, and started toward the door.

Suddenly the sound of voices came to them. The butler was protesting and the second voice was talking him down. "Nuts, he'll see me, you know he'll see me!"

Heavy hangings jerked aside, Dicey Decker hardheeled into the room. He saw Anthony, his thick lips drew back in a snarl, his little eyes blazed. "You," he raged, and dragged at his pocket.

"Dicey!" Moroni's voice alone stopped gunplay, for Dicey had a gun almost out of his pocket. Slowly it dropped back. But the pig eyes continued to glare, and Jim noted with amusement that the marks of his fingers were still on the fat man's face. "Beat it," snapped the little Italian, "and never barge into my place unless I send for you! I'm about half off you anyway!"

Half off, Jim knew, because Dicey couldn't control his own fighter!

THE VOICE OF a news announcer filled the room. As a matter of fact he had been speaking for some few moments, none of them paying any attention. Now, however, because a familiar name was mentioned, all three men froze, listening.

"—the little man from the Philippines who won his fight so spectacularly earlier in the evening at Madison Square Garden took the final count not more than half an hour ago in his own apartment. Police were brought to the prizefighter's apartment by a phone call which advised them that two corpses were to be found at Kid Bolo's address. The bodies found were those of Kid Bolo and his wife. The lightweight had suffered a terrific beating. The room where he was found was a shambles. He was killed by a knife, which was left in his heart by the killer. His wife of only a few weeks was found throttled to death on a bed in the rear bedroom, evidently the victim of an assault. Police at first evolved the theory that the Kid and his wife had become embroiled in a terrible argument, that Bolo had slain his bride and afterward killed himself. There were some smudged prints on the handle of the knife, but a fingerprint expert says they were smudged by a hasty wiping which failed to remove them completely. Also Bolo was a wonderful fighter. It was not reasonable to believe he could be so badly injured by a woman as slender and light as his wife, who could not have weighed over a hundred pounds. The passing of Kid Bolo is to be—"

Where the gun came from Jim never knew. First Moroni was listening to the radio announcer empty handed, and suddenly, as if by magic, it was in his slim fingers, pointed at the trembling Dicey Decker.

"Sit down, Dicey, sit down." The voice was low and cold as ice. "You bungled again, didn't you? I sent you around to discipline your own fighter and you not only knifed him to death but killed the kid's wife. Sit down, Dicey, we'll talk."

CHAPTER VIII

GAMBLER'S DEAL

DESPERATELY DECKER SAID, "PUT it away, Big Boy, put the rod down! Bolo was alive when we left, we only beat him up! But this Anthony guy, he was there at Bolo's when we took off!"

Moroni looked surprised. Harshly he cracked, "Quit stalling! What would a millionaire like Anthony be doing knocking off a prize-fighter? What—"

"I was there," interrupted Anthony calmly, and Moroni looked his disbelief. Jim shrugged. "There was nothing hard about adding it up, Moroni. Bolo was to take a dive earlier tonight. He meant to, had the scene all set to go down in the eighth, but some fellow whispered something in his ear that changed his mind. This fellow evidently whispered that he had Bolo's wife, and Bolo better go through on the up and up with the fight!"

"And how do you figure that?"

"Because after he knocked his opponent out he went into hysterics, crying 'Return her to me' in his native tongue, Spanish. Who could she be but someone he loved to the point of adoration—which was his wife. Tom Gentry and myself went up to Bolo's flat and found some of Decker's plug uglies beating Bolo." He wheeled on the frightened Decker. "What happened when the door opened?"

Dicey gibbered, "One of the boys knocked. After a couple of minutes the door opened and the Kid was there gibbering like a crazy man. Somebody smacked him back into the room and the boys begin. He didn't say nothing after he was hit the first time!"

"And none of you went into the back bedroom, none of you saw his wife?"

"Hell, no. We'd been at him only two or three minutes when you and that other guy came and—"

"And what?" snapped Moroni, as Dicey faltered.

Jim laughed. "He's bashful. Tom and I threw Dicey and his boys out. They're not so tough," he added modestly at Moroni's incredulous expression. "So Tom had Moroni on the couch and I went to get a towel. I saw the woman, Maria, dead, throttled as the radio said, in the back bedroom. I went back into the front room and found Tom smack unconscious and the Filipino knifed."

"A likely story," sneered Dicey. "One the cops will pick to pieces."

"Call copper," snapped Jim. "I can stand it better than you can. I had no motive, you did. You or one of the others might have slipped back, knocked Tom unconscious and plunged a knife into the poor fighter. One of you might have been up there before the gang, and killed the woman then. I can find out, and so can the police!"

"How can you find out? If one of my boys killed that Filipino and his wife, I'll kill him myself! I believe in discipline, not just cold blooded murder!"

Slowly Jim said, "Never mind how. Get all the men that went with Dicey to the flat in here, let me send for a microscope, and I'll tell you who killed the woman. Kid Bolo is another proposition entirely."

Moroni pushed the button, the butler appeared. He gave instructions for all the men who had accompanied Dicey to Bolo's flat to come up. "See the Professor," he went on, "and tell him to bring in that microscope he's always fooling with, along with some glass slides." The butler hurried away. Moroni turned to Jim. "For the past five years I've heard of the way you do

The statuette, like the miniature, was of Myrna Karnes.

things. Now I'm going to watch you. And as for you, Dicey! If Anthony tells me you had a hand in that killing, so help me, I'll blast you myself!"

FIVE MEN SPENT a nervous sweating half hour in Big Boy Moroni's apartment. Five men who glowered and alternated looks of bravado with fearful stares at the two men who alternately peered into the Professor's microscope.

It was odd, Jim thought afterward, the pleasure he took explaining the thing to Big Boy Moroni, the avidity with which the gangster watched, the quickness with which he grasped each specimen. Specimens of skin scrapings were taken from all the men who participated in the "disciplining" of Kid Bolo. From the envelope in his pocket Jim took some of the scrapings that were beneath the nails of Maria, Kid Bolo's wife. These he mounted on the first slide, studied them intently for long moments, then invited Big Boy Moroni to have a look for himself.

Excited as a kid, Moroni peered through the microscope. And Jim explained what he was looking at, pointed out the variety of skin texture, and designated it by the letter A.

"There are," he explained, "many skin textures. But, we know that the man who fought with Maria had the type we have called A. Personally, I can recognize it, because of intensive studies. Should we become fortunate enough—or perhaps unfortunate—to match this skin, I'll make a comparison slide for you."

"And only one man can have this type A?"

"No. It won't be definite proof, Moroni. The man who killed her had type A skin. All of these men were there. Naturally it follows that if only one has type A, he is more suspect than the others!"

Moroni wasted a precious moment glowering at the sullen five, then turned back to Jim, who was mounting a specimen of skin scraping from one of the suspects. Like an eager child Moroni peered into the microscope. Almost with disappointment he said, "It wasn't Dicey, damn it! The texture is different." And one by one they went through the specimens, with the same result.

When they were finished, Jim shrugged. Moroni wheeled, "Scram, you bums. You stay, Decker. We'll talk this out." And when the four had shuffled out with sighs of relief, he turned to Dicey. "Now you was at the fight, Dicey. Who was this guy that whispered something or other to Kid Bolo?"

Dicey shook his head. "It was all over before I got to him, and the bell rang and the Kid was killing his man. But I remember he had a bruised nose, tape all over his face!"

"A busted nose shouldn't be hard to find, should it, Mr. Anthony?"

Jim grinned. "The busted nose was probably faked in order to use the tape as disguise. Look, Moroni—don't forget that Shapiro crashed out of the hospital in time to make that fight."

"He wouldn't—the hell he wouldn't! That guy had too much guts. You figure he deliberately crossed my play by holding the kidnaping over Bolo's head?"

Jim nodded. "It looks that way, Moroni. Don't get me wrong, I'm tickled to death he crossed you, glad your fixed fight came out the way nature meant for it to come out. It's the murders that I'm fighting. The assault of that poor girl, the knifing of Bolo."

Dicey nodded solemnly. "I never knew Shapiro to use a knife, but he was hell on dames."

Moroni winced. After all Shapiro had stolen Myrna Karnes!

"You seen Shapiro with his new face, Dicey?" Jim asked.

"Not that I know of," said Dicey slowly. "He had guts living right there in the neighborhood, and he might have come in for smokes or something. I never recognized him."

AND JIM TUCKED this away in his memory, for future reference, for Dicey was lying. Not only had he seen Colbert-Shapiro, but he'd paid him money for some reason, he'd talked to him, argued with him.

Moroni spoke slowly. "Shapiro's hatred of me is what I can't understand. We did a lot of business together, got along fine, until he fell for Myrna. Then he developed a hell of a lot of hatred for me. I can't understand that." He shook his head, puzzled, and Jim almost explained the psychological fact that a man always hates the person he has wronged. But Moroni went on:

"Someone, evidently Shapiro, has been taking over in a small way, football pool tickets and the like. Some of my policy and numbers writers have even been rolled and beaten, but this fight thing is the biggest Shapiro attempted. It cost me lots of money. We got to pin him down some way."

Dicey put in, "They'll get him. The cops are after him, you got a bunch of guys after him, and Anthony here is after him, aren't you, Tony James?"

Jim flushed, cursed himself. Did everybody in town—except the cops—know he was Tony James?

Back and forth went Moroni. "The point is that Shapiro is mean. He knows the cops want to hold him, want to find out just who the guy was that was machine-gunned in his clothes a few months ago. Now there's this Bolo kill, for I figure Shapiro was the bandaged man who kidnaped Maria. He has to be! So what happens? The cops corner him and he shoots it out with them—and where am I?"

Dicey didn't get it. Jim did, at once. The little man's face was strained, his eyes anxious. For with Dale Shapiro dead, no one could possibly learn the whereabouts of Myrna Karnes! And Jim knew this little gangster, this pitiless little man before him, loved Myrna Karnes better than life itself.

Jim looked at Dicey, said, "I want to talk to your boss." Dicey looked at Moroni, who motioned with his head. Dicey arose, walked slowly toward the door.

Softly Jim said, "What makes you think she's alive, Moroni?"

Moroni winced. "Hunch, I guess, Anthony. And I figure Shapiro was pretty crazy about her. He must have been, he was jealous enough." Back and forth he went again, on the thick, soft carpet. "If—if she's—dead, well I'd feel better knowing it, that's all. For if she's alive, she's suffering. Sticking to a man that's on the lam is plenty tough, and pleasing a killer like Shapiro must be even more so."

"You'd rather see her dead than living with him?"

MORONI MIXED HIMSELF a drink before answering. When he turned, there were tears in his eyes. "Why I talk to you I don't know," he half snarled. "But God knows I can't talk to any of these mugs I've got around here. Would I rather see her dead? In a way, yes, in a way, no. You mean do I want to find her in order to kill her, to punish her for deserting, me? No! A thousand times no!"

He gulped his drink, talked into the glass rather than to Jim Anthony. "It was my fault she ran off with Shapiro. I could have and should have treated her a lot differently, but I didn't realize it until too late. I want to find her so I can tell her it was my fault, so I can beg her to come back to me, to give me another chance. I know in my heart she didn't really love Shapiro. And I know she's going through pure hell every minute she's with him."

"What would you give to have her back—or to learn that she—she is dead?"

"A million bucks, cash on the line!"

Jim shrugged. "What would I do with a million bucks, Moroni?"

Moroni was on his feet in a split second. "You mean you'd try to find her for me? I don't get it!"

"Because Tony James is going to be searched for by the police, is being searched for right now. I'm in it slightly anyway. I want to find out about that bombing, for my own protection. It involves Shapiro; and maybe I can kill two birds with one stone. Likewise the Bolo deal didn't sit so well with me."

Moroni shook his head. "Don't stall, Anthony. Guys like that went out with Robin Hood. If you're willing to find Myrna for me, you've got a reason for doing it. Out with it, man. I'll do anything you say, anything possible for me to do."

Jim snapped, "Would you drop out of the rackets? Would you take her and leave the country?"

Moroni looked at him, hard, then shook his head in disbelief. "We're from opposite sides of the track, Anthony. I told you they rigged the markets, they rig all the big stock deals, they—"

"Never mind that. Yes, or no, to my proposition. There's no catch in it. I happen to be a guy that hates crooked sporting events, I happen to know you fix everything from horse races to golf matches. Yes or no. I give you Myrna or definite proof of her death. You take her and get out of the country."

Moroni digested it. Suddenly he gulped. "If you'll shake hands with a gambler on it—here it is!" And the two men shook hands, the big man and the little man. "But what about Shapiro."

"He goes to the cops, of course. He's not for you, just Myrna."

"Turned up for killing Bolo, eh?"

"If he killed him. After all, he killed a couple of men when he escaped from the hospital, he killed the poor devil in his clothes the night he disappeared."

The phone rang. Moroni moved toward it, said hello. "For you," he said, with raised brows. Jim took the phone.

"Jim? Tom! Get to St. Paul's Hospital, Jim, pronto. It's Dolores! A couple of parkers found her on the highway north, practically dead. St. Paul's, Jim, and hurry, they just called."

CHAPTER IX

A CLUE FROM DOLORES

THOUGH DOLORES COLQUITT WAS pretty badly scratched up, and bruised, it wasn't nearly so serious as Tom Gentry's excitement had led him to assume. Moroni insisted on sending Jim to St. Paul's Hospital in one of his cars, and the way the driver cut in and out of traffic was a marvel.

Dolores' blue eyes crinkled in greeting as her fiancé plunged into the room. Her hair was pressed tightly down by the bandage that encircled her head. Long strips of plaster decorated the loveliness of her face, and she was scratched from foot to throat by the briars in which she had been tossed. But she could talk, and she insisted on talking. Holding Jim's hand she plunged into her story.

"First, Jim, I thought I'd have at this Lora Martin face to face, and play the old mistaken identity gag. You know, pretend to have mistaken her for an old friend from my home town, wherever that is!"

Jim squeezed her fingers and nodded. He knew the gag. The victim is supposed to smile and say, "But I'm not from *there* at all! I'm from Portsmouth!"

"But a big fat woman, kindly and nice, said she'd just gone out. So I said I was a friend from Miss Martin's home town and couldn't I wait for her in her apartment, as I'd been ill. The lady was real nice, and let me."

That would be Mrs. Zimmerman, of course.

"Naturally you know what I did once I was inside. I began going through her things. Funny, Jim, most girls save a few letters or pictures or something, but this Lora Martin had absolutely nothing! Now here's a funny one. I was so busy I didn't hear the key in the lock, and a man said, 'Miss Martin just phoned and said she can't get back tonight.' And there I stood with a drawer open and my hands in the drawer! I felt like a

"I was going through her dresser when the door opened and a man came in."

fool. Then the man stood there with the door open waiting for me to go—so I did."

"What did he look like?" She described him quickly and Jim knew it was Frank Zimmerman who had walked in on her.

"I was parked about half a block down the street, Jim. Well, before I ever made the street, and all the time that horrid little man was staring after me, here came the girl you'd described to me. But how could I speak, with the man standing there in the door? He'd have told her I was going through her stuff. So I went down and sat in the car wondering what to do now, which way to turn. Before I had fully decided, she came out of the house and caught a cab—stayed in the house maybe ten minutes, maybe a bit longer." The last was in answer to Jim's question concerning time.

"WELL, I TAILED her, and she drove right to the M&S Hospital!" Jim wasn't surprised. He knew that part of the story anyway, except for details. The cab had waited only a moment and had driven on. But Lora Martin had walked to the street north of the hospital, where a sedan was parked, empty. She had entered for a moment, then went back to the hospital.

"I waited for a while where I could see both this sedan and the hospital entrance, in case she came out and hailed another cab." Then she told of the shooting that followed. How two men had leaped from another parked car and started blazing away at the man who came from the front door of the hospital with the black gun in his hand.

"Lora Martin ran for the sedan," shuddered Dolores, "and after that fellow—his name is Shapiro—had shot his way clear, he jumped in and the sedan sped away."

"And you tailed it, I suppose?"

"Not right away, Jim! He'd just killed two men, I was afraid. But I used the phosphorescent tracer, clipped it on the left rear wheel after Lora Martin went into the hospital."

Jim chuckled at her resourcefulness. The phosphorescent tracer was another little gadget of Jim's that had come in handy on innumerable occasions. It was a flat tube, about the size of a pint bottle, with a clip to hold it to its object. Inside was a phosphorescent chemical, which did not, however, glow white, but cast off a red glow. There was a timer built into the tube, that automatically opened a small hole every fifty yards or so—it could be set—and allowed a small bit of the red phosphorescence to escape. And Dolores had clipped this tracer to the rear wheel of the sedan!

"So when the excitement died out and I could get away, I just had to follow the trace. They went on north, Jimmy, clear to Dobbs Ferry, where they turned east. They took a side road then and went down to what seemed to have once been one of those roadhouses. I parked quite a way off and went afoot, not knowing what I was bucking up against."

Jim could picture her, stealing down that old road, standing in the bushes and viewing the dilapidated roadhouse while her heart played a tattoo on her ribs. For she didn't know exactly what had happened. All she knew was that the woman she was supposed to learn about, had just helped a man shoot his way out of a hospital in a gun battle that cost two lives. If she took a chance in messing with the beautiful Lora Martin, she took a double chance in messing with a known killer! And she'd gone on!

"I WASN'T SURE from where I stood, but I thought I could see a light in what should have been the kitchen. And sneaking around to the back I found the sedan in the barn, so the tracer didn't fail me. Well, I stole back toward this definite crack of light beneath a window. And I kneeled down and was just glueing my eye to the crack when it happened. Blooie!"

"Blooie? What do you mean?"

"Silly, I mean somebody hit me, knocked me out.

"Before they came out I had a chance to put the phosphorescent tracer on the wheel of the sedan."

When I came to with my head ringing I thought I was in total darkness, and thought it funny they were all talking in a dark room. And I sensed they were standing over me, looking down at me! So, I realized then that my eyes were taped, and that my wrists and ankles were tied. There were three of them, and one was bragging. He said, 'You know who it is, don't you?' and the other fellow said he didn't. 'Jim Anthony's girl' the first one bragged and said he'd seen her picture in the papers often enough."

Dolores fell silent. "Go on," prompted Jim. "Go on."

"Some of it I don't understand, Jim! The fellow growled he'd hate to have Jim Anthony after him and what the hell was the idea of kidnaping your girl friend. The first fellow laughed and said Jim Anthony already was on his trail, that Jim Anthony was Tony James. What did he mean, honey? Who's Tony James?"

And again Jim Anthony had to grin wryly at the thought that everybody else in New York—but the cops—knew who Tony James had been! "Never mind, go on."

"There isn't much else. The first fellow wanted to hold me as hostage, for some reason, and the one who killed the fellows at the hospital said that was foolish on account of the cards were stacked against him anyway. So they tossed me in another room and left me for hours and hours."

"You couldn't hear anything?"

"Nope. Not a word. But I managed to get my hands loose, just as the door opened again and they all came in. This second fellow said to take me back to town and let me out gentle like and the first one, the one who had hit me, growled that they were making a mistake. Well, in a few minutes the girl and the second man left and the other one came over and dragged me off the bed. He said, 'Damn if you aren't a fine looking babe!' And he made me so mad that I scratched him good!"

Jim's heart bounded. Scratched him! He picked up her right hand fingers. Yes, the nails were faintly outlined with grime and dirt—and skin?

"So he brought me back to town, in my own car, because I know the sound of it, and just this side of Yonkers threw me out. That's how I got these bruises. Hey—ouch!"

For Jim was taking the dirt from beneath her nails and carefully putting it into an envelope.

BY THEN TOM GENTRY had arrived. "Tom," snapped Jim, "you stay right here the rest of the night, right here in this room. If anything happens to Dolores I'll hold you responsible, personally. Dolores, north all the way to Dobbs Ferry, then east toward White Plains?"

"Yes, Jim. But don't go out there alone. Take the police. The man is a killer!"

"You just don't worry. I don't suppose you know whether the man who hit you at the window and pushed you out of the car was big or little?"

She shook her head. "I didn't see him when he hit me, and afterward my eyes were taped."

"Funny they'd tape her eyes," put in Tom.

"Not at all," answered Jim. "Either one of them was someone she knew, or they figured from the start to eventually release her and didn't want to be identified." He leaned and kissed her swiftly, gave Tom a meaning look, and strode out.

Ten minutes later he was in his laboratory at the penthouse examining the cleanings from beneath Dolores' nails. It was almost unbelievable. He lifted the phone, called Moroni.

"Moroni, I'm on the track of something. I want about three or four men who will fight and keep their mouths shut, if necessary. I don't want the police in this yet."

"I'll send them right over. You've dug up something already?"

"With a little luck I'm going to get Shapiro as well as the man who killed Kid Bolo and his wife. Have those men wait in the lobby." He slammed up the phone, went back to his microscope for a last lingering look.

There was no doubt about it. The scrapings from beneath Dolores' nails matched those taken from the nails of the murdered Maria, Bolo's wife!

CHAPTER X

DOUBLE DOUBLE-CROSS

TWO MEN AWAITED JIM in the lobby. There was another at the wheel of the big sedan outside. Dicey Decker joined them on the sidewalk outside the hotel. To Jim's cold inquiring look, he said, "I'm going, Anthony. Big Boy said so. After all Bolo was my fighter and this guy killed him. I'll take a crack at him myself for that!" His fat hand patted his bulging pocket and he moved off toward the car.

Once in the front seat beside the driver Jim Anthony said, "Dobbs Ferry. And all of you fellows listen to me. I think I've got Shapiro located—and I want him alive. I don't want any man to use a gun unless I tell him to. Understand?"

They made the long drive in silence, picking up the red phosphorescence easily. At Dobbs Ferry they turned east, still in silence, and before long, following Jim's directions, they were parking the car off a little used side road heading to the north. After some few minutes walk, when the ex-roadhouse eventually came into view, Jim said, "All right, fellows, the bird has flown." There was disappointment in his voice.

Dicey said, "Don't be stupid. It's two thirty, there naturally wouldn't be any lights. Let's close in."

"The last thing I knew was when I was peeping into the window of that roadhouse."

But Jim knew the sedan had left the roadhouse, for almost side by side on the gravel road, one to the east, one to the west side, glowed twin red spots. Which meant, of course, that not only had the tracer-rigged car driven into the retreat, but also had left it. And it followed, of course, that the quarry would have left the roadhouse immediately after Dolores was taken back to town.

"They're gone, nevertheless," persisted Jim, and turned his great flashlight on the one time inn. It was in sad state of repair, just as Dolores had described it. The front door stood open, but all the windows were boarded up, and as they approached, the light illuminated the cavern-like interior. Jim's practised eye immediately picked out the footprints that led across the dust covered dance floor toward the rear. At the door he paused.

"You fellows stay here," he commanded. "I want to look the place over by myself. No doubt they left some clues of some kind, and I don't want them all trampled up." Through the empty dance hall he went, bearing to the right, along one wall, wishing to preserve the tracks. Tomorrow he would send Tom Gentry out here to take film-moulages. He flashed the big light into half a dozen rooms which once served as private dining places, and at the seventh, found what he wanted. A place where people had recently been. A crumpled cot stood against the left wall, a table in the center of the room bore greasy paper sacks, as if sandwiches had recently been brought. The floor was littered with empty coffee containers.

A heavy but faded curtain half covered one of the windows, extending nearly to the floor. It rustled with the wind through a broken pane as Jim's flash found it. And he saw the toe of a man's shoe beneath that curtain. He snapped, "Come out, you're covered!"

THE REST HAPPENED so quickly it startled even Jim Anthony. Although his sense of hearing was many times more acute than that of an ordinary man, he had heard nothing behind him. The first intimation he received that his command to stay behind had not been obeyed at all, was the rapid sputter and roar of the gun by his ear. He almost dropped the flashlight. Seven times Dicey Decker fired, then, breathing heavily, tore the empty clip from his automatic, slipped another into place with lithe fingers and would have resumed firing had Anthony not literally torn the gun from his hand.

Strangely enough, when the smoke cleared away, there was no dead or wounded man in the room. The powerful light disclosed the shoe exactly as it had been, with the toe pointed directly at the doorway.

Jim growled fiercely, "If that had been Shapiro or any one else you'd have killed him—in spite of what I said! Get out of here, before I lose my temper!"

Dicey's eyes were protruding now as he stared at what was obviously a shoe, a shoe without a foot to fill it. He cursed in heartfelt manner, caught himself, clipped, "Sorry, I lost my head." And turned and hardheeled back across the dance floor, scuffling his feet, before Jim could protest. Any footprints across that dusty floor would now be worthless!

Jim closed the door behind him, started a minute search of the room. He found the letter behind the cot, and reading it, found therein the answer to a puzzle. For it was addressed to Lora Martin, Seventy-fourth and West End Avenue, New York City. The stationery was heavy and expensive, the handwriting, aristocratic, and it was signed, "Your loving mother."

He reread the letter, thoroughly. In part, it said, "…and your scheme seems so mad and unnecessary to your father and to me, dear. If your sister were alive, surely one of the hundreds of detectives we have hired would have found her before this. If you are certain that this Colbert is Shapiro, you should call in the police. You say if the police come in he will either be killed defending himself, or will refuse to talk. This may be true, but he is far too dangerous for a girl like you to fool around with. How you expect to influence him, to make him tell you where Myrna might be, I cannot figure. Please, please abandon the mad plan you have in mind…."

SO, THOUGHT JIM ANTHONY, Lora Martin was Myrna Karnes' sister! Somehow, Lora had proved to her own satisfaction that Colbert was Shapiro, and she knew that Shapiro alone could settle the fate of Myrna Karnes, could tell whether Myrna was living or dead. Which, of course, explained the rescue from the hospital.

As Lora Martin, she doubtless had made a play for Shapiro at the West End apartment, for it was obvious to Jim what means she intended using to gain her information. What did a beautiful woman have to fight with, except her very beauty, her feminine charm?

Shapiro's capture by the police was her opportunity. She rescued him from that hospital to gain his gratitude—even at the price of the killing of two other gangsters. Jim didn't blame her. Compared to news of her sister, the lives of a dozen scummy, ratlike members of the underworld, was not too big a price to pay. And Shapiro had evidently fallen for it—at least he still was carrying Lora with him. They had come to the hideout together, and they had left together. The letter in her purse, she realized, would be a giveaway should Shapiro read it, so she had gotten rid of it.

Why, then, Jim asked himself, had she slipped that snapshot and that clipping into his book? And his keen mind found but one answer to that, an answer that made that same wry grin appear on his face. For somebody else, Lora Martin, had recognized him as Jim Anthony, living under the alias Tony James. No doubt Colbert-Shapiro, at the apartment, had been too hard a nut to crack. Hence, she slipped the picture and clipping into Jim's book, in order to arouse his curiosity concerning Colbert-Shapiro, knowing that Jim Anthony usually worked without recourse to the police. She had meant to keep her own identity in the background so that, if Jim failed, she could take up her desperate work where she had left off.

HE FOLDED THE letter and thrust it into its envelope, put the envelope back into his pocket. An atomizer-like object was next employed. Carefully but swiftly he went over the room, squeezing the bulb swiftly and surely, to throw out a fine stream of fingerprint powder. Jim read fingerprints like the Indian trailers read signs. It took him but a few moments to learn that the third person, the man who had hit Dolores in the head as she had peeped through the window, had taken good care not to touch any object where his prints might remain.

The shoe that had stood beneath the long curtain intrigued him. From it he learned much. For a bullet had neatly pierced the heel, just above the sole. The shoe was full of dried blood and the laces were cut, proving that Shapiro had been hit at the hospital, that his foot had swollen so much that he had had to cut the shoe away once the hideout was reached.

Back into the car a few moments later, they headed once again for New York. At intervals of some fifty yards the ghastly red light recurred on the pavement, but Jim's quick eye noted that each mark was growing smaller and fainter the nearer they approached their destination. The fluid was giving out! The small flask with its automatic dropper was running dry. And before they reached the outskirts of Yonkers there was no trail left by Shapiro and Lora Martin. They were again lost, evidently, in the maze of Manhattan.

ONE OF THE chief reasons for Jim Anthony's success in the tracking down of criminals was his thoroughness. He left nothing to chance. He allowed for every eventuality, and foresaw that eventuality always with uncanny vision.

Back at the penthouse atop the Waldorf-Anthony, sleep was the farthest thing from his mind. He had a job to do, a job with a good many facets. He had, first of all, or rather, most important of all, to clear his own skirts in the attempted bombing of Shapiro, that had caused the death of the little hanger-on, Hymie Swartz. For the sake of justice, he wanted to bring to light the killers of Kid Bolo and his new wife. Shapiro must be located, and the woman, Myrna Karnes, dead or alive, through Shapiro. By finding the woman he removed the unmoral, conscienceless Big Boy Moroni from the scene, for Jim knew the little man's word was his bond in such an instance. Knew that when he, Jim Anthony, fulfilled his end of the strange agreement, Moroni would fade out of the picture, just as he promised.

Stopping the car, they threw her into the brambles, tied and taped.

Concerning the first part of his task, the clearing of his own skirts in the bombing, Jim didn't worry much, for Swartz was of no importance in the scheme of things. The police would hardly investigate too thoroughly there.

The search for Tony James would be desultory. True, it might cost him a bit of money, for already too many blackmailers and crooks seemed to know the facts. None of these would report the Tony James-Jim Anthony angle to the police as long as there was a chance for a payoff. Nevertheless, Jim firmly believed that when one angle of the mess was cleared up, the entire mess would at once fall into the category of solved crimes, solved cases, *in toto*.

He made three radio calls from his laboratory to three key men of the tremendous and far reaching Anthony Organization. This was a network of undercover men, throughout New York City, who worked for Jim Anthony for the love of the game, for the love of the good fight against crime. There were stockbrokers, lawyers, truck drivers, bartenders, messenger boys, newspaper vendors, and men from a thousand and one other occupations, who liked nothing better than to drop what they were doing and pursue strange quests for Jim Anthony.

Speaking on his own private wavelength to his three key men, he gave them two requests. One was a necessity, the other was a precautionary measure. The first was the finding of Dale Shapiro and Lora Martin. He wanted an investigation of every man with a bandaged nose and a bad limp in the right foot. Literally hundreds of his agents, taxi drivers, garbage men, delivery boys and many others would be alert for such a man.

The second request was to search from the northern edge of Yonkers into the Bronx, for a small flasklike object—the phosphorescent tracer Dolores Colquitt had attached to the wheel of the sedan that bore Shapiro and Lora Martin from the M&S Hospital.

That finished, he began work on the letter he had found behind the tumbledown cot at the old roadhouse. By iodine vapors and silver nitrates, as well as other tests known only to Jim Anthony, he soon brought out numerous fingerprints not only on the envelope but on the letter itself. Later, he enclosed it in a glassine cover to protect those prints, and stared long and thoughtfully at them. His jaw was grim when he filed them away, for a new avenue of suspicious thought had opened up to him.

HE WAS STILL experimenting at his long tables and benches when dawn came. Shortly afterward he sent for Tom Gentry, sending Mephito up to the hospital to serve as guard to Dolores. "If Dolores did her work well," he said, "when she searched Lora Martin's rooms, she picked up something with the girl's prints on it. Awaken her, Mephito, ask her, and have Tom bring the object when he comes."

Dolores, trained by Jim Anthony himself, had not overlooked the prints. They were on a single stocking that she had thrust into her purse from the floor of the closet, and Jim's advanced methods of latest print handling brought them out in no time at all. He compared them with the prints of Lora Martin on the letter from Boston, and found them the same.

Tom said, "Look, Jim, you're running hither and thither and here and there and getting details together without telling any of us what it's all about. Suppose you—?"

"Get the *Thunderbird* ready," answered Jim, and clapped his friend on the shoulder. "We're going to make a short trip, I'll tell you what it's all about on the way." When Tom had departed, Dawkins, the valet brought in Jim's breakfast of concentrated juices, the diet he always clung to when working. And most certainly Jim was working, concentrating that agile mind of his on ways and means of solving not one, but four problems, simultaneously.

Dawkins knocked discreetly, entered to find Jim shooting a fluid into the shaved belly of a white guinea pig. "Pardon, sir, but there's h'an h'obnoxious party to see you who won't depart, sir, 'e says to simply tell you your h'old landlord, Mr. Zimmerman, is 'ere."

Jim was instantly alert. Another person knowing that Anthony was James! He might as well proclaim it to the world himself! But he was aware of the implications, aware of the opportunity presented by Zimmerman's greed.

"Show him in," he snapped, and tried to put a look of fear and despair on his face. Zimmerman, however, was plainly more frightened than the man he'd come to blackmail. He closed the door and leaned against it, his eyes rolling.

"Look, James, or Anthony, don't get no ideas! I told my wife where I was coming and told her to call the police if I wasn't home in an hour!"

Jim nodded, laughing inside himself. "I—I—don't i-i-intend anything," he quavered. "W-w-what do you want?"

His evident fear gave Zimmerman courage, he walked forward with a bit of a swagger and tossed the morning paper before Jim. "Right there," he said, extending a slightly dirty forefinger, "is an account of what happened at my house yesterday evening. You'll note the police are searching for Anthony James as a killer, on account of they even found the pot in which he boiled off his nitro."

He paused. Jim said, "You put that pot there, Zimmerman, I didn't even have one!"

"Maybe," admitted Zimmerman, "I did. The point is, how would you like for the police to know the great Jim Anthony for some reason or other was pretending to be Tony James, pretending to be a cripple, and all that? Embarrassing to a man in your position, eh?"

"That's what you said over the phone! Your money's ready and—" He paused. A slightly bewildered look was overspreading Zimmerman's face.

Suddenly Zimmerman swore. "Why the dirty double—never mind! How much you willing to pay me to forget it?"

THE PHONE RANG. Jim picked it up. A hoarse voice said, "You know who this is. You got that five grand?"

"Yes. Certainly, to be sure."

"There'll be a Checker Cab standing at the Lowery Street El Station at exactly nine o'clock, and the driver will be missing. You or your messenger is to get in, leave the dough, then get out and go upstairs and get on the train to the city again. Got that? Nine o'clock!"

"It'll be there," said Jim, and hung up. So, he had two blackmailers already! He turned to Zimmerman, said, with shaking voice, "Look, Zimmerman, I don't want any trouble, you ought to realize that. How about five thousand to forget what you know?"

Without waiting for Zimmerman to accede he went to his safe, came out with the packet of money which he had prepared, and tossed it on the table. "Take it," he quavered, "and for God's sake, keep your mouth shut!" He could see Zimmerman's crafty brain working in his eyes. Zimmerman was assuring himself that the dough couldn't be marked, because he had seen Anthony take it directly from the safe. He picked it up, thrust it carelessly into his pocket, turned without a word and left the room.

No sooner had the door closed than Jim leaped for a panel and a master switch that threw off the elevator power serving the penthouse. A touch on an independent buzzer brought Dawkins on the run. "This man that's leaving, tail him, Dawkins! And when you come back, pick up the stack of bills in the emergency fund and take them to Lowery Street—"The last thing he said was, "And don't touch the flat surfaces of the bills you find!"

Dawkins hurried away, to grab hat and coat to take a private lift down to the lobby of the ornate hotel, in order to be waiting for Zimmerman when the elevators resumed operations. Jim gave him three minutes, then threw the switch that allowed Frank Zimmerman to go on his unsuspecting way. Already Jim was at work with $5,000 in bills spread out on the table, a strange mixture of chemicals being mixed in a test tube and the camels-hair brush ready for use.

CHAPTER XI

POISON MONEY

FROM THE ANTHONY AIRPORT to the city of Boston, as the crow flies, the distance is practically two hundred miles. The *Thunderbird II*, powered by engines whose secret was known but to one man, Jim Anthony, ate up those two hundred miles in less than twenty-five minutes. During those twenty-five minutes he took Tom Gentry into his confidence, although he flushed when explaining how he had been at Seventy-fourth and West End rather than in Mexico, for no reason at all except his ennui and boredom.

Tom's eyes threatened to pop from his head. "Gosh," he said, "Jim, we've cut ourselves out something this time, sure enough! Find the bomber of Swartz, who was aiming at Shapiro! Find the killer of Kid Bolo and his wife! Locate Shapiro! Through him find out the facts concerning Myrna Karnes! Give the facts to Big Boy Moroni—and the girl if possible—and thus force Moroni to get out of this crooked betting ring that's ruining so many sporting events!" He emitted a low whistle, and Jim laughed.

"It won't be as tough as you think, Tom. We can locate this Shapiro, I'm pretty sure. The thing is I have to pop the results all at once, if you see what I mean. Even when and if we locate Shapiro we'll have to work carefully—"

"I know." Without visible effort Tom set the big amphibian down on Boston Bay. "You mean to protect the other Karnes girl. Is she pretty, Jim?"

Jim nodded, grinning. "Quite, my romantic laddy, quite. Now you're to wait for me here, I won't be gone any longer than necessary."

He was gone less than an hour, and his brow was gathered when he returned. He had been to see P. Oliver Karnes, that frosty old Back Bay-er, whose family pride was even larger than his purse. He had glared at Jim across the desk, had colored, swallowed, and said stiffly, "Mr. Anthony, I have one daughter, Lora. At present she is in England as a nurse. At one time she had a sister, Myrna. Where Myrna is now, I do not know, and I may well add, that I do not care. Suffice to say, she is no longer my daughter!"

When Jim told Tom all that had occurred, Tom nodded sympathetically. "Poor old guy, proud as a peacock. See what he means?"

"Not exactly, Tommy. What do you think?"

"The way I recall it, this Myrna was the older sister, and a wild one from the word go. Okie-doke, she broke family traditions, and the old man disinherited her, but don't let him fool you. Those gruff old guys are usually pretty soft under their veneer. Him saying Lora was in England was another stall. They're just covering up, that's all. Easy to see, Jim, my boy."

Jim neither agreed nor disagreed, but kept his counsel.

DAWKINS MET THEM as they got out of the elevator at the penthouse. Peering back over his shoulder toward the penthouse proper, ending up his explanations with, "H'and, sir, she was so

"He made me so mad that
I scratched him good!"

h'obviously frightened, h'I hallowed 'er to stay h'in spite of your h'instructions."

Gentry said, "Lora Martin Karnes! She got away from the guy. Come on, Jim!"

"Just a minute," laughed Jim, "I have some work for you to do. You can meet the beautiful Martin Karnes a bit later."

Tom paused in disappointment.

"I want some dust samples, Tom, of several places, and you may have trouble getting them. Use the small vacuum—and your head as well." He told him how to get to the deserted roadhouse near Dobbs Ferry. Instructed him to get dust samples from the dance floor itself, as well as soil samples from outside the window where Dolores was knocked unconscious. He was to obtain similar dust samples from Kid Bolo's flat, from the basement of the house at Seventy-fourth and West End Avenue, from the back room at the Federal Cigar Stores, and several other places.

"How you get them I don't care," snapped Jim, "and take anyone you want to help you."

He saw the downcast look on Tom's face and again his sense of humor got the better of him. Tom's weakness was pretty women. Jim said, "All right, all right, come on in and meet her. I'll be in directly."

So while Tom headed eagerly for the living room where Lora Martin was awaiting Jim Anthony, Jim hurried into his laboratory and to his radio. An automatic receiver recorded all messages that had come in on his private wavelength during his absence.

While he was adjusting it, Dawkins came in to report that he had placed the money in the taxicab at the Lowery Street El Station on Long Island as instructed. And also that Zimmerman had gone directly from the hotel to the Federal Cigar Store at Seventy-fourth and Broadway. Jim nodded. The reports from the three key men of the Anthony Organization came to him. They were strangely alike. For once the immense and well trained organization had failed to turn up their men in a short time. Many limpers as well as many men whose noses were apparently broken had been investigated and checked, but there was no Dale Shapiro to be found.

Jim flipped the switch of his own broadcasting system and a moment later had his three key men. "Redouble all efforts," he directed. "Put the B Units to work."

The B Units were men and women, children and youths, who followed instructions of their actual leader without ever knowing they were working for Jim Anthony himself. Hardly had he given these instructions when one of the key men said laconically, "I had my set in my hand, Mr. Anthony, to get you. That flask thing has been found. A filling station man in upper Yonkers remembers the incident well. A woman took it off the left rear wheel of a car that had stopped for gas, and threw it away. That's all—I have it, if you want it."

Jim sat quietly for a few moments, turning this newest bit of information over and over in his mind. The woman, then, who took off the tracer and threw it away, was Lora Martin. No doubt she did it under the instructions of Dale Shapiro. He arose, and walked toward the living room where Lora and Tom awaited him.

TOM, THOUGHT JIM amusedly, had wasted no time. For the two of them were on a divan, and the woman's head was on Tom's shoulder, his great hands patting her and soothing her. Nor did he cease when Jim entered the room. He simply said, "Poor little thing, she's been through hell, Jim!"

Lora Martin looked up with tear dimmed eyes. Funny, Jim thought, that no matter how much a girl goes through she manages to keep on looking her best.

"Mr. Anthony, Mr. Anthony! Did you find my letter at that awful roadhouse?"

Nodding, he said, "Now calm yourself, my dear. I want this whole story from the start. I've been to Boston to see your father. I know that you're supposedly in Europe, and I know from the letter from your mother that your people are not in accord with what you are doing. Let's start at the very beginning so I can keep things straightened around."

So, with a bit of prompting here and there she told her wide-eyed story, shuddering at the exciting points. She refused to tell how she had come to know that the man Colbert was in reality Dale Shapiro, for, she said, she had given her sacred oath not to reveal the source.

She had moved to the Seventy-fourth and West End house, meaning to—well, as she explained it: "Shapiro was a dangerous man, Mr. Anthony, but his love for women was well known! Oh, I investigated him thoroughly! A pretty figure and a meaning smile could always do wonders with him. But he wouldn't have anything to do with me there at the apartment house!"

Tom put in, "He was pretty scared, I guess, though his lack of taste is amazing!" She rewarded him with a smile.

"And so," went on Jim, "you recognized me in spite of my makeup?"

She nodded. "A woman notices details a great deal more than a man. I used to visit the woman who had the apartment right under yours. You'd pace your floor, and you didn't limp. That started me thinking, and the first thing I knew I placed you. After all, your picture has been published in every paper in the United States, at one time or another."

"Then," nodded Jim, "because I was in disguise you figured I was hiding out for some spectacular reason?"

"NATURALLY. AND I figured the reason was Colbert—or Shapiro. My folks have hired so many detectives, hundreds of them, and I thought they'd managed to interest you. So, thinking maybe you weren't quite sure yet, I put the snapshot of my sister and Shapiro, as well as the clipping, where you'd be sure to find it. Maybe it was a foolish thing to do, but it was the only way I could think of to get you into it without bringing my own plans out into the open."

Tom beamed approval, said, "Smart girl, Miss Martin, smart girl!"

"Then that terrible explosion happened, I suppose before you could do anything, and I knew Tony James would simply disappear."

"Jim didn't cause that explosion," said Tom stoutly, but Jim's raised hand stopped him.

Lora Martin dropped her voice. "After the police took Shapiro to the hospital I recognized my opportunity to really do some good! I—"

"Just a minute," interrupted Jim. "Now think hard. The night of the explosion did you call Zimmerman and give him a message for Colbert, saying that there was a spy planted in the house?"

Her eyes grew wide and round, a hand fluttered to her breast, and her eyes, momentarily, narrowed suddenly. "No! Zimmerman? Did be know Shapiro? Why—"

"Never mind, go on. We know how you rescued Shapiro." And, he thought, how two men were killed in the rescuing! "I know Shapiro was hit in the heel, know you went to the roadhouse, of course."

"Your fiancée followed us, didn't she." Jim nodded. "Well, Shapiro knew where to go, to this roadhouse. And I just told him the truth, that I was Lora Karnes, looking for my sister, and that I really thought he owed me something!" She shuddered. "At first he was going to kill me, even though I had rescued him! And I talked and talked and talked. That was when I put the letter behind the cot. No—! I didn't do that until that other man hit your fiancée on the head and brought her in! He—"

"I don't suppose you'd ever seen this 'other man' before?" asked Jim dryly.

She shook her head. Tom said, "She wouldn't know any of the underworld rats that associate with Shapiro, Jim. Of course not!" He patted her shapely shoulder and again she flashed that meaning smile on him.

"Then you left the letter because you knew Dolores was my fiancée, thought perhaps I wouldn't be too far behind her?"

She nodded. "That was it You see I was terribly frightened of that Shapiro! But—" she beamed triumphantly, "it all worked out! Myrna is alive!"

She waited for approbation, got it from Tom, but only a question from Jim.

"Why in the world did Shapiro ever come back to New York, Miss Martin?"

HER EYES NARROWED. "I've made quite a study of that man, Mr. Anthony. A fellow like Shapiro is a colossal egotist. He stole poor Myrna from Big Boy Moroni, and day by day his hate for Moroni grew, as is usually the case. He kept remembering the easy money Moroni made with his various football pools and baseball pools, the numbers racket, and all kinds of fixed and rigged sports. He just had to come back and try to muscle in, that's all. But he's cured now, all he wants is to get away!"

Tom put in, "With everybody after him so strongly—police, Jim, and Moroni's gang—I don't blame him for wanting to fade. Is your sister with him now?"

She shook her head, her eyes filled with tears. "He swears she's alive and well! And because he's grateful to me for helping him, he promises to surrender her to me—for enough money to get him out of the country."

"Which is how much?"

"Fifty thousand dollars!"Tom said, "If we'd have known, we'd have gotten it from your dad this morning."

She shook her head, her eyes were pleading, tear-filled again. "I don't know whether or not I can make you see this. You've got to understand how this Shapiro is. He'll never be captured alive, by police or anyone else. He has the blackest and most spiteful heart of any living man! Myrna is being held in an institution, her mind has gone blank with her hardships, he says. Now, if he thought there was a cross up anywhere, he'd die laughing, never revealing that institution! He wants his money tonight. I happen to know my father would have a hard time raising it because of many things. He would eventually pay it back to anyone who was kind enough to advance it, in such a case of life or death and—"

Tom said, "Jim," and he gulped hard, "it is an emergency. This brave little girl has gone this far, we can't let her down. We—"

Jim snapped, "Miss Martin, I'll advance the money myself, of course. But I refuse to allow you to take it to this man by yourself. I'll go along."

She flew across the room, threw her arms about his neck, pressed close to him and sobbed, "Oh, I always knew you were kind and good, and sweet! Daddy will raise it some way and pay you back, once poor Myrna is home again!" Tom cleared his throat and blew his nose. The woman said, "You can pick me up around seven tonight, Mr. Anthony, at the drugstore on Seventy-second, and you know I'll be eternally grateful, don't you?"

"Hmmmmm. Pardon me." It was Dawkins. "A gentleman, sir, h'a Mr. Moroni!"

The woman stiffened. She drew away from Jim. "Please," she said tremulously, "I can't see him. After the way Myrna treated him—! I'll run!"

And, as Dawkins obligingly took her through another door, Tom followed her sinuous figure with his eyes, his cheeks flushed. When she had gone, he said, "A wonderful, wonderful woman, Jim!"

Jim shrugged, answered, "The dust, Tommy, my lad. And get back as quickly as possible." And, when Tom had closed the door behind him, Jim, still grinning, said, "A wonderful, wonderful liar!" Wheeling, he said, "Hello, Moroni."

THERE WAS THIS about Big Boy Moroni. When he went into anything he went all the way. He placed himself in Jim's hands entirely, answered Jim's questions without reservation. It was patent to him now that the man who had been breaking in on his rackets was Shapiro. "Of course," he went on, "leaving out the Kid Bolo double-cross, the only thing Shapiro has butted into so far has been the football pools." He grinned. "If you're successful, Anthony, it won't make much difference who butts into what racket, will it. My word is pretty good. I'm stepping out when I find out the truth concerning Myrna or get her back."

"The truth," said Jim, "may not be pleasant."

"Knowing, pleasantly or unpleasantly, is worth what I'm paying for it," answered the little racketeer. "It's eleven tonight, eh, here in your place?"

"Eleven," answered Jim.

Moroni had a pad and a silver pencil, checked off the list. "All the guys that went with Dicey to work on Kid Bolo, Dicey himself, me, a friend of Dicey's named Zimmerman, and a cab driver whose corner is Seventy-fourth and Broadway and whose hands are swollen like feet and a black and blue color."

"Right." Jim admired Moroni. He couldn't help it. The little fellow didn't even allow his curiosity to show in his olive face!

When he had gone, Jim picked up the phone and dialed a number. A moment later Frank Zimmerman's snarl came to him. "Damned right they're swollen, and red as beets! How'd you know?"

Jim kept the laughter out of his voice. "Listen, Zimmerman, I'm sorry as the dickens, I gave you the wrong money! That was some money I'd prepared for experimental purposes, and it was inoculated with germs!"

"What?" shrieked Zimmerman, and went into a string of curses.

"No, no," pleaded Jim, "don't go tell the police that Tony James stuff! Don't! It was a mistake, I tell you! You get up here right away, I'll give you a shot of something to counteract it, to kill those germs! But you better hurry!"

Zimmerman's hands looked like a pair of inflated rubber gloves. He swore and mouthed threats as Jim fussed over them, Jim again pretending to be half frightened to death. He laid the right hand on the table, carefully scraped back a place with a peculiar knife, and injected a hypo of fluid into the shallow wound. The swelling began to go down almost immediately.

"The money is very good money," said Jim humbly, "as long as you keep your gloves on when you handle it!"

When Zimmerman had cursed his way out the door Jim very carefully added his skin scrapings to those of the others, which he had collected the night before.

Someone said, "Ugh! How, Jim."

"Hey," smiled Jim affectionately, "I thought you were supposed to stay with Dolores?"

"Squaw go home, send me back. Squaw say Mephito smell bad."

Jim roared with laughter, for that tendency of Mephito to carry various unmentionable charms in a shaman bag that hung at his waist, did—occasionally—bring a slight odor, to speak lightly.

"All right," he managed, "Tell you what you do. You go down to the garage and fix the roadster, the white one. Have it ready for a trip around six-thirty tonight, understand? And be sure a couple of those heavy fire-sticks of yours are in that rear compartment. You may need them!"

CHAPTER XII

TRAP FOR KILLERS

RIGHT AFTER LUNCH TOM returned with his various dust samples, which Jim immediately examined under a spectroscope. A man brought in the flask that was the phosphorescent tracer, which had been attached to the wheel of the escape sedan by Dolores. Jim brought the fingerprints out, compared them with the prints on the silk stocking snitched from Lora Martin's room as well as the letter received from Boston, found behind the cot at the road-house. And what with one thing and another it was soon time to pick up Lora Martin, who was to take him to Shapiro.

She was nervous and distrait when she stepped into the white roadster. Naturally she would be. Jim assured her that he had the money for Shapiro, and showed it to her. As they sped north through the heavy traffic, she clutched her coat around her throat and said, "You don't know what this means to me! And you know, of course, that you mustn't do anything to Shapiro until he reveals where Myrna is, until we can check and see that he hasn't crossed us?"

He nodded, assured her that he understood thoroughly all that he was to do, that, in fact, he had made adequate preparations. He smiled a bit grimly, but she did not note the smile. Just past One Hundred Eighty-first Street, they twisted and turned into a narrow avenue of small homes, as alike as peas in a pod. At the very end of the street, which was a dead end, she stopped him and indicated the house before which they were parked.

"You want to wait here?" she whispered, gazing at the darkened windows with apprehension, her shoulders trembling.

"I want to see him. I'm unarmed, he can hold a gun on me all the time. I want to pay him this money and warn him what will happen if he crosses us, if he gives us a bad address or something. You're positive your sister is alive?"

"I'm sure!"

Far back in the shell-like house a bell tinkled. But no one came to the door, though a light was visible in the rear of the house. Before he could ring again, the woman tried the doorknob. The door was open.

She called, "It's Lora, Dale! We're coming back." Down the dim hallway she led the way, to where the light seeped from beneath the closed door. She stepped aside. Jim tapped. No answer. "Go on in," she whispered, "he's waiting."

Jim opened the door. Dale was waiting all right. He'd never go any place again! But that was as much as Jim Anthony got to see right then! For the woman yelled, and as he half turned his head, it seemed as though the entire ceiling came down on Jim Anthony's head. He pitched forward on his face and lay still.

AFTER A WHILE he sat up and shook the cobwebs from his eyes. His head was sore. The package of money was gone. Shapiro was still there, though the woman had disappeared. He got to his feet, suddenly became aware that he had something in his hand. It was a gun, a .38 automatic He smelled the muzzle. It had been recently fired. While he was out? He leaned over Shapiro, touched him with his hand. The corpse was not cold, yet it was easy to see that he had been dead a couple of hours at least. The bullet hole directly beneath the point of hair in the center of his forehead, had even ceased to bleed.

Off in the distance Jim heard the sound of sirens, then, and knew it was time to go. A hasty glance through the front door showed his roadster gone. He wiped the gun with a handkerchief and laid it beside the corpse before going out the rear door like a shadow, climbing easily over the fence and flitting down the alley. He felt pretty good. He had the whole thing at his fingertips, now.

At eleven o'clock, he pulled back a wall panel and peered into his own laboratory, where a group of men awaited him. Small amplifiers were so arranged that he heard all conversation as well.

Moroni sat alone at the head of a table on which sat the spectroscope. Tom sat close to him, his eye on various specimens and impediments that he had arranged for Jim's entrance. Moroni looked very sad. He said, to Tom, "What a shame! Shapiro dead before Jim Anthony got a chance to question him! Wonder where Jim is?" The report of the death of Shapiro, of course, had come in over the telephone.

Dicey was there, too, morose, suspiciously eyeing the group. The two plug uglies who had beaten Kid Bolo so unmercifully huddled together. Frank Zimmerman, frowning portentously, snarled conversation with a heavy-set cab driver, both of whose hands were bandaged. "The nerve of the guy," sneered Zimmerman, "insisting on everybody wiping their feet before they come into his precious little dump! Wait till I see him!" The Italian whose subconscious brain waves had started Jim on the right track smiled serenely. "He ain't a bad guy," he returned. "This'll be interesting!"

Jim opened the door and walked in. "Gentlemen," he said, "how do you do?" He walked to the table, glanced over the various objects assembled for his use.

MORONI SAID, "ANTHONY, it's too damned bad about Shapiro. We heard he was found dead by the police, it came over the radio. Looks like we've lost out, doesn't it?"

Jim smiled. "Let's not be too hasty. I've got a lot of possibilities. Will you please repeat our agreement, here before witnesses? And I might as well tell you that everything said here tonight is being taken down automatically."

Moroni rose. He shook his head. "I agreed to drop out of the rackets, to leave the country, if Jim Anthony could set my heart at ease concerning a woman I loved better than anyone or anything in the world."

"You will be satisfied with knowledge of her whereabouts, or assurance of her death?"

"Yes," acceded Moroni, "that was the agreement. Anything to get rid of this worry about her."

Dicey Decker sneered openly, little Zimmerman tittered.

"Gentlemen, each of us knows part of this story, none of you know it in all its details." He started at the very beginning, where he was living as Tony James at Seventy-fourth and West End. He told of the bombing, told of the snapshot and clipping in his book, gave all his movements after coming back to the hotel. "Twice," he went on, "I have paid blackmail willingly, wishing for results. You, cabbie, what's wrong with your hands?"

Shapiro was waiting, all right. But he wouldn't go anywhere again.

The cabbie looked as though he'd like to eat his hands. At last he managed something about poison ivy. Jim laughed. "This is the cabbie," he said, "that opened his door to me when I came out of the alley behind the house after the explosion. He drove me to the hotel, where he learned I was Jim Anthony. When he heard the police were looking for a man that fled in a pair of yellow swim trunks, he decided to make some easy money. Right, cabbie?"

The cabbie simply stared, dully, dumbly.

"He probably told it—in the Federal Cigar store." Dicey started to protest. Jim's glare stopped him. The cabbie nodded. "I know this, because I paid blackmail twice, as I say. Once to the cabbie, once to Mr. Zimmerman." Everyone stared at Zimmerman.

Zimmerman said, "The police would still like to hear about the Tony James-Jim Anthony angle."

Jim's smile was meaning. "They shall—later tonight—from Jim Anthony. What I'm pointing out is that this whole devious plot is laid at Seventy-fourth and Broadway, where we have four characters of our story concentrated within a block of each other. We have our friend, Mr. Decker, we have Zimmerman, we have Shapiro and we have the woman Lora Martin, whose real name is Karnes. I think we can take the keystone from the arch, that we can collapse the whole structure by proving who was associated with each other in what."

Decker said, "And that don't make no sense. I got things to do, Anthony."

"Take your hand out of your pocket!" It was like the crack of a whip. Reluctantly Decker took his right hand from his pocket. It was slightly swollen. Jim snapped, "You, Zimmerman, let's see your left hand! I fixed your right!"

IT TOOK MORONI'S plug uglies and the Italian to hold the two men. The hands were almost identical as to coloring, though Zimmerman's was swollen much the worse.

"You see," smiled Jim, "I inoculated both packages of payoff money with certain germs and chemicals. The cabbie's hands, you will note, are black and blue and purple. Mr. Zimmerman and Mr. Decker here possess hands of an identical color, red. Zimmerman took his payoff and went directly to the Federal Cigar Store where he split with Decker! Which, I believe proves association between Decker and Zimmerman!"

"It don't prove a damned thing," snarled Decker. "The guy came in and bought a cigar. I simply made change."

Across the room Moroni's eyes were narrow and contemplative. The big Italian moved close to the smaller Italian, who was Big Boy Moroni.

Jim said, "Now, let's move on. When Dolores went to the house and into Lora Martin's apartment, she was practically caught searching—by whom? Frank Zimmerman. She trailed Lora Martin and Shapiro from the M&S Hospital to their Dobbs Ferry hideout—and in turn was trailed by someone else! Someone who saw her attach a tracer of my own to the Martin woman's car. Someone who let her get to the point where she was ready to peep into a window before he knocked her unconscious—and taped her eyelids!" He paused dramatically. "The eyes were taped because the girl had seen her assailant, and might see him again, in another capacity. Who was in a position to keep an eye on her? Who was suspicious of her? Frank Zimmerman!"

Zimmerman's laugh wasn't nice. "After a while I'll be the guy that sank the Lusitania! How you going to prove all this? The Colquitt woman didn't see who hit her according to your story, Shapiro's dead and where's the Martin gal? Nuts, say I."

"The point I'm making," smiled Jim, "is that *if* it was Zimmerman, he was connected not only with Decker but with Shapiro as well!"

A silence followed that cracking remark. Moroni broke it. "*If*," he said, "that is so, then it's rather logical to believe that Decker, Zimmerman's associate in blackmail, also knew things about Shapiro which he didn't tell his boss!" Though his voice was soft and silky there was so evident a threat in it that Dicey Decker blanched, and started to protest.

"To go on hypothetically," said Jim, "suppose Shapiro came back here to New York, and started an opposition football pool. Small stuff, but a start. Suppose Decker here and Zimmerman decided to go against you, Moroni, and with Shapiro!"

"It's a lie," howled Decker.

Moroni said, "Shut up!" Decker subsided.

"Then let's say Decker had another scheme or so, which Shapiro wanted none of because he wasn't ready for it! Suppose that scheme was the dumping of the Kid Bolo fight plans, made by Moroni!"

You could feel the tenseness. Jim waited a few seconds and went on.

"The man who killed Maria and Kid Bolo had to be the kidnaper of Maria, didn't he, Moroni?"

"According to the way I figure!"

"THEN, WHAT IF I can prove that the man who killed the two Filipinos was the same man who trailed Dolores Colquitt to the Dobbs Ferry roadhouse and hit her in the head. I think this farce has gone far enough, Moroni. You know what a spectrograph is?" He touched the apparatus on the table and explained its use. How by its prisms and lights it counted the elements to be found in dust, or any other spectra, so that it could be matched and classified.

She slapped his face and snarled, "Get away, you fool, and let me talk!"

"In other words," he concluded, "I have samples of dust and dirt from the roadhouse and from the Bolo flat. Every man in the room scraped his feet tonight before entering. By actual chemical comparison, that will stand up in any court in the country, I can prove that two men in this room were also in Bolo's flat, as well as in the Dobbs Ferry roadhouse! Those two men were Dicey Decker and Frank Zimmerman!"

"No, no," said Dicey. "Shapiro must have killed them, he must have! Sure, I was in both places, but that don't prove I committed any murders!"

"Bolo's killer," went on Jim, "stood for a long while behind the door of the middle bedroom. Oddly enough, that floor is matting covered. The spectrograph shows particles of straw, Decker, in dust taken from—" He whirled, "Zimmerman's shoes!"

"That's enough," snapped Zimmerman. He was up from his chair now, a gun had appeared like magic in his hand. "You'd never make it stick, but I ain't going to hang around and let you—" He opened the door.

Mephito raised one of his fire-sticks and brought it down on the man's head. He dropped.

Jim went on. "Zimmerman knows a lot about explosives. He made the nitro that was used in the attempt on Shapiro's life. I know how it was done. Decker... you want to talk?"

The fat man shook his head. Jim shrugged. "Moroni," he said, "this is something for you to judge." He told about Decker talking to Shapiro before the cigar store, told what he had said, told how he picked up Shapiro's paper and folded it, gave it to him.

"The nitro, made by Zimmerman and given to Decker, was folded into that paper," he said. "You see, Decker and Zimmerman wanted to re-fix the Bolo fight by snatching Bolo's wife, and evidently Shapiro wouldn't agree. Zimmerman pulled the snatch, taped his nose and went down the aisle to tell Bolo they'd done what they'd threatened to do. Bolo won the fight. Afterward, carried away by the beauty of the girl, Zimmerman killed her, and killed Bolo on the way out, for Bolo knew who had warned him, who had forced him to do what he did."

"A hell of a mess," snarled Decker. "I never messed around with Shapiro, boss. You going to believe me, or believe him?"

Before Moroni could answer, the door opened. A woman stood there. A beautiful woman, whose fair face was twisted with desperation. Tom said, "Lora Martin!"

Moroni knocked over his chair, stood staring as if in a trance. Jim said, "Gentlemen, Myrna Karnes. Her face and features were rebuilt at the same time Shapiro's were rebuilt."

Moroni walked slowly toward her, his eyes bright, his voice trembling with emotion. "Myrna! Ah—Myrna!"

Crack! She almost slapped him off his feet. She snarled, "Get away, you runty little fool! I hate you, hate you! Now let *me* talk!"

AND TALK SHE did, Moroni listening with his head sunken in his hands. She told how she and Shapiro had come back to New York, their faces altered, how Shapiro had determined to make a bit of easy money by muscling in on the football pools. She told how Decker, whom Shapiro had contacted, had wanted to fix the Bolo fight, as well as many others, and how Shapiro had asked to be counted out.

"It's like Jim Anthony has said," she told them. "I know Zimmy made that nitro, I know Decker put it in Dale's paper. They were afraid of him, and mad at him the same time. I took Dale out of the hospital because I loved him—and I hated him at the same time! A man can't understand that! I was tired, tired of always hiding out, tired of being struck and growled at because his nerves were on edge! But I couldn't see the police get him! When I recognized Jim Anthony at that awful apartment, I determined to bring it all to an end. But Anthony is right all the way. Zimmerman killed the Bolos, but Decker killed little Hymie Swartz."

She swayed on her feet, seemed about to collapse. Dolores Colquitt came out of the next room and led her away.

Jim said softly, "I think that concludes the performance, gentlemen, except for the calling of the police. All of this has been recorded for their information. Moroni, your promise is also recorded. I did my part. The real Lora Karnes is in Europe. I gave you—Myrna."

"My word is good," snapped Moroni, who had recovered himself. "I'm quitting and I'm leaving the country. Will you shake hands on it?"

Jim gripped his hand.

"As for Myrna," he said ruefully, rubbing his cheek, "I give her right back to you! What happens to her?"

"I'm letting her leave here of her own free will, Moroni. You're well rid of her. She crossed you, she crossed Shapiro. She's simply a female black sheep, that's all."

Moroni said, "All right, you fellows. Gather up Zimmerman and Decker. We'll drop them off at the police station for Mr. Anthony."

TOM SAID, "BUT it all isn't told yet. What happened when you took the fifty thousand to Shapiro? When did you suspect Lora Martin?"

"The letter caused me to be sure of my suspicions, the letter she purposely dropped behind the cot at the roadhouse. You see even then she'd decided to take me personally for getaway money—from Shapiro. When Zimmerman told her she and Shapiro were trailed all the way to the roadhouse, and that Dolores was my fiancée, she knew I'd be along sooner or later. She'd already planned what to do, in another way, and the letter was ready. She simply dropped it there, where I'd find it."

"But how did it confirm your suspicions?"

"Fingerprints, my boy. The letter was covered with them, all belonging to Lora Martin! If Mrs. Karnes had written it, some of *her* prints would have been on it. Obviously something was screwy. Then, this afternoon she didn't want to see Moroni. She told three or four other lies, and the request for $50,000 was pretty bold. Consequently, I had

Mephito tuck himself away in the rear of the roadster. He was outside the door with his handy little fire-stick when she emerged, after crowning me with a gun and leaving it in my hand. Mephito took care of her. Some of the neighbors must have heard the rumpus and called the cops."

"Boy, she was a mean one! And how in God's world did you persuade her to talk?"

"Simple." Jim walked to the table, picked up a piece of thin paraffin.

"Here's a nitrate test of her hand. She fired the gun that killed Shapiro. I promised her forty-eight hours start if she'd ratify my findings on Zimmerman and Decker. She did. Rotten all the way through, Tom, all the way."

Dolores said softly, "Men are chumps, aren't they, Jim?"

"In what way?"

"When she walked out of the hotel twenty minutes ago a man helped her into a limousine."

"And the man was—?"

"Big Boy Moroni," said Jim and Dolores together.

EPISODE VIII

THE HORRIBLE MARIONETTES

"DEAD MEN DANCING!" THOSE OMINOUS WORDS RANG IN JIM ANTHONY'S EARS, AND HE GAVE ALL HE HAD TO SAVE THE LIVES OF DOOMED MEN. BUT WHEN HIS FIANCEE AND HIS FRIENDS WERE THREATENED WITH DEATH, HE FOUND THAT MORE THAN THE FATE OF AMERICA'S DEFENSES WAS AT STAKE.

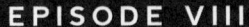

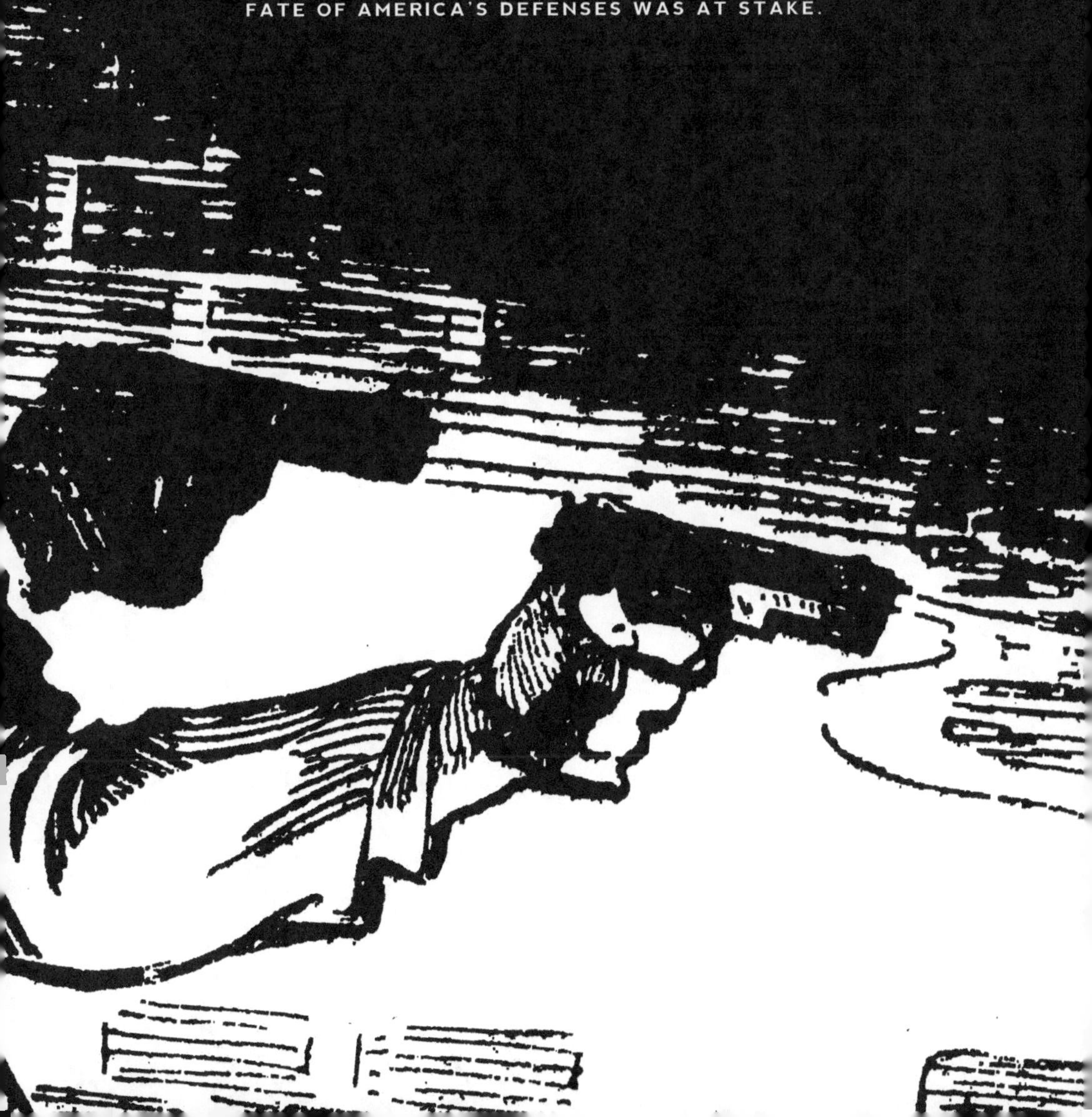

CHAPTER I

VOICE OF DOOM

ON THAT OMINOUS WEDNESDAY night in October, shortly before 10, the phenomenon known to the world as The Voice of Inspiration prepared to go on the air as usual. In the magnificent Westchester mansion bought with the offerings of millions of followers, The Voice—in the small, pudgy person of Maxwell Baldwin—gargled and spat, hemmed and coughed and addressed a few ringing words with appropriate gestures to the beaming bald head reflected in the bathroom mirror.

Satisfied that his miraculous vocal powers had not deteriorated since last week's broadcast, Baldwin rang for his valet to bring his full dress coat, slid into that beautifully tailored garment, and went downstairs with the exaggerated dignity of a little man who remembers that Napoleon, also, was no bodily giant.

Proceeding with mincing steps across rich carpets, regarding with bright blue eyes the luxurious appointments of the rooms through which he passed, Baldwin smiled, feeling no premonition of danger. He had come a long way since the days when he had hit the sawdust trail as a non-sectarian evangelist, preaching to motley crowds in Chillicothe and Uniontown. He was proud of the fame and prosperity that had visited him, and most people would have agreed he had a right to be.

It began when a small-town radio station asked him to deliver a religious talk. He preached one of his stock sermons, largely sentimental, and thought no more about it for a day or two. Then the laudatory letters began to pour in upon the station, many times more than any other program in its history had evoked.

The broadcasters were not slow to recognize that rare find, a voice which can project through the ether, whatever words it may speak, much the same charm as a great actor exerts upon an audience no matter how inept his role. It was such a voice as announcers strive for and some politicians would sell their souls for. It was a true radio voice, ordinary enough on the platform, but transmuted by the magic of vacuum tubes into a thing of wonder.

Baldwin had signed a contract with that small radio station, had broken it when a sponsor offered him a more remunerative one to sing the merits of certain reducing tablets (which he tried without success), had grown so popular that eventually he reneged on that contract, too, and organized his widespread League of Inspiration.

The idea behind the league was fetchingly simple. Anyone could join by paying ten cents for a green celluloid button. Any member could recommend philanthropic movements and causes in need of financial help, and The Voice would select those he considered most worthy and ask the world for contributions, mentioning the total amount he thought adequate.

Be it said to his credit that Maxwell Baldwin was an honest man, and the specified sums were sent promptly to the specified beneficiaries. But with the overflow—and once The Voice requested $4,000 to

The glare of the searchlight reached out from the boat and a burst of machine gun bullets splattered about him.

build a playground for an orphanage, and received $73,406.14—he dealt according to his own conscience. Not all his charities were widespread; a great many of them began and ended at home.

He did not always tout the merits of some needy cause over the Inter-Ocean Broadcasting network, which gave him half an hour of time without cost. Frequently he merely exhorted his listeners to be good churchgoers and staunch patriots, in all sincerity. And now and then he varied things by launching a blistering attack against some group which he considered subversively un-American.

This night he was prepared to hurl his incomparable voice into battle against an organization which, he had been informed on the

very best of authority, was deliberately undermining the peace and safety of the United States and all its Baldwin-conscious millions.

BALDWIN TURNED THE wrought-iron handle of a door and stepped into the long office in which his secretarial staff worked, counting stamps and coins and banknotes received by mail, answering thousands of letters and sending out pamphlet reprints of radio talks. Most of the staff had gone home, but two men and a bronze-haired girl in an office smock looked up as he entered. The girl, Lois Church, was there to answer the telephone and attend to various clerical tasks; the thin man with the careworn face was an Inter-Ocean technician, and Myron Linster was a bright young fellow whom Baldwin had hired recently, on unimpeachable recommendations, to be his personal secretary, replacing another bright young fellow who had been killed in an automobile smash.

Linster smoothed his dark hair, which was already smoother than it need be, and with his free hand offered a sheaf of typescript to Baldwin. Linster's brown-velvet eyes were respectful.

"If I may say so," he said, "it's dynamite, sir."

Baldwin nodded, pleased to be considered a juggler of dynamite as well as a dispenser of cheer and comfort.

"It'll make people sit up and take notice," he predicted. "It'll finish Anson Marner and his Apecia forever. It's just one more service I'll have done for my country."

The bronze-haired girl remained concentrated upon her notebook and the radio technician, not being on Baldwin's payroll, merely looked bored. But Linster, knowing how Baldwin hated Anson Marner and the Apecia, murmured agreeably.

Professional jealousy had a great deal to do with Baldwin's hatred. Marner was a radio orator, also, and the head of an organization whose full designation was the Association for the Preservation of European Cultures in America, but which was better known by the name coined from its initials—A-P-E-C-I-A. Marner had gathered under his banner thousands of persons of foreign birth and descent for the ostensible purposes of making better Americans of them and enriching American culture with the best features of their own various arts and cultures. A large number of people thought this a noble purpose and supported Marner liberally, and among them were several multi-millionaires.

Baldwin envied Marner those multi-millionaires, not one of whom wore the green celluloid button of the League of Inspiration. Baldwin's devotees were legion, but most of them were common people, poor or middle class, and some critics had suggested that their average intelligence was not of the highest.

However, it had been whispered lately that the Apecia was not the noble organization it pretended to be—was, in fact, a front for a group of spies and saboteurs, whose real task was to betray America into the hands of her potential enemies—and this was the sort of stuff Baldwin had been praying for. To make matters perfect, Baldwin had received evidence to support that theory from the one source no man, woman or child in America would doubt.

No less a person than James Anthony, world famous scientist and adventurer, arch-foe of traitors and criminals, had taken the trouble to look into the rumors. Anthony's agents had investigated the workings of the Apecia from within and without, and had learned things so significant that they deserved to be more widely known.

Anthony had elected to make Baldwin his spokesman, not because he admired The Voice of Inspiration, but because he realized The Voice's power over the masses. When Baldwin spoke, millions listened and other millions read his words in the newspapers. The coverage of the nation was complete.

Because he was busy with another matter even more important to the welfare of America, Anthony preferred not to broadcast the message himself and publicize it in his chain of newspapers, headed by the *New York Star*. That might have been even more effective, but it would also involve him in a controversy for which he had neither time nor inclination.

Holding the crisp sheets of typescript in his plump fingers, Baldwin passed into the small soundproof room which was his private broadcasting studio. Carefully he closed and locked the solid door behind him.

IN THE CENTER of the room was a reading stand, to which was affixed the microphone that carried his heaven-sent voice over the telephone wires to the Inter-Ocean broadcasting station on Long Island. There was no control booth, with engineers watching the speaker through a plate-glass partition. Baldwin was a veteran performer and a temperamental one; since he could not have a large visible audience, he preferred none at all, and the broadcasting officials agreed that he was experienced enough to need little or no supervision.

There was, however, a huge mirror covering one wall of the room, and it was the peculiar habit of The Voice to deliver his talks to himself as reflected therein. Immaculate in his evening clothes, he would strut and gesture enthusiastically, and his image would strut and gesture back at him.

He took two steps and fell, and knew nothing of the two men who stepped through the window.

If he admired himself and drew inspiration from his own elegance—if he was candidly vain in the solitude of this room with its curtained window—that was strictly his own affair.

The electric clock on the side wall said 9:58. A red light beneath it would flash when it was time for Baldwin to begin speaking. He placed the typed sheets on the reading stand and cleared his throat again, gazing fondly at his reflection.

The feeling of sleepiness that came upon him all at once brought a frown to his ordinarily serene forehead. He had napped for three hours, as usual, before dressing for his broadcast. There was no reason for him to be the least bit tired.

But he was, and he rubbed his eyes and passed a hand over his brow. He was suddenly so sleepy that he knew this talk would not be numbered among his best in point of delivery, and the knowledge annoyed him.

Could his drowsiness have anything to do, he wondered, with the faint scent of lilacs that permeated the air of the room? It was so subtle a fragrance that he had hardly noticed it when he entered, but now it seemed to have grown stronger.

Perhaps if he opened the window and let in fresh air....

He took two steps and fell, his face striking the carpeted floor. There was a flavor of blood on his lips and his strength seemed to flow away like water squeezed from a sponge. A terrible fear swept over him and he tried to scream, but the hoarse croak that came from his throat could never have been heard through the locked door, even if it had not been soundproofed.

Lying with his cheek against carpet, Baldwin saw the red light glow beneath the clock. He was supposed to be on the air, but he couldn't get up. What would his millions of listeners think? What about his triumph over the hated Anson Marner?

He would have wept, except that he hadn't strength enough to squeeze a tear from his heavy-lidded eyes. He slept, instead, and so knew nothing of the two men who came in through the window, their faces concealed behind grotesque gas masks, their right fists gripping respectively the butt of an automatic pistol and the handle of a glittering dagger.

BUT THE VOICE of Inspiration went on the air, nevertheless, according to schedule. It pulsed and rippled as vibrant waves in the ether, was snared by a million aerials and crashed forth in familiar rolling periods from a million loudspeakers throughout the length and breadth of the land. It stirred the followers of the League of Inspiration as it had never stirred them in the past, delivering one of the bitterest diatribes they had ever heard.

It mentioned names so august that Inter-Ocean officials trembled in their polished shoes. They thought of cutting the program off the air, and refrained only because The Voice had achieved tremendous popularity and it was well understood that Baldwin alone would stand responsible for all his utterances.

The Voice had called down the wrath of loyal Americans on the distinguished head of Jasper Logan, head of the world's greatest industrial organization, and upon four powerful businessmen known to have spent the last few days in Detroit in mysterious conference with Logan.

The Voice cried out to the nation:

"Jasper Logan is scheming to enslave America! He is planning, with the help of fascist-minded associates who dance when Logan pulls the strings, to destroy our sacred institutions by means of new and fearful weapons! He would set himself up as a dictator and grind the people beneath his heel for personal gain and glory!

"If America is to be saved from this new and awful threat, this arch-traitor and those who have allied themselves with him must perish! There are times when it is necessary to be cold-blooded, to do away with the few who threaten the welfare of the many...."

On and on rolled the sonorous accents, more like a voice of doom than a voice of inspiration, awakening fear and indignation and hatred in millions of hearts.

Not once during that part of the tirade which was permitted to reach the ears of the people was Anson Marner's name mentioned. Not once was there any allusion to the Apecia.

CHAPTER II

NIGHT RAID

A **THOUSAND MILES NORTH** and west of Maxwell Baldwin's pretentious domicile, a campfire gleamed in the aromatic darkness of the pine woods of Michigan's upper peninsula. Its yellow rays sprayed over two young men who lounged at either side of the curling flames.

One of the men sat up. He was a huge, battered hulk of a fellow with tousled red hair and a guileless freckled face. He wore high boots and corduroy breeches and was bundled up to the neck in a heavy sweater against the autumn cold of Lake Superior.

He glanced at his left wrist. "Holy cats!" he exclaimed. "I left my watch in the plane, Jim. It must be close to 10. Shall I tune in on Inter-Ocean?"

His companion, who was stretched full-length on the carpet of pine needles, turned his head to note between the treetops the position of Ursa Major in its celestial swing around Polaris.

"Not yet, Tom. According to the stars you'll have to wait a few minutes to hear The Voice of Inspiration."

And James Anthony returned to his brooding thoughts, reflecting briefly that watches and clocks could lie, and all the creations of men were fallible one way or another, but the stars and the sun and the seasons could always be depended upon if one had the wisdom to understand them.

Such primitive wisdom was Jim Anthony's by inheritance from his mother, who had been Fawn Johntom, last of the Comanche princesses. Because of it he lay almost naked on the pine needles, wearing only a breechclout and buckskin moccasins, and would have been comfortable even without the warmth of the little fire. To have a body that could withstand extremes of cold and heat without discomfort, to bring muscles and nerves and all physical attributes to the highest possible state of perfection—that was the very first culture of the primitives.

He was no less a child of nature because his uncanny brain dealt with scientific problems beyond the comprehension of most men. His inexhaustible energy was drawn from the solitude of forests and mountains and expended freely among the teeming masses of humanity.

For the past week he had consulted daily with America's five ranking business and industrial leaders and had worked nightly over drawing boards and tables of specifications, outlining a colossal program for the production of a secret device which would make the United States forever safe from invasion.

Now, those tiresome preliminaries ended, he had sought the seclusion of the wilds to clear his lungs of smoke and dust and his mind of petty details before proceeding with the next step of his self-appointed task.

THE FIRELIGHT TURNED his smooth bronze skin to gold, highlighting the banded muscles of his arms, shoulders and chest. His was the kind of heroic figure that has been too seldom seen in the world since the days of the Greek athletes—tall and solid, but supple as a willow wand and perfectly proportioned.

The most amazing of Anthony's attributes, however, were not apparent on the surface. Those glowing eyes could see in the dark like a cat's; that bold nose could interpret scents that normally would be significant only to hounds; those keen ears could hear the farthest and faintest sounds.

Great as was his debt to his dark-eyed mother, Jim's inheritance from his swashbuckling Irish father equaled it. Shean Boru Anthony had been a scientific genius and an adventurer on a grand scale. He had made the world his playground and workshop, raising sunken ships, uncovering ancient treasures, enriching the world by his amazing discoveries and his son by his teachings. His death had placed in Jim's capable hands one of the truly immense fortunes of modern times.

A product of two great civilizations, young Anthony was all American. In the wilderness, where he was happiest; in the laboratory, where he solved problems of the future and invented for his own use devices for which the world was not yet ready; in the field of crime detection, where he matched wits in perilous combat with the world's master criminals—in all his farflung activities, his first thought was for his country, his last for himself.

The newspapers called him the greatest detective of all time, resourceful guardian of his nation, champion of the poor. It was one case where the press did not exaggerate.

Tom Gentry, who was Anthony's closest friend and constant companion, lacked the shatterproof calm of the bronze giant. He squirmed, uneasy in the vast silence and eyed the portable radio beside him.

"Holy cow!" he grumbled. "Isn't it pretty near time?"

Anthony grinned faintly. "I'll tell you when."

"If only something would happen!" Gentry mourned. "You ought to be spoiling for excitement after organizing ten billion dollars' worth of industry to build a hundred thousand Triple-A Ray units."

This time Anthony did not grin. His dark eyes clouded.

"There'll be plenty of excitement, Tom."

"You've got a hunch?"

Anthony grunted. "Hunch" was as good a word as any for the strange foreboding that had come to him as he lay beneath the wheeling stars. It was a thing that had happened often before and had always presaged danger. It was the operation of a mystical seventh sense that might have been compounded of Irish "second sight" and

"There will be dead men dancing!" Mephito proclaimed. "The evil one comes, and the devil magic strikes!"

the queer foreknowledge of Fawn Johntom's people—such a blending of instinct and intuition as once was the property of men in common with the animals of the woods and plains, but has been buried beneath layers of artificial civilization until now, when it is occasionally encountered, it seems superhuman.

What kind of danger? He could not say, nor guess its source. But that it would concern the Anthony Anti-Aircraft Ray Projector, the most efficient defense weapon ever developed—and that it would menace the trusted friends who had been associated with him in its construction— he had not the slightest doubt.

His brow furrowed as he thought of one in particular who might become a target for the machinations of his enemies—a blonde, lovely girl named Dolores....

THOSE MYSTERIOUS DANGER-SIGNALS reached others than Jim Anthony. Five hundred miles south and east of the lonely campfire they penetrated earth and rock, making themselves felt inside one of the rolling green hills of lower Michigan, where Anthony had established temporary headquarters in what he called The Cavern.

Dolores Colquitt was worried. Her woman's intuition had suddenly become lively, stirring warnings in her breast. An ordinary girl might have been frightened by that inner disturbance, but Dolores, the daughter of Senator Ward Colquitt of New York, was in no way ordinary. She was extraordinarily beautiful, wise and fearless—and she was Jim Anthony's fiancée.

Mephito, who had been Fawn Johntom's father, added to her worries. He squatted on his withered haunches within a fireplace carved out of the rock wall of The Cavern. A toothless mummy of a man with white hair hanging to his shoulders and a loincloth about his lean middle, he sniffed at the smoke of a nine-stick fire.

Into the fire had gone sundry unpleasant items from the buckskin pouch at Mephito's hip—the dried front leg of a toad, the head of an adder, splinters of bone and pinches of brown powder. While the Comanche shaman chanted an unintelligible mumbo-jumbo, the flames sputtered into many colors and gave off a foul odor.

Closing his eyes, swaying back and forth in the smoke-wreathes, Mephito proclaimed, "The evil ones come! There will be dead men dancing when the devil-magic strikes! Oh, Jim, son of my daughter, beware!"

Dolores did not laugh at the old man's mouthings. She was an able scientist in her own right and had no faith in witchcraft—and yet she had seen too many of Mephito's predictions come true to take them lightly.

That one phrase, "dead men dancing," stuck in her mind.

Sitting in an armchair beneath a reading lamp in the subterranean chamber, which resembled an ancient alchemist's den equipped with modern machinery and experimental paraphernalia, she forced her hazel eyes back to the book in her lap. But the lines of type blurred before her eyes and she found it impossible to concentrate.

No one knew better than she the risks Jim would face in this new undertaking, should news of the Triple-A Ray leak out. Spies would be after its secret, as would power-seeking interests which sought in devious ways to gain control of what other men had created. The Anthony organization was strong, but so were other organizations that might be pitted against it—and those other organizations would have the advantage of being underhanded and unscrupulous in their methods of attack.

Dolores had not heard from Jim for two days. If only she could be sure he was safe....

"Devil-magic comes close!" the old Indian grunted. "Mephito go see."

He straightened with a motion exceptionally lithe for one so weighted with years. He padded into the tunnel that was one of the exits from the hidden workshop.

Dolores sighed with relief. In her anxious state of mind the weird old fellow's mumblings had got on her nerves. Now that he had gone, she might be able to get on with her reading.

But her intuition continued to send out disquieting alarms and the printed pages kept blurring. She looked longingly at the radiophone which was always tuned to Anthony's private wavelength. She would not call him, however, knowing that he might be engaged in some important task that would be hindered by needless interruptions. Sooner or later he would call The Cavern or, as he often did, return there unannounced.

She hoped it would be sooner.

THE TUNNEL INTO which Mephito had trotted so abruptly led to an elevator shaft which soared to a concealed door in the cellar of a trim white farmhouse atop the hill. Bill Roarty, a middle-aged farmer, lived there and tilled some of the fields at the back of the hill, away from the steep cliff that overhung a dragon-shaped lake.

Bill Roarty's neighbors, the nearest of whom lived a mile and a quarter away, knew only that he was a bachelor and an unsociable man. They were surprised, therefore, when he took in a boarder, weeks after the summer guest season had ended. The fact that the boarder was more aloof than Roarty himself, and a foreigner into the bargain, did not tend to lessen their astonishment.

The masked man fired, but as Dawkins plunged forward he did not hear the shot.

The boarder's name was Dawkins. His manner was fastidious, even snobbish to a degree, and his accent was unadulterated cockney. Abe Heckels, the grizzled proprietor of the general store in the village, never tired of telling how Dawkins had once asked, " 'Ere, my good man, cawn't we h'obtain h'enny h'imported caviar h'in this h'establishment?"

Tonight Dawkins, his thin body clad in a red velvet dressing gown, sat in the living room of the farmhouse and toasted his slippered feet against the fender of the Franklin stove. Roarty, a stocky, unshaven man in overalls, puffed a corncob pipe at the window. The tin alarm clock on the shelf said 9:55.

"Being Mr. h'Anthony's valet 'as h'its good points," Dawkins was saying. "H'I've lived h'an h'adventurous life, but never so h'adventurous h'as since h'I went h'into the mawster's service. Tyke the times we 'ad

cornering Rado Ruric, who thought no more h'of killing a 'undred people than h'I'd think h'of squashing h'a mosquito—"

"You c'n have yer excitement," Roarty interrupted. "Me, I like the job I got, taking care of this place fer Anthony. I only farm five acres an' he pays me more'n I'd make if I farmed five hundred. A life o' ease is what I allus wanted."

The little Englishman sighed. "H'it tykes h'all kinds, h'as the saying goes. Now, h'I couldn't live without h'a bit h'of h'action now h'and—" He broke off, listening to a sound from the kitchen. "What 'o!"

"It ain't nothin'," Roarty said placidly. "Old houses is allus makin' noises."

Dawkins glanced at a clear glass ball on the whatnot in the corner and was mollified. The farmhouse was lighted by gasoline pressure lanterns, but it was ringed by electrical safeguards. Beams of "black light" guarded the foot of the hill and the shore of the lake. Should a trespasser break one of the beams, the glass ball would glow blood-red.

"H'as h'I was saying—" he began, when he had to yawn. It was strange, for he had felt wide awake five minutes ago. He breathed deeply and caught a scent of lilac perfume. He looked at Roarty and was astonished to see that rustic gentleman's head nodding.

Dawkins' astonishment conspired against his sudden sleepiness, and a second later a footstep and a shocking vision jolted him into temporary wakefulness again.

THE VISION WAS of two bent figures whose bodies were human, but whose faces were made hideous by goggles and rubber masks. Between them they carried a large metal container with a thin spout from which a cloudy gaseous substance hissed. Their free hands pointed black automatic pistols at the wide-eyed valet.

The brain of Dawkins operated swiftly, even though the smell of lilacs had grown suffocatingly strong. He understood instantly that enemies had somehow penetrated the supposedly foolproof alarm system, bringing with them a highly anesthetic, if not deadly, gas. That gas, released into the fans that ventilated The Cavern, no doubt would kill or render unconscious whoever breathed it.

Anthony's sweetheart and grandfather—the two people Jim loved all above others—were down there. So were the plans and working models of Jim's precious Triple-A Ray projector, which could make

America forever secure if used rightly, or could destroy America if it fell into the hands of her foes.

Dawkins was not a reckless man, but he was an intensely loyal one. He owed Jim Anthony a debt of gratitude greater than he could ever hope to repay, and never for a moment did he forget it. He would have laid down his life for his employer cheerfully, if by so doing he could further Jim's plans or protect that which was dear to him.

His hand moved without hesitation inside his dressing gown toward his left shoulder, where he carried a neat .32 automatic in a shoulder clip. His fingers touched the butt of the gun and closed about it as he held his breath against the enervating gas.

The masked men fired simultaneously. Their pistols packed the farmhouse with thunder, but Dawkins did not hear it. He felt a white-hot pain cleaving his skull, burning into his brain, for a fractional second. There was a burst of blinding light that seemed to come from within his eyeballs, and then there was nothing at all.

CHAPTER III

ANTIDOTE FOR VENOM

ANTHONY SAID, "ALL RIGHT, Tom. It's time."

Eagerly Gentry turned his attention to the portable radio. He touched a switch and the tubes whined, picking up WGLO, *The Globe* station in Detroit, an Inter-Ocean unit. Jim, who was the chief owner of *The Globe,* heard the announcer's voice:

"...and now, for the one hundred and eighty-fourth consecutive Wednesday night, we bring you the charm and wisdom of The Voice of Inspiration...."

A moment later Jim tensed, hearing with incredulous ears the words that poured from the loudspeaker to echo in the stillness of the forest.

"Jasper Logan is scheming to enslave the nation...."

"Gee-man-EEE!" gasped Tom, his blue eyes distended. "Holy cats, he's doublecrossed you! He's sold out to—"

Anthony silenced him with a gesture. He leaned toward the loudspeaker, sensing a false note, recognizing what not one in ten thousand of Baldwin's regular listeners would have recognized.

"It isn't Baldwin, Tom. It's someone imitating Baldwin—good, but not good enough."

"Sounds like The Voice to me, Jim. It'll fool everybody. What'll we do?"

Jim arose, his splendid muscles moving rhythmically beneath his skin. He strode swiftly through the trees surrounding the clearing and his eyes picked out the *Thunderbird II* resting on the surface of the river, a quarter-mile back from the shore line of Lake Superior. He waded through cold water that reached his knees, opened the cabin door and hoisted himself within.

The interior of the huge four-motored Douglas transport plane had been converted into a complete efficiency apartment. Jim

A shudder ran through her as she saw
the needle. The man was dead.

switched on lights, seated himself at a desk and set dials in a sloping surface before him. He fitted a telephone headset around his neck and over his ears. There was a high-pitched hum of power.

"WQ210," Anthony said into the transmitter, giving the Inter-Ocean call letters. "Anthony calling WQ210. Urgent!"

Tom clambered aboard. He carried the portable set in one hand and his boots under his arm. His teeth were chattering.

"Calling WQ210—"

A voice purred in the phones, "Come in, Mr. Anthony."

His face grim in the cabin lights, Anthony gave terse orders. Half a minute ticked by. Then another voice came on.

"This is Robert Lawton, Mr. Anthony. We were thinking of trying to reach you. Is it about the Inspiration program?"

Lawton, executive vice-president of Inter-Ocean, was one of the few men who knew that Anthony was the majority stockholder in the broadcasting company.

"Something's happened to Baldwin," Anthony snapped. "That's another man talking. Cut him off the air immediately and put me on in his place."

"Certainly, Mr. Anthony. One of our sound engineers thought it didn't seem natural, but the rest of us—"

"Immediately, Lawton!"

JIM GLANCED INTO Tom's bewildered face. The latter still held the portable radio and the counterfeit voice still blared from the loudspeaker, pouring not inspiration, but hatred and confusion, into millions of hearts.

"There are times when it is necessary to be cold-blooded, to do away with the few who threaten the welfare of the many. Better that five men should die than that a nation be—"

Silence cut across the sentence. The doom-laden voice was obliterated by a switch thrown in Long Island. Anthony had a vision of people all across the country, stunned and shocked and distrustful.

He addressed those people, not waiting to be introduced.

"This is James Anthony speaking. Men and women of America, you have been listening to an impostor! Something has happened to Maxwell Baldwin, The Voice of Inspiration—something that has yet to be explained. I suggest that the police station nearest his home investigate right away!

"The attack you have just heard upon Jasper Logan and his associates was untrue and unfair. You have my word for that—the word of Anthony, which has never been false! I have spent this week with Logan and the four men he has summoned to help him in this hour of America's need. It is their one desire to safeguard the United States from the fate of Europe. By pooling their resources and bringing other industrialists into line, these five can build impregnable defenses in less than half the time Washington has estimated would be needed!

"I ask that you keep open minds until the truth about that unprecedented occurrence can be known fully. As soon as news is available, it will be broadcast through these stations. James Anthony signing off!"

Jim spun the dials to another wavelength. He spoke briefly and pointedly to Gibbons, managing editor of the *New York Star,* and Allen, night editor of the *Detroit Globe.* Through *The Globe* switchboard he put in a long distance call to Marquette, Michigan, where Arthur Fallon, the rich mine owner lived. Fallon was one of Logan's four associates in this all-important enterprise, and Jim had flown him home in the *Thunderbird II* that afternoon.

Anthony's brain functioned nimbly, scanning possibilities, making tentative plans, while all the time that mystical seventh sense spoke of imminent peril. He was as certain as he had ever been of anything that the false voice in the ether had not been jesting when it prescribed death for the men it had denounced.

"You wanted excitement," he said to Gentry, who stood beside him in his wet socks. "Start warming up the motors. Soon as I get some information we're moving—and if we don't move fast, you and I and America are apt to take the worst licking of our lives!"

Tom's freckles were dark splotches on his pale face. He dropped the boots and sprinted for the controls in the nose of the ship. The whine of the starters came back to Anthony.

OLD MEPHITO REACHED the elevator at the end of the tunnel. He had a deep distrust of mechanical contrivances and would have preferred stairs or a ladder, but there were none of those about The Cavern. He stepped reluctantly into the metal cage, closed the door and was wafted soundlessly upward.

A section of the rough stone wall of the farmhouse cellar swung out before Mephito's hands. He crept through blackness up a flight of stone stairs to the kitchen.

The kitchen door was ajar. The heavy scent of lilacs filled his nostrils. But Mephito knew that lilacs would not bloom until April.

"Devil-magic!" he muttered, and held his breath.

The *blam-blam* of two shots, fired almost in unison, stung his eardrums. Mephito hesitated, not in fear, but in caution. The kitchen was dimly lit by the reflection of lantern rays from the living room and his obsidian eyes fell upon stovewood stacked against one wall. He selected a heavy length of oak.

Making no more noise than a shadow, the white-haired shaman moved to the living room doorway. First of all he saw Dawkins lying on the floor, his greying hair matted by blood, and Bill Roarty sleeping in his chair.

Then he saw the masked men standing at either side of a metal tank on the floor. No gas issued from the tank now.

"Elevator's downstairs," one of the intruders said. "We shoot the nerve gas down the shaft into the ventilating fans. Then we go down and grab the girl and whatever else looks worth taking."

The other man made a sound of assent. "It's duck soup, Karl. This bird Anthony can't be as tough as they say. We make the dame give us the plans, or else use her to force Anthony to turn 'em over. It's a pipe!"

Mephito acted quickly. His lungs were clamoring for air, but he did not want to breathe in any scent of non-existent lilacs. He lifted his stovewood club and brought it down expertly on the head of the man called Karl, and the man thudded to the floor, quivering.

The other swore hysterically and wheeled, bringing his automatic into line with the skinny body of the Indian. Mephito had no time for finesse. He swung the oak with all his strength.

The second gunman died then and there. His skull collapsed horribly, caving into his brain, and the pistol dropped before he could squeeze the trigger. He crumpled in a grotesque heap.

Calmly Mephito smashed the glass from a window, thrust his head outside and gulped fresh air. When he turned back his wise eyes told him that Dawkins had only suffered a scalp wound and Roarty was sunk in what appeared to be a natural sleep.

"Ugh!" he grunted. "One devil-man die, but other devil-man can talk." He grabbed Karl's arm and dragged him through the kitchen, down the stone steps and into the elevator. He muttered, "Dolores make him talk in his sleep with brain-wave machine!"

DOLORES DROPPED THE book she had been trying to read unsuccessfully. She sprang to her feet, her lovely face pale, when she saw the unconscious man in the gas mask.

"What happened?" she gasped.

Mephito grinned toothlessly. "Evil ones come like fire-spirits say. Mephito fixum!"

He hoisted the limp body effortlessly upon a couch. With a pair of heavy shears he snipped threadlike cord from a reel on the workbench. The cord, a special invention of Anthony's, was light as common string, but possessed the tensile strength of a quarter-inch woven steel cable. He tied the man's thumbs together behind his back, took off his shoes and socks and tied his big toes together.

Dolores stripped off the gas mask. The man's face was hawklike and swarthy, the nose like a sharpened wedge, the lips cruel. It was the crafty face of a criminal.

"The dream-machine," Mephito said.

The blonde girl brought it from a cabinet, a box no larger than a portable typewriter case. Upon it was a stylus which drew a green line upon a revolving cylindrical graph. Working rapidly and efficiently, now that she had something definite to do, she fitted a pair of electrodes to the insensible man's temples.

The brain-wave interpreter was one of the newest of Anthony's amazing contrivances. It worked on the simple principle, long accepted by scientists, that the human brain sent forth electrical impulses and was in fact a miniature radio broadcasting unit.

Men think, consciously or subconsciously, in words, and the thought-concept of a word is a grouping of letters. As the stylus moved and the cylinder turned, the green-ink line traced a series of peaks, each of a different height, each corresponding to a letter of the alphabet. By means of long experimentation Anthony had found—and taught Dolores—a means by which the broken line could be read almost as easily as print.

Dolores would see what she could learn from the ceaseless stream of thoughts passing through Karl's subconscious mind. Then she would call Jim and inform him of the attack on The Cavern.

Mephito said, "I go for Dawkins and Roarty." He vanished on moccasined feet into the tunnel.

The cylinder began to revolve, the stylus to trace a serrate line. Dolores bent close, her bright eyes reading the letter-signs.

"…get the dame and torture her…. She may know about Triple-A Ray…. If not Anthony may tell to save her life…. Destroy faith of country in leaders…. Great scheme, that of Marner's…. Dead men dancing…."

DOLORES JUMPED. DEAD men dancing! Those had been the very words of Mephito! And Marner—that could only be Anson Marner, leader of the Apecia, which Jim's agents had recently inves-

"Somebody's playing jokes—
sent me that marionette
that looks like me—"

tigated. Jim had said something about the Apecia being an enemy group formed for espionage and sabotage activities!

She bent over the graph again—but the man's eyes were open now, and they were hard, daring eyes.

"Where am I?" he demanded. "What are you doing?" He tried to move, but gave it up when he felt the cords binding him.

"I'm finding out things about you," said Dolores. "What's your name?"

"None of your damn' business!" the man snarled—but the green line spelled out "Karl Ogrund."

She said, "Karl Ogrund. Thank you. And you work for Anson Marner. You were going to torture me to learn about the Triple-A Ray. You see, it's no use trying to hide things. I can read your mind!"

An expression of consternation crossed the pinched face. The serrate line said, "Mustn't tell anything. Sure death if I do. Might as well die with my mouth shut." The man squirmed, his hands moving behind his back.

"What is the meaning of 'dead men dancing?'" she asked. "What men are dead or will be? How will they dance?"

A shudder ran through Karl Ogrund's frame. His face contorted, his eyes rolled upward, his mouth sagged open. Dolores shook him and his head rolled loosely. She turned him and saw his fingers gripping an object concealed in the lining of his coat. The gleaming point of a hypodermic needle pierced the cloth of the coat and penetrated his hip.

He was dead. Rather than betray his master and run the risk of that betrayal, he had killed himself, as spies had frequently been known to do.

Dolores bit her lip, chagrined at not having made Mephito search the prisoner. Jim would never have made that mistake. Jim would have learned all that was in the man's mind. He would have read instantly the thought-line which she saw only now on the graph:

"I'll use the hypo…. Prussic acid works fast…."

All her worries returned, redoubled in strength. She had absolute proof that terrible danger threatened herself, her fiancé and the nation they both loved above all else—but her only chance of discovering when and where it would strike, so that it might be warded off, was gone!

CHAPTER IV

THE MARIONETTES

THE MEN WHO RAN the Anthony newspapers were trained in speed and accuracy. With scores of telephone lines at their disposal and reporters awaiting assignments in key positions, they were in better shape to find out things than was Jim, with his single radio in the Northwoods.

Allen, night editor of *The Globe,* was the first to call. His staff had located three of the five men whose safety was important to Anthony and to America, and had a clue to the location of a fourth.

Most important, Jasper Logan was secure in his suburban mansion. The gaunt, grey man, whose industrial empire gave a livelihood to a million men and influenced the lives of a million more, had laughed at the radio attack as the product of a disordered mind. At sixty, the self-made chief of Logan Motors Corporation was a hard-bitten, fantastic, dominant figure, without whom the Triple-A Ray production program would have difficult sledding; but with him his factories could turn out the weapons as easily as now they turned out automobiles, airplanes, tractors, locomotives and many other products.

At Logan's home, as his guests, were two of the others—Royal Phail, the fat and affable chairman of the board of the Seaboard & Prairie Bank and directing genius of numerous subsidiary trust companies, whose job it was to finance the vast plant expansions that would be needed, and James Bessingham, the slim, elegant and sickly head of Bessingham Steel of Pittsburgh, which controlled half the steel mills in the East.

There was no immediate word of Guy Van Rucker, president of Great Eastern Electric. But the clubfooted old Dutchman, whose ambition was to outlive the doctors who warned that his heart would stop unless he retired from business, had left for his Philadelphia home by automobile that afternoon, and probably was spending the night somewhere in Ohio or western Pennsylvania.

That left only Arthur Fallon, the mine operator. Jim had personally delivered that jolly, red-faced little Irishman to his home six hours

ago, and as soon as *The Globe* operator completed that long-distance call to Marquette, Fallon could be warned.

The *New York Star* came through as soon as *The Globe* had finished, reporting what its men and the police had been able to discover. According to Gibbons, managing editor, Baldwin had disappeared and there were no clues to the mystery of what had happened to him, unless a stain of blood on the carpet could be counted as a clue. Moreover, Myron Linster, Baldwin's secretary, had left the house before the police arrived and could not be located. A hundred yards

As he walked in with the two
murderers he saw the lifeless
body dancing in midair.

from the house they had found the spot where phone wires had been tapped and a microphone cut in so that Baldwin's impersonator could deliver his scurrilous talk.... Anson Marner, founder of the Apecia, claimed to have been in his suite in the Waldorf-Anthony Hotel all evening. He had expressed surprise and indignation at the radio attack upon Logan and his associates, some of whom he knew, and all of whom he professed to respect highly....

None of Jim's Comanche ancestors could have been more grimly patient than he, sitting like a bronze statue at his radio in the Northwoods, waiting for the clue or intuitive urge that would dictate his first move. Yet, behind his calm eyes, his brain worked with flashing speed, assorting and cataloging the meager facts in his possession, giving each item its proper place and significance.

Logan, Bessingham and Phail were safe enough for the present. Logan's home and offices were guarded by armed sentries, and short of bombing from the skies it would be next to impossible for any harm to reach them.

But what of Van Rucker and Fallon? Had they heard the broadcast? Did they have any inkling that daring and resourceful enemies had declared war upon them? Were they taking measures to protect themselves from the fate prescribed for them by the false Voice?

A FEMININE CALL broke through the hum in the earphones. Anthony smiled fondly, recognizing Dolores Colquitt's voice; and then he stiffened as he caught her undertone of tension. He listened without comment while she described the invasion of the farmhouse, the wounding of Dawkins, the heroism of Mephito and the experiment with the brain-wave machine.

When she had finished, he said, "Are you sure that was the phrase, 'dead men dancing?'"

"Positive, Jim. Mephito used exactly the same words when he was burning his shaman sticks!"

"I'll be at The Cavern before dawn if I can make it," he said tersely. "Otherwise I'll call you. The switch just inside the tunnel turns on a second alarm system. Have Roarty seal the tunnel with the airtight door and shut off the ventilating machinery. There's plenty of air, but if it gets stuffy you can open an oxygen tank. Nobody can get to you without using a hundred tons of dynamite, but if there's any alarm call me immediately!"

"All right, Jim, dear. Take care of yourself!"

Jim ended the conversation abruptly. The portable radio was blaring forth the first of the news broadcasts on the affair at the Baldwin house and a part of it sounded interesting. "…Myron Linster, Baldwin's missing secretary, whom the police are seeking, had only been with the radio orator about ten days. He replaced a former secretary who was killed in a highway collision under circumstances which police called mysterious. Linster was formerly the secretary of Alfred Ericson, who was chief engineer of the Logan Motors Corporation until recently, when a reported quarrel with Logan brought about his resignation.

Alfred Ericson! Dead men dancing! Hadn't the bogus Voice of Inspiration spoken of men dancing on strings pulled by Logan?

ANTHONY'S EYES GLITTERED as he took a day-old copy of *The Globe* from a rack near the desk. Jim knew Ericson well and admired the grizzled engineer's inventive genius as much as he deplored his irascible and violent temper. He opened the paper to the third page and looked long and earnestly at the curious picture beneath the caption:

ENGINEER'S PUPPETS STOLEN

The picture showed five marionettes created by Ericson, whose hobby was making animated dolls for his own and his friends' amusement. It was generally known that since his resignation from Logan Motors, Ericson's resentment against Logan, whether justified or not, was keen. The inventor had seized upon the meeting of Logan with the four other leaders of industry to express his scorn of his erstwhile employer.

These newest marionettes were so ingenious that the newspapers had not hesitated to publicize them in a spirit of harmless fun. There was a large figure representing Logan, ludicrously recognizable in carved wood, pulling strings at the ends of which his four collaborators danced upon a stage.

When a crank was turned the strings moved and the slender Bessingham waltzed, his feet fastened to revolving discs; Van Rucker performed a heavy-footed clog, his clubfoot thumping; Fallon's hands and feet jerked in a lively imitation of an Irish jig, and the rotund body of Phail, suspended between rubber bands, went through vibratory motions reminiscent of that terpsichorean phenomenon of the 'twenties, the shimmy.

It was undeniably funny. Nearly everyone laughed, including the men who were thus caricatured. And then someone had broken into Ericson's home and stolen the animated figures, and the theft had been reported to the police.

WITH HIS DEEPEST instincts telling him that something ominous and threatening lay behind the Baldwin affair, Anthony began to think of it in connection with the theft. The speech and the marionettes disparaged the same five men. The authorities had been unable to guess why a burglar had bothered to take articulated dolls of little or no monetary value.

He got *The Globe* by radio again. "Connect me with Alfred Ericson's house," he directed.

He recognized the voice of Ruth, Ericson's 19-year-old daughter. She said, "No, Mr. Ericson isn't in. Who's calling? ...Oh, Mr. Anthony, I wish I could tell you where he went! He didn't say a word except that he might not be back for three or four days. Somebody phoned

Jim raced to the end of the pier and dived into the iciness of the lake.

him from New York and he went out ten minutes later. He didn't take any luggage."

"He never went away like that before, did he?"

"Never. Mr. Anthony, he's been so queer the last few days—ever since he had that row with Mr. Logan! He's always been high-strung and impatient, but never like this...."

A thoughtful frown creased Anthony's brow. No one knew better than he the terrible changes that could take place in brilliant but erratic minds, like Ericson's, when hatred lodged there. Moreover, Myron Linster had been Ericson's secretary, and Anthony was aware that the young man not only held his employer in high regard, but happened to be in love with Ruth Ericson!

Why had Linster left Ericson to work for Baldwin, after Baldwin's secretary had died violently? Did Linster's presence, and his flight from the house, indicate that he was involved in the murder or kidnaping of Baldwin? And if so, was Linster thereby carrying out some mad plan of Ericson's?

Jim hated to believe it, but he had to admit that it was possible. Unbalanced by his row with Logan, Ericson might have determined to strike at his erstwhile employer through the latter's most important venture—the mass production of Triple-A units. To that end he might have enlisted Linster's aid.

It was even conceivable that the two of them had joined forces with Anson Marner and the Apecia!

Tom Gentry, huddled in one of the pilot chairs up forward, toasting his feet in the hot draft from the heater vent, looked over his shoulder. "Find out anything, Jim?"

"Plenty," Jim growled. "Soon as I find out one more thing—"

A VOICE FROM the radio interrupted him. "We've completed your Marquette call, Mr. Anthony. Here is Mr. Fallon."

The Irish mine owner chuckled, and the chuckle was borne five hundred miles over telephone wires to Detroit and hurled back five hundred miles through the ether to where Jim sat, only a twentieth of that distance from Marquette.

"Hello there, Jim! Operator says she been trying to get me for half an hour. I stopped at a friend's for dinner. Is anything wrong?"

"That's what I want to know. Did you listen to The Voice of Inspiration on the radio?"

"Not me. I don't care for that sentimental bunk."

"Tonight's talk wasn't sentimental. Someone kidnaped Baldwin and made a speech in his place. He said you and Logan and the others were traitors and ought to be killed."

Fallon's rich chuckle sounded again. "Somebody's playing jokes. Know what I found waiting for me when I came in? That marionette of Ericson's that looks like me—the one that jigs—or else its double. It's the damnedest, funniest—"

A note of sharpness crept into Anthony's tone. "Was there any message?"

"Not unless a poison label is a message. There's a skull and crossbones pasted on it!"

This was the clue Anthony had been waiting for. He sat straighter in his chair. "Who's with you, Fallon?"

"I'm alone. The wife and kids went to Milwaukee to see her folks. The servants had a holiday while I was in Detroit."

"I'm coming up," Anthony said. "I'll see you within an hour. Lock your doors, Fallon, and if you've got a gun keep it handy. Don't let anyone in but me."

Fallon was concerned. "You really think there's danger?"

"I think so. I can't be sure. We'll find out."

"What do you suppose—?"

"We'll talk when I get there. Anybody might be tuned in to this wavelength. Sit tight and be careful."

He slipped off the headset and got up. Through his magnificent frame ran the not unpleasant tingle that invariably thrilled him when combat lay just ahead. He knew now in which direction the peril lay, and his dark eyes glowed with eagerness to meet it.

CHAPTER V
DEATH IN JIG-TIME

TUGGING GENTLY AT HER mooring line, the *Thunderbird II* pointed her nose downstream toward the impenetrable blackness of the lake. Her motors purred outside the insulated cabin and her metal propellers made glistening transparent circles in the night.

Anthony opened the cabin door and leaned down toward the step beneath it, where the line was attached. He cast it free.

"We're going back to Marquette," he called to Gentry. "We're going as fast as ten thousand horsepower can take us."

Under an open throttle the plane swam downstream, her motor roar shattering the forest stillness. Floodlights under her metal wings sprayed brilliance over the surface of the water, showing it free from obstructions.

Pulling a black sweater over his head, thrusting his long legs into dark slacks, replacing his wet moccasins with rubber-soled canvas shoes, Anthony slid into the chair at another desk, where an illuminated map lay under a ground-glass surface. In the reflected light from the instrument panel his craggy face was purposeful.

The river mouth widened ahead of them and the mysterious expanse of the lake stretched out like an ocean. The great ship gathered speed, its pontoons skimming the surface. It bounded like an overpowered hydroplane and slanted upward into the night, and Gentry switched off the wing lights. When they were well out over the lake and five thousand feet aloft he swung the nose westward and set the Anthony Robot, which would hold them on their course more accurately than any human pilot, and went back into the cabin to join Anthony.

On the Radio Beam Map in front of Anthony a moving point of light, brighter than the overall illumination, marked the progress of the plane toward Marquette and gave its exact position over the lake at every moment.

"What's up?" Tom asked, lounging on a couch. "Fallon in trouble?"

"Looks that way. One of those marionettes stolen from Ericson was sent to him with a death's head attached to it. If somebody's actually going to try to kill Logan and that crowd, as the fake Voice of Inspiration recommended, it looks as if Fallon is picked for number one."

"Golly!" Gentry's honest face was twisted in amazement. "But look here, Jim, how do you know that means anything? If they wanted to kill Fallon, why should they warn him?"

"There could be two reasons. First, the death trap might be so carefully set, they don't think he can escape it, even if he's warned— and they hope the warning will scare the others. Second, they might not be as interested in warning him as in bringing me to the scene. A man who would want to sabotage Triple-A Ray production would want to get the secret of its operation, too. Unless I'm mistaken, there'll be a reception committee waiting for us!"

"But no one was supposed to know there was such a thing as Triple-A Ray! No one was supposed to know you had anything to do with Logan and the rest, till you admitted it on the air a few minutes ago."

"Someone knew," Jim said grimly. "Someone knew my agents learned the truth about Marner, and Baldwin was going to make it public. Someone knows practically every move we've made lately."

"Could any of Logan's bunch have told?"

Anthony thought of the five industrial and financial leaders. They were all capable men with flawless records. Each of them was rich enough to disregard considerations of personal gain. All of them, capitalists though they were, had been fair to labor and had championed democratic institutions.

HE HAD LITTLE fear of danger from within the group. But there were secretaries and personal attendants who might have talked for money. Ericson's long service with Logan Motors had doubtless made him many friends within the plants and its laboratories, who would not hesitate to discuss financial matters with him. And Marner's spy organization was probably the most efficient ever to operate in America.

"Don't ask me riddles," Jim said shortly. "It isn't likely that any of them would have told deliberately, but one or another might have dropped a careless word at the wrong place and time."

Another problem was bothering Gentry. "If they're waiting for this plane at Marquette, how are we going to keep from getting killed? Suppose they have machine guns, grenades—?"

For answer, Jim reached into a compartment and drew forth a small black pack. It contained a light silk parachute of his own design. He slipped his arms through straps and buckled other straps about his waist and thighs.

"I get it," Tom said.

"Keep the plane up over the lake. When I leave Fallon I'll swim out and fire a flare. You can set the plane down near me."

He thrust a signal pistol into his belt.

The dot of light on the map was getting very near the dot of ink that indicated Marquette. Anthony went forward and saw, through the curved windows, a tiny pattern of twinkling lights far ahead and a mile below.

This was the mining metropolis of the upper Great Lakes, the crowded little city that, barring Duluth, was the most important port of Superior. Here the deep-hulled freighters were loaded with iron and copper ore to be floated through Lakes Huron and St. Clair to Detroit, and through Lake Erie to rail points connecting with the busy steel mills of Pennsylvania. In this part of the world originated half the raw metals that supplied the heavy industries of America.

Arthur Fallon's house, topping a hill at the edge of the city, was shrouded in darkness. Anthony's night-piercing eyes picked it out, however, as the *Thunderbird* swooped low over the town. He issued rapid orders to Gentry, who took charge of the controls.

At a thousand feet Anthony opened the escape-port of the cabin and plunged head-first toward the earth. For seconds he fell like a plummet. Then the black folds of the chute billowed above him and his descent was slowed. In his dark sweater and slacks he was perfectly camouflaged from any human gaze that might be turned upward.

He pulled at the shrouds, guiding his fall toward the hilltop where the house stood. Why, he wondered, were no lights burning within it? Had Fallon thought he would be safer in the dark? Or had something happened to him already?

HIS BODY CRASHED through bushes and his feet thudded against the earth two hundred feet from the large brick structure. He spilled air from the chute expertly, disengaged himself from the straps and stood listening.

Someone asked in a hoarse whisper, "What was that, Pete?"

An answering whisper replied, "Prob'ly a bobcat or bear. Animals come right up to the edge of town at night. Don't get jumpy."

Jim grinned thinly, making out the crouching shapes of the two men near the front of the house. They were so distant that ears less keen than his could never have heard their cautious conversation.

He listened while the whispers went on:

"You reckon that was Anthony's plane we heard?"

"Must of been. Chances are he'll come down on the lake. The boys at the dock ought to take care of him."

"What if he gives 'em the slip?"

"Then it's up to you and me, Oscar. That's what we're here for, to grab him if he manages to get this far."

"They say he's a bad one to tangle with."

"Who's going to tangle with him? All we got to do is wait till he goes in the house and turn on the nerve gas, and then gather him up. If that doesn't get him, the chief said to shoot and keep on shooting till we're sure he won't bother us no more!"

BETWEEN ANTHONY AND the pair was a wide expanse of lawn, dotted sparsely with trees and shrubbery. No red Indian, whose life and well-being depended upon stealth, had ever moved more silently and invisibly than Jim moved across that space. He flitted from tree to tree, a shadow among shadows, and knelt finally in the shelter of a bush not ten feet from the men who thought they were ambushing him.

"The plane ain't come down yet," one of them breathed. "I can hear it over the lake."

"Keep your shirt on, Oscar. It's bad to get rattled."

Anthony's groping fingers found a pebble, tossed it. There was a sharp sound as it struck one of the colonial pillars of the house and rattled across the porch.

"What was that?"

Before the other man could reply, Anthony was upon them in two mighty strides. He carried no weapon—it was seldom that he placed his reliance upon firearms, and such weapons as he might use were apt to be strange and disconcerting ones of his own devising—but he had trained himself painstakingly in every known art of physical combat. Both these crouching men were armed, and yet they were helpless against his cunning attack.

His hands clamped simultaneously around the backs of their necks, fingertips pressing nerve centers. Oscar gasped, "What the—!" Pete squirmed for an instant. Then they hung limp in Anthony's powerful grasp, rendered unconscious by a ju jitsu trick that was more effective and less harmful than a blow from a blackjack.

Wrapping an arm around the chest of each of the men, Anthony lugged them toward the front door of the house, letting their feet drag. When he gained the porch he saw that the door was open. He pressed the bell button, hearing the clamor it started inside.

He called, "Fallon! It's Anthony!"

There was no reply. He had felt certain from the time he discovered the two gunmen that there would be no reply.

He pushed his way into the house, through the vestibule, through the arched doorway to the big living room. When he saw what was suspended in another arched doorway, leading from the living room to the dining room, he halted and allowed his prisoners to fall heavily to the carpeted floor.

He was too late to help Fallon. There was no longer any doubt about it. A slow wave of dull anger mounted within him.

For all his ability to see in the dark, Anthony wanted light to examine in detail what had been done. He spied a wall switch and pressed it and a crystal chandelier blazed in the center of the room.

Arthur Fallon had been hanged in a wire noose in the doorway. His ruddy face was purple with trapped blood, his eyes protruded from their sockets and his swollen tongue had forced his mouth open. Other wires, descending from behind the arch, were attached to his ankles and wrists.

As Jim Anthony watched, those other wires began to move, jerking the arms and legs. Slowly at first, and then faster, the limbs moved up and down in a macabre rhythm, until Fallon's lifeless body was dancing in a furious jig in midair!

CHAPTER VI

BOMBS AND BULLETS

CARVED AND JOINTED BY Alfred Ericson, an eight-inch puppet supplied the clue to the corpse's animation. The figure was upon a table near the dancing dead man. It had been removed from its original setting among the other four and placed in a special frame, suspended by a noosed thread. Other threads, fastened to the wooden hands and feet, ran to a wire crankshaft at the top of the frame, and the turning of the crank supplied the motion.

Anthony stepped within the doorway arch and saw the larger steel crankshaft spinning behind it, lifting and lowering the wires that jerked Fallon's arms and legs. One end of the shaft was geared to an electric motor, from which a power cord ran to a wall plug. When he snapped the light switch, Jim realized, he had started the motor and begun the dance.

Now he pulled the cord from the plug. The motor ran down; the arms and legs of the dead man ceased to move. Touching the body,

Jim found it warm from the blood that had been coursing through Fallon's veins only a few minutes ago.

Jim swore, clenched his fists, set his jaw so that its hinges bulged in his cheeks like walnuts. He had liked the tough little Irishman, who had done a man's job in a man's country, blasting and drilling miles of shafts and tunnels through volcanic rock to supply a nation's industries with its most precious raw materials.

Fallon had been a rich man, but he had earned his wealth by hard work and had used it all in developing his mining properties, giving employment to thousands and increasing the wealth of the whole country.

Moreover, Fallon had been a warm-hearted human being with a wife who loved him and two sturdy boys who looked upon him as a hero.

The murder had been wanton and needless. The men who perpetrated it had nothing to gain, except possibly the hope that it would unnerve the other men concerned in the plan for building Triple-A Ray units.

Fallon's job was to have been to increase the production of ore so that the mills would not be handicapped by having to turn over great

quantities of their highest grade of ingot steel for the ray guns; but now that he was dead, Logan and the others could still speed up work at the mines.

All five of the associates had signed an agreement, giving temporary control of their businesses to the others in the event of the death of any of them, until the construction of the ray units was ended. Now the wisdom of that arrangement was shown clearly.

But if murder struck again among the little group of industrialists—if, incredibly, it did away with all four who were left—the program Anthony had mapped out so painstakingly would be shattered beyond repair.

And while Jim did not worry about himself, the fact remained that if he, too, fell a victim to the killers, there would be little hope of ever putting the revolutionary ray to work for the safety of America.

Instead, in that case, the enemies of America would almost certainly gain possession of the ray and use it to destroy the last peaceful stronghold of democracy in the world!

HE STOOD FOR perhaps twenty seconds, considering these things, and then moved swiftly through the rooms. He did not cut the body down, for he wanted the authorities to see exactly how the murder had been accomplished; nor did he bother about such details as fingerprints, knowing the state police were quite competent to manage those details, and he could make use of their findings later.

But he did find behind the draperies of a half-open living room window, a metal tank with a valve at the top, like an oxygen tank. If Jim had entered the house without discovering those two men who lurked outside, they would have opened the valve and flooded the rooms with what one of them had called "nerve gas."

Jim turned the valve handle, releasing a tiny puff of white vapor. He caught the scent of lilacs. His keen sense of smell instantly gave him the chemical composition of the gas.

Returning to the unconscious gunmen sprawled in the living room, Anthony relieved them of two .45 caliber Colt pistols, which he put out of reach on top of a bookcase, and fumbled at his belt. Around his waist, under the belt, ran yard upon yard of the same steel-tough, thread-thin cord with which Mephito had bound Karl Ogrund in The Cavern.

A spring in the buckle, which acted as a reel, fed out the gleaming twine, and the pressing of a button in the buckle cut the fiber with a special blade. Jim knelt beside the men and bound their wrists together, tying them back to back, and then their ankles. He left them not only helpless, but burdened hopelessly each with the other, in case they tried to roll or hobble from the house.

He drew the cords tight, not caring that they cut into the flesh. He was neither cruel nor vindictive, but he found it impossible to pity the men who had been responsible for that dangling corpse in the doorway.

That task completed, Anthony went to the telephone and called the state police barracks at the edge of the city, near the Marquette State Prison, and spoke to the officer in charge.

"This is James Anthony. Arthur Fallon has been murdered in his home and the two men who did it are tied up in the living room. I put their guns on the bookcase. Beside one of the windows is a tank of gas; be careful not to open it, or it will knock out all your men—and keep it away from fire, because it could blow up the whole house. I'm telling you these things because I've got to leave. I'll get in touch with you tomorrow and see what you've found out from the prisoners, if anything."

"Wait!" yelled the officer. "Mr. Anthony, you can't walk out on a homicide like that! Even if it's really you, there are formalities—"

JIM HUNG UP. He had no aversion to working with the police—preferred to, in fact, when his activities were not of too delicate a nature to be entrusted even to the guardians of the public safety—but in this instance the red tape of official investigation would only result in needless delay.

He had to return to The Cavern and, through his own private communications system, set in motion the farflung elements of the Anthony organization. He had to be free to depart for any section of the United States at a moment's notice. At any second his radio might warn of danger in another quarter, and he could hardly attend to it if he put himself at the disposal of the authorities, who had their own ponderous and uninspired methods of doing things.

He left the house immediately, running to the garage. Fallon's car was there. The keys were not in the ignition lock, but Anthony knew how to start a motor without keys.

He swung into the driveway, down the hill and through the streets of the city, skidding around turns, swerving around slower cars. The sidewalks were crowded with men, most of them lumberjacks and mine workers, and the windows of saloons were ablaze with light. When they learned of the atrocious murder of their first citizen, the people of the town would be shocked and infuriated and a little frightened, but for the present they were enjoying themselves recklessly.

Parking Fallon's car close to an ore dock, where the police would be sure to find it, Jim raced to the end of the pier, stripping off his sweater on the way. He paused long enough to divest himself of his slacks and make sure that the signal pistol was secure in his belt, then dove expertly into the lake.

The iciness of the water took his breath away. Its very coldness would have defeated an average good swimmer, but Jim found it exhilarating. He swam with long, powerful strokes, his hard body cleaving the fluid blackness, until he was half a mile off shore. He heard the motors of the *Thunderbird* in the distance, circling, coming back toward the spot where he waited, treading water.

He drew the thick-barreled pistol from his belt, aimed it skyward and pulled the trigger. There was a loud pop as the flare cartridge left the barrel.

Three or four seconds later it exploded, high up, showering red and white balls of fire across the sky.

A BIG MOTOR thundered back among the shadowy docks. A speedboat motor, Anthony knew, hearing the curious flat echo of cylinder exhaust close to the surface of the water. He saw the wide-beamed stubby craft emerge from the shelter of a pier and head in his direction. The sharp bow lifted and the motor-roar was deadened as the exhaust ports at the stern were submerged.

The Douglas swooped above him. The floodlights came on, gilding the lake. The plane passed him, turned back into the light wind and drove toward the water.

The glare of a searchlight reached out from the boat and burst over Jim's head and shoulders. A submachine gun chattered and bullets slapped close to him, glancing and whining away toward Canada. He held his breath and went under, swimming with practiced ease four feet below the surface. The propellers of the speedboat sent out strong vibrations that made his ears ring.

He heard the plane's floats hit the water and come up, twenty feet directly in front of them. He grasped a strut as it rushed past and pulled himself up, reaching for the handle of the cabin door.

Bullets drummed against the metal side of the ship as he hauled himself, dripping, into its interior.

"The compressed air!" he shouted to Tom, whose hands gripped stick and throttle.

Tom tripped a lever with his foot. The *Thunderbird II* shot ahead like a plane hurled from a catapult as hundreds of pounds of air, compressed in the pontoons, was discharged against the solid water. At the same time Tom yanked the throttle and all four motors chorused wildly, literally snatching the great craft into the air.

Once aloft, Tom cut out two of the motors. He turned a white face, mottled darkly with freckles, upon Anthony. He gasped, "Golly, that was close! Gee whiz, did any of those slugs hit you, Jim?"

Anthony shook his head. "It's hard to hit anything, even with a machine gun, from a boat that jumps from wave to wave at fifty miles an hour."

He got a coarse towel out of a locker and began to rub his glowing skin. "Circle over the town and let's see if we can get an idea of what's happening at Fallon's house."

"Was he all right, Jim?"

Anthony's face hardened. "They got him. He was the first victim of whatever outfit staged that lying broadcast. We're going to get them, Tom, if it's the last thing we ever do!"

"Anson Marner's outfit," Tom said, banking and ruddering the plane. "Count on me for all the help you need, Jim. Fallon was a good guy."

Jim could not hear the sirens, up there above Marquette, but he could see the head-

The steam came in like a live torturous breath and soon the little man was screaming for mercy.

lights and the big red signal lights of the state police cars, streaking down the long hill from the barracks, through the streets of the city and up the hill toward Fallon's house. He wondered whether the cops would manage to learn anything from the two men he had left there.

SUDDENLY THE ANSWER came, and it was spectacularly negative. Fallon's house vanished in a tremendous burst of flame. The roof split and lifted, the walls burst outward, while the nearest of the police cars was still blocks away. The *boom* of the explosion jarred through the air, loud above the song of the motors.

They wouldn't talk, those two murderers—except perhaps to the devil down in hell. Like the man whom Mephito had captured at The Cavern, they had killed themselves, had found some way, perhaps, of firing the tank of nerve gas when they heard the sirens and realized they didn't have a chance. The blast would have torn them limb from limb, and the corpse of Fallon, too.

Probably it would have destroyed all evidence of the manner in which Fallon died, and even the hideous little marionette that had heralded his death.

Already scarlet flames were thrusting forked tongues through the ruins of the house....

"They'll never get the boys in that speedboat, either," Tom predicted when he had swerved the plane over the lake again. "They didn't head back for shore; they tore out for some point north of town. Want to chase 'em?"

Jim's smoldering eyes raked the darkness along the edge of the lake. Nowhere was there any sign of a fleeing boat. It was entirely possible that the criminals had landed already at some spot where cars were waiting to help them make a getaway.

"No," he said glumly. "Set the Robot for The Cavern. I'll radio the state police to look for them. Chances are they'll make a clean getaway, but if they don't the patrol can run them down before we could."

He went back into the cabin and sent out a message on the police wavelength. Then he stretched himself on a couch, noting that it was well past midnight.

Notwithstanding his activity of the night and his long labors of the past week, he was not especially tired. His great store of reserve strength had hardly been tapped. But Jim Anthony believed in preparedness, and he realized that the demands already made on his energy might be only a mild indication of what was to come.

He closed his eyes. At the command of his brain his every muscle relaxed completely. In less than half a minute he was sleeping as soundly and dreamlessly as a baby.

There was no telling how long it would be before he would have another chance to rest.

THE ANTHONY CALL

MAXWELL BALDWIN DREAMED, HIS pink lips curving blissfully, a pardonable pride swelling in his heart. He dreamed that his exposure of Anson Marner had succeeded beyond his most sanguine hopes—that his enemy was already in prison and the name of Baldwin was acclaimed by grateful Americans everywhere. Moreover, all the respectable members of the Apecia, including the multimillionaires, had flocked to join the League of Inspiration, their checkbooks fluttering, their potent fountain pens uncapped.

Nor had officialdom been slow to recognize Baldwin's greatness. He saw himself standing upon a platform banked with flowers and bunting, overlooking a hall filled with dignitaries. Senators and cabinet members shared the platform with him, and beside him was no less a personage than the President himself!

The President, smiling his famous smile, was saying something to the assembled thousands about awarding the Congressional Medal to Baldwin for his inestimable service to the nation.

The medal dangled from the President's hand—a disc of yellow gold attached to a colored ribbon. The hand prepared to pin it upon Baldwin's fluttering bosom.

Kleig lights came on, newsreel photographers cranked their cameras, the crowd roared.

"For distinguished service to the United States—"

But something went wrong. The sharp pin pierced the satin lapel of Baldwin's dress coat, slipped through his starched shirt and stabbed cruelly into his flesh.

The fat little man had never been able to endure the slightest physical pain. His dignity evaporated like mist in a breeze. He sprang back and yelled, ungracefully, "Ouch!"

That involuntary cry shattered the dream....

BALDWIN OPENED HIS eyes in yellow light that showered from a naked bulb. He was lying on his back, closed in by whitewashed concrete walls that made him think of a prison cell. A man stooped over him, withdrawing a hypodermic needle from the flesh of his naked chest.

"Help!" Baldwin roared. "Help me, somebody!"

The man towered above him, tall and broad shouldered, his face hidden by a black silk mask. Through slits in the mask greenish eyes glittered with contemptuous amusement.

"Careful of that golden voice," said the man. "We wouldn't want to damage it, would we, just when we've got important work for it to do?"

"W-work?" Memory was flooding back into Baldwin's dazed mind. He hadn't been able to deliver his speech, after all. There had been a heavy perfume, making him drowsy, and he had fallen....

"You're starting your biggest crusade," the man informed him. "You are going to have the honor of telling the world that James Anthony and Jasper Logan and their friends are traitors and crooks. Then, when they are assassinated, the authorities will realize that it could have been done by faithful members of your league!"

"No!" Baldwin croaked. "You can't make me do that! I won't stand for it—"

The door slammed. The masked man had not bothered to listen.

By heavens, Baldwin thought, he'd show them they couldn't make a tool of him, whoever they were! They'd find out they couldn't get away with kidnaping a famous man with a following....

Through small openings in the walls white vapor hissed. It came under pressure, scalding hot, filling the narrow cell in half a minute. It was live steam, searing and suffocating, drenching Baldwin with its murderous breath.

The little man's voice cracked, screaming, "Turn it off! I'll do anything you say! For God's sake, turn it off!"

The naked flesh of his plump chest was getting red. In another minute it would blister, and the blisters would burst, and the layers of fat beneath the skin would start to bubble. He was being cooked alive!

"I can't bear it!" he shrieked. "I'll do anything—"

He collapsed, groveling.

AT THAT VERY minute Anthony awoke, his subconscious time-sense functioning accurately, telling him that the *Thunderbird II* was nearing its destination. He glanced at Gentry, snoring at the opposite side of the cabin, and grinned. He consulted the Radio Beam Map and saw that the moving point of light was within a fraction of an inch of the red circle which designated The Cavern.

He went forward and took over the controls from the robot. His gaze pierced the black night, scanning the round hills and flat lakes.

There could be no radio eavesdropper in this silent visual call.

He pointed the Douglas toward a dragon-shaped lake surrounded by sheer cliffs, turned out the lights and cut the motors.

The *whoosh* of the wind was loud in the cabin, but the farmers of the vicinity would not be aware of the shadowy monster swooping over their houses, settling in their midst and vanishing inexplicably.

Without using the wing lights, Jim touched the floats down on the surface of the lake. The plane coasted, urged ahead from time to time by blasts of compressed air, straight toward the wall of a cliff.

He aimed a reflector, pressed a button and sent a beam of "black light" streaking invisibly toward the rock. The beam found a photoelectric cell and started silent machinery.

A section of the cliff opened inward like double doors and the *Thunderbird* taxied into a vast subterranean hangar whose floor was covered with water!

As the plane came to rest beside a rock and the huge doors closed behind it, Gentry sat up and rubbed his eyes. He muttered, "Holy cow!" and fumbled for a flashlight.

When the cone of light showed him where they were he said apologetically, "Golly, Jim, I didn't mean to fall asleep!"

"Skip it," Anthony said. "Let's see what's been happening since we were away."

They made the plane fast and went to the back of the cave, where the sloping stone floor was dry. A natural tunnel bored into a hill, and

as they strode through it the rays from Tom's flashlight made shadows dance eerily.

A steel door blocked their path. Anthony drummed his fingernails against it, high up, and machinery responding to that particular vibration withdrew a bolt. They stepped into the tunnel that led from the laboratory to the shaft beneath the farmhouse and saw lights in the main chamber.

Shean Boru Anthony had discovered The Cavern years ago, while exploring the rock strata for Neolithic remains of early civilizations. He had never utilized it, nor had his son, until the latter had decided to have his new Anti-Aircraft Ray units manufactured in Detroit. Then Jim had seen the advantage of having a secret base within eighty miles of the Logan plant.

Neither as elaborate as The Tepee, Jim's underground castle in the Catskills of New York, nor as luxurious as The Pueblo, his exclusive

"This, gentlemen, is the most important thing in the United States today!"

resort hotel in the heart of the Mojave Desert, The Cavern was still a valuable asset.

Until tonight, he had thought that no man outside the circle of his trusted friends knew of its existence—and even though enemies had somehow succeeded in reaching Bill Roarty's farmhouse, he knew that the tunnels and rooms were still impregnable.

He stepped into the doorway of the main chamber, and Dolores Colquitt came out of her chair with a little cry of gladness. A négligée clung to the curves of her sleek figure, and her hazel eyes shone with relief as she flung herself into his arms.

"OH, JIM," DOLORES pleaded, "I've been so worried! Let me go with you after this, when you have to be away. I'm not afraid of danger when I can see it."

He smiled, stroking the soft waves of her honey-colored hair. "We'll see." He glanced at Mephito, squatting on his heels in a corner. "What does your magic tell you now, old one?"

Mephito's gaunt face was somber. "You know as well as I, son of my daughter. You have seen the dead dancing and have rubbed shoulders with death. It is not yet over."

Jim said, with a lightness he did not feel, "It'll be over in a hurry. The ray units will be in production soon, with the Army on guard, and it'll be too late for spies to interfere. All we've got to do right now is track down the criminals who have been pestering us and who killed Fallon."

"Marner and his gang," Dolores said. "The thought-wave machine told us that much."

Jim went to where Dawkins lay on a couch, bandages swathing his head. He asked, "How's the skull?"

The valet's eyes were steady. "H'it 'urts a bit, Mr. h'Anthony, but h'I'll be h'up and h'around when h'I've rested. H'I was a fool to get myself shot, sir."

Knowing the fierce loyalty and heroic courage of the little Englishman, Jim was sure he had not been a fool. He gripped Dawkins' shoulder to show he understood.

"I wish I had a thousand fools like you. Where's Roarty?"

"Sleeping, sir. The gas knocked 'im h'out and 'e was sickish when 'e got h'over h'it." His voice dropped. "H'I was thinking, Mr. h'Anthony— h'it was queer, the way those chaps slipped h'in. D'you suppose Roarty—h'I mean to say, sir—"

Jim's eyes narrowed, but he shook his head. "We won't accuse anyone till we're sure." He turned to Tom. "Check the alarm system and make sure the periscopic vision apparatus is working, will you? Turn on the Triple-A Ray barrage, too, in case anyone tries to fly over. After that you can go back to sleep."

Crossing the room, Jim sat at what appeared to be a low dressing table, except that the mirror above it was ground-glass and the table top was studded with knobs, switches and dials. He pressed a button and the mirror glowed blue-white. He set dials in various combinations and scribbled code words on slips of paper.

Into the glass field came a succession of images of men and women in full color, remarkably clear. They looked at Anthony with eyes that seemed to recognize him, seemed to read the code messages he held up before them. They made signs that they understood, and vanished.

THERE COULD BE no radio eavesdroppers as this silent, visual call went out to the hand-picked agents of the Anthony organization. The two-way visoradio was Jim's own invention, reserved for the present for his exclusive use.

In Detroit, a buzzer sounded on a bedside table in the sleeping chamber of a noted minister. That individual sat up, rubbing the drowsiness out of his eyes.

He slid out the drawer of the table and saw in its opaque glass bottom the bronze likeness of Anthony, holding up a sheet of paper upon which meaningful words were scrawled. The reverend gentleman nodded eagerly, hopped out of bed in his old-fashioned nightshirt, got an automatic pistol from under the mattress and checked its magazine, chuckling as he thought how horrified the nice old ladies of his congregation would be if they could see him now. Still chuckling, he struggled into his pants....

On West End Avenue in New York, a redheaded blues singer from an uptown cabaret was drifting dreamward between pale green sheets when she heard a faint buzzing in her pocketbook. Arising in her filmy pajamas—a lithe and lovely figure she snatched at the bag and extracted a gold compact.

In the small mirror she saw the lean face of the man she would have dreamed about, in all probability, and read the message he had written. Into her topaz eyes came a warm light, and her coral lips whispered, "Okay, Jim."

Not until after she had put away the compact did she add, *"dream man!"* to the sentence....

In Philadelphia a reformed safecracker named Schmidt received his message and prepared to practice his well-remembered art.... In Pittsburgh a young fellow named Brown read his orders in a shaving mirror and got into paint-stained overalls.

In New Jersey, Illinois, Florida and California, men and women dropped whatever they were doing and prepared to go into the underworld, into centers where the Apecia was powerful, into many dangerous quarters in search of information for Jim Anthony.

Most of them would have given their lives, if necessary, to carry out their assignments.

CHAPTER VIII

THE SECOND DOLL

IN THE EARLY MORNING sunshine, a sixteen-cylinder sedan turned off the Jackson Highway, sped dangerously through curving hill roads and climbed toward Bill Roarty's farmhouse. Three men and a dark-haired girl of nineteen got out. They were met by Roarty and escorted to the elevator in the cellar, and at the bottom of the shaft were welcomed by Anthony, who had watched their approach through multi-mirrored periscopes hidden in trees about the hilltop.

"Good morning, gentlemen," Jim said heartily. "And you, Ruth. You haven't heard anything from your father?"

The girl's violet eyes were not far from tears. She shook her head. "When that preacher woke me and said you wanted to see me, I—I thought something had happened to him!"

"Nothing has," Jim assured her, "and we'll try to see that nothing does. Jasper, how do you like being up early?"

Jasper Logan's gaunt face was untroubled. "I never sleep after six. I was up before the Reverend Mr. Parkhurst started arguing with my guards. But my guests didn't like being flown to Jackson and driven here before breakfast!"

Bessingham, the steel man, grimaced. "It's as much as your life is worth to ride with Logan. He brought us all the way from Jackson Airport at ninety miles an hour, and I'll swear he touched a hundred on every curve!" The man's face was pinched and pale; he took a glass tube from his pocket and shook pills into his palm, explaining, "In the rush I even forgot to take my medicine!"

The third man, Royal Phail, was inclined to be testy. There were dark circles beneath his eyes and his fat face was unhappy.

"I couldn't get to sleep for hours, thinking about Fallon," he mumbled, his five chins quivering. "Then, when I finally dropped off, Logan made me get up. Damned if I can see why we had to come all the way to this hole!"

"For one thing, to have breakfast," Jim said. He led them into the main chamber, where Dolores waited. They sat at a table and Dawkins, who insisted upon being up despite his scalp wound, served scrambled eggs and bacon and fragrant coffee.

Logan growled, "I'd give a million dollars to catch the one who had Fallon killed. I don't suppose there's any doubt, Jim, that Marner's behind it."

"Certainly Marner," Jim agreed. "And someone else, too—possibly someone in your organization."

Bessingham frowned, poking at his food. "Why not say what you really think, Jim? The man who's working with Marner used to be in Jasper's organization, and still has plenty of friends there. He's sore at Jasper, and there's the evidence of those ugly puppets—"

"If you're speaking of my father," Ruth Ericson flared, "I won't stand for it! Dad would never have anything to do with killing! He's cranky and mean sometimes, but down underneath his heart's as soft as butter!"

Bessingham bowed. "I'm sorry. I forgot about his being your father. Even so, you'll have to admit it looks odd. Myron Linster was your father's secretary before he went to work for Baldwin, and now Linster's disappeared."

"That's even more ridiculous!" the girl cried. "When Dad left Mr. Logan, Myron knew he'd have to find another job. He heard of Baldwin losing his former secretary, so he wrote to Baldwin, and—" She began to cry.

Dolores put her arm around Ruth. "Don't let them upset you," she soothed. "They're only men! They look at the outside of things, but we women know the truth in our hearts!"

PHAIL'S ROTUND BODY was trembling so violently that he could hardly fork his food to his mouth. Jim saw that the banker was in the grip of violent fear. If Marner succeeded in scaring the men associated in the Triple-A Ray program, he would have done almost as much harm as if he had killed them.

Hoping to allay that fear, Jim said, "I'm taking all possible precautions for the safety of the rest of you. Phail, I'm sending a new girl to work in your office—a redhead named Cynthia Arnold. She's a skilled investigator and you can depend upon her. And I've sent a man to your house in Pittsburgh, Bessingham, ostensibly to redecorate your study, but actually to keep his eyes open. I'd appreciate it if both of you would make long-distance calls, arranging for their admittance to the premises—"

Logan broke in, "No pretty girls for me, Jim?"

"You're all right," Jim retorted. "Your bodyguard could protect you against a *blitzkrieg!*"

Phail burst out, "How can a girl help me? I've got a good notion to back out of the whole thing. I'm no coward"—his trembling left some doubt about that, although he did not seem to realize it—"but I have the financial welfare of a lot of people in my hands. If I should be killed, the stock market would crash!"

"Stock market gamblers aren't more important than other Americans," Jim said soberly. "If the war ever spreads this far, what will happen to stocks and bonds?" He arose, went to a control panel against the wall and threw a switch. "This, gentlemen, is perhaps the most important thing in the United States today!"

A section of the floor, ten feet square, swung up and back like a trap door. A platform beneath it began to rise, lifting into view a glittering machine of brass and steel, resembling in some ways a large telescope, and in some an aerial defense gun mounted on a swivel base.

It was the Anthony Anti-Aircraft Ray Projector, so-called by officials of the War Department. Instead of shells, it could throw a stream of electrical energy twelve miles into the air, powerful enough to put any airplane motor out of commission. It could also be used against tanks and automobiles.

There was a defense against the ray, an armor energized with electricity, which could be used to shield vulnerable parts of a motor. With that, American planes would be safe in areas in which enemy ships, unprotected by the armor, could not fly.

Logan's slate-covered eyes were shining. He knew the theory of the ray, but he had never before looked upon one of the projectors, nor had any of the others. His voice was vibrant with enthusiasm.

"Think of it!" he said. "We'll build a hundred thousand of them and place them all along our national borders, ten to the mile. Enemy planes would be forced to land undamaged and would augment America's air fleet! There could be no bombing of our cities, no killing!"

Anthony nodded. "Between us we've got everything it takes to make that possible. Fallon's mines can deliver plenty of ore, even though Fallon is dead. Bessingham can produce the special types of steel I've specified. Van Rucker can fill the orders for the necessary electrical equipment. Logan's shops are equipped to forge, machine and assemble the parts, and Phail is in a position to do what financing is necessary. By doing the job quietly, with the secret cooperation of the War Department, we can keep the risk of sabotage at a minimum. Men, we've got the opportunity of a lifetime! It will be the greatest job any of us has ever done for our country!"

Suddenly Jim dropped into blackness beneath the numbers overwhelming him.

ANTHONY WAS RICHLY endowed with personal magnetism. His words went far to dispel whatever fears a part of his audience may have entertained.

Bessingham sat straighter. "I'll see it through," he asserted. "All over the world people are dying in the hope of winning wars. I'll take a chance on dying in the hope of making wars impossible!"

"That's the stuff!" Logan said, slapping his shoulder.

Even Phail's manifold chins were steadier. "I'll stand by, too. I'll hire private detectives and watch my step. No reason why anything should happen to me."

CYNTHIA

Jim was gratified. "If only we had Van Rucker here—"

"Van Rucker!" Bessingham frowned. "You know, Anthony, it's funny about him. He never seemed very anxious to get into this. I know something of his personal history—how he built his business by smashing little competitors—and I also know he has connections in Europe. Do you think—?"

"No!" Logan thundered. "We don't think anything of the sort! If we're going to start suspecting each other, we might as well chuck the whole business!"

"I was only wondering out loud," Bessingham apologized. "Quite likely there's nothing to worry about."

Jim's jaw was grim. "If anyone in this crowd is against us, we'll find it out soon enough. The minute anything suspicious happens, I'll hear of it and get on the scene as fast as a plane can take me. God help any double-crossers!"

The three men left when breakfast was over. Logan was to drive them to Jackson, where his private plane waited to return him to Detroit, and Anthony had ordered another fast plane to take Bessingham and Phail to their respective homes. Bessingham should reach

RUTH

Pittsburgh in two hours, and Phail should be in New York an hour or so later.

Ruth Ericson was to have returned with Logan, but she had other ideas.

"Let me stay, Mr. Anthony!" she begged. "My father and the man I'm going to marry are involved, and I've got to try to help them! If you won't let me stay with you, I'll try to find them alone!"

Pitying her, Jim consented. There was nothing she could do, but at least he could protect her while she remained with him. Left to her own devices, she might get into serious trouble.

He turned her over to Dolores' sympathetic care and went into a private laboratory to work on a tiny device that had been in his mind ever since he had perfected the Triple-A Ray. He had put it off under the pressure of more important work, but now he foresaw a possible need for it.

FOR TWO HOURS he worked, utterly absorbed, interrupted only once by the radiophone. That was when Schmidt, the ex-safecracker, reported from Philadelphia:

"I went all t'rough de jernt, boss, an' didn't find nuttin'. Dis guy Van Rucker ain't got back, but I hoid de soivants say dey was expectin' him dis aft'noon."

Remembering Bessingham's indirect accusation of Van Rucker, Jim's brows drew together....

At the end of two hours he tested an innocent-looking black tube with the aid of an electric motor. An exclamation of satisfaction escaped his lips. Now he had one more weapon with which to

DOLORES

confront the forces arrayed against him in this battle for America's safety!

It was then that the radiophone spoke again, this time bringing positive information:

"Brown speaking from Bessingham's place in Pittsburgh, sir. Western Union messenger just delivered a dancing doll! Bessingham not at home, but butler has message saying he'll arrive about noon. Any orders?"

"You bet there are orders!" Jim snapped. "Keep your gun ready. When Bessingham comes, guard him with your life till I get there! I'm leaving now!"

He darted into the main room. "We're going places, Tom!" he yelled. "Dolores, stick here at the radiophone and relay all messages to me. I'll be tuned to the private wavelength every minute!"

He and Tom sprinted through the tunnel to the secret hangar. Not till they had boarded the huge plane and Tom was warming up the motors did they realize that Ruth Ericson had followed and clambered into the cabin. Jim tried to send her back, but she refused to go, and his mind was too full of other things to argue with her.

CHAPTER IX

A SUSPECT FLEES

HEADLINES IN THE MORNING papers had a curious effect on the white-haired man in the Pittsburgh hotel lobby. His body, clad in a worn tweed suit, literally jumped with nerves, and his deep-set black eyes squirmed like those of a hunted animal. He looked at the sleek clerk behind the desk, where he had registered falsely in the small hours as "J.C. Johnson, Chicago," and at the three or four men lounging in the lobby. He read again the story from Marquette, which occupied a full column under the streamer:

MINE OWNER DEAD IN BLAST
FOLLOWING BROADCAST HOAX

Alfred Ericson—for the thin, shabby man was he—folded the paper, put it in his pocket and went out of the lobby. A harassed gleam came into his eyes and the lines around his mouth were taut with desperation.

"Damn them!" he muttered. "Damn them to hell!"

There was a taxicab at the curb. He got into it and gave the driver an address he had found in the telephone directory. He was driven through steep, crowded streets to an imposing marble home in a fashionable suburb of the city.

A butler in livery answered the door.

"I have an appointment with Mr. Bessingham," said Ericson—although he hadn't. "I'm Alfred Ericson, a good friend of his."

The butler knew the name and expected his master soon. He bowed. "You may wait in the library, sir. Mr. Bessingham should return from Detroit very shortly."

Ericson followed the butler through carpeted halls to the gracious book-lined room. The smell of paint assailed his nostrils and he became aware of a man in overalls in a small adjoining room that appeared to be a private office or study. He felt the keen eyes of the painter upon him.

"We're redecorating," said the butler apologetically. "I hope the fuss won't disturb you. You'll find the latest magazines on the table."

MUMBLING HIS THANKS, Ericson sank into a leather-upholstered armchair. His apprehensive glance traveled about the room, took in its luxurious appointments scornfully. He became uneasy about the decorator, a young man with blunt features and a grim mouth, who worked facing the library just within the open door of the other room.

A section of the bookshelves was devoted to technical works. To avoid the painter's scrutiny, Ericson got up to look at their titles. He halted abruptly, his mouth open, seeing in an open space in one of the shelves a curious object suspended by threads within a frame of wood.

"The dirty rats!" Ericson snarled beneath his breath.

He recognized the object instantly, for his clever hands had fashioned it within the week. It had been taken from its original setting, in which four other similar objects kept it company, but there was not the faintest doubt that it was the animated marionette he had made of Bessingham!

The feet of the wooden figure were attached to discs that revolved when a crank was turned. Ericson picked up the thing, turned the crank. As the feet moved the slim figure swayed, the threads moving the arms and torso in languid gyrations. It was an almost perfect representation of an elegant man waltzing.

In spite of the tension that gripped him, Ericson could not help grinning maliciously.

THERE WERE FOOTSTEPS in the hallway and a man stood in the library door, his pale face surprised and worried.

"Well, Ericson," Bessingham said. "I didn't expect to find you here. What brings you?"

"Circumstances," Ericson answered vaguely. "You know about them."

Bessingham crossed the room gracefully and seated himself at a carved teakwood table. His lips were drawn in a straight line and before he spoke he slid the top drawer of his desk two inches and looked at the gold-plated automatic pistol lying there.

In the other room the decorator, Brown, who was Jim Anthony's operative, fitted into his ear a tiny device which would enable him to hear clearly any conversation that might pass between them.

"Look here," Bessingham said slowly, "I suppose you know one of your marionettes was sent to Art Fallon just before something happened to him?"

Ericson blinked. "I didn't know. The paper didn't say anything about it. But I suspected it."

"The marionette was there. Fallon told Anthony about it by radio. Anthony found it beside Fallon's body when he reached Marquette. An explosion and fire destroyed all traces of what had been done, but Anthony knew. Fallon's body was rigged up just like that wooden doll, and it was dancing!"

"The marionettes were stolen," Ericson growled. "A stranger wanted to buy them, and I wouldn't sell, and the next night a burglar got them."

"That's your story! How do I know it's true?"

Ericson sighed. "You don't know. When I heard that phoney radio talk I knew you wouldn't know, nor anybody else. Right afterward I got a long-distance phone call warning me to hide if I didn't want to be killed, and my daughter with me!" The engineer's gnarled hands curled into fists. "I beat it, but not to hide. I wanted to find out things. I was going to New York to see Linster, but when I heard he was missing I decided to drop off here and talk with you."

Jim's car crashed into the curbing
and lurched into the grass.

Bessingham took a long time about replying, but said finally, "Alfred, we've been friends for years. I'd be willing to give you the benefit of any doubt, even though it's known you have a nasty temper and don't forgive your enemies easily. You've quarreled with Logan and it's pretty well known you hate his guts. You've never quarreled with me, but how do I know you don't hate my guts just because I've joined forces with Logan in a new job?"

"You don't know," Ericson said again. "On the other hand, how do I know you or Phail or Van Rucker—or even old Jasper Logan himself—aren't behind all this, trying to make me the goat? You were all cutthroats in the beginning. I understand that if any of you dies, the others take over his holdings for the time being. Suppose all of you but Logan were killed, and he controlled all your mills and factories and other properties. How long would it take him to make that control permanent?"

"That's preposterous!" snapped the steel man. "We've got all we can manage, as it is. None of us ever committed murder, or ever will. Don't start suspecting me till you find those marionettes in my possession!"

The malicious grin returned to Ericson's face. "Take a good look at your bookshelves, my friend!"

BROWN, THE DECORATOR, loosened his revolver in the holster concealed by his baggy overalls. He quit pretending to work and stood watchfully in the doorway, seeing Bessingham spring to his feet, his eyes bulging from their sockets and his mouth working convulsively.

"You brought it with you!" Bessingham screamed to Ericson. "You're the man who murdered Fallon! You came here planning to murder me, but you won't get away with it!"

"Take it easy," the old man said—and strangely, in this emergency his voice was calm. "If you kill me, you'll only direct suspicion against yourself."

"I'll kill you if you make a move!" Bessingham swore. "If you sit perfectly still, I'll let the cops have you alive!" He lifted the ivory phone from its cradle on the desk and said, "Operator, get me the police!"

"I didn't bring the marionette here," Ericson said. "I saw it when I came in."

"We'll see about that! If you handled it, probably your fingerprints are on it…. Police headquarters? This is James Bessingham. Someone is trying to kill me. Send men out to my house right away!"

"You'll be sorry," Ericson murmured. "Just wait a little while, then see if you're not—"

He broke off as the pistol wavered in Bessingham's grip. The steel manufacturer passed a bewildered hand across his brow. He moved away from the desk, walking languidly, his slender body swaying.

Bessingham was naturally elegant in all his movements, but he was not given to exhibitionism. Neither Brown nor Ericson thought it funny when suddenly he began to waltz, sliding his feet gracefully over the rug, waving his arms as if keeping time to lilting music, while all the time his face was rigid with horror!

Brown rushed toward Bessingham. Ericson, too, had sprung to his feet. But Brown waved the engineer back.

"Keep away!" he warned sharply.

A hoarse rattle came from Bessingham's throat. He tried to speak, but could not. His body crumpled and writhed for a second, then lay still.

"Dead?" Ericson asked.

With his hand pressed over Bessingham's heart, Brown nodded wordlessly.

"I'll get help!" Ericson cried, and dashed from the room. A minute later the butler entered, wringing his hands.

"Oh, this is terrible!" the butler wailed. "Oh, whatever shall we do?"

Brown's ears caught the wail of approaching sirens. That would be the police, responding to Bessingham's call. He thought belatedly of the man who had been responsible for the existence of the horrible marionettes.

"Where did that fellow go?" he demanded.

"Mr. Ericson? He went away. No sooner had he told me the master was dead than he ran into the street as though the devil himself was after him!"

CHAPTER X

ENTER ANSON MARNER

HIGH OVER AKRON, THE *Thunderbird II* roared, her four metal propellers shredding lofty cirrus clouds. Anthony crouched at the radio desk, phones clamped over his ears, his dark face inscrutable as he listened to Brown's report.

"…There wasn't a thing I could do, sir. I had my gun ready and didn't take my eyes off either Ericson or Bessingham all the while. But the damage had already been done. I'm convinced Bessingham was finished before he ever returned to his home, Mr. Anthony, but whatever finished him didn't take effect till a few minutes ago."

Jim was no longer in the same spot. In that fight he was
almost like a ghost, rising where least expected!

"Ericson ran away right afterward, eh?" Jim asked.

"That's right. The police have broadcast his description, but so far there's no trace of him. They picked up a carload of armed men down the street, but there was nothing to show they had any connection with Bessingham's death. I think, sir, they were waiting in the hope you would show up."

Jim broke the connection, realizing more than ever the supreme cunning of the forces that opposed him. Brown was probably right about Bessingham having been finished before he reached Pittsburgh, perhaps before he ever left Michigan. Marner's plans had been laid cunningly in advance, and Marner's death traps were already in existence. Jim's task was not to prevent weapons being aimed at Logan, Phail and Van Rucker, but to create shields against weapons that were already aimed—strange, secret weapons at whose types he could only guess.

He became aware of Ruth Ericson beside him, her pretty face filled with desperation.

"I heard you mention Dad's name," she said. "Where did he run away from? Why? What lies are they telling about him?"

He shook his head pityingly. "I hope I'll be able to tell you all the answers soon."

He had no heart to stun her with the news that her father had paid a visit to Bessingham and the steel man had died in his presence, aping the antics of the marionette Ericson had made. Why terrify her with things he did not understand fully himself?

He signaled to Gentry, who lounged opposite him, reading his favorite detective magazine, while the Anthony Robot guided the plane.

"We're not stopping at Pittsburgh, after all, Tom. We're going on to Philadelphia."

"Gosh!" Tom exclaimed. "Did they beat us to Bessingham?"

"They beat us." Jim let it go at that. The one thing clear to him was that his only hope was to take the initiative. Instead of waiting for the marionettes to appear and then hurrying to the men who received them, he had to reach those men first and surround them with safeguards, and that was a job he could not trust to his agents.

Van Rucker in Philadelphia and Phail in New York would be next on the death list. Logan, too—but of all the men threatened, Logan was the best able to take care of himself.

The *Thunderbird* was as fast as anything its size ever to take the air, but nevertheless it was two more hours from Akron to Philadelphia. During the intervening time Jim kept the radio busy, checking with Dolores at The Cavern, with Cynthia Arnold in New York, with trusted operatives in many cities. There was no definite news, and he was no wiser when the amphibian swooped to a landing in a private airport in the Germantown section of the city of Brotherly Love.

PHILADELPHIA WAS BLANKETED by a drizzle of rain. Over the slacks and sweater he had donned, Jim pulled a raincoat. He issued rapid directions to Gentry.

"We're splitting up here. Take Miss Ericson to the Central Hotel and wait there till you hear from me."

Jim's eyes swept the landing field, searching for signs of suspicious persons, seeing no one. He herded his companions toward the hangars, where private cars, ordered ahead by radio, waited to pick them up.

Gentry knew better than to question the orders of his friend and employer, but Ruth pouted at the arrangement.

"Why can't I go with you?" Her dark eyes were pleading. "I know you'll be finding things out. After all, it's my father and my sweetheart—"

"No argument!" Jim made his voice harsh to dispel further talk. He pushed them both into a limousine chauffeured by a man he knew to be dependable and courageous—an expert driver and a qualified bodyguard—and himself took the wheel of a fast roadster. He waved. "Be seeing you!"

It would not have helped their peace of mind to know that his sole reason in ordering them to the hotel was to spare them a share of the danger he expected to face. Even if members of Anson Marner's gang had not picked up the radio signals from the *Thunderbird,* they would expect him sooner or later at Philadelphia, and would be ready for him.

Anthony was eager to face whatever arrangements might have been made by his enemies for his reception. He did not for a minute underestimate the peril to himself, or relish needless risks, but he clung to the hope that, by taking advantage of some unguarded move on the part of Marner or his men, he could trap or destroy the criminal leader and end once and for all time this very real threat to America's safety.

As he speeded the roadster over the wet concrete of a sparsely traveled road, in a direction opposite to that the others had taken, his seventh sense of danger was tingling. He wondered whether he would encounter the next spurt of action at Guy Van Rucker's home, or whether it would concern Tom and Ruth in some manner, or strike in his absence at Dolores or Jasper Logan, back in Michigan.

So brooding, his constant guard of wariness was lowered just for a moment—and it was in that moment that the lightning struck. He had not noticed the big sedan coming up from the rear. What happened came with such shocking abruptness that even his swift reflexes could not respond in time.

With a burst of speed, the sedan cut in sharply. Its right rear wheel struck the left front hubcap of the roadster. Tires screeched, sliding sidewise. Jim's car crashed against the curbing, lurched into the wet grass, rolled over. He flung himself clear before the heavy machine crushed him, but the force with which he was thrown to the ground stunned him momentarily.

Men leaped upon him, four, six, a dozen of them—he could not be sure. Their boots and fists thudded into his ribs, stomach and face, and blackjacks in their hands smashed against his skull. His assailants, doubtless having been warned repeatedly about Jim's skill and strength, took no chances and gave no quarter. The man beneath them absorbed a beating that would have killed an ordinary person.

Jim made one powerful effort, half rising to his feet, throwing men left and right as he struck out with groggy aim. But a slugger stood ready behind him, waiting for just such an opportunity. Rockets and pin-wheels exploded within Jim's brain as that last blow landed. His knees crumpled and he dropped swiftly into blackness....

SOME TIME LATER, consciousness surged back painfully. Jim became aware that men were carrying him up half a dozen steps in the rain, into a house and down more steps. He did not open his eyes, but other senses than sight told him he was in a house that had stood empty for a long time. His ears noted the tread of feet over creaking boards, his nostrils caught the musty smell of a large dwelling that has been closed and airless for months or years. More than that, his wrists and ankles felt the squeeze of steel cuffs biting into the flesh—cuffs too strong to be snapped by human strength and too snug to be wriggled out of by any Houdini tricks.

He lay limp, pretending to be still unconscious, not wincing when the rough movements of his bearers caused special agony to his multiple cuts and bruises. He was carried into a cellar room that smelled of steam and, more faintly, of the lilac-scented gas he had sniffed in Fallon's house. There he was dumped unceremoniously upon a plank bench.

A heavy voice said, "Here he is, boss—signed, sealed and delivered. I hope I never have to knock out another guy as tough as him, or carry one as heavy!"

Then Anthony thrilled, for the smooth accents that purred in reply were known to him all too well.

Supported by the cord, he dropped to within thirty feet of the ground.

"Yes, here he is! You have done well, men, and I have done even better. Nothing can stop me now. I shall make first a fool of this overrated man, then a traitor, and finally a corpse. Leave him with me while I bring him back to life with the adrenalin!"

The men left, and Jim looked up at a tall, broad-shouldered man whose face was covered with a black cloth mask, through which green eyes appeared as malevolent slits.

"You won't need your adrenalin, Marner," he said. "You won't need that mask, either, with me. I know you."

The mask moved, as if the face beneath it might be smiling. "Ah, Mr. Anthony, you will know me much better before we are through with our brief business! Meanwhile, this bit of camouflage is not for you. It is for certain of my own men, in case they should fall into the hands of the authorities and be persuaded to try to identify me. Only a fool trusts other fools!"

Anthony lifted his manacled hands to rub a bruised place on his jaw. "I've been looking for you, Marner. You needn't have dragged me here by force. I'd have come of my own accord, if you'd sent me the address."

"But probably not alone. You see, I have no real wish to quarrel with you. I only want to obtain from you the secret of the Anthony Anti-Aircraft Ray, and then dispose of you quietly, so that I shall be the only man in the world in possession of it. I think that secret will make me as rich and powerful as I care to be!"

"Supposing," Jim asked, his eyes narrowing, "I won't tell you the secret?"

The mask moved again. "I have no worries about that. As you may know, I have some very clever scientists in my employ. They have discovered a certain derivative of scopolamine, vulgarly called truth serum, which is usually effective. Unfortunately—or fortunately, depending upon one's viewpoint—the drug is invariably fatal, too, though not immediately. There is ample time for a man to carry on a technical discussion before death seals his lips!"

THOUGH HIS BLOOD was chilling and there seemed to be no prospect of escape, Jim pressed for more information. "Why did you have Fallon and Bessingham killed? They didn't know the secret of the ray, and if they had, killing them wouldn't have helped you get it."

"Those two and three others had associated themselves with you for the production of the ray projectors," the masked man informed him. "Even if they didn't know the details, they knew the general plan, and probably would have known where to point the finger of accusation if you had vanished. Besides, I wanted to create a diversion. As far as the public is concerned, those men weren't killed by me, but by bands of patriotic vigilantes, inspired by a great and sincere radio orator"—the voice grew mocking—"one Maxwell Baldwin. You will recall that he informed the world last night, before he was cut from the air, that those men were foes of the nation."

"And how about the marionettes stolen from Ericson? Was their purpose simply to cast suspicion upon the man who made them?"

Anson Marner chuckled. "My friend, you do not know what clever and powerful men have joined in my enterprise. Ericson? Ah, even though you are about to die, I shall not tell you everything. But this much I shall show you."

Marner clapped his hands and issued an order. An instant later a short, pudgy man entered the concrete room in which Anthony lay. He came unflanked by guards. Jim looked in amazement at Maxwell Baldwin, The Voice of Inspiration, standing in the disheveled remains of a full dress suit, gazing shamefacedly at the floor.

"Tell Mr. Anthony," said Marner, "that you are on my side against his gang—which is practically helpless, anyway, since we've captured its leader."

Baldwin did not lift his eyes, but the toe of one patent-leather shoe scuffed the floor.

"Th-that's right," he muttered.

"It's of your own free will, and all that?" pursued Marner. "We haven't used—ah—persuasion of any kind?"

Baldwin's voice was scarcely above a whisper. "Of my own free will. No persuasion."

"Very well. You may go." Marner turned again to the helpless Anthony. "You see how it is?"

Jim Anthony saw how it was.

CHAPTER XI

BATTLE IN DARKNESS

RINGING FORTH IN ALL its familiar magic from the pulsing throat of its authentic originator, The Voice of Inspiration was heard again that evening upon the ether waves, giving the lie to all that Jim Anthony believed in and had fought for.

In his soiled and drooping finery, Maxwell Baldwin stood before a microphone in the cellar of an old house on the outskirts of Philadelphia. This time he did not strut in solitude; rather he cringed before an audience dominated by Anson Marner, the masked man with the blazing green eyes. Near him hummed a generator which powered a secret radio station, whose aerial was concealed by a nearby wood.

Upon a bench against a wall in the foreground, Anthony was one of the little man's visible audience. Although Jim's hands and ankles were still gripped by the torturing manacles, two of the men who had slugged him upon the highway stood close, watching. They were taking no chances with their distinguished captive.

Marner had told the young giant, "I wouldn't have you miss Baldwin's talk for anything! The scopolamine derivative is prepared and you won't be alive in the morning, but I want you to die knowing how thoroughly you—the mighty Jim Anthony—have been beaten by the man you tried to ruin!"

And Marner had chuckled, vastly pleased with himself.

But a glimmer of hope had come to Jim in these last few minutes. It had to do with the tiny weapon he had devised at The Cavern before beginning his flight east. That weapon was still clipped in the breast pocket of his black sweater, left there by his captors, who evidently mistook it for nothing more dangerous than a fountain pen.

Now Jim leaned forward and fixed Baldwin with his glowing eyes while the scared speaker read the script which had been written for him....

"Friends of America, this is Maxwell Baldwin, The Voice of Inspiration, appealing earnestly to you to rise up and annihilate the menace that confronts your country! Because my life is in danger, I have been forced to flee from my home and address you from a secret place...."

Baldwin may have trembled, but his tones did not. The words that were being broadcast from that hidden station, being poured into tens of thousands of radio receivers, sounded as convincing as any the pudgy spellbinder had ever uttered. People would hear and believe, and those that did not hear would read it all in tomorrow's newspapers!

"...James Anthony, who poses as a patriot, but who is actually the most dangerous enemy the United States has within its borders, has sworn to kill me! Jasper Logan, whose scheme I exposed last night, has scores of men seeking me, to murder me...."

Marner was smirking and applauding silently. He did not appear to have noticed the unblinking, penetrating gaze Anthony had fixed upon Baldwin.

"…Royal Phail, the money-mad banker, has put a price on my head! Men and women of America, those monsters would destroy you as well as me…."

Baldwin's small eyes were held completely by Anthony's stare. One might have thought him hypnotized.

IN THINKING THAT, one would not have been entirely wrong. Not only had Anthony studied hypnotism and experimented widely with its possibilities, but even without his knowledge of that mysterious art, his will was powerful enough to project itself into the persons of weaker men and dominate their wills.

Baldwin was a weak man. Some of the magic faded from his tones as he continued, "…for these men and their hirelings are prepared to trample underfoot the cherished ideals of the nation and—er—to suck its very—er—lifeblood…."

Anson Marner frowned suspiciously.

Strangely, under his vanity and his fear, Maxwell Baldwin, was becoming a man. Righteous anger was swelling within his breast. Goaded by that indomitable will of Anthony's, he was rising to new heights of heroism. He *had* to do something!

He did it dramatically, shredding the script between his plump fingers, shrieking into the microphone with all the power of his lungs:

"Men and women of America, I have been lying to you! I have been forced to lie! The men I have condemned are patriots! James Anthony and myself are prisoners of the real enemy, who is—"

But Marner's hand had thrown the switch that disconnected the microphone. Cursing, Marner literally danced in his rage.

"Kill him!" he roared.

A gunman leveled an automatic at Baldwin.

Anthony was already on his feet, hopping forward, diving headlong at the gunman. He struck the man's legs and they rolled together on the floor, while the bullets meant for Baldwin skittered wildly about the room. Oaths and cries arose on all sides, and loudest of all was Marner's threat, "You'll pay for this, Anthony! Not only you, but the girl you love and your friends shall die!"

Jim's ironed hands were at his breast pocket, withdrawing the tube. He was not certain whether his plan would work, but if the electric generator controlled the lights of the house as well as the radio transmitter….

He caught up Baldwin
and slung him over
his shoulder like a
sack of flour.

IT DID. THE invisible beam from the miniature Triple-A Ray projector was instantly effective. The lights in the cellar blinked out, the hum of the generator died.

Guns made streaks of fire through the sudden darkness, bullets chipped the concrete where Jim had lain. But Jim was no longer in that spot. Able to see in the dark where the others were blinded, he was on his knees, working his way toward one of the gangsters who had carried him into the house. He rose up behind that man and his hands clamped around the back of a thick neck, pressing nerve centers. The man collapsed without a struggle.

In the fellow's vest pocket Jim found what he wanted—the keys to the irons at his wrists and ankles. He sat down, fitted them to the locks, felt the grateful rush of blood into his numbed hands and feet.

"Make a light, one of you!" Marner was bawling. "Shoot the little one—we can't trust him any more—but take the other one alive! He can't get away with his hands and feet fastened!"

Anthony's keen ears sorted out the rustle of a match folder from the general pandemonium. He saw one of the gangsters about to strike a match. He lunged instantly, thrusting with his shoulder at Baldwin as he passed. The uninspired Voice of Inspiration still was standing at the microphone, probably more astounded than any of them at his own audacity; he was catapulted by Jim's thrust into a comparatively safe corner behind the metal bulk of the generator.

Jim smashed a balled fist into the jaw of the man who had the unhappy thought of lighting a match. He grabbed a pistol from the one who, hearing Baldwin's whimpers, was trying to aim by sound at the spot where the pudgy man lay. Disdaining to use the weapon for the purpose for which it was intended, he threw it at a man who had taken a flashlight from his pocket and was blinking it aimlessly about. The man dropped and the light vanished.

ANTHONY WAS ENJOYING himself hugely, but he did not forget that the stake in this fight was more than fun. Marner was the prize he was after. The erstwhile prisoner went like a tornado through the cellar, bludgeoning one man with his closed fist, shouldering another into insensibility against a wall, his eyes always seeking the arch conspirator.

But Marner was not to be seen, and all at once the roar of a car's motor outside the house told why. Realizing that the battle was going against him, the leader of the Apecia had fled, leaving his men to whatever fate might befall them.

Raging inwardly, Jim caught up Baldwin, slinging him like a sack of flour over his shoulder. The killers in the cellar were still fighting in the darkness, blundering into one another, striking and firing blindly. Cries of fear and pain echoed through the house as Jim vaulted lightly up the stairs, smashed a locked door and sped through empty rooms. He plunged through a window, saw cars standing in the driveway, and piled his blubbering burden into one.

"You can quit crying," he snapped. "You're safe. You can go back on the air with a police bodyguard and tell the story of what happened, and you'll be a hero!"

Baldwin sniffled, peering up in the light of the instrument board as Jim started the car, assuring himself that he was really rescued. His spirits mounted swiftly.

"Y-you really think so, Mr. Anthony? A h-hero?"

"The whole country will sing your praises," Jim said gravely, gunning the car down the driveway. He grinned behind his hand at the thought, but he knew it was the truth, and he was glad of it. Baldwin craved glory, and as far as Jim was concerned, he was welcome to all he could get.

The adulation of the crowd was never to Anthony's taste. He could not always avoid it, but he did so whenever possible, thereby gaining a measure of privacy in which to carry forward those tasks of scientific research and criminal detection to which he had devoted his life.

He followed a highway toward the glow in the sky that marked the city of Philadelphia. Soon he was threading his borrowed machine through heavy traffic. Within three-quarters of an hour he was drawing up beside the Central Hotel.

TOM GENTRY GOGGLED at the two battered, bedraggled creatures who presented themselves at the door of his room, having passed the doubtful scrutiny of the hotel attendants.

"Holy cow!" he gasped. "I heard Baldwin's broadcast, Jim, and was just going to—"

"This is Baldwin," Jim broke in. "Get him some clothes and see that he's given plenty of police protection. How about Miss Ericson?"

"She's in the next room. She wanted to go out, but—"

Jim strode to the door of the next room and knocked. There was no answer. He opened the door. The room was empty.

He turned with blazing eyes. "You were supposed to take care of her, Tom! God knows what may happen to her if she starts chasing around by herself!"

Gentry's honest face was troubled and embarrassed. "Gee whiz, Jim! She promised to stay put. I couldn't very well keep a pretty girl like her in my room, could I? A girl's got to have some privacy—"

Jim was in the bathroom, washing some of the mud and grime from his hands and face, cleaning the worst of the dirt from his clothes.

"Well, you won't have to be so bashful about Baldwin. Don't let him out of your sight for a minute. Understand?" He started for the door.

"I get it, Jim. Where are you—?"

"I'm going to try to save Ruth's life, keep Guy Van Rucker from being murdered, grab Anson Marner, and take care of a few other little details. You'll be hearing from me—or of me!"

He jabbed his thumb ferociously against the elevator button.

CHAPTER XII

SONG OF DEATH

VAN RUCKER, PRESIDENT OF the Great Eastern Electric Corporation, lived—or "resided," his neighbors would have said—alone with his servants in one of those massive houses of another day in an old and aristocratic section of Philadelphia. He was a native Hollander, not of the pre-Revolutionary American stock that occupied most of the houses surrounding his, but his wealth and national prominence made him not too odious to the community. For that matter, it was a fast-deteriorating community, due to the encroachment of modernism. Directly opposite Van Rucker's mansion, for instance, was a ten-story apartment building with glass-and-chromium trimmings, futuristic in design, and therefore disgusting to the more conservative element.

Jim Anthony approached his destination by stealth, leaving his car three blocks away and proceeding on foot, keeping much in the shadows. He was rewarded for this caution when he saw pairs of men lurking unobtrusively at the corners nearest Van Rucker's house, their hat-brims down against the drizzle, their coat collars high.

That they were killers, sent by Anson Marner to watch for him, Jim had no doubt. Let him approach the door of the mansion and his body would become a target for silenced pistols, thrown knives, or other deadly missiles.

Jim did not approach the structure directly. Instead he circled the block and crept through a delivery alley into a trade entrance of the apartment building. He rode the automatic elevator to the top floor, unchallenged, and climbed the short flight of steps to the roof.

Peering down into the street he judged with mathematical eyes and brain the width of the street and the height of the fourth-floor windows of the house he wished to enter. He had a delicate problem, for he could not approach his goal directly, but because of the positions of the two buildings must reach it by a course that curved both vertically and horizontally.

He then fed from the reel in his belt buckle yards of the thin, enormously tough cord that was wrapped around his waist, and made one end fast to a cornice at the front of the roof. Going toward the rear of the building, paying out the threadlike stuff as he moved, he reached a drainpipe. Down this he half-slid, half-climbed, past lighted windows from which issued the mixed music of many radios. Between the fifth and sixth floors he poised, ran over his calculations once more in his mind, and then launched himself into the air.

SUPPORTED BY THE cord, he swooped along the side of the building, dropping to within thirty feet of the ground, and out over the street. There was little risk of his being seen by the waiting killers, for the rain made a fine haze and his passage was swift, and anyway their hat-brims were down and their eyes watching the streets. The only danger was that he would miss his objective and fall back, in which case they would surely see him, and he would be helpless to defend himself against them.

As he reached the end of his breathless downward sweep, the cord slipped from the side of the building, swung him to the left and lifted him. He rose against the face of Van Rucker's house, stretched out feet and hands, and perched on a wide fourth-floor windowsill as nimbly as a bird alighting!

He grinned, looking down at the lurking shapes at the street corners. But there was no time for self-congratulation, even had Jim been given to that indulgence. He severed the cord by means of the special blade in his belt buckle, took a thick-bladed jack-knife from his pocket and in twenty seconds had slipped back the catch of the window. Raising the sash carefully, he stepped into the darkness of a room.

THE FOURTH-FLOOR OF the house, evidently, was given over to servants' quarters. The room in which Jim stood was empty, but he heard the voices of women in another room nearby. He slipped quietly through the hallway and down the stairs. The third floor was dark, but there were lights on the second floor, where, Jim had judged from his survey of the house, the drawing room and library were located.

He found the wide doorway to the library and lingered beside it, hearing the conversation of two men. He recognized Van Rucker's gruff voice, which still retained the accent of his mother-tongue.

"I tell you, Linster, dere iss no cause to be afraid! I shall not call der police. Because someone has sent me a little dancing doll—"

The voice of a younger man interrupted, "But, Mr. Van Rucker, you know what happened to Fallon and Bessingham!"

Jim stepped into the doorway. He saw Van Rucker sprawled in an easy chair, his cane by his side, his clubfoot in its oversize shoe thrust out before him, his jowls pink with anger where they were not hidden

As she touched the cabinet, the current leaped upon her like a live thing.

by mutton-chop whiskers. Opposite the old Dutchman sat Myron Linster, the missing secretary, his dark hair smooth as glass, his velvet-brown eyes veiled.

But what held Jim's gaze longer than either of the men was the grotesque figure on the table at Van Rucker's side. It was one of the Ericson marionettes, the clubfooted one, suspended by threads within a frame to which a crank was attached. Van Rucker's stubby fingers were turning the crank absently and the figure was stamping its wooden feet in a passable imitation of a clog dance!

"Good evening, gentlemen," Jim said. "I seem to be in time, for once."

Both men started. Over Van Rucker's ruddy face came a smile, and into Linster's eyes an inscrutable expression.

"Ja!" Van Rucker exclaimed. "My boy, it iss glad I am to see you! We were joost talking about you."

Linster wet his lips. "Yes, Mr. Anthony. I've been wanting to get in touch with you ever since—what happened last night."

Jim studied the younger man. "A lot of people have been trying to get in touch with you, Linster. You picked a bad time to run away, and a bad time to show up."

Linster spread his hands in an empty gesture. "Why should I have stayed? The police would have blamed me for what happened, and I'd have been in trouble. The fact that Baldwin's former secretary died violently, and I took his place less than two weeks ago, would look suspicious as the devil to them. I knew you'd been in touch with Baldwin about Marner, and I thought possibly you'd know something that could clear me and save me from spending time in jail."

"How do you happen to be here?"

"I'd met Mr. Van Rucker through Mr. Ericson. At one time he offered to make me his secretary if I ever left Mr. Ericson's employ. I thought he'd know how to get in touch with you and I managed to reach him by phone at his Akron factories while he was on his way here from Detroit. He asked me to meet him tonight."

"Der lad iss right," Van Rucker declared. "I told him I vould do all dot I could to help him."

Jim pointed to the dancing marionette. "And that?"

VAN RUCKER SNORTED. "Dot liddle toy iss supposed to mean danger, I understand. How can it hurt me, *hein?*"

"How did you get it?"

"It vas here ven I returned, deliffered by a messenger. Dere iss der package it came in. I joost opened it."

Jim picked up the flat cardboard box. It told him nothing, but a flat circular object still within it, which Van Rucker seemingly had missed, caught his eye. He lifted it out gingerly, removed its tissue-paper wrapping and held a phonograph record in his hands. In the center of the disc was pasted the title—*Song of Death*.

"Music!" said Van Rucker. "Dot iss nice. Let us play it and see vot it iss like."

"It may not be as nice as you think." Jim scowled. He examined the material of the record, scraping it with his knife blade, tasting it with the tip of his tongue. Satisfied that it was an ordinary record, neither of poisonous nor explosive construction, his scowl deepened. He picked up the marionette and examined it. His eyes searched the room thoroughly.

That room was packed with danger. Jim could feel it with that extra sense, which never lied, but he could not place it. He knew that earlier in the day Schmidt, the reformed burglar and safecracker, had searched the house from roof to cellar without finding anything suspicious. He had no fear of anything so crude as an attack from without, and a bullet could hardly be fired through the heavily curtained windows with any chance of finding its target. And yet he felt that the life of at least one man hung in the balance.

"Put it on der phonograph," Van Rucker insisted, pointing with his cane to the ornate cabinet in the corner. "Or else let me put it on. I am not frightened of such foolishness!"

"No," Jim said. "I'll play it. You others keep back." Whatever deadly trick of Anson Marner's might be forthcoming, he knew that he was more capable of dealing with it than either of the others.

He examined the phonograph cabinet carefully before putting the record on the turntable. It had not been tampered with, he was certain, and no wires ran from its legs to the floor. He chose a fresh needle and fitted it to the playing arm. He started the electric mechanism and waited a moment before lowering the needle point into the wax grooves.

He could think of no further precautions to take.

A sneering laugh came out of the machine as the needle vibrated. Then a strain of thin violin music, and a nasal voice:

Guy Van Rucker, traitor, sucker,

This shall be your knell. Death's advancing, so start dancing—

Clog your way to hell!

A girl's voice in the doorway spun Jim around. He saw the solemn figure of a baldheaded butler in livery and, darting around him, Ruth Ericson!

THE DARK-HAIRED GIRL cried, "Myron!" and flung herself into the arms of the man who had been her father's secretary and Baldwin's. She said, "I couldn't stay in that hotel room! I was sure something would be happening here, so I looked up the address in the phone book—"

The nasal voice was still issuing from the phonograph, jeering and insulting, but there was so much commotion Jim could not make out the continuing words of the song. Most of the commotion was made by Van Rucker, who had heaved himself from his chair and was thumping toward the machine, brandishing his cane.

"I smash dot damn' insult!" Van Rucker roared. "By *Gott*, I show dem—!"

"Wait!" Anthony shouted—but Van Rucker either did not hear or did not choose to obey.

And suddenly a strange and terrible thing happened. Van Rucker halted in front of the phonograph, as if frozen. A curious, frightened expression came over his face. He lifted first one foot, then the other—lifted them as if that act were laborious, and set them down hard, so that they banged against the floor. He began to stamp the floor rhythmically in time to the music—began, actually and unmistakably, to clog!

Even while Anthony leaped toward him, the old man turned an ashen, appealing face to him and dropped. He was dead before Jim could reach his side.

In the very presence of Jim Anthony, in the face of all the precautions that could humanly be taken, the hand of Anson Marner had for the third time in two days struck down one of the men vital to America's safety! It was uncanny! Almost it seemed beyond belief, except that the crumpled body of the Dutchman, there on the floor in front of the squawking phonograph, was not to be denied.

Jim turned incredulous eyes on Linster and Ruth. "Did either of you see—?" he started to ask.

The pistol in Linster's hand silenced him. The pistol covered Jim and the butler, and behind it Linster's face was that of a desperate, ruthless man.

"You're not going to frame me for this!" he cried shrilly. "If either of you try to follow us, I'll shoot to kill!"

Ruth clung to Linster's free arm, her cheeks drained of color. She moved with him as he backed from the room. The thick door slammed, an old-fashioned heavy bolt was shot, and there were the sounds of running feet on the carpeted stairs.

CHAPTER XIII

WALL STREET AFFAIR

CYNTHIA ARNOLD FOUGHT DOWN an almost hysterical impulse to giggle. No one knew better than this lovely titian-haired agent of Jim Anthony, who had lately been a blues singer in an uptown cabaret, that what was happening in Royal Phail's fortieth-floor office above Wall Street was hardly a laughing matter; yet there was an irresistibly funny resemblance between the small wooden doll that had just been delivered there and the man to whom it had been delivered.

The doll—undoubtedly one of the horrible Ericson marionettes—was fat and pompous, and it was held in a frame by taut rubber bands. At the slightest provocation—sometimes it seemed at none at all—those bands quivered and the ridiculous figure shimmied.

Sunk in the padded depths of his swivel chair, Royal Phail, without benefit of rubber bands, sped the tremulous movements of the marionette. He shimmied, too, as much as a fat man sitting down was able to. His overfed belly heaved and rippled, his various chins distended and contracted, his chubby hands fluttered like blown-up leaves, the chair beneath him vibrated.

Beyond that, Phail's pale eyes popped from their folds of tissue as they regarded the token of doom, and sweat beaded his forehead.

"Get Anthony immediately!" he gasped. "I don't care where he is or what he's doing, Miss Arnold—tell him to come here this minute!

Three men have died already and I'll be the fourth unless he gets here in time!"

Cynthia's shapely legs flashed as she hurried to her desk just outside Phail's private office. Call Jim Anthony? There was nothing on earth she would rather do, at any time. She knew that Dolores Colquitt was Jim's fiancée and that the bronze man of miracles had little enough time to devote to Dolores, let alone other girls— but she had a right to her dreams, hadn't she?

Leaving Phail to his horrified contemplation of the carved messenger of death, Cynthia phoned a certain number in midtown Manhattan. From there her call would

His body struck the ledge and bounced out and downward—forty stories.

be relayed by radio to The Tepee, Jim's underground castle in the Catskills, and from The Tepee it would be broadcast on a private wavelength, in code, throughout the nation. No matter where Anthony might be, he would hear that call, either directly or through some of the operatives who were always near him....

The girl glanced up, frowning, as a stooped, bearded man entered the outer office, piloted by one of Phail's numerous assistants. She said, "I'm afraid this is a bad time—"

"But Miss Arnold," protested the assistant, "this gentleman wishes to invest a quarter-million dollars with us, and he's carrying it around in his hands! He insisted upon seeing Mr. Phail personally."

The stranger apologetically displayed a manila envelope from which the corners of ten-thousand-dollar bills peeped forth. "I wanted some expert advice," he explained.

"If you'll wait outside—" began Cynthia.

But Phail had seen and heard through the open door. Phail had not risen to the top in the banking profession through ignoring large sums of money. Habit proved stronger than fear in him.

"A quarter-million?" he asked, achieving a smile. "Of course I'm not too busy to see the gentleman. Come right in, sir."

The bearded man went into Phail's private office. The assistant withdrew. Cynthia Arnold's topaz eyes widened suspiciously.

"ALWAYS READY TO welcome a new client," Phail said, rubbing his hands. "What exactly did you have in mind, Mr.—er—?"

"Mr. Anthony," said Jim, thrusting the envelope into his pocket, smiling through the false beard. "I had a feeling that something might be wrong here, and I wore the disguise to keep from being killed on the way up." He looked at the shimmying puppet. "Maybe it's a good thing I'm here."

Phail relaxed, torn between relief at Jim's arrival and disappointment at not adding another large account to his business, which did not handle the Anthony affairs. He drew a damp hand across his damp brow.

"Miss Arnold has been trying to reach you. This—er—monstrosity was just brought in by a messenger boy."

Cynthia had come into the private office, her eyes shining. "Oh, Mr. Anthony! I was sending a message to The Tepee, as you instructed me. I've already contacted the messenger service, but all they know is that a stranger left the parcel with directions to have it delivered here. I didn't know what else to do."

"Nothing out of the ordinary happened earlier?"

She shook her head. "Mr. Phail cooperated fully. I read his mail, searched his office and listened to all his phone calls. There have been no callers, except close friends and business associates of Mr. Phail."

The banker chimed in, "I have twenty extra guards scattered through the outside offices, all from a reputable agency. I don't see how any harm can reach me. And yet, Anthony, I'm scared enough to drop dead!"

Behind its hirsute disguise Jim's face was worried. He didn't see how harm could reach Phail at this moment, either. But harm had reached Fallon and Bessingham and Van Rucker—sensible men, who had been warned and had taken all reasonable precautions.

He said slowly, "That's how Van Rucker died—he was scared enough to drop dead, and he did. It was a devilish scheme, and whoever planned it knew all about Van Rucker's heart condition. The doctors had been telling him for years that the least exertion or excitement might kill him."

Phail's cheeks were pasty. "How—how did they do it? The papers said it was a mystery."

"It wasn't a mystery when I finished my investigation. Somehow they'd got into his house and fixed a big electro-magnet beneath the floor in front of the phonograph. Somehow they'd got hold of Van Rucker's shoes and placed steel plates in their soles—an especially thick plate in the sole of the shoe on his clubfoot.

"They counted on his playing the record himself, or at any rate going near the phonograph while it was being played. The sound vibrations of the music sent a fluctuating current into the magnet. Van Rucker found his feet sticking to the floor, then suddenly being released. In a fix like that, you or I would stamp our feet, and that's what he did, not being able to help himself. The record was ordering him to clog himself to death and he was doing it. His rage and fright killed him!"

"GOOD GOD!" PHAIL breathed. "What sort of man would think of a thing like that?"

"The same sort of man that thought of a way of killing Bessingham through one of *his* weaknesses. You know, he was always taking pills for his liver and stomach and what-not. Well, the murderer simply slipped a deadly pill into his supply."

"But the papers said he waltzed!"

Jim muttered, "He did, or seemed to. I was up most of the night superintending the autopsy. We found that he had been poisoned by an enteric pill—one coated with a substance that will not dissolve in the stomach, but must pass into the intestine first. Probably he took the pill before he left Michigan.

"Beneath the outer coating of the pill was a layer of laudanum. When that entered his system, it made him reel and stagger, and his natural gracefulness gave him the appearance of dancing. Beneath the laudanum was potassium cyanide."

"How are you going to save me?" Phail whispered. "How can you combat a fiend like that?"

"If I could guess who it was, I could probably figure out what he would be apt to do next. Marner is behind it all, of course, but it isn't Marner's brain that's planning out these murder methods."

Phail wet his lips. "You know who is guilty, as well I! Alfred Ericson has thrown in with Marner and is trying to kill us all to satisfy his grudge against Logan. The man was always a genius, and now he's a mad genius. He knew all of us well. He knew about Van Rucker's heart and Bessingham's pills. He made those puppets!"

Cynthia said, "The very fact that he made the puppets and let the public know about them ought to count in his favor, hadn't it?"

"A smart man might have planned it that way, knowing how people would look at it," Jim said. "Still, there's not enough evidence yet for us to confine our suspicions to any single person."

"There's another," Phail said hesitantly. "I've kept from mentioning him because he's a good friend of yours, Anthony. But has it ever crossed your mind that Jasper Logan might want to add Fallon's mines, Bessingham's mills, Van Rucker' factories and my banks to his hold-ings? He could do it, you know, given control of them for a year or so with the rest of us out of the way."

"It has crossed my mind," Jim admitted.

"He's been a Napoleon of industry. He started out to build the greatest industrial empire on earth, and he's done it by fair means and foul. A man like that is ambitious for power, and the more he gets the more he wants. His appetite becomes insatiable and his methods ruthless."

"That agreement the five of you signed gives full control of all those organizations to the survivor or survivors during the Triple-A produc-tion program," Jim recalled.

"I think it does that very definitely." Phail began to heave himself laboriously from his chair. "I have a copy in the top drawer of that filing cabinet...."

"I'll get it," Jim offered.

But when he turned, Cynthia was ahead of him, eager to perform even the slightest service for the man she admired above all others.

She cried, "Let me, Mr. Anthony!"

JIM SAW HER feet quicken. Then he saw something glinting through the carpet ahead of her. His brain clicked, grasping the truth, and he sprang forward.

"Stop!" he shouted.

She turned her head in bewilderment, but her hand reached automatically for the handle of the filing drawer and touched it. Electrical sparks hissed and crackled. The girl's slim body became rigid, quivered. Her wavy red hair straightened and sparkled. A blue flame ran along her spine.

Jim's shoulder struck her with the force of a tackling fullback. He felt the numbing shock of tremendous voltage jerk his nerves and muscles, but the violence of his lunge carried both their bodies free of the deadly current. He rolled on the floor, got his breath and sat up, staring dazedly at the girl.

One glance at her blackened flesh and rigid features, at the wisps of smoke curling from her hair, was enough to tell him that she was dead—that, but for her, he would be dead in her place.

He lifted a face that had become a mask of fury toward Phail. The banker was not shimmying now—he seemed literally frozen with horror. But if he had touched that filing drawer, completing the electrical circuit between the wire matting beneath the rug and the metal of the cabinet, his fat body would have been suspended there, quivering, exactly as the ghastly little marionette was quivering even now!

"God in heaven!" Phail mumbled. "What—?"

The door burst open. A grey-haired, wild-eyed man dashed into the office, waving a revolver. He shrieked at Phail, "The electricity missed you, but this won't, damn you!" He triggered a bullet which shattered a photograph high on the wall.

Anthony dove for the gunman. The fellow wheeled, aimed briefly and fired again. The bullet scraped Jim's shoulder, but Jim's arms went around the man and Jim's head butted up against his chin with a knockout impact.

At the same instant Phail, galvanized into action, swung a heavy metal ashtray against the gunman's skull.

"Who is he?" Jim asked, his foot prodding the senseless man upon the rug.

Phail leaned weakly against his desk. "One of the guards I hired to protect my life, Anthony. What can I do now? Who can I trust?"

Jim's jaw was rock-hard. "You can trust the New York police department," he said. "I'm going to have headquarters send men up here, and then I'm going out and put an end to this killing in a hurry!"

He kicked the revolver out of the reach of the would-be assassin and went to the phone Cynthia had used ten minutes before. He dialed police headquarters in Centre Street and spoke briefly to an inspector of the homicide bureau.

Sounds of scuffling brought him back into the private office. He saw the banker and the gunman locked in a desperate embrace near the window. As he raced toward them the fat man thrust suddenly. Glass shattered. The grey-haired man vanished from sight.

Leaning from the window, Jim saw the hapless man's body strike a ledge, bounce outward and drop forty stories into the thronged traffic of Wall Street, turning slowly and hideously in its descent.

"I couldn't help it!" the banker wailed. "He came to and went after me again. If he hadn't been stunned, I'd never have been able to manage him! Oh, God, I'll dream of this for the rest of my life!"

Staring at the charred form of Cynthia, Jim knew that he, too, would remember this day for a long time to come.

CHAPTER XIV

DOG FIGHT

WHEN DOLORES' WARNING AND call for help reached Anthony, the *Thunderbird II* was two-thirds of the way back to The Cavern.

Jim had already relayed code orders by radio to the Reverend Mr. Parkhurst, the adventurous Detroit minister who was one of his most trustworthy operatives. Jasper Logan was to be informed that his life was in imminent peril and that he must go into hiding. Knowing the

The plane swooped past and dropped crazily to the ground.

resources of the industrial king, Jim did not state where or how Logan should hide, leaving that to the man himself; but Jim did want to be notified of Logan's whereabouts as soon as the move was effected.

Phail had been left with a bodyguard of policemen. The banker had seemed happier, with the discovery and destruction of the electrical trap in his office. He had offered, moreover, to do whatever money could do to make up for the death of Cynthia Arnold—an offer which Jim had rejected brusquely.

Whatever money could do for the family or relatives of Cynthia, Jim would take care of without stint. But all the money in the world could not bring back the eager, bright-haired girl who had asked nothing more than to serve him loyally.

The Anthony Robot flew the plane while Tom Gentry plied Jim with questions.

"What do you suppose happened to Linster and Ruth? Do you think they had a hand in what happened at Van Rucker's place?"

Jim's answer was a grunt that might have meant anything. He was stretched in the cabin of the plane, relaxed in body, but by no means at ease in his mind.

"How about old man Ericson?" Tom went on, undaunted by his chief's taciturnity. Golly, it's beginning to look more and more as if he's Marner's little helper, isn't it?"

Jim's grunt was even less committal.

"As for Jasper Logan, the old pirate—"

Tom never finished that particular observation. Jim's arm, moving with seeming effortlessness, hurled a heavy cushion across the cabin, and the impact of that soft missile drove the burly Gentry against the wall and left him breathless.

"So that's the way you feel!" Tom said sulkily. "Okay—keep your thoughts to yourself!"

He withdrew into the tiny galley in the tail of the plane and glumly set about preparing coffee.

JIM'S IMPATIENCE WAS not so much due to the insistence of Tom's urge for conversation as to the fact that so far he had no answers for Tom or himself. He had deep suspicions that were crystallizing and gathering weight in his mind, but they were badly in need of verification.

And that seventh sense of impending disaster was bothering him again. Somewhere danger was brewing, for himself or someone for whom he held himself responsible. He was quite willing to face it, but how could he be sure that he was moving in the right direction?

He couldn't fail now, he told himself fiercely—not with three key industrialists murdered and only two left of his original syndicate to manufacture Triple-A Ray projectors for the safety of the United States. Other men might die, but if Jim Anthony had anything to say about it, they would be Anson Marner's men!

If only some clarifying message would come through....

It did, almost at that moment. The weight in the upraised hand of a model of the Discus Thrower statue in a niche of the cabin wall glowed red. Jim arose with a single lithe motion and went to the radio.

"Come in," he said.

It was Dolores.

"Jim, dear, I'm afraid there's going to be trouble at The Cavern. The ray barrier is still working, but something has put the alarm system out of action and Roarty and Dawkins can't seem to fix it. Two fast planes have been circling for half an hour, keeping just beyond the rays. Roarty is watching them and says they don't seem to be up to anything, but Mephito's shaman sticks tell him there will be a raid here!"

JIM GLANCED AT the Radio Beam Map, checking the *Thunderbird's* position. "Mephito is probably right," he said. "Tom and I will be there in less than an hour. Anything else?"

"Nothing, except… darling, I've been so worried about you! Are you all right?"

"Of course I'm all right!" Jim's expression was a combination of grin and scowl, his voice a mixture of fondness and sternness. "Let me do the worrying for this outfit."

"But you never seem to worry!"

"It's a good example for you to follow. Tell the others I'm on my way and let me know as soon as anything happens."

He removed the radio headset and replaced it with an instrument resembling a physician's stethoscope, attached to a case covered with a complicated system of dials and knobs. As he turned the knobs the beat of many distant motors vibrated against his eardrums—planes riding the skies on all sides of him, near and far.

With the aid of the Radio Beam Map he set a directional sound-wave finder to bear on The Cavern, thereby tuning out most of the sounds. He heard the rumble of a twin-motored transport crossing his course and the snarl of a Coast Guard scout over Lake Erie.

Then he singled out the planes he wanted, long before any visual apparatus could have located them—two speedy ships circling a small area nearly two hundred miles ahead! He called Tom.

"Here's news for you. Two planes are waiting for us above The Cavern, probably armed with machine guns and prepared to blast us out of the sky!"

Tom's freckles were like splotches of black paint on his cheeks. All he said was, "Holy cow!" But he knew as well as Jim that the *Thunderbird* was not built for fighting and was unarmed.

"We could land, get fighting planes and take them on," continued Jim, "but that would be a waste of valuable time. I think I can knock them both down, but we'll have to take some lead in doing that. Are you with me?"

Tom's blue eyes were steady. "You know darned well I am!"

THEY CLIMBED TO eighteen thousand feet to face that battle, but even so they found the enemy ships above them as they neared The Cavern. The *Thunderbird* was easily recognized, and the first of the planes came streaking out of a drift of fleecy cloud, opening fire at a distance of a thousand feet. Tracer bullets ruled thin grey lines ahead of its gleaming propeller.

"Gee-man-EEE!" Tom exclaimed. "Look, Jim!"

His trembling finger pointed to the right wing of the big Douglas. Along that wing a row of dots advanced swiftly toward the cabin, striking the motor cowls in passing, but not damaging either of the motors.

"Watch when he tries to pull out of that power-dive!" Jim said grimly. He had lifted his arm and was sighting the tiny Triple-A Ray tube at the plunging attacker. He held it steadily on the nose of the plane, even when bullets ripped through the glass and metal of the cabin and snarled within inches of him and Tom.

The enemy shrieked past, headed toward the earth three miles below. They saw the plane flatten as the pilot tried to pull out of the plunge—flatten and go into a deadly spin. Without power there was no recovering from a dive at that speed, and the Triple-A Ray had stopped the engine dead!

Tom watched the plane drop crazily. "Poor devils!" he muttered, forgetting that a moment before the "poor devils" had been trying their best to kill him.

Grasping the controls, Jim shouted, "Snap your belt, Tom!" Behind and above them the second plane was wheeling over to dive. This time, however, Jim did not intend to take a shower of bullets.

He dropped the nose of the *Thunderbird* sharply, aiming for the white speck beside the dragon-shaped lake that was Bill Roarty's farmhouse. Instead of a flat surface, the Douglas presented the smallest possible target as she dove with all four engines roaring.

ORDINARILY IT WOULD have been a suicidal dive for a ship that large and heavy. But Jim had confidence in the *Thunderbird*, into which he had built special braces of corghium, the new lightweight steel of incredible strength he had developed in his own laboratories. While Tom bit his lips till blood ran, Jim gunned the motors to their limit.

Even so, the plane behind was swifter, and the pilot knew his gunsights. More than one bullet ripped through the cabin and one of the motors was conked out. But the enemy was still riding his tail when Jim passed over the invisible line that marked the boundary of the Triple-A Ray barrier sent aloft by the powerful projector in The Cavern, and that was what Jim wanted.

Then, and then only, Jim began to level out the huge craft, very gently, to ease the strain on the wings. Two of the motors still sang their song of power, being unaffected by the rays because of the special shields with which they were equipped.

It was not so with the smaller ship. Decoyed into the path of the rays, which it had somehow been wise enough to avoid during its period of waiting, it streaked beneath and past them, harmless as a swallow. Its pilot managed to level off to a degree and avoid the fatal spin that had destroyed his comrade, but he could not avoid a crash.

Jim and Tom watched the plane pancake in a cloud of dust in a far-off meadow. They saw a single man crawl slowly on hands and knees from beneath the crumpled wings.

Then Jim circled for a landing upon the lake.

Tom vowed, "Jim, I wouldn't trade that little tube of yours for fifty machine guns! Boy, how your ray will revolutionize aerial warfare!"

Jim placed the *Thunderbird* neatly upon the smooth surface of the lake and guided it toward the cliff that concealed the secret hangar.

"I don't want to revolutionize warfare," he said. "I want to end it. If this weapon doesn't get into the wrong hands, Tom—into the hands of men like Marner, who would sell it to gangster nations—there won't be any wars after this one!"

"Holy cats! No more wrecking of cities like London! No more useless killing of women and children! An end of barbarism. Jim, sometimes I think you're the greatest man in the world today!"

Taxiing the ship into its secret cave, Jim flushed. "Shut up!" he growled. "You're talking like a fool! I'm trying to do the thing I know best how to do for the world, and every decent man on earth is trying to do the same!"

CHAPTER XV

FARMER'S HARVEST

DAWKINS WAITED FOR THEM in the tunnel that led from the hangar to the main chamber of The Cavern. The little Englishman's face was grave in the light of Gentry's flash, but his grey eyes sparkled.

"H'I saw you 'andle those planes, sir," he said to Jim. "H'if h'I may say so, sir, h'it's the most h'exciting spectacle h'I've witnessed since the last war! H'I don't mind saying h'I was worried h'at first, for h'I knew they meant to shoot down the *Thunderbird*."

Jim dropped behind with the valet, letting Tom go on ahead. He knew Dawkins had more than congratulations to impart.

"How did you know they meant to do that?"

Dawkins lowered his voice. "H'I didn't say h'anything to Miss Dolores or the h'others, sir. There was no need to worry them. You'll remember, sir, that yesterday h'I ventured to suggest that Roarty might not he h'exactly loyal."

"I remember."

"Well, sir, when the h'alarm system went h'out of h'order, h'I investigated, h'and found the control board smashed beyond my h'ability to repair h'it. Mephito won't 'ave h'anything to do with your scientific contraptions—'e mistrusts them, h'as you know—h'and h'it would be madness to suspect Miss Dolores. H'only Roarty or myself could 'ave done h'it, sir—h'and it wasn't me."

Jim's lips tightened. "Go on."

"'Alf h'an hour ago, sir, Roarty was standing h'outside the farm'ouse, signaling with a white cloth to those two planes!"

Anger blazed up in Anthony's brain, and died almost as swiftly as it had come. He felt something like pity for the big, stupid farmer. Marner's men had approached him, of course, and turned his thick head with bribes. It had been a mistake on Anthony's part to trust a man of so little intelligence or principle.

But, at the same time, it might turn out to be a lucky mistake.

"Bring him down to the laboratory, Dawkins," he ordered. "If he's really working against us, he may prove to be more valuable than he ever was working for us."

"Yes, sir."

A slim shape in white appeared in the gloom of the tunnel as Dawkins turned away toward the elevator shaft. A soft voice cried, "Oh, Jim!" and a second later Dolores was in his arms. He held her briefly, stroking her honey-colored hair.

"Why, you're trembling! Don't tell me you've been scared! I thought you were the bravest—"

"Not for myself," she said. "I've been frightened for you, Jim. It's been terrible, sitting here with nothing to do, while the radio was telling me all the things that were happening to you. I heard that you were a prisoner of Marner's, that you couldn't keep them from killing Van Rucker, that if it hadn't been for poor Cynthia Arnold you'd have died in the trap set for Phail! I saw those planes waiting to shoot you down, and didn't know how you could defend yourself against them! If it was me going through all those dangers, and you couldn't help, wouldn't you be afraid?"

He squeezed her shoulder. "I'd be scared stiff," he assured her.

THE EVIL SMELL of Mephito's nine-stick fire filled the main room of The Cavern. Squatting in the fireplace, the old Comanche bowed gravely in greeting to his grandson.

"You are in time, son of my daughter," he mumbled. "There will be devil-magic loosed upon us tonight that only you can contend with. There will be bloodshed and danger, and once again the devil will dance!"

Jim looked at the skinny shaman sharply. Man of science that he was, he did not laugh at the ancient magic of his mother's people. He had seen too many of Mephito's dire predictions come true not to be alarmed at this one.

"What dead men will dance?" he asked. There were only Logan and Phail left of the original five caricatured by the dancing marionettes. "Old one, tell me all that you see!"

But Mephito squatted back on his heels and lowered his white head. "The fire spirits speak the truth," he said through toothless gums, "but the pictures they show are dim. Mephito has told all that he has seen."

Jim crossed to the visoradio table and flooded its mirror with blue-white light. He set dials and waited until the lean face of a man who wore a clerical collar appeared before him. Jim scribbled code words on a slip of paper and held them up.

The image wrote certain symbols on a desk pad and showed them to Jim. The Reverend Mr. Parkhurst's lips formed the eager question, "Anything you want me to do about it?"

Jim shook his head, and the minister's face showed keen disappointment before it faded from the television screen.

According to the minister, Jasper Logan had gone aboard his yacht, the *Ilium,* and would spend the night cruising in Lake Erie. Assuming that all members of the yacht's crew were to be trusted and the vessel kept out of sight of shore, Logan would he safe enough.

To make sure, however, Jim sent out a radiophone call on the *Ilium's* wavelength, and within a minute was talking to the industrial czar.

"Hell, yes," Logan exploded. "I couldn't be safer in the vault of one of Phail's banks, Jim! Nobody knows where I am except a few people I can trust absolutely, and no one will know the position of the yacht. Seems like damned foolishness to me, running away like this, but if you say so—"

"I'll keep this radio tuned to you from now on," Jim said. "If there's anything you should know, I'll get in touch with you. If anything out of the ordinary happens aboard, or anywhere around you, call me immediately."

"Just as you say, Jim. Too bad you didn't send Phail along with me. We could play pinochle for a tenth of a cent a point...."

Jim turned his head at Dolores' sudden exclamation. She was staring in consternation at two bloody men who had just come from the tunnel.

DAWKINS' LEFT SHOULDER was stained with gore and he staggered feebly beneath the weight of Bill Roarty, who was slung across his shoulders. Roarty was bleeding, too, from a chest wound, and his blood dripped over the valet's clothing.

Just as Jim reached them, the little Englishman collapsed, his pain-contorted face turned apologetically to his master.

"H'I'm terribly sorry, sir. 'E must 'ave suspected we were onto 'im. H'I told 'im you wished to see 'im, sir, h'and 'e pulled a gun h'and shot me, h'and h'I 'ad to return the fire h'in self-defense. H'I tried not to kill 'im...."

Jim lifted the valet in his arms and carried him into an adjoining room, where he stretched him on a cot. While Dolores stood watching, he cut away Dawkins' coat and shirt at the shoulder.

"YOU'LL BE ALL right, Dawkins," he said affectionately. "The bullet went right through, leaving a clean wound. Don't worry about whether you killed him or not. Dolores will fix you up and I'll attend to Roarty."

He returned to the side of the farmer. The latter was not dead, but it took Jim only a few seconds to make sure that he would be soon. Dawkins' bullet had punctured a lung and no surgery of which Jim was capable could save the man

Jim turned. Dolores was staring at two bloody figures coming into the room.

from the terrible internal bleeding that was killing him.

HE CARRIED ROARTY gently to the couch upon which Karl Ogrund, Marner's spy, had committed suicide the previous day. He gave the half-conscious man a drug which would ease the pain of the wound. He brought the thought-wave machine from its cabinet and fitted the electrodes to the dying man's temples.

"Roarty," he said, not unsympathetically, "you've played a losing game, and now you're paying off. I'm sorry—I wouldn't have wanted you to die for turning against me—but you're dying now because you tried to kill another man."

"I—I'm sorry, too," Roarty murmured weakly. "I guess I was jest crazy fer money an'—"

"Don't try to talk. Just relax. If you want to help me, and make up for the harm you tried to do me, try to think over carefully all your contacts with my enemies. Your thoughts will be recorded on this machine."

"I was a f-fool...." Roarty's voice faded and he appeared to sink into a coma.

But the cylindrical graph upon the machine was turning and the stylus was tracing an uneven line in green ink. Jim bent over it, understanding its message far more clearly than if the man had spoken.

"Feller in grocery store gimme five thousand dollars an' promised five thousand more.... All I had to do was wreck the alarm system an' let 'em in.... I lived a hard life an' never made much money, an' it looked like a chance to get rich easy.... Then they told me to find the limits of the ray barrier an' signal 'em to the planes.... Tonight they're comin' with gas an' guns, an' I'm supposed to see the alarm system is busted an' let 'em in the house.... They promised just to steal the ray plans an' not to kill nobody.... Now I guess I been a fool.... Reckon I'll die an' go straight to hell.... Should 'a'... known... better...."

The line of the stylus was straight now. There was a gurgle in Roarty's throat and his chest sank for a last time.

Jim straightened slowly to find Tom at his shoulder. Gentry had read the traitor's thought-message, too. His blue eyes were wide.

"This is one time a double-crosser did us a real favor," Tom said. "We can fix the alarm system in a jiffy. We can seal The Cavern, Jim, and electrify the hill. Once they're here, they won't be able to get away without electrocuting themselves. Then the cops can take 'em! How's that for an idea?"

Jim shook his head. "We'll leave the alarm system as it is and let them carry through their plan, Tom."

"But golly! Don't you want to grab Marner?"

"We'll grab him. But I don't want to grab him alone. I want the man who's working with him—the one who knows so much about my affairs and the affairs of Logan and the rest."

"How about the gas? If it knocks us out—"

"It won't knock us out," Jim promised.

Stripping to his favorite costume of breech-clout and moccasins, he went into his small private laboratory. He spent two hours working with a complicated arrangement of oscillators and vibrant metallic strings, arranged like the strings of a harp. Then he went to work on the extensive air-conditioning system of The Cavern, overhauling it single-handed, too absorbed in his work even to hear Tom's thousand and one questions.

When the early autumn darkness came over the countryside, Anthony's plans for the reception of his expected visitors were complete.

FROZEN IN SOUND

SHORTLY AFTER TEN, THE raiders came in the moonless night, slipping from automobiles on the highway and creeping across fields and up the hill. Through the periscopic vision apparatus above The Cavern, Anthony saw them with his night-piercing gaze. He counted twenty or thirty figures converging upon the farmhouse and saw that all of them wore gas masks and several carried metal tanks.

Dictaphones in the farmhouse brought their voices to loudspeakers in the subterranean chamber. Dolores listened apprehensively, sitting beside the sleeping Dawkins in an alcove; her face was pale, but her hazel eyes, fixed upon Jim, were trustful.

Beside Jim, Tom Gentry kept whispering, "Gee whiz! Gee whiz! I don't know what surprise you've got for 'em, Jim, but I hope it's a good one!"

Only old Mephito, squatting in a corner, appeared oblivious to the excitement. For more years than he could count the white-haired shaman had seen men come and go, live and die, and his fatalistic calm was practically impregnable.

Jim's fists clenched as he recognized Anson Marner's tones in the loudspeaker. He had doubted whether Marner would have the courage to lead this raid personally.

Marner said, "That's it. Release the gas into that shaft. According to Roarty, it's an intake for the ventilation system, and in a minute or two it ought to be all through the place."

The hissing sound of the gas escaping from its valves was plainly audible.

What Marner did not know or suspect was that, in overhauling the ventilation system, Jim had altered the only intake shaft that

He swept up Ruth with his free arm and led Dolores out of the tunnel.

opened in the farmhouse. The gas would now be sucked into the shaft by fans and discharged harmlessly through another vent a quarter-mile away!

Meanwhile, machines set in the walls of The Cavern kept the air pressure a degree higher than normal. Fresh air came in from the lake in sufficient volume to clear the underground rooms of any gas that might seep in.

Marner appeared to be arguing with someone. His voice said, "What if the farmer isn't here? Probably he got scared and ran away. As long as the place is unguarded and the alarm system out of order, we don't have to worry about anything. When we go down, we'll find them all knocked out by the nerve gas."

Then Tom started and gripped Jim's arm, for Marner's next words were, "Where's Ericson? Send him here. I want him with me."

Tom breathed, "So it was Ericson! The dirty skunk! And I'll bet Linster was helping him all the time—"

"Don't get excited," Jim advised him. "We still have work to do." He glanced at all of them. "Are you wearing those earplugs I gave you?"

Tom and Dolores nodded. Mephito said, "Ugh! Devil-plugs hurt ears. Don't like!"

"Keep them in just the same," Jim said. "In a little while you'll be glad of them."

They heard the purr of the elevator motor, and a moment later the scuff of feet in the tunnel leading from the shaft beneath the farmhouse.

"Gosh!" Tom said. "There must be a dozen of them! They'll have machine guns and everything. What if they shoot the minute they see us, Jim?"

"They won't shoot." Jim was sure of that. Marner would have given explicit orders on that account. Even more than he wanted to kill Anthony, Marner wanted the secret of the Triple-A Ray. When he had that—not before—he would be willing enough to murder them all.

TWO MASKED MEN appeared in the tunnel entrance. They had machine guns clamped beneath their arms, and when they saw Tom and Anthony sitting there, watching them, they swung the muzzles swiftly to cover them.

Jim arose. "Come right in, gentlemen! You have no idea how glad I am to see you!" He smiled at the tall, broad-shouldered man who came next—a man with green eyes that glittered through the goggles of his gas mask. "Ah, Marner—nice of you to return my visit!"

Marner's gaze darted suspiciously about the room. "What's this? What have you got up your sleeve, Anthony? Speak up, or I'll have my men chop you down with their Tommy guns!"

Jim shook his head. "How will you ever learn about the ray if you shoot me?"

"I sent gas down here. Why didn't it affect you?"

"A simple matter of air pressure," Jim said innocently.

"Where's Roarty?"

"Dead, Marner. He and my valet had an argument about something, and shot each other. Roarty was killed, but I expect Dawkins will come to before long and tell me what it was all about."

Marner called, "Ericson!" A thin, shabby man with white hair came into the room. "Take a look around, Ericson, and see if you can spot any traps!"

Other men came into the chamber—grim, silent men, armed with machine guns and pistols. Jim started, recognizing Ruth Ericson and Linster among them, despite the masks that concealed their features.

Ericson returned from his tour of inspection. "I don't see anything that looks dangerous."

Marner drew a breath of relief. There was jubilance in his voice now.

"Then we did take you by surprise," he said, "and you're just trying to pass it off with that damnable nerve of yours, Anthony! Well, you know what I want, and I'll take it in a hurry! Show me the ray projector and the plans, and tell me and Ericson all about it."

"No," said Jim.

"I suppose you'd rather see your sweetheart tortured?" Marner turned to two of the gunmen. "Bring that girl here. Go to work on her face with penknives and see if the great Jim Anthony won't relent when he sees her features turning to ribbons!"

The men started ominously toward Dolores, who shrank back.

"No," said Jim again. He brought his hands together and pressed the glowing emerald ring on one of his fingers. His sensitive ears caught the faint click of an electrical contact made back in his private laboratory by the microscopic radio control within the ring.

A HUNDRED NESTS of hornets released within the chamber might have made such a sound as filled the air then—angry, snarling hornets, bent on vengeance. The sound grew louder and shriller, torturing the eardrums. Jim felt it along all his nerves, even with the special plugs in his ears; he saw Dolores commence to tremble, saw Mephito's lips move in some primitive incantation against evil.

The sound climbed the scale and passed beyond the range of hearing, but still it could be felt, an intangible force in the air, freezing all it touched in the grip of vibrations too swift for human nerves to withstand or absorb.

The two men who had started toward Dolores halted in midstride. Their features twisted in anguish and remained that way.

Marner had flung up an arm, pointing an automatic at Anthony. The arm grew rigid, the muzzle of the gun bore squarely on Anthony's chest, but the finger did not tighten against the trigger.

The twenty-odd men within The Cavern were held as motionless and powerless by the sound-waves as if they had been twenty-odd statues, cast in threatening postures, but incapable of carrying out their threats.

Jim grinned. "I know those tingles hurt, but with those plugs in your ears, the sound-waves can't paralyze you. But I'm afraid our visitors won't have much freedom until I turn the power off—which won't be until the state police send an army out to take charge of them!"

"I'll be darned!" Tom muttered. "Jim, looks like we've got the whole kit and kaboodle. One thing I don't understand—are Ruth and Linster guilty, too, or just her old man? It's hard to think of a pretty kid like her being mixed up in a business like this!"

Once more Tom's question struck against heedless ears. Jim had caught the flicker of the red bulb above the radiophone he had left tuned to the *Ilium*. He hastened to the instrument.

"Hello, *Ilium!*" he cried. "Anthony speaking. Anything wrong?"

There was no answer.

Jim checked the set, making sure it was in working order. "*Ilium!*" he called. "Come in, *Ilium!* What's the matter?"

He could hear the whine of power from the yacht's transmitter, but nothing else.

"Here comes the windup, Tom!" he snapped. "Logan's in trouble on Lake Erie! We'll all go. The sonic waves will keep these crooks safe till we get back."

"Golly, what if something goes wrong? What if Marner gets away?"

There was sense in that. "Tie Marner up and we'll take him along," Jim decided. "Bring the Ericsons, too, and Linster. You needn't tie them, but make sure none of them is armed. Dolores, grab the thought-wave machine and come along! We'll start warming up the *Thunderbird* and leave Mephito to take care of Dawkins."

The old Indian arose. "Mephito take good care of Dawkins." His fierce glance swept the trapped gunmen and his gnarled fist lifted a steel bar from one of the work-benches. "Mephito take good care of paleface statues, too, if they make trouble."

"They won't make trouble," Jim said. "They'll be good boys from now on, Mephito—here and in prison!"

HE TOOK DOLORES' hand, swept up Ruth with his free arm and went through the tunnels to the hangar. He had two of the *Thunderbird's* big motors roaring evenly when Tom appeared, panting under the weight of Marner, who was bound securely with straps. Linster and Ericson marched ahead of Tom, having been freed from the spell of the sonic vibrations by earplugs.

Ignoring the baffled, hateful expression on Marner's face, Jim addressed the three other prisoners.

"You've been traveling in bad company. You've run away when you shouldn't have. There's some reason to suspect all of you of being as guilty as Marner of the murders that have been committed. I don't suppose you intend to admit anything of the sort."

"You know why I ran away," Linster said.

Ruth pleaded, "Believe him, Mr. Anthony! He's telling the truth! Dad is innocent, too!"

"They captured me in Pittsburgh," Alfred Ericson declared. "They got Ruth and Linster in Philadelphia. Marner threatened to torture my daughter if I didn't help him get the secret of your ray. I agreed, but I was planning all along to trap him. I—"

Jim held up his hand. "Never mind. I haven't time to listen to a lot of lengthy explanations. If you'll all agree to let Miss Colquitt work on you with my thought-wave machine while Gentry stands guard, I'll give you the benefit of the doubt till we see what the machine says."

"Of course we agree," Ruth said. "We haven't anything to be afraid of!"

Leaving them, Anthony took his place at the controls. The cliff opened before the beam of "black light" and the *Thunderbird* skated across the surface of the lake and slanted into the air.

Through earphones clamped over his head, Jim could hear the high, thin wail of the *Ilium's* radio, voiceless, but nevertheless a guiding beacon. By means of a directional aerial he could follow that beam straight to the yacht, wherever she might be.

As his ship thundered beneath the stars, he regretted the machine gun bullets that had put one of the engines out of commission, leaving him only two effective ones. Jasper Logan's life was worth all the four lives of his associates in the Triple-A production plan—was perhaps more valuable to America today than the life of any other man—and if Logan died tonight Jim would never cease to reproach himself.

Far beneath him the water of Lake Erie was a vast, black expanse of mystery.

CHAPTER XVII

DERELICT

JIM CIRCLED THE *THUNDERBIRD*, his eyes scanning the darkness beneath. The radio beam had swelled to a crescendo and was lost. The *Ilium* was black-hulled and finished all in mahogany, which did not make her stand out against the background of the lake, but he spotted her finally—a ship drifting helplessly, without lights or power, with no sign of life about her.

As he dropped the plane toward the surface of the lake, he remembered Mephito's words of the afternoon, *"Once again the dead will dance!"* If he were too late to save Logan from the death of the dancing marionettes, his great scheme to safeguard America from the ravages of war might well be lost, even though Anson Marner was a prisoner. There was hardly another industrialist in the nation equipped to take on the vast manufacturing program involved, and certainly not another who would be willing to in the face of any such disaster as this!

Fallon had died in a jig, Bessingham while waltzing, Van Rucker doing a clog dance, and Phail had narrowly missed a fatal shimmy.

The marionettes that represented those men had been engaged in those same dances through the mechanical ingenuity of Ericson. But, he remembered, the marionette resembling Logan had not been dancing at all, but had been pulling the strings at the ends of which the others danced.

Jim's brow was corrugated in a thoughtful frown as the pontoons slapped the water.

Tom came forward from the cabin, peering at the dark hulk of the *Ilium,* drifting fifty yards away. "Found her, huh? Holy cow, Jim, it looks like we're too late—"

"What about Linster and the Ericsons?" Jim interrupted. "What did the thought-wave machine say?"

Tom took a deep breath. "Either your machine is wrong, or they're all innocent. Ericson suspected something was up when his dolls were stolen. He left home because he got a threat by phone that Ruth would be killed if he didn't disappear. He ran away from Bessingham's house because he realized he was in a tight spot and couldn't prove his innocence, and Marner's men picked him up in the neighborhood, where they were waiting for you. Then Marner's men grabbed Ruth and Linster in Philadelphia, and used them to force the old man—"

"That's enough," Jim said. "I get the general idea. We'll count them as being on our side, then. I'm going to swim to the yacht, Tom. I'll carry a line with me and make the plane fast to her. You inflate the collapsible boat and wait. If I call you, come aboard and bring the others."

"Marner, too?"

"Marner, too. I don't want him un-watched for a minute."

"Okay," Tom said, "And good luck, Jim."

It would be good luck, Jim thought grimly, if he found Logan alive.

HE OPENED THE cabin door, looped an end of the light cord beneath his belt about one of the struts, and slipped into the cold water. His powerful stroke brought him to the side of the *Ilium* in a matter of seconds. He grasped the rungs of a boarding ladder and hauled himself up.

The scent of lilacs greeted him, too faint to be dangerous now. But it told him why the ship drifted without a hand to guide her. Everyone aboard had been overcome, apparently, by Marner's nerve gas. Somewhere in Logan's crew there must have been an employee of Marner.

Through the windows of the closed bridge and the saloon he saw men sagging in chairs, sprawled on the floor. He opened doors and windows to clear the gas from the enclosures, making his way aft toward the master's cabin.

He flung open the door of Jasper Logan's stateroom and saw the form of the manufacturer spread-eagled on the bed. At first he thought Logan was dead, but his hand beneath the man's coat detected a faint heartbeat, and he sighed with relief.

He plunged into the icy water and a few strokes brought him to the *Ilium*.

Then he noted the ropes that had been tied to Logan's wrists and ankles and stretched through portholes at the four corners of the cabin. He glanced through a rear window and saw with a surge of horror that they were fastened to a winch on the afterdeck.

Had that winch been turned, the ropes would have tightened and literally pulled the man to pieces!

He slashed the ropes with his knife, and as he did so noticed the fifth marionette lying in a wooden frame on a table beside the bed. It was the largest of the five Ericson had made—the one intended to represent Logan—but it no longer pulled strings at the ends of which other men danced. Instead, it was spread-eagled as Logan was, and the strings were attached to a crank in such a way that, once the crank was turned, the wooden figure would be torn limb from limb!

It was a diabolical device—more diabolical in its conception than any of the methods by which the others had died!

Why hadn't the winch turned? Why had all power aboard the yacht been cut off? True, the radio was operating, but that would be energized by batteries. No motors, no generators turned aboard the vessel.

JIM LEARNED THE reason when he found the main switchboard just forward of Logan's cabin. A man wearing a gas mask lay on the floor before it—a dead man, whose hands and arms were terribly burned. Jim looked at the board and saw that the master switch had been pulled.

He thrust the handle forward, and the *Ilium* came instantly to life. Lights glowed aboard her from stem to stern, dynamos purred in her hold. The winch on the afterdeck turned with a clatter winding up the ropes that had been fastened to Logan two minutes before.

Marner's spy, it appeared, had been overtaken by a kind of poetic justice. He had gassed the crew, had trussed up Logan for the killing, had everything prepared. But in seeking the switch that would start the winch, he had pulled the master switch by mistake, and in the ensuing darkness, while trying to remedy that mistake, had electrocuted himself.

Doubtless the radio operator, feeling the first effects of the gas and knowing something was amiss, had attempted to send out a call. He had managed to close the key for sending, but had been overcome before he could put a message on the air....

Jim strode to the rail. "All right, Tom!" he yelled. "Come aboard, all of you!"

He sought out the cabinet in which the *Ilium's* medical supplies were kept and found a vial of adrenalin there. Filling a hypodermic needle with a weak solution of the drug, he returned to Logan's cabin and injected it beneath the skin over the manufacturer's heart.

A moment later Logan sat up violently. "What the hell!" he roared. "What's happening here? Who are you?... Oh, Jim! How in the devil did you get aboard this tub?"

Jim explained briefly.

"So they tried to get away with that!" Logan said furiously. "Get the crew in here, Jim. I'll find out which one did it and make him walk the plank!"

"The crew's still out," Jim said, suppressing a smile at the older man's impatience. "The gas must have got those who were below decks and indoors immediately, and overcome the others when they left the deck to see what was the matter. As for the one who did it—he's dead. If he hadn't blundered and killed himself, you'd be in pieces now!"

Logan rubbed his forehead. "What a screwy business! All I remember is smelling lilacs and feeling sleepy. I lay down here, just for a minute, and I guess I passed out. That was right after I talked to Phail."

"You talked to Phail?"

"Sure. Why not? I didn't want to come on this scow in the first place. I only did it because the preacher said you insisted. I began to feel lonesome, and I got on the ship-to-shore phone and called Phail in New York. He said he was surrounded by cops, but I convinced him he'd be safer here, and he agreed to charter a plane and fly out. What time is it, Jim?"

"Couple of minutes after midnight."

LOGAN FROWNED. "HE said he'd be here before midnight. I told him about where the *Ilium* was and said all the lights would be on. I wonder if he flew over while she was dark and missed her?"

"I don't think so." Jim's ears had picked up the distant hum of a plane's motor. "I think maybe he's coming now. If he is, the lights are all on, and he won't miss you."

Hearing the sounds of voices and footsteps, Jim went on deck. He found Dolores, Ericson and his daughter already aboard the yacht, and Tom and Linster sweating to get Marner's trussed-up bulk over the rail. Jim grasped the straps that bound the erstwhile head of the Apecia and swung him inboard, standing him upon his feet.

"How does it feel to have lost out, Marner?" he asked.

The square, heavy-featured face of the man was flushed with anger. "I haven't lost out, Anthony, till I'm dead," he said. "If you think your prisons can hold me, you're making a big mistake."

"How about our electric chairs?" Jim asked. "There isn't any capital punishment in Michigan, but Bessingham and Van Rucker died in Pennsylvania, and there was a girl who died in New York. You caused them to be murdered!"

"You may have a hard time proving that, my friend."

Jim shrugged. He doubted whether it would be hard to prove. Of all those prisoners back in The Cavern, some would certainly testify against their master, now that he had fallen. But the point was hardly worth arguing now.

He listened to the sound of the plane motor coming nearer, and turned to Dolores. "Do you think you could get some of those sailors on their feet again? The least touch of adrenalin seems to counteract the effects of the gas. We're going to have company, and somebody ought to put over a boat."

"Company?" she asked.

"It seems Royal Phail is on his way to pay Logan a visit."

He wondered briefly at the faint smile that curved Marner's lips. But Ericson began to grumble at that point, and it took Jim's mind from the subject of the prisoner.

"Couldn't I go back aboard the plane, Mr. Anthony? You know I don't get along with Logan these days. I don't like being on his yacht."

"Whether you like it or not, Ericson," Jim said, "you're staying. If Logan can stand it, you can. I want to finish up this case tonight—I want to have a showdown before we set foot on shores—and I'm going to need all of you for that."

The strange plane was circling the yacht. Jim signaled with the searchlight and then sent a broad beam downwind across the water to give the pilot a path for landing. Tom drew away from the others and approached him.

"Jim," said Tom, "let me in on this, will you? If Ericson isn't the man who tipped off Marner to all the inside stuff, could it be Logan? You know, all this business of gassing the crew and being trussed up could have been faked by him, to give him an out. He may have been darn near killed, but I notice he's as lively and healthy as any of us at this minute. Are you sure he didn't plan it all that way himself?"

Anthony grinned mysteriously. "When you're up against clever men, Tom, you're never sure of anything till it's all over. It's like playing stud poker with experts—the pot is anybody's till the last card is played!"

CHAPTER XVIII

SHOWDOWN

JIM ANTHONY WENT IN the small boat with two sailors to meet Royal Phail's plane. He helped the fat man into the stern sheets, steadying the boat when it rocked dangerously. During the short row back to the yacht he gave Phail a brief resume of all that had happened during the evening.

The banker's small eyes gleamed. "You're sure Marner's safe? He's a dangerous man to be carrying around this way. If I were you, Anthony, I'd have shot him on sight."

"He's all right," Jim said. "I'm only worried about catching his chief accomplice."

"You've got him. He may be Ericson or he may be Logan, but he's got to be one or the other." Phail shivered. "It makes my blood run cold to think Logan might have invited me here just to kill me. The fact that you found him tied up that way doesn't mean a thing!"

Jim reserved comment as the boat bumped the side of the yacht. He had his hands full for the next couple of minutes, getting the fat man aboard. This he accomplished by following Phail up the ladder rung by rung and boosting his broad posterior.

Marner was standing close to the head of the ladder, guarded by Tom. Phail squinted at him.

"You dirty rat!" Phail sneered. "You rotten killer! Try to electrocute me, would you?"

In an excess of bravery, the banker slapped the bound man's face.

"Cut it out, Phail!" Jim seized the furious man's arm. "Marner will get all the punishment that's coming to him legally."

Logan appeared from the corridor leading to his cabin. "There you are, Phail! You know, this idea of yours of using the yacht as a hideaway wasn't so hot. It came damn' close to being my last voyage!"

Jim's eyes narrowed. "Was it Phail's idea?"

"Sure it was. He mentioned several days ago that it would be the safest place if danger got too close. This afternoon, just after I got your message through the preacher, Phail phoned me from New York to remind me that I was the only one of the five who hadn't had trouble, and suggested again that I take a cruise. In view of your warning, Jim, I took his advice. Later I got the idea of inviting him to join me."

"Why, then—" Jim began.

DOLORES' SCREAM INTERRUPTED him. He spun, his muscles tightening, and saw Anson Marner sprinting for the rail. The arch-criminal was free from his straps, which lay on the deck where he had been standing. His obvious intention was to jump overboard and swim for one of the planes.

Jim sprang toward the man, but someone's pistol bullets were swifter. Marner staggered, fell. As he lay twitching, Phail calmly pumped three more bullets into his body.

Phail pocketed his pistol. "Lucky I was keeping an eye on him. I was afraid he'd try something like that. The man was a fiend, and I'm glad he's dead!"

Tom lifted a stricken gaze to Jim. "I only turned my back for a second," he muttered. He stooped and picked up the straps that had bound Marner. "Look, they've been cut cleanly—and this is the knife!" He held a small gold penknife in his palm.

Jim took the bit of glittering metal from Tom. He said dryly, "I should have anticipated something like this. It's Phail's knife. Phail killed him deliberately because he was afraid Marner would betray him!"

The banker stared incredulously. "You don't mean that, Anthony! You don't really think I had any part in this terrible affair!"

Jim nodded. "I do. I've thought so ever since I went to your office this afternoon. Now I'm sure."

"Why, it's preposterous!"

Ericson thrust himself forward. "No, it isn't, Phail. I thought I saw you slip something into Marner's hand when you slapped him. You gave him that knife and he thought you would help him escape."

"But," Logan objected, "how about that attempt on Phail's life this afternoon? If he'd touched that filing drawer—"

"He wouldn't have touched it for anything," Jim said savagely. "He had the marionette sent to himself as an excuse to get me into his office. He wanted me to grab the drawer and almost tricked me into doing it. Marner had given up trying to capture me, and they thought if they could kill me they'd have an easier time stealing the ray plans from The Cavern.

"Phail had a gunman planted to kill me in case the electrical trap failed. The man pretended to be after Phail, but the first shot he fired was intentionally wild. He took careful aim at me, though, and came close to getting me. He was out cold after that, but Phail was afraid he might talk when he came to, so Phail dragged him to the window and threw him out. I watched the poor devil drop, and he didn't scream or struggle, because he was still unconscious!"

The spy had pulled the master switch by mistake and had electrocuted himself.

Phail's mouth twitched. "If that were true," he said, "what would I be doing here?"

"If the plan to kill Logan had succeeded, coming here would give you a perfect out. Logan had invited you, and the detectives guarding you knew it. They'd never suspect you'd fly here if you'd known what was going to happen. The pilot of your plane would help alibi you by telling how you'd found the crew gassed and Logan dead."

LINSTER BROKE IN, "I still can't believe it! Phail is a rich man, a famous man. Why should he enter into a scheme like this?"

"Because of his peculiar psychological makeup," Jim explained. "Phail has been talking about Logan's hunger for power, but his own appetite was far greater. Greed made him go into the banking business, where by means of money he could gain control of what other men had sweated to create. Before he died, Phail wanted to be the richest and most powerful man in America, if not in the world. He wanted to control not only money, but men and vital industries, also.

"When he learned from me what Marner and the Apecia really stood for, Phail pretended to be indignant, but actually he saw a chance to make Marner help him attain his ambitions. He made Marner a proposition. Phail would provide the necessary information about our moves, and Marner and his crooked scientists and gangsters would work out the methods of procedure and take care of the dirty work."

Jim glared at the banker, whose moon-shaped face had turned the color of putty. "Phail was to get control of all the industries represented by the syndicate, and Marner was to get the Triple-A Ray secret. But I doubt whether either trusted the other. I think Phail planned from the first to kill Marner when it was over and let Marner take the blame, and I wouldn't be surprised if Marner planned to kill Phail for the same reason!"

Phail made a pitiful attempt to draw himself up. "You can't prove a single one of those accusations! My word is as good as yours!"

"You're mistaken," Jim said quietly. "It happens that I possess a little machine that interprets thought waves, by means of which you will confess to everything. There'll be fingerprints on the penknife you slipped to Marner. I'm not so sure about the other murders, but I know you'll go to the chair for the death of Cynthia Arnold." He pointed along the corridor to where the body of the masked man lay beneath the switchboard. "You'll die in the same way as the spy you planted aboard to kill Logan, if ever he should take your advice about a yachting trip. You'll pass out with high voltage tearing through your body!"

"No!" Phail shrieked. His hand darted into his coat pocket and brought forth the pistol again. "No, by God, I won't—"

Jim had been watching for just such a move. He leaped for Phail, feeling the white-hot pain of a bullet scraping his ribs. The edge of his right hand chopped down on Phail's wrist, knocking the pistol to the deck. His left hand slapped Phail against the cheek, hurling the banker against the edge of the doorway.

BLUBBERING, STUMBLING, PHAIL ran into the corridor. "You won't send me to the chair!" he cried. "I'll cheat you of that satisfaction, if it's the last thing I ever—"

His feet struck the body of the dead spy. His plump hands reached purposefully for the master switch. He grasped its two poles, and the lights of the *Ilium* were dimmed as current coursed through his flesh.

Hanging there, Phail shimmied. The rolls of fat that upholstered his frame rippled and jerked while the smell of burning hair and flesh filled the corridor. Long after he was dead he kept up that horrid dance—exactly like the dance of the rotund marionette—until Jim pried him free from the copper electrodes with a boat-hook....

ON DECK, BENEATH the bright stars, Jim filled his lungs with the cool night air. He asked Logan, "How do we stand now?"

"You mean about the manufacturing program? Hell, Logan Motors can handle that all right! The mines, the mills and the electrical factories will keep on running, even with their owners dead, under my temporary direction. Phail's banks can finance us now as well as they could before. Those ray projectors will start rolling off the assembly line within a month, Jim, and within a year we'll have the United States ringed with 'em. We can start sending them overseas, too, and stop those criminal air raids!"

The manufacturer paused, his gaze going wistfully to a thin, shabby figure standing not far away. "Of course it'll be a bigger job than any I've tackled, and it'll take a lot of good men. If only I had a first-class chief engineer...."

Alfred Ericson snorted, "If you wouldn't pick fights with your engineers, you old billy-goat, you'd keep 'em longer!"

"Me pick fights?" Logan asked innocently. "I don't remember ever starting one. But I do remember a cantankerous old coot who was always arguing with me—"

"That's enough!" Anthony's long arms reached out, right and left, grasping the shoulders of the two old men, bringing them face to face. "You're not kids any more. Shake hands and make up!"

They shook hands, grinning foolishly.

JIM SQUARED HIS shoulders, forgetting his weariness in the knowledge that all was well again. The nation had nothing to fear now from what had been the most powerful enemy within its borders. A criminal gang of unprecedented menace had been wrecked, and the men whose insane greed and ambition had been responsible for a long record of murders were themselves dead.

Now he could go back to his peaceful work in which his real interest lay. Not for long, perhaps—for in a world so largely dominated by selfishness the threat of evil was forever recurring, and there seemed to be no end to the fantastic crimes demanding Jim Anthony's unique talents—but for the present he could relax.

Someone nudged his arm. Looking down, he saw Dolores, small and lovely in the dusk. She was smiling, and her bright eyes were directed along the rail.

Jim glanced that way. Linster and Ruth Ericson were embraced so tightly that at first he thought he was seeing a single person.

"Romance!" he said. "Those poor kids deserve it. They've been through hell these last couple of days."

Dolores whispered, "Jim, now that it's all over, I feel a little bit romantic, myself!"

Laughing softly, he put out his arms and drew her close. He held her a long time.

Back in the shadows, Tom Gentry's eyes widened at this rare gesture of sentimentality on the part of his usually undemonstrative chief.

"Gee-man-EEE!" he murmured. "Holy cats! What next?"

THE TEPEE

WHERE SUPER-DETECTIVE READERS CAN GET TOGETHER

Editor *Super-Detective:*

For several months I have been meaning to write to you. I have two sons, sixteen and nineteen, both of whom read *Super-Detective* each month.

It's hard some times for a parent to keep up with and to thoroughly approve of the reading of his children, but in this case the boys' mother joins me in expressing hearty thanks to Jim Anthony.

In these trying times, when schools, pulpits, newspapers, radio programs, and all sorts of social clubs are likely to be used by un-American propagandists, preaching their various isms, believe me, every parent is glad to find his children interested in something completely wholesome and completely *American.*

I am well aware of the insidious methods used by the enemies of our country who talk through text-books, who spread their poison on every street corner. And I realize how difficult it is for our form of government to combat these various evils in a land of free speech and free press.

I truly believe that it is through such magazines as Super-Detective, magazines that have a definite appeal for the younger generation, that our democratic ideals can best be upheld.

Thank you again for Jim Anthony! The more readers you get, the more I and thousands like me will feel safe!

S.S.C.
Des Moines, Iowa

To the Editor of *Super-Detective:*

I have followed Jim Anthony's adventures with great interest since the first issue; and in particular I have paid attention to his marvelous scientific inventions. A good many of these have to do with defense measures for the United States. Now what I want to ask is this: Are they taken from true facts? Are there such things in existence? Are they only a figment of John Grange's imagination? Why don't we hear more about them?

M.C.
Norfolk, Va.

They may be related to actual discoveries, M.C., but if not, then neither are they figments of an author's imagination. They are expressions of our believe that Jim Anthony is the spirit of American youth. We haven't, for that matter, met anyone quite like Jim Anthony, in real life. But we don't think he's very hard to believe in. He represents the ultimate development of the American heritage of courage and youth and scientific achievement—and the right and true guidance of these qualities that are part of us. So Jim Anthony's inventions, if they aren't actually in existence as yet, lie well within the capabilities of the men and women who are giving all their energies to make our country better and protect it in a strife-torn world.

The Editors

EPISODE IX

BORDER NAPOLEON

GOODLOE'S RANCH WAS A WORLD OF ITS OWN. GOODLOE
WAS THE LAW, THE JUDGE AND THE JURY, ON THE
BOXED G. HE IMAGINED HE WAS GOD. BUT HE WENT
TOO FAR WHEN HE TRIED TO PUT PRESSURE ON A HIGH-
SPIRITED GIRL. THAT BROUGHT JIM ANTHONY INTO THE
PICTURE, AND THE WAR WAS ON—A WAR INVOLVING
FORCES EVEN GREATER THAN ALL GOODLOE'S POWER.

IT MIGHT WELL HAVE been a scene from one of those mad Broadway successes that so enchant theater audiences, wherein each member of the family has his own particular screwball hobby and follows it at every opportunity. Although it was daylight, the room was further lighted by one continuous fluorescent tube which encircled the room, set in a reflector some eight feet from the floor itself. This reflector cast a white light against a slightly curved, or domed ceiling, whence it was distributed to every corner of the room.

Cabinets containing strange chemicals and pieces of equally strange radio and electrical apparatus lined the walls. A bench of some rare plastic material, impervious to acids and impervious to fire, ran completely about the room. This was littered with electrical retorts, a thousand test tubes, various microscopes, and countless pieces of odd looking gear and accoutrements which might have puzzled a Steinmetz or an Einstein!

Take that contraption in the far corner, for example, that resembled nothing so greatly as a device from a Rube Goldberg cartoon. Small though it was, it was a complete cyclotron, used in the smashing of atoms and the releasing of atomic power. The queer gadget which looked like a radio, except for the roll of graph paper atop it, was an electronic tube outfit used to inscribe thought waves issuing exactly like sound-waves from a conscious or subconscious mind.

At the far end of the room, his back turned to the other occupants, a man hunkered over a fire, built on a specially prepared piece of porcelained steel, backed by a couple of inches of fireproof, and non-heat-conductive plastic. He was old and wrinkled, with black eyes and the nose of a hawk, and he wore a red blanket about his skinny body. His hair hung in two shiny braids over his shoulders, tied at the ends with bright, crimson string. From time to time he licked his thin lips in anticipation. For he was broiling a thick and juicy steak over the coals.

The man flat on his back on the polar bearskin rug in the exact center of the room, was slight and thin. He wore a soft white shirt and a black bow tie, a sedate jacket, rather short, and striped black and grey trousers. He looked exactly the valet which he was. The long five foot rodlike object in his mouth was an African pygmy blowgun, which he held with both hands. His cheeks puffed alarmingly, his blue eyes bulged, he expelled his breath with a mighty puff.

The three inch feathered dart quivered in the cork target, attached to the ceiling. He removed the blowgun, peered upward from his couch on the floor. "It cut the line, sir! A nine, a direct 'it h'on the bull's-eye!"

The sentry snapped to attention as Jim threw the gravel. Then Jim and the girl were through the gate.

The man on the couch said, laughingly, "Wrong, Dawkins. Get your glasses! It's at least a thirty-second of an inch from the bull's-eye. Now watch this."

Dawkins didn't argue. He knew the phenomenal eyesight of his opponent, knew that the man on the couch had the sort of eyesight possessed only by birds of prey. Dawkins turned his head to watch the shot.

The man on the couch wore a pair of yellow swimming trunks—nothing else. He was not swarthy, rather he was a tawny cream color, and every muscle in his magnificent torso moved beneath the satin of his skin as he raised his own blowgun carelessly to his laughing lips. His gun was short, some eight inches in length. The dart itself was hardly an inch long. He seemed scarcely to aim. The magnificent bellows of his great chest expanded for a brief, split second. There was not even a *pffftt* as there had been when the little Cockney valet blew his dart. Faster than the eye could follow it, the dart emerged from

the blowgun to quiver exactly in the center of the silver disc that was the bull's-eye.

"Dead center, Dawkins," he announced, and rolling off the couch, walked across the room swiftly on his hands! The ancient Indian who was broiling the steak over the coals, watched his grandson with satisfaction in his obsidian eyes.

The steak sizzled alarmingly, he turned back. A wisp of blue smoke arose from the hot meat juices, boiling on the plate beside the coals. The old Indian's eyes narrowed slightly. Swiftly his ancient fingers undid the greasy buckskin pouch at his waist, opened it, emerged with a pinch of dampish powder. This he tossed into the few drops of boiling meat juice.

One cloud of smoke arose, like a miniature, grey-tinted rain cloud. It floated slowly upward, no larger than a man's handkerchief, and the old Indian's eyes followed it. Ages ago this old man had been a feared and respected shaman, or devil doctor, with his tribe, the Comanches. His name was Mephito, and Mephito's magic was strong, strong enough, at times, to rival the modern, scientific magic of his grandson, Jim Anthony, the man in the yellow trunks.

He said, "Ugh! Tom Gentry no longer lost. He come now, very close, he here any time."

Jim Anthony, scientist, explorer, adventurer, and criminologist extraordinary leaped lithely from his hands to his feet in one motion that resembled nothing so greatly as the easy release of a steel spring.

"Wait until I see him!" he said, but his smile belied the threat in his words. "Worrying me like this! He should have been back days ago—well, day before yesterday, at least. Close, eh, Mephito?"

The ancient red man nodded, and sampled his steak, smacking his lips with satisfaction at its savor. "Close," he agreed, and fell to with a will. Dawkins eyed him askance for a few seconds. Mephito's ability to read the future in the smoke from his magic fires always frightened Dawkins a little. Then he shrugged his thin shoulders, picked up his blow-gun, sprawled again on the bearskin rug. He said, "Shall we finish, sir?" Jim Anthony was staring thoughtfully out of the window and did not answer. So Dawkins sucked in his breath, filled his cheeks, and huffed and puffed his dart toward the target on the ceiling.

JIM ANTHONY, WORLD famous for his physical prowess as well as his mentality, continued to stare out the window unseeingly, wrapped in thought. He was the son of an Irish-American father,

Shean Boru Anthony, and a Comanche Indian princess, Fawn Johntom, and from them both, he inherited the strange conglomeration of qualities, instincts, and impulses which had aided so greatly in his rise to fame.

Shean Anthony had left him more than a sizable fortune. He had given Jim the impulse toward the study of strange sciences and strange inventions which placed Jim at the forefront of modern scientific wizards. And from his mother, the Indian princess, Jim had inherited those many instincts of the forest and plain without which no Indian could have survived a thousand years ago. The instinct, for example, which might awaken him from sound sleep, to tingle along his nerve system like electricity, to cause the hair at the nape of his

"Death rides on that plane," the old Indian said.

neck to arise and quiver, like the hackles of a startled wolf. The instinct of a threatening danger, either to himself, or to one he loved.

Tom Gentry was Jim Anthony's pal, his very best friend. He was Anthony-trained, yet possessed a strange propensity for getting himself eternally in trouble. Several days previously he had taken Jim's plane, a huge twin-motored Douglas, and had flown Jim's fiancée, Dolores Colquitt, to the west coast for a visit. Tom had been due to return the day before yesterday, but nothing had been heard of, nor from, him.

Several times Jim had tried to get in touch with Tom via his own wavelength on the radio. This failing, the powerful broadcasting station of the *New York Star*, a newspaper owned by Jim Anthony, had gone into action—and obtained the same result. Tom Gentry had completely dropped from sight. Jim had tried not to worry, and there, too, he had been unsuccessful. For Jim realized of course how many enemies, vindictive and relentless, he had throughout the world. No man could send so many criminals to justice as had Jim Anthony, without incurring many mighty enmities, enmities which would allow their owners to stop at nothing for revenge. And on more than one occasion these enemies had struck at Jim through a person he loved.

So, the night before, when he had awakened from his deep and dreamless sleep to find every nerve in his body tingling, to feel his throat tight and his blood pounding through his veins, to hear an animal snarl on his lips and feel the hackles at the back of his neck, he had felt sure that this danger-warning concerned Tom Gentry or Dolores Colquitt. Dolores he had reached by radiophone almost immediately, and was reassured of her safety—and happiness. But once again he had been unable to reach Tom Gentry.

THIS MORNING HE had chided himself for his fear. "Tom's a man," he told himself, "and you've trained him; he's no fool. Quit worrying about him, Jim Anthony! Relax, relax!"

Which was when he had started the blowgun contest with his valet, Dawkins, the Cockney.

"He comes in the plane," announced Mephito, peering into another small cloud of smoke arising from his fire, the result of another pinch of his powder. "But he does not come alone. There is a face that peers over his shoulder, a face that smiles. It is—" His voice died away, he arose hurriedly, gathered his blanket about his skinny shoulders, and started for the door.

"Who is it, Mephito? Who rides with Tom? Whose face looks over his shoulder?"

But the old Indian, steak forgotten, was padding across the room toward the door. Jim sprang to intercept him, and again that strange sense of impending danger gripped him, flowed through his veins like acid, electrified his nerves. His voice was almost harsh as he whirled his grandfather about. "Tell me, Mephito, whose face does your magic show? Tell me!"

The eyes of Mephito were strange, his lips were grim. "He wears a robe of black, my grandson. A robe with a cowl that covers his shiny head. He reaches with his fingers for the shoulder of Tom Gentry, my grandson, and the fingers bear no flesh! The fingers are bone! The eyes are but black and empty sockets, the face is fleshless, the terrible mouth lipless! It is the face of—!"

"The face of—?" prompted Jim, hoarsely.

"The face of Death," said Mephito and, opening the door, pattered down the hallway, leaving Jim Anthony and Dawkins staring after him.

CHAPTER II

SOUND OF THE WHIP

HE LIKED TO BE called General Goodloe, and indeed, his bearing was military. Goodloe had officered in the U.S. Army from Valley Forge to Bull Run. From the time of its inception a Goodloe had always attended West Point. When Teddy Roosevelt organized his Texans into the world famed Rough Riders and led them up San Juan Hill, a Goodloe had been well in the van. The World War had brought about the deaths of two of the remaining three brothers.

It had always been a bitter drop in Warren Goodloe's cup that he could never serve the United States as had the rest of his family, that he must content himself with the ruling of an immense ranch that was a kingdom within itself, and satisfy his craving for glory by ruling some three hundred employees with military rigor.

For Nature had taken Warren Goodloe's left leg and twisted it malignantly into a mass of ugly blue flesh; he had been born a cripple.

He was a large man, with deeply set eyes, and a jaw that jutted aggressively; a mouth that was a thin purple line; and a thin bridged nose forever quivering when he was angered. He sat as stiff and straight as a poker player behind a massive carved desk in the study—or what he liked to call headquarters—of his ranch. His shirt was of brown whipcord, his tie black silk, and the leather strap that went over his shoulder to help support his holstered pistol, was remarkably like a Sam Browne military belt.

Warren Goodloe pressed a button beneath his desk. Almost at once the door came open, a Mexican in dark clothing entered, closed it softly behind him, clicked his heels, and standing very erect, said, "Yes, my general?"

"My wife, Chico," growled Goodloe, and the mozo departed as swiftly and as silently as he had entered. Goodloe picked a quirt from where it hung on the back of his chair, stood up, turned his back to the desk and thoughtfully slashed at his specially made boots with it.

The door opened, and Nada Goodloe, his wife, entered. Once she had been beautiful—now she was broken and cowed, broken by this man who eternally hungered for power. She was a faded blonde, no longer caring about her looks. She wore no makeup, her skin seemed coarse and rough; her hair was stringy, with careless strands straggling about her forehead and neck.

Abjectly she approached, stood with bent head on the opposite side of the desk, facing her husband's broad back. Her eyes fell on the heavy, pointed letter opener, with its leather handle and glistening blade. Fascinated she stared from it to a spot directly between her husband's shoulder blades. Her tongue slid out of her mouth to dab at her dry lips, her thin body shook spasmodically.

Without turning, he said, harshly, "You wouldn't have the nerve, Nada. Or would you care to try?" He could hear her teeth chattering behind him; the sneer in his voice was malevolent, hateful. "Pick it up, Nada, take it in your hands." She made no move. He whirled, slapped the quirt against the desk with a crack like a gunshot, snarled, *"Pick it up!"*

Fascinated she stared into his eyes, like a bird hypnotized by the stare of a predatory snake. Her hand went out tremulously, her fingers closed around the haft of the heavy knife.

She was powerless against the superior strength of her guards.

"With that knife," he said softly, venomously, "you could do away with the thing you hate, Nada. You could plunge that bright blade into my breast, twist it into my beating heart, and release life from this crippled body of mine. And, of course, the ranch would come to you—perhaps you would sell it?—and with the money you could be very happy."

She did not answer. His lips were writhing with the taunt; his eyes were narrowed and hot.

"You might even find a lover," he sneered. "Perhaps a better lover than Graumann."

"No!" she gasped. "No!"

He roared with laughter. "Believe me, Nada, nothing happens around here that I don't know! Nothing! Shall I tell you what Graumann whispered to you through your window last night as he kissed the palms of your hands?"

"No!" she gasped again, and "No!"

"If I were out of the way, Nada, you would have everything—including Graumann. That is what he whispers, is it not, my dear wife? Well, now is your chance! You have the knife. Walk around here, Nada, and thrust it into my heart! Come!"

AND SUDDENLY SHE raised the knife, quicker than words can tell, raised it high above her head with a little despairing moan. But as she brought that clean blade downward, gleaming in the early morning sunshine that poured through the window, the quirt in her husband's hand flashed upward, the three thongs at its end, weighted with lead, wrapped themselves about her wrist. He jerked her off balance and the knife clattered to the desk top, lighting so that its point penetrated the wood and it stood there quivering, trembling like an aspen in a high wind.

"Good morning, general." The voice was soft and suave, and came from the door.

Goodloe peered at the man who stood there, and literally fought down his anger. He leaned across the desk and unwound the quirt from his wife's wrist before speaking. His nostrils flared, white and quivering, but he managed a smile and an evenness of speech that fooled no one.

"Good morning, Graumann. Come in. We were discussing my wife's visit to San Antonio. She leaves shortly. I would suggest that you pack and dress at once, Nada. Conchita will accompany you, of course."

With head bowed, nursing her quirt-welted right wrist with the fingers of her left hand, Nada Goodloe hurried from the room. No need to protest further—she knew that. She was fortunate that Graumann had entered when he had. Otherwise her back even now would be bleeding from that merciless quirt in the hands of an even more merciless man, her husband. "Conchita," she thought, scurrying across the flagstoned patio.

Conchita, who hated her, because she, Conchita, aspired to be mistress of the Goodloe ranch. Conchita, who would haunt her like a shadow all the time she was in San Antonio, who would report every move and every word to Warren Goodloe! Ah well! Anything, anywhere was better than this hell on earth. Anything!

CARL GRAUMANN WAS as tall as Goodloe, but much more athletic, not so bulky. The tailored shirt of brown silk which he wore accented the broadness of his shoulders. Trim riding breeches and well polished boots set off his muscular figure to perfection. He was blonde, burned red rather than tan by the Rio Grande sun, and his hair was cut close to his head, except for the fore part, which stood erect like the bristles of a light colored brush. The man's cheeks were crisscrossed with scars, dueling scars, saber marks from Heidelberg, and he eternally wore a gleaming monocle in his left eye.

Now he seated himself on the corner of the desk, took a long, Russian cigarette from a case and inhaled lazily. "I have talked to the south, my friend. The trucks must be ready tonight. There will be eight plane loads."

Goodloe nodded, lit a heavy black cigar, and leaned back in his enormous chair. "They will be ready, as usual."

Graumann nodded affably. "And the fool on the Flying L, I can never recall the name. What says he now?"

Goodloe grimaced. "Kroschel, damn him. He says, as usual, that I can go to hell, that he will sell his ranch where he pleases." He paused a moment, and again anger made those sensitive nostrils flare and tremble. "That damned fellow Gentry! If he hadn't been around, we'd have wiped the fool out. Now—?" He shrugged his heavy shoulders. "Perhaps if we doubled our offer?"

"He would be too suspicious," snapped Graumann. "There must be a way; there has to be! Damn my eyes, we have to have that ranch of his, the Flying L. It is necessary to us!" He moved his left brow, the monocle fell from his eye, to be caught deftly. From his pocket he withdrew a black silk handkerchief and began polishing the glass vigorously.

Chico, the servant, opened the door, clicked his heels again. To Goodloe's inquiring gaze, he said in Spanish, "All is well, my general. It worked as you expected. She is here."

Goodloe's scowl slowly changed to a smile. "Wait a few minutes and bring her in."

Chico departed.

To Graumann, Goodloe said, "There is a way, now, Graumann. A fine way! I do not think this Kroschel will sell to anyone but us, *now*."

"What do you mean? What have you done?"

Goodloe smirked. "That daughter of his, she is very curious even for a woman! Many times during the past few weeks she has ridden south to the river to see what she can see. Naturally she was within her rights on her father's property. But the time came when her curiosity got the better of her, and she crossed the river into Mexico." He threw back his head and laughed. "Led by that great curiosity of hers she formed a habit of recrossing the river—onto my property! This morning my *vaqueros* caught her!"

Graumann put the monocle back into place, his face grave. "And—?" he prompted.

"The signs are plain along the river, Graumann! The warnings! She was trespassing. Perhaps she can be persuaded to write a note to her father concerning the sale of his ranch?"

Graumann shook his head slowly. "I don't like it. We're just really getting under way, Goodloe. Don't fool me, or rather, don't try to fool me. Not trespassing you mean, but kidnaping! And if the government sends a man—?"

"Not to my ranch!" snarled Goodloe. "You forget that I am master here! Not even the government sends men to the Box G without specific permission from me!" His broad palm slapped the desk, so that the knife, still embedded there, trembled all over again.

THE DOOR OPENED with a bang. Two *peons* entered with a woman. The two *peons* had their hands full, for the woman was a veritable tigress. She kicked at them, twisted her lithe body this way and that, contorted herself into knots that suddenly unraveled into a fury of flailing boots. Her fingers clawed, and her teeth snapped at them.

Before the big desk they paused, panting, and the woman ceased her struggles to glare angrily at the smiling Goodloe and the suave Graumann. Her high, firm breast, beneath the silk of her sweater, moved angrily as she fought for control. Her hair was as black and as gleaming as a raven's wing, her eyes a curious, deep green. Her red lips twisted, so that white teeth gleamed between them as she snarled, "Damn you! Tell them to loose me, kidnaper, murderer!"

Goodloe smiled. "Release the trespasser, *hombres*." The two *peons* stepped back, as though happy to be rid of this tigress. Proud and erect she stood before the two men, one seated at the desk, one standing stiff and erect beside it.

"Nazi!" she spat at Graumann, who bowed deeply and mockingly from the waist, his eyes sweeping over her lithe body insolently.

"You are very beautiful," he said in German.

"Do not speak to me in that hateful tongue! I am a Czech!"

He shrugged. "It is the same now, my dear."

Goodloe purred, "And did you enjoy your morning ride, Miss Anna Kroschel? You learned much, you saw much?"

"Only what I already knew! That you are a killer, that you and your *vaqueros* are murderers! I saw the two dead Mexicans in the shallows of the river, shot down by your men as they attempted to cross!"

"They were trespassers—as you are," purred Goodloe. "My men have instructions to fire upon all who would cross to Box G soil. We are, shall we say, an unofficial Border Patrol?"

"With political power enough to get by with it," snapped the girl. "Why did they not shoot me? Why—?" And for the first time she seemed to realize the implications of her capture. Her mouth formed a red O, a momentary flicker of panic flashed through her green eyes, but she drove it out quickly and stood straighter than ever.

"You can't hold me here against my will," she managed. "No matter how powerful you are! This is kidnaping!"

"I am not holding you against your will, Miss Kroschel! I have brought you here to ask a favor of you; that is all. I merely want you to write a simple note to your father. Is that too much to ask? I only expect you to advise him to cancel the option on the Flying L which he gave to that man, Gentry, and to make arrangements to accept my generous offer."

"I'll see you in hell first! Do you think we are blind, on the Flying L? Do you think we don't know what goes on here? The planes flying across by night, the trucks, loaded and covered. The fake attacks by false Mexican bandits! No, my father sells the Flying L to Gentry, and Gentry is the friend and companion of Jim Anthony!" She laughed wildly. "Jim Anthony, the hunter of men! He'll smash your finely laid plans for you! You can't buy him! The roar of your motors will puzzle him, the passage of your laden trucks across his ranch, his friend's ranch; a man like Jim Anthony will investigate those things! You know of him, you know his reputation!"

She laughed again, triumphantly, her head thrown well back, so that the white curve of her bowed throat was a thing of utter beauty.

Graumann cursed beneath his breath. "The dog! So that is the reason! The son of a dog!"

Goodloe was on his feet by now, the quirt swinging idly from his great hand.

"You will please sit here at the desk, Miss Kroschel, and you will write what I dictate."

FOR A LONG few seconds she gazed at him, eye to eye. Then her hand shot out; she seized the embedded knife. As swift as lightning

Once she had been beautiful. Now she was broken and cowed.

she leaped backward, slashing at the two *peons* behind her. One of them howled as the heavy blade bit into the arm thrown up to protect his face; the white sleeve of his shirt turned slowly crimson.

Now she was at the door, tugging at it, beating on it when she found it bolted from the other side. She turned, like a tigress at bay, and the blade of the knife was red and sticky.

Goodloe smiled, though the smile was not nice. Graumann had a gun in his hand.

Goodloe said, "It would be very easy to shoot her, my friend. We could even put a bit of opium in her pockets and place her body in the river, opposite her own ranch. But we need her. Come, Miss Kroschel, the letter! Be reasonable! Think!"

As he talked, he approached her, a limping step at a time, the quirt swishing against his shiny boots. Desperately she raised the bloody knife and pressed her back against the door. "Don't come any nearer!" she warned him, thinly, shrilly, and there was death and the promise of death to come in those slitted green eyes. Her breath whistled between her teeth, her breast rose and fell tumultuously.

"Let us be reasonable," purred Goodloe, over and over, to the rhythmic accompaniment of the ever swishing quirt. Over and over he said it, but suddenly he raised his voice and shouted, "Chico!" Even as the word left his mouth, he leaped aside, swiftly for all of his bad foot.

The door, which had been bolted from the outside, opened inwardly. As Goodloe had talked, Chico, on the other side, had slid back the bolt, had slowly and soundlessly twisted the knob. Now, at command, he hurled his body against the door.

Anna Kroschel literally flew into the room, hurled by the erupting door. She slashed at the spot where Goodloe had been, and received, for her pains, the quirt, exactly across the eyes. Blinded, she went to her knees, to scream with pain as that vicious reinforced leather fell across her shoulders, protected only by the thin silken sweater. The knife fell from her hand; she was conscious of a *peon* springing forward to snatch it away. Then she lost track of everything but the fire of that quirt, which cut the silk from her shoulders like the blade of a razor. She plunged downward upon her face, tried to roll away, but the quirt was relentless.

Graumann watched momentarily, then, wet with perspiration, turned away. But he could not shut out the terrible slashing sound of the whip, the sounds from the girl, whose screams had died away to one continuous moan. And presently the sound of the lash fell silent, too.

Goodloe, breathing hard, snarled, "Women! Like beasts, like animals! They must be broken! Pick her up, you two!"

The *peons*—one of whom had tied a tourniquet about his cut arm, picked Anna Kroschel from the floor. She sagged between them, only semiconscious. "Chico! *Habanera!*" Chico, breathing like a cat, filled a glass. He thrust a hand beneath her chin, held back her head, and literally poured the fiery brandy into her mouth. She strangled. She coughed, sagged again, and as the heat of the liquor flowed through her, straightened and stood swaying.

"The desk. Set her in the chair," snapped Goodloe. And when she was where he wanted her, he laid a sheet of white paper before her. "Now," he rasped, "you shall write what I say, Anna Kroschel."

The eyes she turned upon him were filled with a strange mixture of hate and fear. She stared full at him, her lips trembling, a red worm of blood crawling down across her chin from the wound where she had clenched her lower lip between her teeth. He glared at her like the beast he was, slapped the desk with the quirt. There was a bit of madness in his eyes, his thin purple lips were flecked with white spittle, like tiny bits of cotton.

"The pen! Or—?"

Slowly, with hands that shook, she drew the paper toward her. The fingers of her right hand inched across the desk. She took the pen from its holder and poised it above the sheet of white paper. A drop of blood fell from her chin, to leave its red horror on the whiteness of the paper. At sight of it, Goodloe chuckled. He spoke slowly, and just as slowly the pen moved across the paper.

CHAPTER THREE

PREMONITION OF DEATH

A BLACK AUTOGYRO, SMALL but powerful, leaped into the air from a spot at the Anthony Airport. Already field men and mechanics were wheeling the big Douglas into its hangar, making ready to service it. The gyro, having gained height, headed directly westward, soundlessly, being operated by batteries and a generating device invented and built by Jim Anthony. Soon, for the gyro was extraordinarily speedy, it was over Manhattan proper, flying at an altitude of some 2,000 feet.

Presently it began dropping downward toward an immense building of black and chromium. For a few seconds it hovered over the rooftop of this building, then suddenly settled down like a bird of prey, to alight on a specially constructed runway, to wheel slowly along not more than fifty feet and come to a stop.

A plastic and transparent cover over the cowling flew up, a man thrust out his head, like a jack-in-the-box. A great bandage, like a turban, encompassed the head, and the man's freckles stood out like spots of black, rather than brown, due to the whiteness of his features. Now he stood up, threw a long leg to the small step, and eased himself from his cramped position behind the gyro controls. His left arm was in a sling.

As he touched the roof he turned, and with his good arm, pushed the gyro slowly toward a white square, not far away. Once it was on the square, he walked to the parapet and pulled a lever. The plane sank slowly downward, and as it disappeared, a protective layer of dark material took its place. The white spot was an elevator that bore the gyro to a hangar, in the basement of the Waldorf-Anthony Hotel.

Limping, Tom Gentry crossed the landscaped roof toward Penthouse A. There was no knob on the entrance door, but it swung open before he reached it, controlled by a photo electric eye. Tom's presence was made known to the others in the same manner, the room lights momentarily turning red when a newcomer cut the beam of another eye.

The laboratory door flew open, Jim Anthony and Dawkins, the valet, hurried out to meet him. "Tom, you dog, where in the world— you're hurt! Did you crash? Come in here, boy! Dawkins, get him a drink! Sit down here, Tom, lie back! How badly are you hurt?"

Jim Anthony clucked around his friend and confederate like a hen with one chicken. He got him installed on his own couch, a couple of pillows beneath his head. Dawkins drew off his shoes and substituted slippers, in spite of Tom's protests. They slid a long, tall drink into his hand, which he accepted gratefully.

Only when the drink was finished did Jim Anthony speak, from where he sat on the floor, cross-legged, near Tom's feet.

"Now, boy, where'd you crash? Why didn't you radio?"

"I didn't crash, Jim. I've been shot." And, as Jim's eyes widened, "Don't look so worried. The scalp wound is just a shallow furrow, just enough to put me temporarily out of action. The other bullet went through the fleshy part of my arm. I'm all right, honestly."

The door opened and Mephito came in, said, "How, Tom Gentry!" He hunkered down beside his grandson.

"Who shot you, Tom? I don't understand this."

"You'll never believe it, Jim. I was shot by Mexican bandits, Mexican rustlers! On the Flying L, a border ranch in Southwest Texas!" He paused a minute, then said, curiously enough, "Jim, did you ever see a woman with hair so black that it gleamed, like—like—obsidian, and whose eyes were a deep green? And whose mouth—?"

"Yes," sighed Jim, "I've seen all sorts of women! I might have suspected there was a female mixed up in this. Now, if you don't mind, my lad, will you start at the beginning and tell me this story, if story it is? You left Dolores in Los Angeles, and what happened?"

Tom Gentry grinned and a little of his color seemed to return as he flushed. "Then is when I met her," he said. "She's beautiful. Jim, she's—well—anyhow—her father owns the Flying L, has for the last seven years. It's right next to the Boxed G." He paused significantly, but Jim shook his head.

"Never heard of them. Sounds like a Zane Grey story. Now how did you get shot by Mexican rustlers?"

And eventually he got Tom on the proper track, got the story rolling breathlessly from his lips.

HE HAD DELIVERED Dolores safely to the friends with whom she was to visit in Los Angeles. Then, since it had been some time since he had seen the town, he had set out to do it properly. "The newest and swankiest place on Wilshire," he said, frowning, "is Ganzi's, sort of a cross between Ciro's and the Brown Derby, only more so. Well, sir, the bar was three deep, and all the tables were crowded. A row of booths goes along one wall, Jim, and I walked to the rear hoping to find one vacant. And I thought I had. So I slid in, and suddenly above the music I heard sort of a muffled sobbing. It worried me, Jim. Before the waiter came, I stood up and looked around the booth. Half lying on the other seat, hidden from me by the table-top, her head down on the seat itself, was a woman! She was sobbing her little heart out. Guess who it was?"

Jim said, "Madam Lupescu," and Tom looked hurt.

"Nope. Anna. Anna Kroschel."

Which, of course didn't mean a thing to Jim! Could he have used a bit of Mephito's magic to peer into the future he would have known how much the thread of his life during the next few weeks was to be mixed with that of this girl, Anna Kroschel, and how Death and destruction, and blood and torture and vicious, unreasoning cruelty, all of these were to be tangled and matted into that Gordian knot of mystery!

TEN MINUTES LATER, the tale partially told, the two of them, Tom and Jim, were bent over a large map of the state of Texas, both on hands and knees on the floor. "Here," said Tom, "where the Rio Grande cuts southeast, only to turn suddenly and cut back northeast, in this triangle, is the Big Bend National Park. Now, go back northwest from the apex of the triangle, and you cross the Alamito River, which empties into the Rio Grande, and a few miles the other side of it, the town of Presidio. Between Presidio and the limits of the Park, lie the two ranches, the Boxed G and the Flying L. Honestly, Jim, haven't you ever heard of the Boxed G?"

Jim answered, "You know this screwy brain of mine. Maybe I've heard of it, but I forgot it right away to make room for more important information."

"The Boxed G belongs to a man named Goodloe, has been in the family since before there was a state of Texas. Jim, it's a little world of its own, with Goodloe as God. Believe it or not, it's a whole county, complete, and Goodloe, of course, runs it to suit himself. The east side of it touches the Park, the south side, or rather the southeast side, is on the Rio Grande. The Flying L, in the shape of a letter L, is a narrow ranch that extends clear around the other two sides. Do you follow me?"

Jim nodded. He knew that due to some of the old Spanish land grants, as well as tricky work in the old Texas land office days, that there were some odd layouts of ranches in Texas.

"The Boxed G is not only fenced, Jim, but the fence is electrified, and there are watch towers around its borders and what looks like forts at its gates, especially where the highways stop."

"The highways stop?"

"There's a road out of Big Bend Park that goes right up to the Goodloe fence—and stops. A road from Presidio crosses the Flying L and does the same thing on that side—stops at the fence. I tell you this Goodloe is the last of the feudal lords! He's the law and the judge and the jury in his own county, he does as he darned well pleases."

So, with the layout in Jim's mind, Tom went back to the crying woman in Ganzi's.

Anna Kroschel had come to Los Angeles to try to raise money on the Flying L. Having her father's power of attorney, she had almost consummated the deal, only to have the bank refuse her because of unsettled conditions along that stretch of the Border. There was, for example, at San Carlos, in Chihuahua, a colony of Spanish refugees, many of whom had turned to banditry when the government held up their funds. La Mula, and Ojinaga itself were wild towns, whose people were perfectly willing to shelter any thieves or bandits, and all of whom considered *gringos* legitimate prey! The northern part of Chihuahua and Coahuila was wild and mountainous, providing many places of concealment for wet cattle, cattle stolen on the American side and brought across the shallow Rio Grande.

"Eighteen months ago," said Tom, frowningly, "the Kroschels were running about 4,000 head of cattle. Now the pastures are almost denuded, empty!"

"What's wrong with the law?"

"That's the funny part. He's had Rangers, he's had Border Patrolmen, he's had Cattle Association men. They stay a couple of days and everything is quiet. Then mysteriously enough they get recalled—and the thieving goes right on."

Jim nodded, "And Goodloe, on this Boxed G? They steal from him, too?"

"Goodloe has only a few hundred head of blooded cattle, and he's got men enough to guard them well. He's irrigating and raising crops—cotton, mostly. So, well, I tell you, Jim, she was so pretty and, well, I—"

"Yeah," nodded Jim, "you loaned her some money to pull her through, and I still don't know how you got shot."

"I'm coming to it," said Tom stiffly, "and I didn't loan her any money! I paid five thousand dollars for an option on the place." Defensively, he added, "I always have wanted a ranch, you know that! And besides, they made me a plenty cheap price."

Jim groaned. "What you'll do with a ranch with no cattle is more than I can see."

"I'll get cattle, darn it. Look, I didn't just dive in, I investigated. Land around there is worth seven or eight dollars, and I got a price on 42,000 acres, which the Flying L is, of $3.00 per acre."

"And now," added Jim grimly, but smiling in spite of himself, "all you have to do is raise about $120,000 more!

"Only half. The rest in two years. You can have my note and—!"

"Okay, okay! But don't expect me to go down there. I've got enough troubles of my own without nursing a bunch of cow critters."

THE LIGHTS TURNED red momentarily, indicating that someone was arriving. Jim waved a hand impatiently, said, "Go on. I don't know yet how you got shot, sonny boy!" Dawkins entered with two yellow jacketed telegrams. Jim said, "Put them on the table, Dawkins. And you, Tom, keep talking. This is like pulling teeth!"

Tom explained that he had flown Anna Kroschel back to the Flying L in the Douglas, in order to close the deal, and see the ranch. Riding over the property the next day, he found it exactly as his beautiful companion had described it. It was during this ride that he first saw the Goodloe fence, with its ever present watchman at the gate, in a little masonry tower. Kroschel, he explained, had been ill, having had a nervous breakdown some time before.

"He was jumpy as a cat," said Tom grimly, "like he was waiting for something to happen any moment. We signed the option, and that same night, it happened."

He had been awakened by a voice outside shouting, in Spanish, "Hello, the house!" Footsteps had pattered past his door, and suddenly the night had been split by the sound of gunfire.

"Not only revolvers and rifles," went on Tom grimly, "but automatic rifles, and I could make out the chatter of a Tommy gun, as well. I rushed out of the bedroom and the three of us, the old man, Anna, and myself stood them off."

"How about the help? And the telephone?"

"The telephone wire was cut. As for the help, they've all quit, all but one old fellow they call Kilowat. The bandits had him penned up in the bunkhouse. Well, anyway, we stood them off, and all at once out the window I saw the flare of a torch and saw they were trying to fire the Douglas."

"So what did you do?"

"I—well—I sort of lost my head. I slid a new clip in the rifle they gave me and opened the door and charged the ship." That would be like Tom Gently! Angry enough to charge into a Tommy gun, because bandits were trying to burn his best friend's property!

"And that was when they got me, creased me, and got me through the fleshy part of the arm. When I came to, the fire was out and the bandits had fled and Anna had dressed my wounds. That's about all, Jim. Except I lay over a day and came on home."

Jim said no more. He understood Tom better than young Gentry understood himself. He knew what Tom would do, knew that he would return to the Flying L exactly as he had promised, knew that he would never rest until he had repaid these bandits who had wounded him, who had stolen cattle from the girl he admired so greatly.

And Jim Anthony was remembering that premonition of grave danger that had awakened him the previous night. The bandit attack

on the Flying L had been *two* nights before, so evidently this infallible hunch of his had to do with future danger to Tom, not to the attack which was over and past. And Mephito's smoke-reading. Death flying with Tom through the morning sunshine, Death with its black cowl, its empty eye-sockets, its grinning mouth, reaching, reaching for Tom's shoulder with bony, clutching fingers....

"Pick up the knife!" he urged her. "Let's see you plunge that blade into my heart."

What danger was there down along the Rio Grande? What omnipotent peril brooded so ominously over his friend? Jim walked to the table where Dawkins had laid the wires. Surprised, he handed them to Tom. "Both for you," he said.

TOM OPENED THE first, read aloud: "HAVE PRIOR OPTION KROSCHEL RANCH. ADVISE YOU TAKE REFUND WITHOUT PROTEST AND STAY OUT OF BORDER COUNTRY STOP THIS SECTION VERY UNHEALTHY FOR NORTHERNERS. WARREN GOODLOE."

Tom sputtered, "Why, that big ape! Who does he think he's scaring off! If there'd been another option Anna would have told me!"

He tore the other yellow envelope open. "DEAL CANNOT BE CONSUMMATED RETURNING OPTION MONEY TOMORROW PLEASE DO NOT CAUSE ANY TROUBLE. HENRY KROSCHEL."

He stared at the two wires in disbelief, his face turning red, then back to white. Jim said, "Looks like your deal is off, Tom. Looks like you're not to embark on a rancher's career after all!"

Tom swore beneath his breath. But before he could speak, the lights flickered red again. Two heads turned to watch the door. It opened shortly to admit Dawkins—with another wire. This he handed directly to Tom, who tore it open.

"FIRST WIRE SENT UNDER DURESS," he read aloud slowly, then, picking up speed, "ANNA DISAPPEARED FEAR HELD CAPTIVE CAN YOU COME BACK AT ONCE FOR HER SAKE FEAR THE WORST MAY HAPPEN. HENRY KROSCHEL."

Tom's jaw set grimly. He glared at Jim. Jim said, "What are you going to do, Tom?"

Tom answered, "I'll disregard the first two wires altogether! Will you get me a draft for the money I need, Jim? I'm flying back, at once, I'm buying that ranch just as I planned, and Goodloe can fight me or he can sue the pants off me. And I'm going over that country with a finetoothed comb until I find Anna!"

Jim sighed. Dawkins stuck his head around the door. Jim said, "Get me some clothes, Dawkins. And you, Mephito, you stay here to keep an eye on things. It looks as though I'll have to go to Texas to straighten out a tangle that Tom's gotten into. Darn it."

But his voice was happy; he'd stagnated for several weeks. There were the two danger warnings he'd received, once from his own inherited extra-sense, the second from Mephito. Besides, the whole setup, the whole layout, seemed to have a slightly crooked appearance. Though he could not as yet lay his finger on it, there was something in the story that didn't fit, and such mysteries were to Jim Anthony like a red cape to a fighting bull! A challenge and a dare!

CHAPTER IV

NICE PEOPLE!

ONE OF THE REASONS for Jim Anthony's inordinate success as a criminologist, a solver of man-made mysteries, was the thoroughness of his preparations. He studied his problem from all possible angles, he looked into the future and prepared for any and all emergencies. Naturally, he was but human, and just as naturally on occasions made mistakes, or failed to take some element of his problem into consideration. But, as a usual thing, his thoroughness was startling and astounding to those who were unacquainted with the man or his methods.

The big Douglas plane, stepped up by methods known only to Jim Anthony, sped southwestward with a speed that literally ate the miles. This plane had been originally constructed for one of the big transcontinental airlines. Anthony had removed the passenger seats and converted the rear cabin into a room that greatly resembled an efficiency apartment.

He had slid out of the loose and baggy trousers and the sweat shirt which as a usual thing comprised his costume, and was once again in his yellow swimming trunks. Tom Gentry was beside him at the radio table, and they were speaking to Gibbons, managing editor of Jim's *New York Star*. Up front in the control room, a small black box, correctly set, held the plane on its course and automatically adjusted the big motors to the conditions met at 15,000 feet. The black box was the Anthony Robot.

"Where did you get all this stuff, Gibbons?" demanded Jim.

Gibbons answered, "We syndicate a lot of stuff down in that part of the country. El Paso, Eagle Pass, Del Rio, all the way over to Brownsville, Jim. This is sort of a composite, I guess you might say, of all the information I could garner."

Jim said, "M-m-m. Check me. This Warren Goodloe is the biggest man in that part of the country, a man with a power complex, sort of a megalomaniac."

"Right. And sore at the world, mean and cruel, a cripple who hates even himself. A shrewd dealer in anything that shows a profit, a cotton grower, a little king in his own kingdom. Can swing a heck of a lot of votes in local, state or national elections. Now go on, and I'll check you."

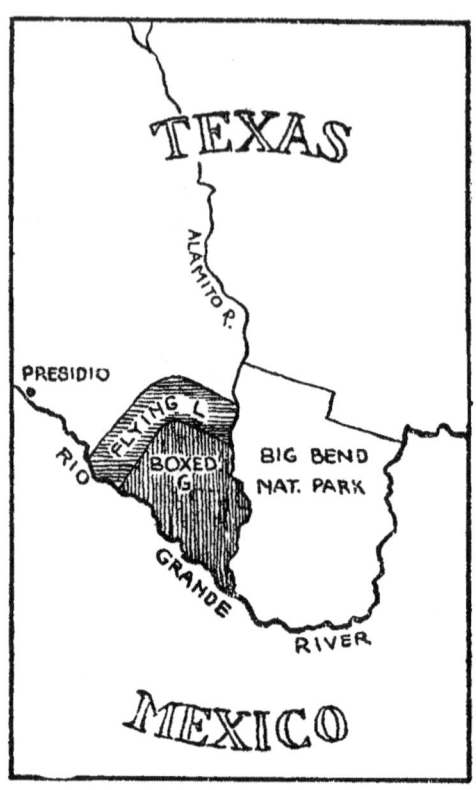

Like the last of the feudal lords, he held sway in that vast area.

"Married the daughter of a banker whom he ruined, you said. Keeps spies watching the doings of important men in order constantly to have something on them. Rules through bribery, corruption, and blackmail and is even thought to have more than a little to say about the Rangers and even the Border Patrol."

"You've got it right, Jim. Now, you understand, none of this was given for publication. It came from customers of ours, and from editors down in that part of the country whom I know. So don't pass it around. Where are you now, Jim?"

Jim looked quickly at the map table. A map of the route between the Anthony Airport and the Flying L ranch was attached to this table, and the top of the table was electrically controlled so that the map was faintly illuminated. By the use of crossbeams, obtained from various radio stations along the way, and tuned into the table itself, the exact location of the *Thunderbird* could be noted at all times in the shape of a tiny pinpoint of yellow light that moved across the map as the crow flies across the heavens. When they reached their destination, this yellow pinpoint of light would converge with another, and turn to red.

"Nearly to Dallas, Gibbons. Anything else? We'll land soon."

"Wait a minute. Here's a report just come in from our correspondent in Mexico City. Wait till I read it." A few minutes went by before his voice, excited and tense, came over the air again.

"Jim, how much do you know about the political situation in Mexico?"

"Not much. They had an election last month, that's about all I know, and a lot of shooting and trouble, as usual."

"Right! More than usual. Alfaro Rodriguez managed to win the election, Jim. General Rafael Guedea is the disappointed candidate. He was supposed to have had the backing of American oilmen, the rich interests, and the Fascists."

"I did read something about it. He disappeared, didn't he?"

"Right, immediately after the election. Remember, he claimed to have won, said Rodriguez was handpicked by the present administration, and the Guedea votes were thrown out? The Mexican president is inaugurated in December, Jim, and just before he dropped out of sight Guedea swore he'd be on hand to be inaugurated, according to law, if he had to march 50,000 armed men into Mexico City!"

Jim answered, "Get to the point. Mexican and Latin politicians are always hard losers."

"Our Mexico City correspondent says local rumors have it that General Guedea is drilling an army somewhere along the Border. Close to the Boxed G, Jim! Drilling them with German and Japanese officers. Here's what fits in—Guedea is a bosom pal of Warren Goodloe. He's obtained guns from somewhere, and the rumors are that Goodloe runs them into his little kingdom, and across the border into Chihuahua or Coahuila, wherever General Guedea is. That's all, Jim."

SO JIM, DIGESTING this fresh information with a corrugated brow, flipped off the radio. Tom ventured, "Say, if that rumor is anywhere near true, maybe it explains why Goodloe is so anxious to get the Flying L all at once, for it would make a sort of No-Man's land around his own place, the Boxed G, and there'd be no danger at all of discovery. If he's gun running—what are you doing, Jim?"

Jim had opened a cabinet door and let down a plastic board which served as a bench. From the shelf of the cabinet he took an alcoholic lamp and a large test tube. Into the tube, measuring carefully and painstakingly with his naked eye, he poured liquid from three opaque bottles. A narrow, tapering spatula went into a brown bottle of powder, from thence to the test tube. Then a lead box gave up a pea-sized chunk of something that resembled paraffin. This, too, went into the test tube, and the tube was placed in the wire rack above the blue flame of the alcohol stove.

Jim smiled. "We may run into a little trouble, Tom. I'm fixing to make some hand loads for my gun."

"Gun?" asked Tom in bewilderment, for never, in their long association, had he known Jim Anthony to use a firearm.

Jim's smile was enigmatic. From the waistband of his trunks he withdrew what appeared to be a fisherman's book of flies. Opening it, he disclosed page after page of miniature darts, feathered at the end with black feathers, their points gleaming and polished, the entire dart being no larger than a victrola needle.

"Hand loads," he smiled, and stirred the boiling liquid in the test tube with the narrow spatula. Soon the gum-like stuff and the powder were dissolved. Very carefully he poured the hot liquid into a shallow porcelain bowl, and using a pair of tweezers, cautiously dipped the points of a half hundred darts in the black, viscous fluid that came from the bowl. These darts he stood up carefully by spreading the feathered ends a bit. The fifty finished, he cleaned up the mess he had made, and by that time the darts were dry, their points no longer gleaming, but rather dull and black. Soon they were tucked away in the book, and the book put back in the trunks' waistband.

"Inee, arrow poison? And a Weber airgun!" Tom's eyes were bright, he thought he had solved the little mystery.

Jim shook his head. He was working at his belt now, and from it took a small aluminum tube, the thickness, perhaps of a soda straw, but only half as long. He thrust one end into his mouth, puffed his cheeks, said, *"Pffftt!"*

"My golly," said Tom, bug-eyed, "you couldn't shoot one of those little things accurately for twenty feet, Jim. That's worse than a toy. If this bunch of bandits from around San Carlos have got Anna, I'm telling you your toy won't do much good against them! I told you

The *peon* howled as the keen blade bit
into the arm that protected his face.

before that they've got Tommy guns and automatic rifles and only
the Lord knows what else!"

"I think it will do nicely," disagreed Jim. "Besides, my common
sense tells me the bandits haven't got your girl. Suppose you wanted
a piece of property and a man wouldn't sell to you? Suppose this man
had a pretty daughter whom he thought a lot of? What would you
do?"

Tom managed, "Surely not, Jim! That would be kidnaping. And the law—?"

"Gibbons said this man Goodloe is a megalomaniac, says he has delusions of grandeur. Maybe he holds himself above the law, Tom. Considering the three wires you received, it's only logical to suspect him. Now, lay the information we've received concerning him on top of it—guns, a friend of General Guedea, and all—and you'll see what I'm getting at. Oh, oh, the radio."

FOR THE RADIOPHONE'S warning light was, indeed, a bright and brilliant red, winking on and off rapidly.

"Hello, hello, Anthony speaking, aboard the *Thunderbird.*"

"Jim, Gibbons again. I've got some stuff on this man Kroschel who owns the Flying L. Same sources, unimpeachable. He's a Czech. Former officer in the Austrian army during the World War. When his native land was freed, went into the army there as a major general. Came over here about nine years ago, resigning from the army. He was a widower, with one daughter, named Anna. Acted as technical advisor in Hollywood on several films, then bought the Flying L and went in the stock business."

The voice of Gibbons went on and on, telling what the border grapevine revealed of Kroschel's trouble with his next door neighbor, Warren Goodloe, how the Czech had fallen in love with Goodloe's wife, Nada, and had beaten Goodloe within an inch of his life in the little town of Presidio, for maltreating her.

"This Goodloe is a big-shot all right," continued Gibbons. "Immediately after that clash, strangely enough, bandits from Mexico began crossing the river and running off Kroschel's cattle. Looks pretty suspicious, doesn't it, when you keep in mind the fact that Kroschel hadn't been bothered until he had the trouble with Goodloe. And Kroschel couldn't get any protection. I understand he couldn't even hire help, and every time he prevailed on the State Department to investigate, or the Cattle Association, someone bigger than he is put on enough pressure to have the guards removed. Looks nasty, Jim, plenty nasty."

Jim agreed that it did, indeed, look worse than nasty, that because of his unlimited political and money power, Goodloe, unscrupulous as he appeared to be, was no mean foe.

"Oh yes," continued Gibbons. "Mrs. Goodloe checked into the St. George Hotel in San Antonio, with a Mexican maid, this morning.

Hotel reporter on the *San Antonio Evening Dispatch* had the information, and when he found I was checking on Warren Goodloe, he passed it along."

No sooner had Jim hung up the phone, when Tom turned from the map table. "Hey, we must be passing over Big Bend Park."

He hurried to a semiconcealed button set in the wall, thumbed it. A panel slid back in the floor of the *Thunderbird* to disclose a large section of thick, unflawed glass. Sure enough, below them, they saw the jagged peaks and the rugged escarpments, the deep *arroyas* and the twisted, windbent trees that made up the Texas *brasada*, or Big Bend country. Breathlessly both watched, for it was one of nature's wonderlands.

Then Jim arose and hurried into the control room. Swiftly he cut off the robot, took the controls and headed the ship into a steep dive. For below him he had glimpsed the thin, winding ribbon that was the highway, constructed through the badlands for the convenience of tourists.

Soon he was flying the big ship only some fifty feet above that ribbon, just high enough to clear the peaks and huge rocks, which seemed to grow shorter in stature as they flew ever westward.

Tom opened the door and came in. "According to the map," he said, "in a minute we'll see the Boxed G. We—hey, look, there it is!"

JUST AS TOM had explained early that morning, the state highway ran directly to a high, barbed wire fence and ended! There was a heavy iron gate set across the road, and on the opposite side of the fence, there was no pavement at all, just a dusty white track leading westward. In the brief split second required to pass the gate Jim saw the stone watch tower, saw the brown, upturned face of the Mexican watchman, saw him throw a modern rifle to his shoulder. Then they were past.

"Nice reception," he grinned. "We'll just look over Mr. Goodloe's little feudal kingdom before we land, Tom. Thank goodness for that bullet proof plastic on this baby, and the fact that the glasses are unbreakable." He chuckled again. "Nice fellow, this Goodloe. He has nice hired help, too!"

The plane roared on, and in the distance they saw the town, known as G-Town, or Geetown to Texans, a town owned *in toto* by Warren Goodloe. Its size rather amazed Jim, for it was not merely a group of *adobe* huts thrown together, with one larger building for a store! They circled it, three times, no higher than a couple of hundred feet above the buildings. There was but one street, true enough, but it was a full block in length. There were a few ramshackle cars parked in it, a few more teams and buckboards, and perhaps a score of saddle horses tied to old-fashioned hitching rails. Back of the town could be seen the spire of a church, and past it, a schoolhouse. The houses, quite a large group of them, were mostly located back in a grove of cotton-woods and live oaks that lined a crooked creek, perhaps a full block away.

Circling over Geetown for the third time, they saw the commotion in the street. The roar of the big plane frightened horses, and they kicked and bucked and plunged at the hitching rail. Men turned angry faces upward and shook their fists at the *Thunderbird.* A heavy, stocky man was in the exact center of the street, and so low did they fly that they could see the star upon his vest.

"Goodloe's sheriff," said Tom, excitedly. And at that precise moment, Goodloe's sheriff jerked a pair of six-guns and cut loose at the speeding plane.

"Nice people," commented Jim again and headed toward the big, rambling ranch house he saw in the distance. More than anything else, he decided, flying over it, that ranch house resembled a fortified castle. Why, the place even had watch towers, with a sentry on duty in every one. The corral, horse filled, was immense, there was a huge storage shed or warehouse, presumably for cotton, the biggest barn either of them had ever seen, innumerable water tanks, silos, and sheds. The whitewashed houses of Goodloe's workmen were more numerous than the houses in Geetown itself.

They circled the ranch house twice, but, except for the sentries in the watch towers, saw no one. Jim straightened out, headed west again, toward the Flying L, their destination. He followed the white ribbon that was the graveled road, and soon came to the fence that was the western border of the Boxed G. It, too, had its masonry watch tower; it, too, had a coffee colored watchman who threw his rifle to his shoulder and emptied it at the plane.

The big, stepped-up plane ate up the miles. It was a matter of minutes before they were circling the Kroschel ranch house. There was no living thing in sight. Even from a height of four or five hundred feet the ranch had a deserted, neglected appearance. Gently Jim set the Douglas down in a pasture behind the barn that offered a smooth surface. It bumped over the ground for a moment, then, engines cut off, coasted to a stop behind the big red barn.

Jim said, "Get that black bag, Tom, and the brown briefcase. No, never mind, maybe I better dress—the lady of your heart's delight might have returned by now."

He was drawing on his slacks and sweat shirt when his premonition hit him again. He sat utterly quiet on the edge of the skin-covered couch, felt that nameless shock flowing and surging like hot acid through his veins, felt again the hackles on the back of his neck arise like those of a dog. Automatically he drew back his lips from his strong white teeth in a snarl. Danger! Danger! Every nerve, taut and tense and tortured, in his great body shrieked the word.

Jim Anthony knew! He knew that Death walked the Flying L, Death with its hideous, grinning face, and its bony fingers outstretched for its newest victim.

CHAPTER V

SUICIDE?

THEY LEFT THE PLANE, Tom carrying the black case and the brown briefcase. Grimly Jim led the way through the shadowy barn, noting that it was utterly empty except for a Ford Model T parked near the front door. They walked through the corral, opened the gate, and approached the ranch house from the rear. The back door was closed.

Jim hammered on it, called, "Hello, inside! Hello!" But there was no answer, only the echo of his voice reverberating into his ears. He tried the door. It was locked. And again that sense of danger flowed through him.

They walked slowly around to the front, noting as they went that all of the shutters were closed, also locked from the inside. Jim hammered heavily on the front door, calling lustily again. And again his answer was the same—utter silence.

Tom said, "Jim, I don't understand it. That Model T is all the transportation they had, I tell you. There it is. Kroschel wouldn't walk any place, would he? And besides, as I remember it, this front door had a big bolt, not a lock at all. Wait a minute, will you?"

He disappeared on a lope only to return a moment later and announce that the key was in the lock on the inside of the back door, and that if his Anthony-trained memory served him correctly, there was a big bolt on that door as well. "Get it?" he asked.

"Of course," snapped Jim, witheringly. "The key's in the back door, all right; I noted it when we were back there, Tom. It seems to me that Kroschel must be inside. Didn't you mention some sort of hired help he had?"

"An old fellow they call Kilowat. He must be around somewhere. Should I look for him?"

"We'll both look," said Jim grimly, picking up his bag and briefcase.

THEY FOUND THE man named Kilowat with no trouble at all. A shed behind the house served as a bunkhouse. Kilowat lay flat on his back in the bunk, his mouth open beneath his greying, handlebar mustache, breathing stertorously as he slept.

He wore a blue work shirt, a pair of blue overalls and a blue jumper. His face was the saddle brown of the oldster who has spent his life in the open, beneath the sun. The hands, folded across his thin and deeply breathing chest, were wrinkled, the nails dirtfilled.

Jim Anthony said, "Light that lamp, Tom." And when the lamp lit, he did an odd thing. Instead of shaking the old man, or calling to him, he picked up one of the hands gently, and felt it with his sensitive fingertips.

Tom said, "Look. The old guy's full of liquor."

On the floor, pushed back beneath the bunk, was a pint bottle. Jim took a handkerchief from his pocket, picked the bottle up carefully. "He couldn't be drunk," he exclaimed. "Look, there's only one drink out of it, and that a small one." He opened the bottle, smelled it, not once but half a dozen times. He nodded his head, his jaw was grim.

From the briefcase he took what appeared to be a cellophane envelope, which he carefully pulled about the bottle. He handed it to Tom, to be tucked away in the black bag. Already Jim Anthony was leaning over the hard breathing old man, sniffing at the breath that issued from the black cavern of his mouth. He worked swiftly. A half dozen grey-streaked hairs were pulled from Kilowat's head, greatly to Tom's surprise. These joined the bottle in the bag. The briefcase gave up a flat wafer of dental wax. Jim flipped back Kilowat's right eyelid, muttered, "Out, clear out. Mickey Finned, Tom." And working as though the man were a dummy, he spread the hired man's mouth, widened his jaws, and took impressions of his teeth!

Tom said, "For the love of God, Jim, quit fooling around. You got an emetic? We've got to find out what's happened."

Jim had an emetic. He also had a hypo and a shot of digitalis for the thin arm of the doped man, another of adrenalin to be injected directly over the heart. In a very few moments they were walking Kilowat around the room between them. He was a very sick man.

At last, when he seemed fully awake, they propped him on the edge of the bunk. Shakily he leaned over, swept his hand along the floor. "Hey," he whined, "I had me a bottle of liquor, I did. You fellers take it? I need me a drink to settle my stomach, I do."

Carefully he coated the foot, working bits of the mixture between the stiffening toes.

Tom said, "You old devil, that's what knocked you out. Someone doped your drinking whiskey." Jim said nothing. He leaned against the head of the bunk and regarded Kilowat with measured stare.

Kilowat's mouth formed a black O beneath his great mustache.

"Couldn't be, mister! The bossman gave me the whiskey hisself, right after that derned Goodloe left. They couldn't be nothing in that liquor. What have you done with it?"

"What did Goodloe want, Kilowat?"

A string of oaths came from the hired man. He told how Goodloe had ridden over that morning with his "danged army," about twenty *vaqueros,* armed to the teeth. How he had clattered into the yard while he, Kilowat, had been talking to the boss in the front room. Kroschel had picked up a rifle and stepped out on the front porch to face him. And Goodloe had smiled and said he was bringing a message.

"What happened?"

"This here now message was in an envelope. Kroschel took a look and turned white as a sheet, he did. Then he told Goodloe, dern him, to come in the house, and they went in. After a while the army left, Goodloe with them, and Kroschel came to the back door and yelled for me."

He'd been sitting in his office with his head in his hands when Kilowat entered. Never, said Kilowat, did he see a man so filled with sorrow and despair.

"What did he say?"

"He'll tell you. He said I'd been working pretty hard and he thought I might like a little drink of redeye. And he gave me that jug, he did, so you fellers see it couldn't have had no knockout drops in it. Reckon it was something I et."

JIM ANTHONY STARTED for the door, flinging back a summons for the others to come on. He had a burglar's jimmy with him. At the east side of the house he paused beside the first window and went to work on the shutter.

"Hey," protested Kilowat anxiously, "you ain't got no business breaking in the bossman's house. I tell you he ain't going to like it a bit, I tell you! You, mister, cut it out!"

Grimly Tom pulled him back, for more than a vague premonition was haunting even Tom Gentry. The shutter swung wide. The jimmy was pressed beneath the crack of the locked window, Jim Anthony exerted pressure. The lock snapped. Carefully he raised the window.

"The front," he said. "I'll let you in." He slipped one foot over the sill and entered the house. His delicate sense of smell told him he was in Anna Kroschel's bedroom. There was the aroma of sachet and cleansing cream, face powder, and bath salts. He drew a pencil flashlight from his belt, flipped it on. And, not knowing what he might find, he loaded the short, thin blowgun, and holding it in his mouth as another man might hold a cigarette, opened the door and stepped into the dark hallway.

He knew, then. For no sooner had he shut the bedroom door behind him than he caught the other scents. His nostrils quivered and twitched. He could smell burned paper, he could smell lignite, and he could smell—blood! Noiselessly he went down the hall. For a moment he paused at the first door on his right. Only a heavy drape closed it from the hall. Jim pulled the drape aside, cast in the beam of light. His search was ended. Kroschel was there.

THEN HE WENT to the front door, and using a handkerchief, threw back the heavy bolt, and swung the door wide. He said, to Kilowat, "Can you drive that Model T?"

Kilowat's eyes widened. "Bossman always takes the car," he said. "Don't reckon for a minute he was going to walk anywhere, do you?"

"The car's in the barn, Kilowat, and the key is in it. I saw it. Get to Presidio as quick as you can and get back with the sheriff."

"Sheriff? Presidio? Say, mister, what's wrong?" He started in, but Jim's wide shoulders cut him off. "Why don't you call the sheriff on the phone? And you better let me in there, if something's wrong I'm the one to see about it. I work here!"

Dryly Jim said, "Didn't you see the dangling phone wire when we came in? It's cut. Go on, and get the sheriff; your boss is dead!"

Kilowat breathed hard through his nose. "Dead? Heck, with the house all locked from the inside? Now what do you think of that! Give me some doped whiskey to put me to sleep, locked up the house and kilt hisself!" He took off his battered hat and shook his head mournfully. "Shore hate to tell Miss Anna that happened. Where you reckon she is, anyway?"

"Get the sheriff," snapped Jim, and there was something about the baleful look in his eye and the jut of his jaw that sent Kilowat running for the ancient car.

Jim stood silently where he was, still barring entrance, until the car went sailing westward to disappear over the brow of a hogback, headed for Presidio. "Bring the two bags and come on," said Jim shortly. "Don't touch anything, we'll have to wait for the sheriff. But we can look around."

They went silently into the room Kroschel had used as his office. Jim had noted a Delco system in the barn. Now, still covering his hand with a handkerchief, he turned on the solitary bulb that dangled overhead.

Tom Gentry gasped. Most certainly Kroschel was not a pretty sight, with the entire top of his head blown away, and his head, itself, dangling sideways, lolling on his shoulder, where he sat slumped in the chair before the old-fashioned desk.

A .30-30 Winchester rifle lay on the floor beside him. His right foot was bare, his shoe, with the sock tucked neatly inside it, standing beside the desk. "My God," said Tom, his voice filled with horror. "He put his gun in his mouth and pulled the trigger with the toe! And the gas from the explosion literally blew his head off."

Jim nodded. He was leaning over a portable typewriter that stood on the desk. Tom joined him, and it was the latter who read aloud, "My Darling Anna: We are beaten, my dear, and I simply cannot face ruin and destruction again. You are far stronger, far brainier than your father; I am positive you will come out all right. Forgive me, my dearest dear, for taking this easiest way, a coward's way, I will admit! Your loving father."

Jim snapped, "We've got less than an hour! Where's the bag?"

It stood on the floor at Jim's feet. From it Jim quickly took apparatus, a spirit lamp, what appeared to be an atomizer. "Take that paper out of there with your nails, Tom, and see about latent prints! Use the vapor that disappears as soon as it is cold. You'll find a micro-camera in the bag, I brought everything. Photograph the suicide note minutely, then get me a separate photo of every key of the typewriter, as well as the space bar, in sections. Don't look at me like a fool, get to work!"

Tom got to work. He might be wondering greatly with consuming curiosity just what Jim Anthony expected to find, but he did not ask. Instead he worked! Behind him he heard his mentor padding about the room, but he did not turn his head.

THE BIG FIREPLACE itself gave up its secret to Jim Anthony. He found a piece of burned notepaper, burned to an ash, yet practically intact. A moment later, handling it so carefully that he dared not so much as breathe on it, he deftly placed it between two sheets of transparent plastic. The same black bag gave up what appeared to be a small bull's-eye bedlamp.

This he mounted on a table, pressed a switch. Apparently nothing happened, no gleam of light seemed to come from it. But the ash of the burned paper between the clear plastics took on a translucent, purple glow, and the writing on it became a brilliant, phosphorescent green.

Grimly Jim said, "Goodloe has the girl, Anna Kroschel. Listen to this." He read the message aloud. "Dad, if you want to save me from the very worst, do as Goodloe says. He is far too strong for us, I am fully convinced of that. Please do it, Dad, for my sake. Anna."

Tom quit work for a moment to stare at Jim. "By the Eternal," he said grimly, "he'll pay for it! Why, Jim, can't you see, as soon as Anna gave up and quit, poor kid, her father killed himself! That Goodloe is responsible for this suicide! Just as surely as though he pulled the trigger!"

Jim put the plastic plates into the bag, put the black ray machine away. "We'll keep this to ourselves, Tom. Don't worry about the girl; we'll call on Mr. Goodloe, tonight. You finished?"

"A couple of more keys. What then?"

"I want a photograph of that door, and I want you to work on that bottle as well as Kilowat's bunkhouse. I want whatever prints you can find out there—then wipe them off!"

Jim screwed a special lense onto the camera to photograph the edge of the door, just above the knob itself. The ordinary eye would never have discerned those scratches, but Jim's eyesight was phenomenal. He had noted them when he opened the door to Tom and Kilowat, and now with the aid of a bright white flare, Tom too saw them as he snapped the camera.

"I don't get it," admitted Tom. And Jim, knowing that time was short, sent him scurrying for the bunkhouse to print Kilowat's private belongings.

FOR A FEW seconds Jim stood grimly on the porch, gazing off in the direction Kilowat had gone for help, the direction of the town of Presidio. He shook his head, and his eyes gleamed. Swiftly he reviewed occurrences. Tom, paying $5,000 for an option on this ranch, and being attacked that very night by bandits from across the river. The three telegrams, the last being a frantic appeal for help. The doped whiskey, the locked house, the suicide note—on a typewriter! He shook his head grimly again and took the black bag and the brown briefcase into the big plane behind the barn. He stowed them safely in a locker, left the plane again and started to see how Tom was getting along.

But a big black touring car whirled over the hogback, leaving a cloud of dust behind it like a low lying fog. It wheeled rapidly into the front yard, the door flew open and a man in a wide Stetson hat and cowboy boots slid out. A star was attached to his vest. Jim went to meet him.

The sheriff said, "Howdy, mister. Feller named Kilowat said something was wrong out here. My name's Dobson, Sheriff Joe Dobson."

Jim stuck out a hand, said, "I'm Jim Anthony, sheriff. Come this way."

The sheriff took his hand and grinned. "Jim Anthony! By golly, Mr. Anthony, I read plenty about you. How come you're down here on the border?" They started toward the house.

Jim explained, "My partner, Tom Gentry, paid $5,000 a couple of days ago for an option on the Flying L. We came down to pay some more money and take over. What's the matter?"

Sheriff Dobson had stopped walking and was staring at Jim as though he was crazy. "Buying the Flying L?" he said in amazement. "Why I'd just as lief buy me a chunk of hell, right here next to General Goodloe and all!" He shook his head, and as Jim shrugged, clumped away on his high heels and up onto the porch.

Long minutes later they were joined by Tom Gentry, who wore a cat-that-ate-the-canary look, which told Jim he had been successful in printing the bunkhouse. Jim introduced them.

The sheriff said, "Too bad, ain't it. Poor guy! The Mexes stole him blind, I reckon, ruined him, and he shot himself. Where's his gal?"

Tom and Jim shook their heads.

"Going to be pretty hard on her," said the sheriff lugubriously. "You aim to go on and complete your deal, Mr. Gentry?"

"Why not? Now, more than ever. Anna needs the money."

The sheriff sighed. "Reckon you're right. Well, I'll have to go back for the coroner. Kilowat said the phone was out of order. If he'd been told what you found in here he could have told me and saved a lot of riding back and forth in the dust. You fellers aim to stay here?" They nodded in unison. The sheriff said, "Reckon that's Kilowat driving in now."

But it wasn't Kilowat. Tom saw the man climb out of the car and said, "Oh oh!" Even Sheriff Dobson grimaced.

The sheriff muttered, "Peters, the fat son. Sheriff over in Goodloe County." For it was the same red-faced man who had emptied two six-shooters at the *Thunderbird* from the solitary street of Geetown. He waddled up on the porch to join the trio, shook hands with Dobson as though he had not seen him for years. He took off his hat and mopped the pink skin of his bald head with a bandana handkerchief.

"What are you doing out here, sheriff?" He fumbled in his hip pocket and found a plug of tobacco, bit off a huge chew, his little porcine eyes shifting from one man to another.

"Kroschel killed hisself," said Sheriff Dobson, and gestured over his shoulder with his thumb. Peters grunted, spat, and started into the ranch house. "Reckon you better not touch nothing," warned Sheriff Dobson. "You're out of your jurisdiction, Peters."

For a few seconds they stood there, then as one man went back into the death room. Strangely enough Sheriff Peters was not even looking at the corpse. He was leaning over the fireplace, examining the ash by the aid of a lighted match. "Fellers that do the Dutch," he explained defensively, "pert near allus burn papers beforehand. Sometimes them papers tell just why they kill theirselves."

Dobson said again, "You leave things alone, Peters."

Peters nodded, made washing motions with his hands. Almost casually he said, "You two fellers just flew in a bit ago, didn't you, in a hell of a big airyplane?"

Tom said, "Sure." And grinned.

"Who 'us driving that airyplane, gents?"

Jim said, "I was, sheriff. Why?"

"Well sir," said the piglike sheriff, "reckon I'll just have to arrest you, mister. Arrest you and take you to jail, over in our county. Flying low like that ain't legal, you ought to know that! Why, you endangered the life and limb of I don't know how many peaceful citizens."

"Well now, sheriff," laughed Jim, placing an arm around Tom's shoulders, "I'm pretty sorry. Of course, if you have to take me back, you have to do it, it's your job. Come along out to the plane with me till I get some more clothes and I'll go along right peaceable, I assure you."

Without awaiting an answer he set out for the plane, pulling Tom along beside him. Sheriff Peters trotted along, huffing and puffing. And Jim's fingers, on Tom's shoulder, where the fat sheriff could not see them, were tapping out a message in Morse code. He gave Tom instructions for procedure that night, and laughing greatly over a joke the sheriff could not see, of course, he entered the plane to pick up a sweater, and to change his shoes.

"Shall we go, sheriff?"

The sheriff eyed him suspiciously. There was something about this bubbling laughter he didn't care about. "Come on," he said sourly. "Reckon you won't be laughing this time next week."

CHAPTER VI

NINE POINTS OF THE LAW

IN THE CAR BELONGING to Peters, sheriff of Goodloe County, the two of them set out. Tom Gentry and Sheriff Dobson, from Presidio, watched it scuttle over the rise and around the turn in the highway headed eastward like a fleeing animal. Dobson turned to Tom, said, "Reckon you better come on into town with me, Mr. Gentry, and see what you can do about a writ to get Anthony out on bond. That Goodloe is pretty mean, just for the sake of being mean. That hand-picked judge of his is liable to throw Anthony in the Goodloe bastille and forget about him for a while, and you wouldn't want that. Come on."

"I'll stay here," answered Tom coldly, "and wait for Anna Kroschel. As for Jim, let them throw him in jail, what do I care. He needs a lesson. I told him not to dive that Douglas at those people in Geetown, but no! He had to play around, like a little kid! The jail will do him good." Dobson looked as though he didn't believe it. He spat in the dust, he pushed his big hat further back on his head. His voice sounded disgusted when he spoke. "Reckon we folks down here don't look at friendship like you folks back east." Tom didn't answer. The only thing that proved he had even heard the remark was the slow flush of red that crept out of his collar, up over his neck and freckled face to disappear into his hair.

Dobson continued, a bit harshly. "I got to get the coroner and somebody to help me move Kroschel. You be damned sure you don't touch anything!"

He turned and strode toward his car, climbed in beneath the wheel and the starter roared the engine into life. The tires screamed madly as he wheeled the car in a circle and shot back to the westward toward Presidio.

Tom kicked viciously at the dirt of the yard and spoke aloud. "Me, darn it, always the ramrod! Born years and years too late! Now that sheriff—and he seems like a swell guy—thinks I'm a heel for not making arrangements to spring Jim immediately! If Jim would only open up with me and give me whys, but no! Years and years too late I'm born! I should have been in the Light Brigade at Balaclava,

The quirt encircled the wrist, and she lost her grip on the knife.

charging into the Valley of Death. 'Theirs not to reason why, theirs but to do and die!' That's me, darn it. Ask no questions, just do as I'm told!"

All the time he talked he was bearing toward the barn. Now he walked through it, toward the plane, still grousing, for time had been very short, and Jim had had but little time to tap out a message on Tom's right shoulder. Part of that message had been to the effect that Tom was not to endeavor to get Jim Anthony out of the Goodloe County jail! Though what his mentor and friend expected to discover in a county jail was more than he could see.

He found the black bag and the brown briefcase where they had been safely stowed in the *Thunderbird*, took the few things he needed and went back into the house, where the dead man still sat at the old-fashioned desk. "I don't see," he muttered, still angry because he had looked bad before Sheriff Dobson, "any good in this. The poor guy killed himself, that's plain and apparent. The joint all locked up and bolted from the inside, whiskey with kayo drops in it for old Kilowat." Tom knelt before the dead man and shrugged. "Well, if Jim says to do it, I've got to do it."

Distastefully—for who likes the cold and clammy touch of death?—he raised the bare right foot of Carl Kroschel, and placed it on his own knee. The square of paraffin had been worked into a thin, oily sheet on the way into the house. This, now, he spread carefully over Kroschel's foot, crowded bits of it down between the stiffening toes, brought it over the instep, patting it, kneading it, working it down with his thumbs and forefingers. Removing it, he was doubly careful. Now that thin sheet of paraffin resembled nothing so much as a plaster cast of Kroschel's foot.

Tom unscrewed the cap from a bottle. Attached to the cap was a small brush. With this brush, wet from the bottle's contents, he painted the inner side of the paraffin mold, the side which had touched the dead man's foot. It turned blue, and, holding it to the light he made out the flecks of powder which had been embedded in Kroschel's foot and which had transferred themselves to the paraffin cast. He grunted, observing these specks and flecks, then using a chemical in a small atomizer, he fixed the powder permanently by spraying it.

BACK TO THE plane he went, to put the cast into a small ice-box, where it would harden again and be ready for Jim's inspection. Tom shook his head, wondering why Jim wanted it, when it was so darned obvious that Kroschel had killed himself. The paraffin test only proved it more definitely. There is a loss of gas and powder at the breech of every gun when a shell is fired, and many a criminal has met a just fate because he was not aware that traces of that powder were certain to become embedded in the flesh of the gun hand. Only, Tom reflected, poor Kroschel had pulled the trigger of the gun with his toe, rather than his hand. Poor guy!

Back again to the house Tom hurried, and once more knelt beside the dead man with a pad and fingerprint paper. Minutes later he wiped Kroschel's ten fingers hurriedly with a handkerchief, for he heard a car in the front yard. He slipped the printing material as well as the resultant prints into his pocket, slid out the back door and was in the barn when Kilowat thrust his head out the back door and yelled, "Hey, where's everybody?"

"Be there in a minute," called Tom Gentry in answer, and went back to the plane once again. To the right rear of the rebuilt compartment of the big Douglas, was Jim Anthony's automatic darkroom. Swiftly Tom adjusted the several levers and dials necessary, swiftly he unloaded the micro-camera and thrust the film into the proper slots. The fingerprints he had just taken he also thrust into a slot, and shortly he slammed the door and pressed a concealed button near the floor.

Now that automatic darkroom simply looked like a paneled section of the wall. But Tom knew that returning shortly he would not only have prints of all the pictures he had taken before the sheriff had arrived, but would also have finished pictures of Kroschel's fingerprints.

He found Kilowat standing mournfully in the door of the bunkhouse gazing toward Presidio and the west. "Passed the sheriff," said the oldster, and gulped. "He gave me hell from who laid the chunk. Said if I'd have told him Kroschel committed suicide he'd have brought the coroner or sumpin out with him and saved hisself a trip." He shook his head dolefully. "Reckon I felt too bad to tell him. I shore liked that Kroschel and I don't like telling Anna her pappy's dead." Tom said nothing. "Where's your pardner?"

"In jail by now, over at Goodloe's. Sheriff Peters came over and got him." Rapidly he explained to Kilowat what had happened.

KILOWAT CURSED. "YOU ain't gonna leave him there, be you? By cracky, that Goodloe wouldn't keep a pal of mine in jail very long. He's mean! He'll throw away the key 'fore he ever notifies Federal authorities he's a-holding Mr. Anthony. He's bad, I tell you, damn his dirty black soul!"

But Tom was in no mood to go through the same humiliation he had experienced with the sheriff. He simply shrugged and walked away, to carry out a few more of the instructions Jim had tapped out on his shoulder. By the time Sheriff Dobson and the coroner arrived with a couple of deputies to help, Tom was finished. He had in his pocket a half dozen slugs, dug out of the house itself. Slugs from the guns of the Mexican bandits who had attacked the house the night he was creased and shot through the arm. Again it was a case of Balaclava and the Light Brigade, for Tom had no idea what Jim wanted with those slugs. He'd been told to get them—and Tom, even though he might grouse and grumble a bit, invariably did as he was instructed.

One of the deputies had formerly worked for the phone company, and went right to work on the Kroschel phone while the coroner questioned Kilowat and Tom rather closely. Kilowat told the same story he had told Jim and Tom. How Goodloe had arrived with his army in miniature at his back, how Kroschel had met them with the rifle in his hand, only to invite Goodloe into the house a few seconds later.

"Where was Miss Anna?" queried the coroner. And for a brief second Tom was tempted to speak up, to tell of the burned letter in the fireplace, which Jim had read by means of the black light. But he held his peace.

Kilowat said, "Danged if I know. There's only one old nag, and sometimes she'd take him early in the morning and go for a ride. Reckon she did that this morning, but I can't see where she'd go to stay so long."

Tom told of finding the house locked and bolted from the inside, told of finding Kilowat drugged in the bunkhouse, and Kilowat confirmed the story. The coroner read the suicide note two or three times and shook his head. By now the telephone was in operation and a few minutes later he was talking to Warren Goodloe.

Goodloe seemed shocked and surprised to learn of his neighbor's suicide. "Why," he said, "I was over there myself this morning. He wasn't feeling so good, but if I'd have suspected he contemplated suicide I'd—I'd—well, maybe I could have prevented it."

"What were you doing here, Mr. Goodloe?"

"Business, of course. Kroschel has had some big losses you know, and he's been wanting to sell. About a month ago he approached me, and though I didn't particularly want his place—outside the county and all, you know—I bought an option on it. I was there this morning to take it up, that is to arrange to take it up. That's about all I can tell you, Mr. Coroner. He was planning to move day after tomorrow, I believe he said."

Carefully he dipped each dart in black, viscous fluid.

Sheriff Dobson took the phone. It was evident from the tone of his voice that he did not like the man to whom he spoke. He said, "Look, Goodloe, this is Sheriff Dobson. When did you say you took an option on the Flying L?"

"Just a minute." He was gone but seconds rather than the moment. "I have my option here, sheriff. It's dated July 29th. Why?"

"This, Goodloe. Kroschel was straight as a string! Why did he take $5,000 for another option on August 23rd from Tom Gentry?"

Tom pricked up his ears. This long, tall drink of water of a sheriff was no dumbbell after all!

Goodloe answered a bit sadly. "It's just come to me, sheriff, that perhaps that was one of the reasons Kroschel killed himself. As you say, he was straight as a string, a strictly honorable man, but desperation forces us to many strange byways. He spoke to me of having something lying heavily on his conscience, and I guess that was it. I hate to speak badly of a dead man, dead by his own hand, but I think he was desperate for money. I think he took that $5,000 from Gentry and found he couldn't return it and shot himself!"

"Couldn't return it? I—?"

"I forgot to tell you, he spoke to me of a large debt which he could not possibly pay at the present time unless I took his ranch and paid part in cash."

Slowly the sheriff said, "Maybe you're right, Goodloe. All right, if anything else comes up, I'll get in touch with you. Wonder what he did with the five grand he got from Gentry?"

"Doesn't his daughter know?" The phone was the old-fashioned sort that requires cranking to get the operator. Most such phones are strident and loud, and this one belonged in that category. Everyone in the room could hear both ends of the conversation.

At Goodloe's suave words, Tom fists clenched. For Tom knew where Anna Kroschel was, knew that even as Goodloe spoke so misleadingly into that phone that somewhere on the Boxed G, Anna Kroschel was being held captive.

AFTER THE CORPSE of Kroschel had been loaded into the delivery truck which was to serve as ambulance, the coroner asked Tom curiously what he was going to do. Tom answered, "Maybe that fellow Goodloe is right, but I'll check all the angles. His option may predate mine, but I can't quite believe it. Kroschel was a former army officer on the Continent and honor means a lot to those fellows. I'll stay here until Miss Anna shows up and have a talk with her."

The sheriff narrowed his eyes and nodded. "Don't blame you, knowing Goodloe like I know him. Just don't forget that possession is nine points of the law. Was it me, I'd get Jim Anthony out of jail and bring him here to help me."

"Jim," said Tom stiffly, "can darned well get out himself. He got in, didn't he." He wheeled to the coroner. "There going to be more investigation?"

The coroner shook his head. "This ain't New York, sonny. This is the border. Kroschel's dead. He had reason for suicide, and that's what I'll call it, keeping in mind the knockout drops in the whiskey, the suicide note and the fact that the house was locked tight and bolted from the inside. Nothing else to do."

After they had gone, Kilowat said, "Reckon I'll fix us something to eat, Mr. Gentry. 'Twon't be much, but it'll fill up our bellies. Dang, I wish Miss Anna would come on, I got to see where I stand. Reckon I've lost a job now."

"Can't you stay on and work for Goodloe?"

"That dirty crook and thief? Not Old Kilowat. Me, I like to work for a boss, not for a king, mister!"

CHAPTER VII

STUDENT
OF HOUDINI

SHERIFF PETERS, DRIVING TOWARD the Boxed G in his big car, the road a smoking ribbon beneath the car's white-walled tires, decided this man beside him, Jim Anthony, was the dawgonedest prisoner he ever had. He lay back in the seat and put his queerly shod feet on the dashboard and whistled tunelessly through his teeth, as though he had not a trouble in the world.

"Reckon you'll whistle another tune, mister, time the general gets through with you." There was no answer, only that low, interminable whistling. "Say," the sheriff's curiosity got the better of him, "what kind of shoes are them, anyway? Plenty big, ain't they?"

Jim's whistle ceased, he looked down at his shoes. As a matter of fact they resembled overshoes more than shoes! "Guess you'd call them big, my fat friend. But they're comfortable and I like them. They're called *ordschkla* and they were made specially for me by an old Norwegian shoemaker who never came south of the Arctic Circle in all his ninety-six years."

This, of course, was mere kidding, but Sheriff Peters nodded solemnly and wheeled the car around a bend. The whistling went on. It began to get on his nerves. Now Jim Anthony had a sense of humor, and Jim Anthony despised this fat man instinctively, despised him for the sneak he was. The thin, toneless whistle that issued so innocently from between his teeth was in reality a tone or tune he had learned in India, some years ago, from the greatest of all Indian snake charmers and magicians, Nanda Singh.

The car went slower and slower, it was with visible effort that the fat sheriff held the wheel. His head nodded. Thickly he said, "Dang me, I never was so sleepy in my life!"

But in the next few moments he awakened sharply—for a split second or so, at least. He dragged his left hand from the wheel and slapped at his sun reddened neck, on the side next Jim Anthony.

"Danged mosquitoes!" His voice was that of either a very sleepy, or very drunken man.

Jim watched him closely, and suddenly reached forward and turned the engine off, tugged at the wheel himself and pulled the car to the shoulder of the highway where it came to a stop. Sheriff Peters' head was down on the wheel itself, he was snoring raucously. Jim grinned, eyed the little object in his hand. It was one of the miniature darts which he had prepared aboard the *Thunderbird*.

The quirt slashed directly across her eyes
and, blinded, she went to her knees.

That curious, dull black mixture was a concentrate upon which Jim Anthony had spent an immense amount of time. Almost immediately upon its entrance into the bloodstream of a victim, it induced sleep, yet, oddly enough, not deep and profound slumber. For another of its concentrated ingredients was scopolamine truth serum, the drug used successfully by many police departments throughout Europe

and the States, and also given in maternity cases to induce twilight sleep. The victim, if such he might be called, lingered in a borderland, halfway between the conscious and subconscious, and a skilled questioner could easily elicit truth and nothing but truth from him.

Jim put the little dart back in its place of concealment. He had hardly pricked the fat sheriff's neck and there was still enough of the ebon concentrate on the dart to attend to another.

Jim slid over into the sheriff's place beneath the wheel, moving the heavy, bulky body as if it weighed but a few pounds. This was so that any chance passerby might not be too suspicious, seeing the parked car. Jim leaned over close to the great hairy ear of Goodloe's chosen man, he placed the sensitive fingers of his right hand on the nerve centers at the base of the fat neck.

"How did you know Kroschel was dead? How did you know Kroschel was dead? How did you know Kroschel was dead?"

The red-rimmed lids did not flick open. The fat lower lip trembled and the words were faint, but discernible. "The—general—told—me—."

Jim digested that quickly. How would Goodloe know that Kroschel was dead in his locked house?

"How did the general know? Where did he find out?" He repeated it two or three times.

"The—general—knows—everything—everything. I—don't—know—how!"

Who could have told him? Not Kilowat. Kilowat was full of chloral hydrate, full of kayo drops, and there had been no stalling about it. The man had been completely knocked out. Jim thought swiftly. He knew Goodloe did not want the Flying L sold to Tom Gentry. Logically then, Kroschel stood in his way. Could it be that he had made the price for Anna's release—death for Kroschel himself? In spite of himself Jim shuddered at the thought.

"Where is Anna Kroschel? Where is Anna Kroschel?"

"Somewhere—in—the—house—prisoner—."

And, under Jim's adroit questioning, a bit at a time the fat sheriff, under the influence of Jim's concentrate, revealed how Anna Kroschel had been deliberately trapped and captured that same morning. But there were so many questions which Peters was unable to answer, that it soon became apparent to Jim that the master of the Boxed G was not one to take subordinates into his confidence.

SO, JIM STARTED the car, the sheriff still dozing beside him, and continued toward the feudal kingdom of Warren Goodloe, which was the Boxed G, or Goodloe County. Soon, in the distance Jim saw the heavy steel gate and the grim watch tower, with its armed watchman or sentry, atop. A quick glance at his companion showed that the unfortunate lawman was good for twenty or thirty minutes more in the arms of Morpheus, at least. Jim grinned wryly—or perhaps in anticipation—and sped up to the gate.

The sentry, a whiteclad Mexican with an evil, pockmarked face, looked down the barrel of an automatic rifle at him. "Stop!" he commanded, "and alight. What want you here, and who are you?" His eyes narrowed a bit. "And what do you with the sheriff's car, stranger?"

Jim got out of the car and stretched lazily like a great cat. The black eyes of the sentry continued to watch him with suspicion over the rifle sights. "I have the sheriff's car and the sheriff as well, my friend," acknowledged Jim, and gestured toward the car with his head. For a moment the black, beady eyes left him, stared at the car.

"What is wrong with the fat peeg? Is he drunk?"

Jim shrugged. "That I could not say. He came to the Flying L to arrest me, and on the way back said he was sleepy, and asked me to drive.

"Arrested you, eh? And then he went to sleep." The man with the pocked face leered. "General Goodloe will like that, of a certainty. You must be the man who flew that giant of a silver plane not many hours ago."

"That was me," said Jim, disregarding his grammar. "Now, you will open the gate and let me proceed?"

"Oh, no, my friend. Now I call the house and tell General Goodloe about this fat peeg. We shall see what he says. And do not reenter the car, for I can see you from the phone."

Jim stayed where he was, as directed, trying not to grin, and shortly the sentry was back. "I theenk you will wait, Mister Jeem Anthony. General Goodloe is a bit annoyed. It will be some few moments before he arrives, so you may sit down if you wish."

To his great surprise Jim Anthony did not sit down—he lay down. He stretched out in the shadow cast by the car, with his arms above his head, and he lowered his eyelids over his eyes. Jim Anthony had the same ability possessed by a cat or a dog to relax utterly. Every muscle in his great body went lax and loose and limp, every nerve was without feeling. His chest rose and fell and Jim Anthony was instantly asleep! It was as though he were an automaton and someone had snapped the switch that turned off the electrical current which was his motive power.

But the sound of the approaching car in the distance pierced that sleep. Indeed, he heard it long before the sentry in the tower, though apparently he slept on. He knew that a large car was speeding toward them. He could tell from the motor roar when the wheels hit a soft spot in the road, knew precisely when it topped the hogback and bore down on the watch tower.

It coasted gently down that rise and came soundlessly to a stop near the gate. Jim's phenomenal hearing allowed him to get the soft, "Ssssst! He sleeps! Easy, you dogs. Easy!"

HE KEPT HIS eyes closed as the gate opened softly. He heard the shuffling approach of many pairs of feet and fought back his grin. Then, from that maze of footsteps he picked a man who limped. A man who walked more easily with one foot than with the other. General Warren Goodloe was honoring him with his presence!

By now, suspecting what would happen, Jim had his hands crossed over his chest, the wrists close together. He sensed someone leaning close to him, smelled him, felt the soft touch of his breath. Then there was the touch of cold steel on his wrists, and a click, as a pair of handcuffs snapped into place.

A foot spurned him, a voice said, "Waken, *borracho!* Waken, drunkard!"

He opened his eyes. It was a *peon*, with another rifle, who had spurned him. Past him Jim saw a man in semi-military dress, a heavy gun holstered at his hip, a man who could be none other than Warren Goodloe, the owner of the Boxed G, the man who delighted in being addressed as "general."

Jim grinned, sat upright, glanced with raised brows at his manacled wrists and shrugged. Easily he came to his feet, the rifle in the *peon's* hands covering every move. Jim said, "Do you think these irons are necessary, Goodloe? After all, your sheriff went to sleep and I came on alone—or practically alone!"

"*Silencio!*" snarled the *peon* and rammed the rifle barrel at him viciously. The only trouble was that Jim's stomach was not there when the rifle arrived. The *peon* looked a bit astounded. "You will speak when spoken to, dog!"

Goodloe was watching stonily as two men were getting the sheriff out of the front seat. He was not deep in sleep, though his eyes were closed tightly and his chin and lips were lax. He stumbled across the sand and rocks toward Goodloe, his head down on his chest, and would have fallen had it not been for the two men who supported him.

Goodloe's face was furious, probably more furious because of Jim Anthony's taunting and disrespectful grin. "Peters! Peters!" snapped the master of the Boxed G. "Get your head up, Peters, and talk to me, damn you!"

One of his supporters thrust a rough hand beneath the double chin and raised the head of the sheriff so viciously that his hat fell off. Still the eyes remained closed. The lips moved, "Don't know, don't you see—general tells nothing—knows everything happens—on—border."

They grinned down as the sheriff
cut loose with his six-guns.

Goodloe stared angrily at Jim Anthony. Jim shrugged. "He just asked me to drive, said he'd been up all night and was plenty sleepy, that's all I know."

Instantly he saw the fire of suspicion kindle in Goodloe's eyes, just as he had meant it should. He knew Goodloe was wondering what Sheriff Peters had been doing up all night. But a second later Jim was truly sorry. For Goodloe snarled, "I'll waken the fat fool, damn him!" For the first time Jim noted the heavy quirt that hung at the wrist of the master of the Boxed G.

It whistled viciously through the air, its leaded thongs smacked down across Peters' bald head, leaving red welts oozing blood, and where the lead touched the back of his neck, taking off pieces of skin the size of quarters. Twice more it came down, the last time on Peters' shoulders as he fell to his knees.

"That," said Goodloe grimly, "usually will awaken the dead."

And in fact it had brought the sheriff back to consciousness. He was on his knees before Goodloe, whimpering, his breath making a sobbing sound as it issued from between his lips, his great forearms shielding his face. "Don't, don't, don't hit me!"

"Throw him in his car and put him in solitary in the hole until he sobers up." He whirled on Jim. "And you! I've heard about your sweet tricks! I suppose you gave him a few drinks to try to get him to talk?"

He half raised the quirt. Coldly Jim answered, "Talk? What would he have to talk about? Options? Suicides? Mexican politics? Kidnaping? Or maybe—*murder?*"

THE QUIRT FLASHED upward. But it did not descend. There was something in Jim Anthony's narrowed eyes, something in his lips which had suddenly become a thin red line, something in the white walnuts that were the contracted muscles of his powerful jaw that deterred the descent. The hairy fingers of the master of the Boxed G slowly relaxed, the quirt dangled for a split second from the thong about his wrist, then the raised arm came down, and Goodloe shrugged.

"Sorry," he smiled, though there was no amusement in the smile. "We are pretty law-abiding around here, Mr. Anthony, we try to live up to the letter of the law. You know what the Federal law is concerning low flying, whereby lives are endangered. So I had nothing else to do but send Peters for you."

"Quite all right," acknowledged Jim. "I was a bit exuberant. Shall we—oh oh!" He held out one hand. The manacles, the handcuffs,

"I think you had best obey," said the jailer.

dangled from one wrist only! "Looks like your man didn't lock these, Goodloe!"

Goodloe glared at the *peon* with the rifle, who muttered beneath his breath, and stepping forward, locked the open cuff about Jim's left wrist.

Goodloe said, "I'll have to make a Federal complaint, Mr. Anthony; I'm honor bound. But I suppose you have made arrangements for bond at once, have you not?"

"Nope," answered Jim cheerfully. "I need a rest, and I have not been in jail for a long time, Goodloe. I hope the bunks are soft in Goodloe County's bastille."

Goodloe almost lost his temper again. But he held on. He nodded, growled, "You may change your mind, Anthony. Suppose you get in the car." He turned to the *peon* with the rifle. "Put him in the jail and bring me the key at the house." He nodded politely but grimly at Jim. "I'll see you a little later, Anthony."

And so Jim Anthony entered the last of the feudal kingdoms, passed through the guarded gate into the Boxed G, Goodloe County, where the only law was the whim and wish of Warren Goodloe.

Before the jail, after a twenty minute ride, the car came to a stop. The *peon* opened the door and motioned with the rifle. Jim nodded, stepped out easily, the man with the gun following. The man's eyes widened, he turned pale, noting the shiny something that dangled in Jim's hands.

Jim followed the direction of his gaze, raised his brows in surprise.

When Jim Anthony was a mere lad, the great Houdini, a friend of his father's, had taken a liking to him. Often he had called Jim his most apt pupil. Now Jim said, "Oh, yes. They came off, *amigo*. I'm afraid you ought to get a new pair, these are not very good."

And he handed the handcuffs to the cursing *peon*.

CHAPTER VIII

HOUSE GUEST

JIM ANTHONY LAY FLAT on his back, his hands beneath his head, and stared up at the iron ceiling. The Goodloe County jail, he reflected, was fairly up-to-date considering its age. Evidently it did a good business, and because of this, had been modernized from time to time as the years went by. It was dark outside now, and the only illumination was from a flickering, flyspecked bulb high in the ceiling of the corridor.

They had taken the blubbering, cringing man who once had been the sheriff, Peters, through the corridor, past Jim's cell, and Jim had heard a trap door clang. Evidently the "hole" was just what the name implied—a hole beneath the floor of the jail proper. Jim's conscience didn't hurt him about Peters. Peters was a weakling, a coward, and a dirty fighter, exactly the kind of man who would work for Goodloe, and do his master's bidding without question. Jim hated the lashing the man had received out by the gate, however. There was something about the sound of blows on a defenseless body that set him afire.

A humpbacked Mexican with a black patch over his eye, called Tuerto by the *peon* who had taken the handcuffs from Jim, had run his hands over the body of the prisoner before clapping him in jail. Finding nothing suspicious—Jim had a thousand places of conceal-ment which could not be found by an expert, let alone a border jailer of uncertain intelligence—he had lifted his hump in a shrug, growled, *"Nada!* Nothing." And he gave Jim a shove, evidently very angry that this *gringo* prisoner had nothing of value which a jailer might retain for his own use and benefit. "Not even a dime, *Americano!"* He shoved him again. This time, to his great surprise, it was a great deal like pushing the wall of the building. Instead of the victim moving, the humpbacked jailer went reeling backward from the force of his own push!

He cursed, more so because his friend, the *peon* of the handcuffs, laughed and jeered at him. His eyes boded Jim no good as he unlocked a steel door and conducted him down the corridor to the cell he now occupied.

Now, from outside the jail, Jim's keen ears knew footsteps were approaching. He did not move; except for a slight grin not a muscle of his relaxed body responded, even when he heard the corridor door clang open, heard the shuffling feet of half a dozen men. The jailer glared at him through the bars as he placed a key in the cell door, swung it wide. "Come out, *gringo,"* he growled. "You are to go to the house to see the general."

"Oh, no," answered Jim Anthony. "Tell the general that I like his jail very much and that I am resting easily. Here I remain."

"Look!"

Lazily Jim raised his head. Five men stood outside the door of the jail, and each of the five was training an ugly gun on Jim Anthony.

"I think," said the jailer grimly, "you had best obey. Unless you wish to be killed, while trying to escape!"

Naturally Jim Anthony got the import of that speech. He knew that more than one political prisoner in the Republic south of the Rio Grande had met death in just such a manner—"trying to escape!" And this was a border ranch! Evidently Mexican methods were often used! Also a quick glimpse at the thin lips and the electric eyes of the humpback, convinced Jim that the man would have no scruples concerning the giving of the command, nor would the five gunmen hesitate to shoot at the word!

As the sheriff nodded, Jim slid over behind the wheel.

Consequently he arose.

IT WAS A strange meal, for Goodloe and Graumann were awaiting Jim's coming, and he was treated as an honored guest rather than as a prisoner. Both of them wore military mess jackets, yet Jim, caring nothing whatsoever for clothes, did not feel out of place in his rumpled, wrinkled slacks and the sweat shirt that covered his magnificent torso. After the sumptuous meal, Jim refused the brandy and cigar offered, and the three of them went into the library.

Goodloe seated himself behind the massive desk, picked the quirt from the back of the chair and laid it in plain view on the mahogany surface.

"Anthony," he said, "just what do you know about me?"

Jim's answer was a shrug, that not only said he knew nothing, but implied that he cared less. The eyes beneath the bushy brows narrowed slightly, but with an effort Goodloe kept his temper.

"Since 1710," he said softly, "the Goodloes have ruled this section of the country. After Texan independence, our brand was registered as the Boxed G, but we still lived like kings. Anthony, I am a feudal lord today, in the midst of a democracy!"

Jim nodded, yawned, tapped his lips politely. "And we come to what point, Goodloe?"

"The point is this—in this county, on both sides of the border for more miles than I know myself, *I am the law!* How I have achieved that position in two countries, you may guess. Suffice it to say, neither the American Government nor the Mexican Government touches me, nor wishes to touch me."

"Tag," murmured Jim, and the monocle fell from the left eye of the man named Graumann, who sat in a reversed straight chair facing Jim. Casually Jim glanced at him—and was rewarded by a wink! As if Graumann were saying: "I've heard this maniacal ranting a dozen times, old man. You can put up with it once!"

"This is no time to jest, Anthony!" Goodloe was angry now. He had arisen and the quirt was swinging—*swish-swish-swish-swish* against his trouser leg. "Should we lay the cards flat on the table, face up? Then listen. I sent that fat fool of a Peters after you for a damned good reason. Do you think I care about your flying low over Geetown?" His lips curled. "That was a pretext!"

"To be sure," acknowledged Jim. "But the only way I could learn your real plans was to allow your sheriff to take me on the low flying charge, Goodloe. So far, it's a Mexican standoff."

Goodloe almost choked, his face became choleric. Slowly the red flowed back inside the collar of his soft white shirt, but the quirt against the black trousers swished swifter than ever.

"Killed while trying to escape," he said hoarsely. "And not a court in the country would touch me!"

NOW JIM ANTHONY was no superman. He was normal, he knew the meaning of fear. This man, Goodloe, who faced him, lowering and making his mouth a thin purple line, swishing that whip against his leg, was mad with power. Power to him was like a dope, like morphine, or cocaine, and Jim Anthony realized it. The more power the man obtained—and he was born with plenty!—the more

The engine roared into life, and Tom leaped aside barely in time.

he required to keep going. He knew the man was a psychopathic case, knew he had killed many times before, and would not hesitate to kill again. He was as dangerous as a locoed wolf, and Jim realized the fact.

So, he simply sat and stared at Goodloe, tense and taut and waiting. Finally he said, "Suppose you tell me what you want?"

Goodloe turned to the desk. A moment later he handed Jim a paper, asking, "You have seen Carl Kroschel's signature?" Jim nodded. He had seen it on Tom Gentry's option for the Flying L. Jim unfolded the sheet of paper, found it neatly typewritten, dated July 29th. It was an option on the Flying L, granted by Carl Kroschel to Warren

Goodloe, and the signature, in purple ink, was undoubtedly the same as that affixed to a similar document held by Tom Gentry. Jim refolded it, handed it back.

"Your friend will listen to you, Anthony. I'm a peaceable man, a man who dislikes trouble and goes a long way to dodge it. I know this man Gentry is a fighter, and I do not care to clash with him. Plainly my option predates his, and when I was over there this morning and arranged to have a check for him tomorrow, as additional payment, Kroschel said he was moving out the following day, when I could take over."

Jim interrupted, "Then you think he simply cheated Tom?"

The big man shrugged. "When a man is desperate he will do almost anything, Anthony. Kroschel was desperate. I can beat Gentry in a court of law, you know that, so why have trouble?"

"And you want me to—?"

"Tell him it's useless to fight me! Tell him to get in that plane with you and go back to New York, where you fellows belong." Now he became a bit too anxious. "Do that, give me your word to do that, Anthony, and you go free—now! I take you clear to the Flying L, a free man."

Jim said, "And what happens then? You don't understand how tiresome and boring my life is, Goodloe. Work! Work! Work! I rather like this little jail of yours, and I can rest and relax and sleep without anyone bothering me. Nope, I believe I'll just let you hold me while you're reporting my low-flying to the Federal Commission."

Goodloe's nostrils twitched and quivered, his knuckles whitening on the butt of the quirt.

Jim arose. "Besides, the devil himself couldn't change Tom Gentry's mind. He's worse than a kid, stubborn, set in his ways." He sighed. "Sometimes I get pretty sore at him, and it doesn't help a bit! Now he's made up his mind to be a rancher on the Flying L, and option or no option, I think you'll have a tough time beating him, Goodloe. What with possession being nine points of the law, and the Flying L being out of the county where you are a little king."

He started slowly toward the door, paying no attention to Goodloe's grim-jawed anger, nor the unmistakeable admiration and amusement in Graumann's eyes.

Goodloe snapped, "I'm afraid you'll learn different, Anthony, and perhaps the lesson will prove hard. Chico!"

Jim smiled as he turned, waiting. Casually he remarked, "And your house guest, Miss Anna Kroschel, is feeling fit, Mr. Goodloe?"

Again that choleric red flowed up under the big man's collar, up his wrestler's throat and onto his cheeks. Again the nostrils whitened and flared, and again Goodloe managed to fight down his ire. "She's doing very nicely, Anthony. A bit too stiff and sore to come down to dinner, but otherwise quite well and—shall we say willing?—to co-operate. Perhaps eager is the better word." His smile was demoniac. "Chico, you will return this *gringo* to the hospitality of our jail, and be very careful with him."

And as he walked away from the house toward the jail, the muscles of Jim Anthony's back twitched and crawled, ached and throbbed, for the crack of a gun and the spat of a bullet would not have surprised him in the least. Jim realized the seriousness of this affair, now! He realized that when Goodloe admitted to him that he was holding Anna Kroschel captive, he was telling him that he, Jim Anthony, was not destined to leave the Boxed G, the last feudal kingdom, alive!

CHAPTER IX

ESCAPE!

BEFORE EIGHT O'CLOCK, ON the Flying L, Tom Gentry was reading a newspaper left behind by Sheriff Dobson, and trying to get Anthony and the beautiful Anna Kroschel off his mind. The newspaper only added to his worry, or reminded him of it, for, published in El Paso, it gave in full an interview with General Rafael Guedea, who had been defeated at the polls in the Mexican presidential election more than a month previously, early in July.

Guedea's present location was not disclosed. He had gone swiftly incognito to an El Paso hostelry, called the reporters and given the interview, then departed as mysteriously as he had come.

According to the disappointed warrior, who was a revolutionary war-horse of long standing below the border, he had been gypped, and badly gypped. He was positive he had received more votes than had his opponent. "And in December," he had roared to the newshawks, "when the time comes for the president of our great nation to take the oath of office, it will be I, Rafael Guedea who takes it, rather than that impostor, Rodriguez! The streets and the plazas will resound to the tramp of marching feet, and those who stand against me will die like the dogs they are!"

"And what kind of government will you give Mexico?" he had been asked. "And armies cost money, General Guedea."

"What kind of government? A strong man leading an uneducated people! The Indian and the *mestizo,* they do not know what is good for them! I, Rafael Guedea, will tell them, I will pound culture into them until they are a great people! All differences will be forgotten; there will be one party, and all shall work for the State and the State alone!"

"Isn't that Fascism, general?" he'd been asked.

"Call it what you will! Sick people go to a doctor! The doctor prescribes! Mexico is sick and I, Rafael Guedea, am the attending physician!"

And again he was questioned about this army, its equipment, and the little matter of money necessary to its maintenance.

"That," he said, "is well in hand. Even now—and Rafael Guedea does not lie!—my men are in training fields. I have airplanes from American factories, bombers and pursuit planes alike! I have American guns, the best made! And as for money! Bah! Perhaps the industrialists of the United States back me, who can tell? Perhaps I have other sources!"

After reading the interview, bombastic and mysterious as it was, Tom Gentry had not laughed. He was remembering the information they had received from Gibbons, of the *New York Star* as the big *Thunderbird* bore them to the border. General Rafael Guedea was a bosom friend of Warren Goodloe. Could it, then, he wondered, be Goodloe who was furnishing the money for Guedea's movement? It would be like the owner of the Boxed G, Tom concluded, realizing that the man was power crazy, a megalomaniac! Why, he might even go on into Mexico with the army Guedea claimed he had in training. He might even give up his American citizenship to be a big-shot in Mexico! There was no telling where a yearning for power such as Goodloe possessed might lead a man.

THERE IS NO moon in the world like a border moon. Tom stood peering out the window of the plane's cabin at it, wondering about Jim, wondering about Anna Kroschel. He bit his lips, smacked his clenched left fist into his right palm. Anything could happen! That fellow Goodloe was dangerous—dangerous even to a man as well versed in taking care of himself as was Jim Anthony! If Jim would only let him in on some of his plans occasionally it wouldn't be so hard. But this uncertainty, this confounded waiting! That was the pure hell of it.

Tom opened a drawer in a cabinet, brought out some of the photos he had taken in the ranch house of the Flying L. There was the suicide note, for example, photographed after the vapor had been blown upon it to bring out latent prints. There were prints all right, and Jim was going to be disappointed. For they were undoubtedly the prints of Carl Kroschel himself. Kroschel had rolled that paper into the machine, into the typewriter. The clear fingerprints proved it, and they were the only things visible on that paper except for a couple of smudges near the upper left hand corner, which clearly were not fingerprints at all.

Tom looked at the series of photographs that were the forty-eight keys and the space bar, on the oversized portable typewriter which stood on the dead man's desk. The photos had been blown up by the automatic enlarger, until each key was saucer sized. Tom whistled through his teeth as he observed these pictures, one at a time, starting at the back spacer which was located in the very upper left hand corner of the machine, and which he had numbered, "1". He wondered what Jim Anthony would make from these. For the numbers themselves, the J, the K, the Q, X and Z, all bore clear fingerprints—of Carl Kroschel. A few smudged prints were on the space bar, as well, but most of these were topped or overlapped by the same sort of queer mess that appeared latently on the suicide note. The rest of the keys, with the exception of those five letters mentioned, also bore this odd smear rather than a clear print.

With wrinkled brow Tom put them aside, picked up the photograph of the edge of the front door. Taken under a strong bisecting light, it showed faint scratches, some eight or ten inches lower than the knob. And again Tom wondered what Jim wanted with this.

"HEY, MISTER, HOW do you get in that thing?"

The voice came from the ground outside, and undoubtedly belonged to the ancient Kilowat. Hurriedly Tom replaced the photographs along with the other paraphernalia. Then he hurried to the front of the cabin and swung the door wide. The moonlight bathed Kilowat in silver, he gnawed at one end of his grey, handlebar mustache.

"Mister," he said plaintively, "this place is getting bad, it's giving me the creeps. Be all right with you iffen I take pore Mr. Kroschel's car and drive into Presidio for a while? Buy me a couple of beers, maybe, to settle my nerves?"

"Sure," said Tom, "go right ahead, Kilowat." He flipped off the lights in the cabin, stepped down to the ground and pressed the lever that swung the door to behind him. Without speaking the two men went toward the Model T which sat in the barnyard. "I'll crank her for you," said Tom, and the oldster crawled behind the wheel.

Tom Gentry was not the man that his friend was physically, but at that he was far above average in strength. Tonight, he was thankful for that

Then sentry's eyes were suspicious over the sights of the rifle.

measure of muscular power! For, as he spun the motor of the model T, the engine roared into life and the car leaped forward, directly at Tom Gentry. It would have knocked an ordinary man down, a man less catlike through physical exercises. As it was, Tom leaped aside, and only the fender caught his hip, to send him spinning in the sand.

Then Kilowat was leaning over him, a hundred apologies on his lips, wiping his face with a handkerchief.

Tom got up, limping. He grimaced there in the moonlight. "Go on and drink your beer," he managed. "Next time anybody cranks a car for you be sure you've got your brakes on, old timer!"

Tom watched the Model T pant over the hogback, headed toward Presidio and the foaming brew. Still grimacing he rubbed his hip and limped back to the *Thunderbird*. He never knew whether it was the near accident that broke his resolution or not. But he did know that he was determined to be in on whatever was going on at the Boxed G, where Jim Anthony lay in jail and Anna Kroschel was held captive.

THE *THUNDERBIRD* WAS a huge ship with an incredible wing span. Tom approached the very tail of the rebuilt transport, worked for a few brief seconds at concealed buttons and knobs and levers, and shortly wheeled out of the shadow a black, cigar shaped object not more than ten feet in length. Back he trotted, took more material from the tail, more oddly shaped objects from the interior of the wings themselves. In exactly nine minutes, had some one been timing him, the little autogyro which was the pride and joy of Jim Anthony, was assembled. So small it was that to a layman it would seem incapable of sustaining a man's weight. Yet not only would those thin, horizontal blades shoot the plane straight up into the air, and those twin propellers with the three blades hurl it forward at an incredible speed—not only that, but the autogyro was soundless. For it operated off concentrated and compressed storage batteries and a miniature generator, and thus was soundless in operation.

A moment later Tom wheeled the little ebony job clear of the *Thunderbird*, where the moon beat down on it like a spotlight. It had a queer, unfinished appearance, and when Tom forced himself into the second seat his legs and most of his body were visible.

Visible to the watcher who crouched behind the row of shrub pines which served partially as a wind-brake to the north.

"Madre de Dios," breathed this one who watched, as the little black ship leaped suddenly skyward as though tossed by a medieval catapult. *"Madre de Dios!"*

AT ALMOST THE same time that his friend, Tom Gentry, set off in the autogyro to accomplish his rescue, Jim Anthony decided that sufficient time had passed to allow him to go to work. He sat on the edge of his bunk and stripped down to the yellow swimming trunks which he laughingly called his jumpers, or his work clothes.

The voluminous slacks he wore were next in his hands. At the very waistband his fingers found the metal object no larger than the head of a pin, for which he searched. A sharp tug and the miniature zipper gave some three inches. His fingers found the end of something thin, unbelievably thin, which seemed to come out in answer to his pull like a strip of the thinnest of silken gauze. Another zipper gave on the other side of the trousers, to give up even more of this thin, black material.

Jim worked for brief seconds, there in the darkness of his cell—the humpbacked jailer having sneeringly extinguished the light an hour before—and shortly he appeared like nothing so much as a figure from one of the comic books so pored over by the younger generation. He was Superman and The Shadow and Flash Gordon and the Blue Beetle, all rolled into one, for the thin black material was in reality a suit of tights, closely fitting, which even covered his face. The more like a shadow Jim looked this night, the better satisfied he would be.

But he was not through. He was too thorough to risk an accident. From the hollow heel of one shoe he withdrew a rubbery object like a child's balloon. Quickly he inflated it, felt it with sensitive fingers, and, unsatisfied, put in a bit more air. This he placed at the head of his bunk. He wadded his clothing, wadded a pair of the blankets, arranged them on the cot with care, and covered them all with the last of the three blankets provided by the generous Warren Goodloe for his prisoners.

An ordinary eye would not have seen him move across the cell, so deeply black was he. In his right hand he carried two pieces of steel, short and thin and narrow. One was stiff, the other springy. With these, almost as quickly as another might have used the key, he opened the door to his cell. For a moment he paused, long enough to insert a miniature dart into a blowgun no larger in circumference than a soda straw, and not nearly so long.

Then, softly, softly, like the shadow he so resembled, he slithered down the smelly corridor to the steel door. For a brief second he laid his ear against that thick portal. An ordinary ear might not have detected the sound—but Jim Anthony picked it up. The soft swishing sound of a man crossing the floor of the office or anteroom.

The humpbacked jailer at least was alone, Jim told himself, for there was no growl of conversation, no undercurrent of words. Should he pick this lock, too, and take a chance on overpowering the jailer? That was not Jim's way.

He threw back his head and screamed like a wolf baying at a full moon. The noise echoed and reverberated from the steel walls, seemed to clang and clatter down the corridor only to rush back full blast and bounce against the door!

THERE WAS THE noise of a key in the lock. The humpbacked jailer swung it wide, a flashlight in his hand. Jim was safely hidden

Silently Jim used the blowgun and the jailer slapped at the back of his neck.

behind the door, the blowgun in his mouth, ready for action. The light painted a silver path down the corridor, the jailer came in, the steel door closing behind him and locking automatically. Cursing to himself he moved down the corridor toward the cell where Jim Anthony had been imprisoned.

"Cut out that yelling, damn you," he snarled, as he cast the rays inside the cell.

Jim tensed. Was it time for action? Had his ruse worked?

Puzzled, the jailer peered into the cell. He saw a blanket clad form on the cot, the blanket well up beneath the chin of the sleeper. Evidently it hadn't been that *gringo* Jim Anthony who called! There he was, deep in slumber! Most assuredly he had not called, not that one. Peters, then?

Jim breathed a silent sigh of relief. His inflated mask had worked, he'd fooled the jailer, at least. So far, he told himself, so good. While the humpback was raising the trap door that led to the hole, Jim was tempted to use his springs on the solid steel door, and thus gain the liberty he sought. He decided against it, however, and held himself in check. The other way would be surer, safer, better.

He heard Peters' whining frightened voice pleading, "For the love of God let me out of here! The place is haunted, it's full of rats! I'll do anything Mr.

Goodloe says, anything at all. Tell him that, won't you? Ask him to let me out!"

"I'll tell him nothing," snarled the jailer. "And if you scream like that again I'll put worse than rats down there with you, you fat pig!"

"Scream? I didn't scream! I heard it, the place is haunted, I tell you. Get me out of—!" The fall of the heavy trap door cut off his whining entreaties. The shuffle of the jailer's huaraches preceded by the beam of the flashlight came toward the spot where Jim Anthony crouched against the wall.

A brown hand reached out to place a key in the lock. The light was only dimly reflected from the door back onto the humpback. There was no noise as Jim fired the tiny blowgun. The jailer slapped at the back of his neck, cursed the bugs. The door swung open, he went through, the steel closed behind him.

Jubilantly Jim darted across the corridor. The shot had been difficult, for he did not want the jailer to be able to pick the dart with its chemical covered point from his skin. So he had shot it in such a manner and at such an angle that it left an inch long scratch on the right tendon, at the base of the hair, then caromed off. Jim had even heard its thin metallic *plink* as it hit the wall.

For a moment he stared into the blackness, then as his eyes became accustomed to it, he saw the dart. Picking it up he thrust it back into his ammunition book, and a second later was using his steels on the door. This lock required a bit longer than had the one on his cell, but soon the door swung wide. Grinning beneath his black mask, he looked down at the humpbacked jailer, who sprawled on the floor, breathing raucously through his open mouth.

Jim picked him up, seated him at the ancient desk in the corner and propped his chin on his palm, his elbow on the desk. Then he crouched down in the shadow of that desk and spoke, low but distinctly.

"Where does Goodloe hold the woman captive? Where does Goodloe hold the woman captive? Where does Goodloe hold the woman captive?"

The raucous breathing stopped as Jim's black clad fingers found nerve centers at the back of a hairy neck. "I—am—not—certain," came the muttered answer. "In—the—house—I—have—heard. There—is—an attic—!"

The palm came away from his cheek, his head crashed resound-
ingly against the littered desk. Grinning even more widely Jim arose
to his feet and skittered out the front door of the Goodloe County
jail like the shadow he represented.

CHAPTER X

PLANES
FROM MEXICO

C URIOUSLY, THE TOWN OF GEETOWN was strange-
ly deserted, so deserted that it aroused Jim's suspicions. That
afternoon it had been teeming with life, and also when the *Thunderbird* had flown over the streets had been busy. Now, all stores were
darkened. By following his nose through the blackness of the south
alley, Jim soon discovered the town saloon, and saw, through the open
back door, that a dim light burned within. His sharp eyes made out
a section of the bar, deserted as the town street.

Softly, softly he opened the screen door, slid in, leaped into the
shadow cast by a stack of beer cases and waited. Now, from somewhere
he heard the low murmur of voices, and by listening closely soon
distinguished two talkers, though he could not make out their words.
He crept on his hands and knees past the cases, and soon could see
the body of the saloon proper.

The place was closed, the front door locked and the shades drawn.
Two men, evidently the bartender and a friend, played cards at a table
near the window, a bottle and two glasses at their elbows. The second
man said, "Can't say I blame you a bit, Henry. Goodloe is too bossy,
too danged Big-I and biggety for his britches. Look at tonight! Good
saloon night, you'd have made plenty of money."

The bartender, Henry, grunted dolefully and tossed a card.

"And what happens," continued his friend. "He sends around word
that everything closes at eight sharp and everybody remains indoors.
Like Hitler! Dang his eyes!" He, too, tossed in a card, shifted his chew
and went on talking.

"You aim to try to sell out?"

"Can't sell out lessen he says so. I'm mortgaged to him just like
everybody else. All I can do is make a run for it."

His friend nodded. "Me too. Heck, I owe so much at his danged commissary that I can't ever pay off. And it gets bigger every month, Henry!" He poured himself a stiff drink, tossed it off. "Now what would you say was the idea of tonight?"

"Airyplanes," said Henry, whispering the word and looking mysterious. "Airyplanes from Mexico, like always. Tell you what, all hell is going to break loose around here one of these days! Airyplanes a-flying in in the darkness, and trucks a-rolling out East. Something is going to break loose, I tell you!"

SLOWLY JIM WENT backward to the door and into the alley, knowing now why Geetown was deserted. Because its emperor, Goodloe, had so ordered it! His was the power to do as he wished, and tonight he wanted no prying eyes about. Why? Something to do with planes, airplanes from Mexico.

Always keeping well within the shadows Jim went at a space-eating trot toward the big castle-like dwelling of Warren Goodloe. He did not approach it from the front. Rather he went to the side, where the seemingly smooth wall towered some ten feet above him. A giant *mesquite*, ages old, cast a lace of shadow at this particular spot, and Jim, rubbing his fingers over the surface of the wall soon found what he sought—a crack.

Up he went—like a human fly—until his fingers curled themselves over the very top. As a boy might chin himself, he pulled himself up cautiously. Hunch had served him well. A maze of delicate copper wires made a labyrinth on top of the three foot wall. He knew that a blundering intruder would set off an alarm that would rouse the guards. A bit at a time Jim drew himself upward until his stiffened arms supported his weight and he could see over the wall and into the patio. A bed of flowers followed the wall on the inside. Luck again!

He swung his muscular body like a pendulum, from side to side, his feet coming higher and higher at each swing. At last, gaining momentum, he cleared the wires, shot over the wall and landed like a cat in the flower bed. For long seconds he listened. There was no challenge, he had not been heard. He scurried through the patio, through the fragrance of semi-tropical flowers, past the fountain, and crouched beneath a lighted window. Cautiously he peered within. It was the kitchen. An ancient crone was mopping the red tile floor, muttering to herself as her tired body moved protestingly. The kitchen was clean. Evidently she was the scullion, just finishing up.

Suddenly the little autogyro leaped clear over the big plane.

Another soft light revealed the library, with its immense carved desk, where Warren Goodloe had lounged while he made his proposition to Jim Anthony that evening. The window was barred. Jim grinned behind his black mask as he found his fingers subconsciously testing those bars. He thought: it would be easy to get in and I could go through his papers. But that was not the purpose of this stealthy visit! The purpose, the reason, was the attic— where Anna Kroschel was held prisoner, if the humpbacked jailer's gossip was true.

Jim went in through the back door, gliding past the kitchen entrance while the crone mopped on, never missing a word of her own muttered monologue. Three times within the quiet house Jim paused, and once a mozo whom he recognized as Chico, the majordomo, passed by him so closely Jim could have reached out and touched his ankle.

Strangely enough, he found the stairs to the attic in Warren Goodloe's bedroom. They were hardly more than a ladder, and the trap door above was securely held in place by a pair of bolts and a padlock. Again the twin pieces of steel came into play. The lock yielded. The trap door was on well oiled hinges and made no sound as Jim pushed it up. He slithered into the attic proper, closed the door, closed his eyes tightly for a moment to allow them to become accustomed to the darkness, then opened them.

Only a vagrant moonbeam came in through the window, set high in the wall. By its dim glow Jim saw the cot—and its sleeper. Suddenly she moaned in her sleep, moved her body a bit, and awakened with a tiny scream of pain! Jim's blood ran cold. For, as perception came to his trained eyes, he saw that her back was turned to him.

There was no covering at all, no garment over that back, and it was easy to understand why. It was a mass of dried blood, it was crossed and crisscrossed with welts from a lash wielded by a cruel hand whose identity Jim Anthony knew. Had he not seen that leaded quirt slash downward across the bald pate of Sheriff Peters?

SILENTLY HE CROSSED to her, and again anger raged within him when he saw how cruelly she was lashed to the cot. There was no pity in this power-drunk monster! A rawhide lash tied her arms across her breast, like the letter X, the lash passing over her back, invisible in the blood and red whip marks. She wore torn riding breeches, through which her soft flesh gleamed where thorns—or something worse than thorns?—had left gaping rents. Boots had been jerked from her slender feet; Jim saw them where they had been tossed carelessly against the wall. And another strip of rawhide bound her shapely ankles together, went down over the end of the cot and was secured to a ring in the floor. She was trussed like a fowl for market!

Jim fumbled at his belt as he leaned close to her, a tiny knife, no larger than the half of a toothpick gleamed in the faint glow of moonlight from the high window.

"Do not scream," he whispered, "I am a friend." Her eyes widened, she peered into the darkness about him, directly at him. She was conscious of her leather bonds being severed, yet—

"Where are you, who are you? I cannot see you." Her voice was almost a whimper.

"Jim Anthony," he replied softly, "the friend of Tom Gentry." As if she did not know! She caught her breath, bit her lips at the wave of hot pain flowing through her body when his gentle hands pulled her slowly to a sitting position.

"I knew you'd come," she managed, "either you or—Tom!"

"We'll go out of here now, my dear, just as soon as you can walk."

She leaned over, moaning with the pain of her welted back.

"Goodloe?" he asked. "He whipped you?"

"Damn him, yes!" And Jim's heart sank at the task that lay before him, for he knew he must tell this girl of her dead father.

"Not now, not now," he said miserably to himself as she managed to get to her feet. His arm slid about her shoulder and she winced with pain. "Let your boots stay here, you'd never get into them."

Slowly, slowly, they went toward the trap door. "A moment," he said softly, and dropping to his knees, opened the trap a tiny crack. And his caution was rewarded, for a light burned brightly in the bedroom of Warren Goodloe. Jim heard the clink of a bottle on a glass rim, heard the approving smack of lips. Then Chico, the major-domo, came into view, wiping his mouth on his white sleeve.

He hummed softly beneath his breath as he turned back the stern and severe bed. He disappeared for a brief moment to return with a plain robe of blue flannel and a white stock, which he deposited on the bed.

Jim Anthony's blowgun was in his mouth now, his eyes were narrowed. Any man as close to Warren Goodloe, as Chico must be, could not be too badly treated. Chico brushed absently at the back of his neck, walked across the room again, and once more Jim heard the clink of glass. The man was helping himself to Goodloe's liquor!

SUDDENLY THERE WAS a crash, the sound of a body hitting the floor. Swiftly Jim snatched up the trap, swiftly he descended the ladder, or steep stair. For a few seconds he worked—after first retrieving his dart from Chico's neck—then back up the ladder, to help the girl descend.

Wide-eyed she looked at Chico, snoring in Goodloe's bed, the bottle clasped tightly to his chest. "Goodloe will practically kill him!" she said.

Chuckling, as if able to foresee Chico's acute discomfiture and Goodloe's unrestrained anger, Jim turned away from the sleeper. From a fold in the black tights he took what appeared to be a handkerchief of the same gauzy material. "Too much moonlight for you to run around like that," he said, and shook out the material. To her amazement, yard after yard was disclosed, and he took it by the corners and passed it over her head so that her upper body was completely covered by the sleezy stuff.

A moment later they passed the kitchen, now dark, and stepped out into the patio. Suddenly Jim paused. For his keen ears had heard the sound of approaching planes, not one, but—he counted them, one, two, three, four, and on up to eight! This, then, was what the bartender had meant about "airyplanes" from Mexico. This, then, was the reason Warren Goodloe had commanded his followers to close up shop and stay in their houses that night!

Jim seized the girl's hand and glided through the shadows for the front gate. There was no time to take her over the wall. And besides, considering the condition of her back, most surely she could never span that maze of wires without setting off the alarm. Jim stooped quickly, picked up a handful of gravel.

There was a whiteclad sentry lolling at the front entrance, all right, a rifle in his hand and a revolver strapped to his lean hip. He was smoking a twisted cigarette when Jim first saw him. Jim drew back his arm, threw three or four pieces of gravel over the man's head and far beyond him. The man froze, turned his head in that direction, spat out the cigarette. A few seconds later, however, he relaxed again. Again Jim tossed gravel. This time the man did not hesitate. He was a good sentry. He grasped his rifle with both hands and set out at a skulking dog-trot.

Jim Anthony grasped Anna Kroschel's arm and hurried her through the gate and in the opposite direction. Once safely about the corner he paused to listen again. The planes were approaching very near now, so near, in fact, that the girl heard them herself and looked aloft through the thin material that shielded her features.

"The planes!" she whispered. "The planes from Mexico!"

"What do they bring, Miss Kroschel?"

"I don't know! But once or twice every week they pass over the Flying L, and make a landing here at the Boxed G."

"And the field; is it here?"

"Not half a mile from the house, straight north."

"Do you think you can make it?" And when she was a trifle too long in answering, Jim Anthony swung her into his arms and set off to the northward, trotting along as though he bore no burden at all!

THE LITTLE BLACK autogyro scuttled through the air like a bat, covering the distance from the Flying L to the Boxed G in very few minutes. If the sentry on duty saw it, he made no move, for Tom was flying high, and felt sure anyone observing him would take him for some species of night bird. Nearing the house that was his destination, he dropped lower, hovered above it while he leaned over the side of the gyro and peered downward with a pair of strong night-glasses. Dim light trickled from one or two windows, and the moon beamed down on the rifle of the sentry at the front gate. Nevertheless, Tom assumed that the house was more or less deserted, and was surprised further, in flying over the town proper—Geetown—to note that it too was conspicuous for its darkened windows and lack of loafers on the dark streets.

Back he went, watching the terrain closely for a small clearing, not too far from the house and the town, in which to land the autogyro. While it was true that the miniature machine did not require much room, Tom had his getaway in mind, and wanted more space than was ordinarily required, because, as he told himself, if there was trouble in collecting Jim and the girl, Anna, they might have to take off quickly as an ordinary plane takes off—with a run, rather than a leap into the air. Consequently the little gyro drew farther and farther away from the house.

Twice Tom stopped and hovered, and twice he decided the spot beneath him lacked sufficient space. At last he heaved a sigh of relief. He saw exactly what he wanted, on the flat and level top of a *mesa* or bit of tableland.

He chuckled aloud, said to himself, "Just like a hand-made airfield. Flat as a bedsheet spread on the floor." The gyro came in easily. A hundred feet from the ground Tom turned off the propellers and flipped on the horizontal blades. He settled to the hard packed earth as easily as a bit of down.

He cut all motors, threw one long leg over the side of the fuselage and drew the other up after it, so that he was in a sitting position. What followed happened so suddenly that all he could do was sit blinking and frozen! For, apparently from the four corners of the compass, huge searchlights flipped on to bathe him in blinding light! And a voice, laughing and sneering, came to him over a loud speaker system.

"Good evening, Mr. Tom Gentry," sneered that voice. "We have been expecting you, my dear sir. And I might add that we are quite prepared to welcome you with any welcome you choose. For example, you can step out of the little toy and advance toward the sound of my voice, and do it gently and easily and carefully. Nothing of consequence will happen to you, I assure you. But should you choose to run, or to be otherwise foolish, this machine gun beside me will go into action. There is one to the east and one to the west as well, to enfilade your line of flight. And again I assure you, I shall shoot. For to me you are merely another trespasser!"

FOR A MOMENT Tom sat there, cursing his own stupidity. And wondering if Goodloe were lying when he said he, Tom, had been expected. How could that be? Nuts. It was just his hard luck that made him land on what evidently was a flying field! Just like Tom Gentry, he told himself bitterly, and slid to the ground.

"This way," said the voice, tauntingly, and, straight into the beam of the south light Tom walked, his head down, in order to shield his eyes from the glow. "Stop there," he was commanded, only this time the voice was not amplified. "Thrust out your hands, my friend and would-be neighbor."

Tom obeyed. He was conscious of a Mexican, grinning broadly, then altogether too conscious of the handcuffs that clicked on his wrist.

Goodloe explained to a listener, "We'll keep him here, it does not matter in the least what he may see. Not in the least!"

And Tom's blood ran cold, grasping the significance of the speech.

CHAPTER XI

THE SECRET MINE

WITH A *PEON* ON either side of him as guard, Tom lolled against a low building, heavily camouflaged to any one in the air, he noted, and watched the strange and eerie scene with interest, his fears forgotten. For now the opposite side of the field seemed a row of bright lights, and it was only with difficulty that Tom adjusted his eyes to the brilliance and saw what made those lights. A group of dump trucks, eight of them, by count!

Then Goodloe came limping his way across the flat ground, a quirt swinging in his hand, his heavy body erect and soldier-like in spite of his crippled foot. He paused before his captive, his nostrils quivering, his eyes glowing like coals. "Some day," he said coldly, "you and such fools as that friend of yours, Jim Anthony, will learn to keep your noses out of other people's business." Swish-swish went the quirt against his booted leg, for he was wearing some sort of semi-military uniform.

"Some day," retorted Tom, giving him glare for glare, "you'll learn that you can't get away with things like this. Kidnaping is bad, my friend, and so is murder, and the illegitimate use of power!"

A man approached, the light gleaming on the monocle in his left eye. It was Graumann. "Look, Goodloe, I don't like this. Fling this fellow in your hoosegow, the less he sees, the better for all of us."

Goodloe snapped, "I differ with you. The more he sees the better he will realize the extent of my power, the hopelessness of fighting against me. Afterward—nothing matters—afterward."

He turned back to Tom. "Gentry, where is the option you obtained from Carl Kroschel? You can save yourself and your—ah, friends—a lot of trouble by giving it to me."

Tom grinned like a Cheshire. "It's safe in New York," he lied. "If you've got one dated before mine, what's the difference? Maybe you're afraid yours won't stand up in court?" There was no answer, save the sudden intake of Goodloe's breath, denoting swiftly rising anger. "Because it damned sure is going to get a chance! I don't know why you want the Flying L so badly, but we'll fight you to the last ditch for it, Goodloe!"

Goodloe's temper snapped. The quirt came upward high above his head, poised there. He snarled, "A dog knows but one thing—the lash!" The quirt started its whistling descent. In spite of himself Tom's manacled hands came up to protect his face. But the quirt never hit him!

Instead, it seemed to twitch aside in midair, and, almost faster than the eye could follow, to leap to the right. Unfortunately for Goodloe, the thong was about his wrist. His great body seemed to fly through the air, in the same direction taken by the quirt. And there he was— once the thong snapped—flat on his face on the ground—empty handed.

A couple of *peons,* very frightened at this miracle, helped him to his feet. He glared at Tom. He glared at Graumann, whose open mouth was a black O. A stream of curses issued from between his purple lips. "My quirt," he eventually roared. "I'll lash the dog to death!"

The *peons,* frightened badly, began a half hearted search. Who, they asked one another, with expressive gestures and raised brows, had ever heard of such a miracle as a quirt that flew through the air and almost jerked a man's arm from its socket? But, spurred on by Goodloe's curses, they scurried about like a pair of beagles. There was no quirt to be found!

Crouching behind the cases, Jim
listened in on their conversation.

Shortly Graumann, whose lips were curled in a smile of amusement, snapped, "Forget it, Goodloe. You threw it out of your hand some place or other. Listen! The planes are coming!"

Goodloe called, "Bring me the keys to these manacles, damn you!"

The *peon* with the keys hurried to him, the other gave up the search thankfully. Goodloe unlocked Tom Gentry's handcuffs, jerked him viciously toward a *retama* tree. "I think this will hold you, Gentry," he snarled, and while a gun muzzle poked hard into his back, Goodloe jerked Tom's arms about the trunk of the tree, and snapped the cuffs again on the wrists.

He could not understand why Tom's eyes were shining and why Tom laughed in his face. It was because Tom knew that somewhere in the shadowy background, Jim Anthony was lurking, unnoticed and unseen!

BACK OF A *chaparral* thicket, impenetrable to an ordinary eye, Jim Anthony rocked with laughter. The quirt lay at his feet, but there was no laughter in Anna Kroschel's face as she gazed down at it. Rather horror, and nausea.

"I don't understand how you did it," she faltered. "You ran a few steps out of the thicket into that deep shadow, I saw your arm come back, I saw you jerk, then Goodloe—damn him!—was in the dust!"

"There is no time now," Jim managed through his laughter. "Later I will show you exactly how it was done."

Of course it had been done with the thin, threadlike material wound into Jim's special belt, the buckle of which, containing a spring, served as a reel. This line, no larger than silk thread, was a plastic, worked out in Jim's own laboratory, which possessed a tensile strength which would support a weight many times greater than the weight of a man. When Jim had noted from his place of concealment that Goodloe's anger was growing at Tom's taunts, that instinct inherited from the primitive people of Jim's mother had come into instant being. He had sprung forward, invisible in the deep shadow. His first instinct had been his blowgun, and indeed, it was between his lips, loaded and ready. But he had realized that should Goodloe be rendered unconscious, perhaps part of the evening's routine might be skipped, and he would never know what would have taken place. So, as he had come to a pause in the heavy shadow, already his fingers were reeling off coil after coil of the threadlike plastic. Quickly he had snapped a pair of tiny brass balls to the end of it, and, swinging it about his head like an Argentine gaucho, had let fly at the exact instant the quirt reached the zenith of its parabola. Retribution had swiftly overtaken Mr. Warren Goodloe.

NOW THE SKY was filled with the roar of planes; Jim could make them out as they passed over the face of the moon, and saw they were flying without lights, diving toward the Goodloe landing field. He slid forward again into the deep shadow whence he had cast at the quirt, crouched there, invisible. The first plane came out of the air, to make a perfect landing, and roar across the field. Everyone, including Goodloe, Graumann, and the *peon* guards hurried toward the plane.

Jim seized his opportunity. A silent shadow, he raced toward the field, crouching low, taking advantage of every bit of cover, no matter how small, and keeping the *retama* tree between him and the flying field. Another plane roared down out of the Heavens, closely followed by yet another. Then Jim was working at Tom's cuffs with a small piece of steel.

"Jim! Listen, Jim, I—"

"Never mind, no time!" Now the cuffs snapped open. "Don't move for a minute and listen to me. Anna Kroschel is back of that *chaparral!* Get her, start making for the fence as quickly as possible. If they notice your escape, I'll divert them somehow!"

"Leave the autogyro?"

"Leave it! I want to use it myself. Wait for me at the Flying L, tell Anna of her father's death, and don't trust anyone at all. Dig out the machine gun and keep watch all night, if I don't get back. Now go!"

Tom slipped quickly behind the tree and, doubled over, scurried away toward the *chaparral.* And the shadow that was Jim Anthony faded across the field toward the autogyro just as another pair of planes came out of the sky and landed.

A MOMENT LATER Jim had Gibbons, editor of the *New York Star,* on the radio phone. He snapped, "Listen closely, Gibbons. Get a picture of General Rafael Guedea on the air at once, to the radio-picture machine aboard the *Thunderbird.* Then get in touch with Dolores at once in Los Angeles. Tell her to go to San Antonio immediately, give her Mrs. Warren Goodloe's hotel address and tell her to exert all her charm, to do everything she can do to win Mrs. Goodloe's confidence. I'll get in touch with her later. Got that all straight?"

"Got it," said Gibbons laconically, and might have added more, except that Jim Anthony, not having any time to spare, snapped the phone off and thrust the tiny instrument into its place beneath the dashboard. He slipped from the autogyro, and crouched in its shadow until the last of the planes from Mexico had arrived and rolled to a stop. Then he skulked across the field to the group in the glare of the lights.

EIGHT MEN WEARING flying helmets stood at attention before the monocled Graumann, who spoke to them not in the border dialect of Mexico, but in the purest of Old World Spanish. He used the intimate "thee" and "thou" and "thy" as he addressed each man in turn, congratulating them on their successful flight, in his own name and in the name of our "devoted general and patron, General Goodloe!"

The flyers saluted sharply, eight pairs of heels clicking. And yet Jim could not be sure whether he was imagining it or not, but it seemed to him that more than one pair of eyes sparkled sardonically and more than one mouth twitched in amusement!

For, stiff and erect, jaw set, chest thrown out, General Goodloe, stood in the background, his right hand inside his hastily donned military jacket in a Napoleonesque attitude.

From out of the darkness emerged a Mexican with crossed cartridge bandoliers on his torso, a rifle in his hand. He presented arms, saluted, and, when Graumann turned to him, said, "General Rafael Guedea, sir!"

Up came every right hand in salute. Aviators, Graumann, Goodloe, the entire company saluted the thin man who stepped into the light. He wore the military uniform of Mexico, well tailored to his slimness, with the insignia of a major-general on the collar, and a great row of medals across his left breast.

Jim peered in disbelief—and perhaps, disappointment. For evidently General Rafael Guedea, the man who was willing to bathe Mexico in blood once more, had had an accident. A thin white bandage almost covered his features entirely, so that only his nose and eyes and a bit of his chin were visible.

His voice, strained through the gauze of the bandage, had an odd quality, unrecognizable, as he, too, congratulated the flyers on once more "getting through" and thus striking a blow for freedom! For justice! Obediently the flyers cheered him. Their spokesman stepped forward to reply that all in San Carlos asked but one thing—to serve!

Back in the shadow Jim's keen mind was working overtime. San Carlos! He knew the San Carlos colony, established just a few miles from the Border in Chihuahua by the Mexican government. It was populated by refugees who had fled helter skelter from Spain after Franco's Moors had pushed into Madrid and the People's Front was no more. But why, he asked himself, should these Spanish Loyalists be serving Goodloe and Guedea, who represented Fascism at its fanatical worst? For Loyalist refugees would very likely be Reds! No, it didn't make much sense!

But Jim had no time for conjecture now. At a word of command, the eight dump trucks crawled out onto the field, each sidling up to one of the planes. A chute attachment was fixed, from fuselage to truck. Nearer and nearer crept Jim Anthony, rendered almost invisible by his black garments in spite of the silver moon.

The planes, then, were cargo planes! Something heavy began rattling down the chutes and pouring into each truck. A man entered each plane with a large scoop shovel. And Jim, jaw set, decided he had to risk it.

HE WAITED HIS opportunity, then slithered forward eight or ten feet and fell flat on his face. A few seconds later he repeated the operation. And in a matter of minutes he was back at the little autogyro with a peculiar chunk of rock—or ore—in his hand, which he had lifted from one of the loading chutes.

It was heavy, streaked with peculiar colors. He smelled it, he dug at it with a thumbnail, then tasted that rock. Jim was a good geologist, he knew the field tests for practically all common ore. Mounted on the dashboard of the autogyro was a strip of porcelain. He rubbed the rock across the porcelain, careful that one of the colored streaks made contact with the white surface. If he were right—? And he was! For the ore left a definite, grey-green streak behind!

He turned and stared at the field again, rapidly computing the load carried by each plane! Molybdenum! Where, in the name of all that was holy did these men get such ore? Its worth, in such pure form and in such quantities, was practically inestimable, due to the great demand created for it by the war. Molybdenum, necessary to harden the steel of airplane parts, motors, fuselages! Used to harden steel to make machine tools! Again Jim examined the lump in his hand, and realized that if this were a fair sample, this ore was the richest in the world. And with half the world in flames, half the nations of the world arming, shouting for machine tools and hardened steels! Whew! And the thought came to Jim—where does this go? Is the United States reaping the benefit of this secret mine—for it could be nothing else—or is Goodloe, by hook or crook, getting it out of here and shipping it to a foreign country?

Soon the trucks were loaded, and shortly afterward, they thundered away to the east, directly toward the Big Bend National Park. Could it be, wondered Jim, that they passed through the park and continued on to a Gulf Coast port? For Jim was convinced that Goodloe was not selling that valuable ore to Uncle Sam.

So Jim Anthony altered his plans. He had originally intended to use the autogyro for pursuit of these planes, to see where they went, afterward leaving it on the Flying L and returning to the Goodloe County jail, pretending he had spent the night safely in his cot. But this was more serious now! The fact that that molybdenum ore, invaluable to the United States, was being run across the border and sent into the Big Bend badlands to God knew where, put an entirely different face on the matter. This was not simply a matter of the death of Carl Kroschel and the ownership of the Flying L! This had resolved itself into a national problem of great proportions.

Eight aviators from San Carlos lingered long enough to drink a toast to General Goodloe, and to General Gueda, *the next president of Mexico!* Then, into their planes they clambered, and, to Jim's surprise, the monocled Graumann entered one himself! They took off. And in the noise and confusion of their going, no one noticed the little black autogyro that leaped into the air and headed after them like a sparrow hawk pursuing its prey.

CHAPTER XII

ENTER, THE F.B.I.

FORTUNATELY, JIM ANTHONY WAS prepared—even for this! The eight airplanes broke formation, scattering a bit, yet all holding to the southeast at an easy pace. They had nothing to worry about. Most certainly the U.S. Border Patrol could do nothing, for they were not equipped to halt illegal flyers! And, thought Jim grimly, Goodloe and Graumann were too shrewd to fall into any trap set for them. If planes had been waiting to intercept their ore carriers at the border, their planes would have been held in Mexico! No doubt these smugglers-on-a-large-scale had their own information bureau to tell them of such things.

Jim never lost sight of the plane that carried Graumann. Up he went, until he was some hundred feet above it, where he adjusted his speed to the others, and kept pace with them, a few feet in the lead. Quickly he attached an induction coil to the end of a threadlike wire, hooked on various odd appearing contraptions, clapped a solitary earphone to his left ear and lowered the coil. As it was highly mag-netized, careful manipulation easily laid it on the fuselage of the plane beneath him, where it clung like a leech. The roar of Graumann's plane's motors almost deafened Jim, but by adjusting a few dials, he soon had what he wanted.

Raucous laughter came to him, and the admiring voice of the man who piloted the plane. "La, Herman, you sly dog, never have I seen anything like it! You have the man completely fooled, he is, as the Americans say, eating out of your hand!"

Graumann, too, roared with laughter. "Did you see how he stood, Paco? Like Napoleon at Ratisbon! And General Guedea! He is as great a fool as Goodloe!"

"The Falangist dogs, the Fascist pigs! But tell me, Herman, how do you keep General Guedea from coming to San Carlos to inspect his Foreign Legion, the nucleus of his Revolutionary Army?"

Again Graumann laughed. "I tell him he must do the spectacular! That he must leave it all to me and Goodloe! Guedea's job is to issue bombastic statements, Paco. And I explain to him that when the time comes, he must appear to his people as the Man on the Horseback. I tell him that with his Foreign Legion we can take Torreon, that thousands of fighters will then flock to his banner. I tell him we go on to Saltillo then, that nothing can stand against us, Monterrey next, then down the highway to Mexico City!"

Paco giggled. "The Fascist fool! How much reward do you suppose will be on his head by inauguration time?"

Graumann answered, "Who can say? Already he is outlawed, and carries 50,000 *pesos* head money. In three months, if I can get him to talk enough, it should be ten times that much! And when we turn over the rifles and the machine guns and the planes, most certainly Paco, we shall be the fair haired boys of the northern part of Mexico." He laughed again. "I think Mexico will reward us handsomely, I think the government will then trust us fully, and we can get about our appointed work!"

Paco, troubled, said after a few moments, "But my conscience hurts me concerning this ore, Herman. I realize that we are in need of the money but—"

"But you are afraid it is being used by the enemies of the Soviets? Bah! Listen, it is Goodloe himself who pays us for the ore, Paco. This I learned from that colorless fool of a wife of his! He knows that Big

His leap was flawless,
clearing all the wires.

Bend country well, and he stores that ore in a huge cave, just as we mine it in a huge cave. When the time comes, he expects to make a deal either with the United States or with the Mexican Government—once General Rafael Guedea takes over!"

"Bah!" snorted Paco. "I would like to blow all those Fascist dogs to hell!"

A HUNDRED FEET above them in the autogyro, Jim listened, sick at heart. Jim Anthony was not altogether an idealist, he had seen too much, traveled too widely. Yet treachery always sickened him physically, and, hearing these two discuss their double-cross below him, he felt nauseated. For he got it now, he realized there were wheels within wheels, realized that the power-hungry Goodloe and the bombastic General Guedea were to be victimized by as foul a plot as he had ever heard.

Graumann, just as the other refugees at San Carlos, was a Red! No doubt, after some of the refugees had happened on this rich molybdenum mine, he had approached Goodloe with forged papers to show that he was in sympathy with the Fascist cause in Mexico, which cause was represented by General Rafael Guedea, Goodloe's personal friend. Jim's

"Good evening, Mr. Tom Gentry," the invisible speaker said. "We are waiting for you."

keen mind reconstructed what must have followed. How Graumann had offered to organize his San Carlos friends into a Foreign Legion as a nucleus for General Guedea's army, how he had made a deal to sell this ore to Goodloe, provided Goodloe would furnish planes to get it out of Chihuahua.

Wheels within wheels! Led by the sly Graumann, the rebel general would issue his bombastic statements from hiding, statements meant to anger the legitimate Mexican Government, so that the reward for him would grow larger and larger. Then, at the proper moment, General Guedea, Goodloe, and all the guns and planes they had purchased with Goodloe's money, would be turned up! The rewards would go to Graumann and his group of Spanish refugees.

And, as he had told the flyer, Paco, they would then be trusted friends of the government, their appointed work would be carried out! And Jim had no doubt as to the nature of that work! Propaganda, sabotage, revolution… direct from the Kremlin!

Wheels within wheels! On Jim flew, listening to scraps of conversation below him, his agile mind turning all events over and over. Kroschel, a Czech, must have learned too much of Goodloe's affairs. But now Kroschel was dead. And if Goodloe could get hold of the Flying L, it would serve as a buffer to his own ranch on the west and north, just as the Rio Grande and the wilds of the Big Bend Park served as buffers on the east and south.

SOMETHING TUGGED AT the autogyro, it dipped slightly. The other plane was nosing downward. Jim flipped a switch, shutting off the magnetic power of the induction coil, reeled his instrument in and put it away in its proper place. He hovered for a moment while the plane below went into its dive. Another of the planes dived past him without seeing him. Jim's keen eyes peered earthward as he lowered the gyro by decreasing the speed of the horizontal blades. Soon he made out the squat *adobe* structures that constituted the town of San Carlos, saw the first of the carrier planes land on a flat *mesa* directly south of the town.

Twenty minutes later, the gyro safely concealed, Jim regarded the camouflaged aerodrome with amazement. Amazement, that is, until he remembered that these men, these people now abiding in this squalid North Mexico *pueblo* had gone through the Civil War in Spain, where the art of camouflage had been developed to a new high.

The nine men who came in the planes, accompanied by three or four who had been at the concealed hangar, lost no time in making for the nearest *cantina*, where a table was already laid, as if the proprietor was expecting them. Through the window Jim Anthony watched them, listened to them, and again he was nauseated, for it seemed that every Spaniard was fully aware of the great double-cross their leader, Graumann, was arranging.

Her back was a mass of dried blood, covered with the welts of a lash.

Toasts were drunk to Napoleon Goodloe, amid much laughter. Alexander the Great Guedea was also honored, or dishonored. Another toasted the "Mine Which Enriches Us!" and another went so far as to toast the very burros who "carry our riches!"

Jim Anthony waited no longer. The word "burros" was what he awaited.

NO ONE IN San Carlos saw the black shadow of a man who searched the ground like a hound on a trail. No one saw the black shadow glide down a trail left by the hooves of a hundred burros, leading toward the little river that flowed from the *monte,* west and south of the town. Strangely enough, less than a mile from the town, that little river disappeared into the ground! Rather it flowed *out* of the holes, rather than *into* it, for miles northeast of San Carlos it connected with the sluggish Rio Grande.

There was a Spaniard with a very modern automatic rifle at that hole in the ground from whence trickled the river. He slapped viciously at his neck when the night flying insect bit him. He even cursed, and crooked his fingers to scratch the bite, but before his fingers arrived at his neck, he was very, very sleepy. The rifle dropped from his hand, he sighed and lay down on his side. He did not even see the black shadow that plunged into the hole from whence the river emerged.

Presently Jim Anthony, dripping water, came up out of that same hole. He paused just long enough to remove the cartridges from the sentry's rifle and tuck them away in his waistband. Back he raced, the way he had come. In the town, by careful entry, he managed to get into a full half dozen of the little shacks, unseen and unheard. Emerging from each, he tucked more ammunition into his waistband.

The refugee flyers were yet holding high wassail when the little autogyro leaped soundlessly into the air and headed northeast. Grimly Jim Anthony picked up the powerful radiophone, tuned it to a wavelength he knew. Out upon the ether went his call.

"*Policía Secreta Mexicana! Policía Secreta Mexicana!* Jim Anthony calling! Jim Anthony calling! Mexican Secret Police! Mexican Secret Police! Come in, come in! Jim Anthony calling!"

His answer came in sibilant Spanish; he asked for the lieutenant in charge. Shortly Jim was speaking to the officer. He gave the exact location of the molybdenum mine, told how the Spanish refugees were loading the valuable ore into planes and flying it into the United States.

The lieutenant's voice was grim as he thanked Jim Anthony. Mexico has little liking for those who bite the feeding hand. Jim said, "One favor, lieutenant, and one alone."

"Anything, Jim Anthony, that you may ask. Your services tonight are invaluable."

"Do not take over the town and the mine until around eight tonight." It was then about two in the morning. "Do this for me and it is entirely possible that I may remove General Rafael Guedea from the Mexican political picture!"

"*Ai!* That one! You know then where he is?"

Jim hedged. "I will know where he is by tonight." There was a hint of grimness in his words. "I promise you, if all goes well, General Guedea shall lose all interest in Mexican politics after tonight!"

Minutes later, he broadcast, *"FBI headquarters Washington, FBI headquarters Washington! Jim Anthony calling, Jim Anthony calling!"*

He talked to FBI headquarters for nearly ten minutes, and the man in charge there assured him grimly that with daylight a hundred men would be scouring the Big Bend for the storage cave, the cave where Goodloe was hiding the invaluable molybdenum.

"And you agree," snapped Jim, "to back me in my play? I give you my word to break up the worst border combine this country has known, and to bring a killer to justice!"

"Okay, and thanks, Anthony. And I'll have the men you need at Presidio, as you ask. The signal will be just the lifting of the phone receiver?"

"Right," said Jim, "and when the light flashes on in the switchboard, tell the boys not to spare their horses, we may be needing them badly!"

CHAPTER XIII

THE CUPOLA

NOW JIM ANTHONY HAD the same ability to store energy that the camel has to store water. During his inactive periods he lounged around like the laziest man the world, yet somehow all the time his body was making energy as busily as a munition factory makes shells, and storing it away for future use. Right now he drew upon that store of energy and it served him well. For he worked all through the night at his laboratory bench aboard the *Thunderbird* back at the Flying L ranch.

Tom Gentry managed to stay awake until around three in the morning, but the strain was too great. He dropped on the couch across the compartment and slept the sleep of utter exhaustion.

As Jim worked, his mind touched on many things. One magnificent break had come his way. The girl, Anna Kroschel, had not collapsed into hysteria on learning of her father's death. Tom had not told her, and it was not until Jim Anthony returned from San Carlos that she had learned the truth.

Jim's fingers found nerve centers at the back of his neck.

She had drawn herself up proudly then; her eyes had blazed, she had emitted a stream of Czech which neither man understood. Her dry eyes flashed fire as she said, "He did not commit suicide, not my father! He was no coward, I tell you that! He would face whatever came and fight to the last ditch! He was murdered!"

Tom had put his arms about her and held her close for a moment. He shook his head sorrowfully, murmured something about the bolted doors, something about a paraffin test on a man's bare foot. But surprisingly enough, Jim Anthony had nodded.

"I think you are right, Miss Kroschel," he had said. Then, "You can help me, if you will."

"Anything! Absolutely anything!"

"To begin with, Tom paid your father $5000 for an option on this ranch. What happened to the check?"

"I had to go into Presidio for some supplies the next day, Mr. Anthony. My father did not like banks. I cashed the check and gave him the money. Wasn't it in his desk?"

Jim had not answered that. Hunch and common sense told him that the $5000 was *not* in the dead man's desk! Instead he had asked,

Jim was ready, and let fly at the instant the quirt
reached the zenith of its parabola—

"And among those supplies, Miss Kroschel, there was a bottle of purple ink?"

She had nodded, her eyes wide. "He always used black," she had answered slowly, "but the man at the drugstore made a mistake and gave me purple. Why?"

Nor had he answered that question. "Why didn't this man Kilowat leave when the rest of your help was run off?"

"Because he said he wasn't afraid of Goodloe, and because he liked my father and me. Even though he hasn't been with us but a few months."

the tiny balls caught at the quirt, which, attached to his wrist, he couldn't let go.

And so, shortly, Anna Kroschel, worn out by her ordeal, had retired for the night, leaving the two men in the laboratory of the plane. And the silence had grown deeper than Tom could stand, for Jim was immersed in his work and would not talk. Hence, Tom slept.

JIM ANTHONY WORKED swiftly and precisely with many cartridges dug from the walls of the Flying L ranch house, which had been presumably fired into the *adobe* by Mexican bandits the first night Tom Gentry had spent on the ranch. He lingered long over some short hairs, not more than two inches long, turning the ultra-

The flyers saluted smartly as the thin man stepped forward.

violet ray or black light upon them, examined the impression of a man's teeth even longer, going so far as to make a plaster mold from the wax plate.

Moment after moment, until more than an hour had passed, he spent over the group of photographs that Tom had taken, pictures of typewriters keys, a picture of the suicide note, a picture of faint scratches on the edge of a door. He checked on the paraffin sheet with which Tom had checked Kroschel's foot, and saw that the Czech rancher had, indeed, pulled the trigger of that .30-30 rifle with his toe.

Puzzled momentarily, he fed the photos of the typewriters keys back into the automatic developing machine, and setting the dials at the proper spot, waited impatiently for the fresh prints to emerge, still dripping wet. These were huge enlargements. He studied them for long moments through a powerful reading glass, then tucked them out of sight and smiled like a Cheshire cat! If only the rest worked out!

Behind him a red light glowed on a machine that resembled a typewriter. Quickly he padded to it on his bare feet. Like magic a sheet of paper began unrolling from the machine, carrying the transmitted message sent by Gibbons in New York City. Except for a slight fuzziness it resembled nothing so much as ordinary typing.

"Sorry to be late, had trouble," said the first line.

The second: "Major General Rafael Eufemio Guedea, age forty-one years, height, five feet ten inches, weight one hundred ninety-six pounds, swarthy, paunchy, no identifying scars."

Jim's heart sank, for this information knocked one of his pet theories into a cocked hat!

Now a bit at a time a picture emerged. It showed Rafael Guedea in military uniform, heavy with medals and gold braid. And just as the description had stated, the general had an immense paunch! Indeed, it seemed to Jim, upon close examination, that Guedea's one hundred ninety-six pounds were mostly excess, the result of too much rich living.

And he snapped his fingers, and mentally kicked himself! He closed his eyes and conjured up a vision of the scene he had seen at the Boxed G a few hours previously. *The General Guedea he had seen, with his bandaged face, had not been a fat man at all!*

Two women climbed from the plane
and hurried to the house.

But what was this? More information came from Gibbons. Guedea, it appeared, had enjoyed a fine education, in the United States and Europe as well as in his own country. Guedea was admittedly an irreconcilable Fascist, a friend of Mussolini's. He had even spent some months in Spain with Franco's armies, presumably as an observer. Without doubt, thought Jim, this Guedea is a dangerous man.

Now the signature "30" came out of the machine and Jim flipped it off. He hurried again to the radiophone, called Gibbons.

"Anthony, back aboard the *Thunderbird*," he snapped. "You got through to Dolores okay?"

"Sure. She must be in San Antonio by now."

"Get her again, Gibbons. Tell her to get Mrs. Warren Goodloe aboard a plane sometime today and get her here to the Flying L. This must be done if she has to chloroform her. Tell her I'll take no excuses, and I want her here before evening." He said a curious thing, then, a thing that puzzled Gibbons, but which he was afterward to remember. "A megalomaniac is a psychopathic case. Part of his affliction is the need for an audience."

Before Gibbons could ask what he meant, he clicked up the receiver of the radiophone and went back to his work.

AT DAWN TOM Gentry awakened to find Jim still hard at it. Tom yawned, and disappeared into the shower. Emerging, and dressing, he went to the ranch house to find Anna already getting breakfast.

Her smile was brave. "Good morning," she said, "the food will soon be ready. Is Mr. Anthony awake?"

"You don't know that guy! When he works, he never sleeps. He's still hard at it! Not a bit of use in the world to call him."

Nevertheless when Tom and the ancient Kilowat were at the table eating, she fixed a plate and took it out to the *Thunderbird*, covered by a snowy napkin. Jim Anthony did not even see it! He growled, "Bring me that bottle of purple ink and the empty bottle that held the black. Then you and Tom get together and draw up your deal—he's got the money. Only don't touch that typewriter!"

He didn't mean to be short or rude, he was simply all business when at work. Glimpsing the hurt in her eyes, instinctively he patted her shoulder. "Don't worry, my dear, I think I'm on the right track. I have an idea we'll kill half a dozen birds with one stone. Now run along and bring me what I asked for."

Afterward when she had brought the empty bottle and the fresh bottle of ink, he said, "Oh, yes, Miss Kroschel. A couple of drifters will show up here before very long asking for work. Tell them okedoke, that they've got a job, and send them out to Kilowat to be put to work."

By now she felt a great deal like Tom Gentry—hers not to reason why, hers but to do and die! So she nodded, and went out of the

Thunderbird, leaving him to drag a small black box from a cabinet and connect it with the electrical circuit. She did not know it, of course, but the box was a spectroscope.

THE TWO DRIFTERS came to the ranch house around nine, in a battered wreck of a car. They were typical of the men who drift along the border in search of work, overall-and-jumper-clad, tobacco chewing, speaking with a laconic drawl.

Yessum, they'd been workin' over in New Mexico, but they'd got sorta tired of it and drifted east'rd. If they was sumpin' they could do fer a little gas money they'd be obliged.

She hired them, as instructed, and sent them out to Kilowat with instructions that he put them to work cleaning out the barn. Kilowat scratched his head, said, "Damn me, she's getting tender hearted. Hell, that there barn don't need no cleaning, but if she said clean it, you rannies fly at it!"

The two drifters grinned and went to work. From the corner of his mouth, one said to the other, "Mister, this is luck! Hot damn, don't miss a thing!"

Back in the house Anna Kroschel looked wide-eyed at the stack of greenbacks before her, and slowly signed the bill of sale on the kitchen table with Tom's fountain pen.

"Do you know," she said softly, "why I was so willing to sell to you, Tom Gentry, why I went to such pains?"

He shook his head.

"Because everyone knows you are Jim Anthony's buddy. I knew that if you took the Flying L, that he would come, too. And I knew that with him as a next door neighbor that damnable Goodloe would have to cut out this traffic with Mexico."

Tom blew the smoke of the cigarette through his nostrils, said, "You must hate Goodloe, my dear!"

She winced. "Why shouldn't I hate him? He represents everything despicable in the world to me! Limitless power, an iron fist, and an iron heel! And he killed my father!"

Tom patted her shoulder and shook his head. "Darling, he's bad, there's no doubt of that. But as far as your dad is concerned, let's be fair. Remember the bolted doors."

AROUND FOUR O'CLOCK old Kilowat heard the raucous roar of a plane motor, and scrambled out of his bunkhouse to watch. To

**Right between the man's eyes
a black hole appeared.**

his amazement, the plane was landing in the clearing beside the ranch house! It ran a short distance along the ground, lost speed, turned and taxied back, to come to a stop not fifty feet from the front door.

Two women got out of the plane, which was a speedy cockpit affair. Due to the fact that both wore goggles and helmets, Kilowat recognized neither. Both hurried into the house. The plane's motor roared, it went back the way it had come, headed into the wind for the takeoff, and disappeared in the direction of San Antonio.

Now Kilowat had a large lump of curiosity. He walked openly to the rear of the house, then, changing tactics, let himself noiselessly into the kitchen. He was in time to hear Tom Gentry say, "Golly, Dolores, it's good to see you! Seems like months, instead of just a few days. Jim will probably be finished in a little while. We can't bother him now."

Then, "I'm very glad to know you, Mrs. Goodloe, very happy indeed."

Then the sound of soft crying, as if two women who were friendly were comforting one another. He peeped around the door jamb. Anna Kroschel was holding Mrs. Warren Goodloe in her arms, and vice versa, and both were sobbing softly.

AT ALMOST THE same time Jim Anthony became aware of a slight tapping sound. He listened with close attention, realized that someone was tapping out a message on the side of the *Thunderbird.*

Presently, when it ceased, he tapped out a solitary two letters in reply. The letters were, OK.

The message he had received said, "The cupola of the barn. False walls. Clever job."

THE QUIRT

MINUTES BEFORE EIGHT O'CLOCK that night, a horn blew outside the ranch house door. Jim Anthony, Tom Gentry, Kilowat, the two drifters hired that morning, Anna Kroschel and Dolores Colquitt were playing the Mexican game of *fuente* for matches. Jim pardoned himself and went out into the open.

Two large touring cars filled with men were in the front yard. "Evening, Goodloe," said Jim easily, "I didn't think you'd have nerve enough to come over!"

The rear door of the second car came open, a *peon* with an automatic rifle got out, followed shortly by the bulky figure of Warren Goodloe. Goodloe said, "Why shouldn't I have nerve enough? Are you to be feared? As a matter of fact I came to take you back to jail. You'll be charged in Goodloe County with jailbreak, my fine feathered friend, and I've also complained to the Federal authorities concerning your low flying."

Jim's laugh was not pleasant. "Come in, first, and let's get this Flying L business settled, Goodloe. Afterward, if you want, I'll gladly go back to jail with you."

Goodloe was no coward; he was sure of his position. He snarled, "Come on, Graumann," waited until the man with the monocle joined him, then stumped toward the door held open by Jim Anthony.

Jim said pleasantly enough, "Did you bring Sheriff Peters to take me back?"

Goodloe answered coldly, "Sheriff Peters still stays in the hole, Anthony. Chico keeps him company." His nostrils quivered and flared. He forced a smile. "Perhaps you will explain that Chico-sheriff business to me before I leave?"

"Perhaps," said Jim, "and the miracle of the quirt as well. I suppose you remember Miss Kroschel, gentlemen? And this is my fiancée,

Dolores Colquitt, daughter of the senator. All right, you two boys can breeze along. Kilowat, you stay, as a witness."

Goodloe passed it off well, perhaps because he was prepared. He actually smiled at Anna Kroschel, nodded pleasantly at Dolores, pulled a chair toward the wall and straddled it, his arms across the back. "I haven't much time, you know," he said.

Jim nodded. He picked up a sheet of paper, handed it to the master of the Boxed G. "A bill of sale for the Flying L, from Miss Kroschel to Tom Gentry."

Goodloe did not even glance at it. He sneered, "A waste of time, not worth the paper it was written on. My option, predating his, will stand up in any court. She sold him something that wasn't hers to sell."

"You die hard, don't you, Goodloe?"

"Die?"

Jim nodded. "Should I tell you exactly what transpired, facts that I can prove?"

"It might be interesting fiction, Anthony. Suppose you go ahead."

THERE WAS NO movement in the room now, only a great and frozen tenseness, like the prelude to a storm. The end of Kilowat's handlebar mustache was in his mouth, but he did not gnaw it. Even his jaw muscles were so taut they refused to move.

"Anna!"

Slowly, softly, she began to speak, but as she neared the climax of her story, concerning the happenings of the previous day when she had been taken captive by the *vaqueros* of the Boxed G, her eyes blazed, her voice heightened, her breast rose and fell spasmodically beneath the silk of her sweater.

"—and so I was afraid he'd whip me to death! I wrote the note!"

Jim said, "I have a photograph of the note, Goodloe."

"Oh, no, my friend, you could not have that." The nostrils were white now, quivering like those of a thoroughbred horse, the purple lipped mouth was merely a black slot, the eyes beneath the bushy brows demoniac.

"You saw Kroschel burn it," said Jim softly, and read truth in Goodloe's eyes. "You brought the note yourself, Goodloe, and you told Kroschel what you would do unless he wrote you an option that predated Tom's. And you made him burn the note she had sent! When

Sheriff Peters came to arrest me for low flying, he knew Kroschel was dead! He admitted it to me! You told him, you knew, Goodloe! And you also knew I was here!"

"Bosh! You talk like a madman! You—!"

Graumann winked the monocle from his eye and started polishing it nervously with a black silk handkerchief. Graumann's wrinkled brow and blinking eyes plainly denoted—worry!

"And knowing I was here, knowing something about scientific criminology, Goodloe, you instructed Peters to see to it that the burned ash of that note was ground into powder." Jim leaned forward. "He was too late, Goodloe. I already had the note, it had already been read with the aid of the black light, and now it is photographed. I suppose you've heard of kidnaping?"

Goodloe laughed. "You bore me. I thought we were going to speak of this ranch deal, this so called sale?"

Jim didn't dodge, didn't seem to
notice it when his arm dislodged
the telephone receiver.

"We will." Jim looked from Graumann to Goodloe and back again, his teeth white in his smiling lips. "You forced Kroschel to type out that option, Goodloe, and sign his name. But you overlooked a bet. While the option is dated more than a full month ago, the purple ink with which it was signed, was purchased in Presidio but two days ago. And I can prove it by counting mineral particles with a spectroscope! Laugh that one off. And remember that spectroscopic evidence is admissible in any court in the country; it is adjudged absolutely scientific proof!"

Goodloe's face was white now. Probably, thought Jim, he remembers other papers signed by Kroschel, remembers that Kroschel *did* use black ink as a usual thing!

"I won't argue with you," choked Goodloe. "I'll see you in court. Now, if you'll bring my wife, I'll go home."

Jim nodded. "Certainly, a bit later. She's here, but how did you know it?"

"I know everything that occurs in this section," snarled Goodloe.

"Would you like to see what I used on your sheriff, your jailer, and Chico, your majordomo?"

WITHOUT WAITING FOR an answer he took the small blowgun from the belt of his yellow trunks. He held a dart by the feathered end, said, "Observe the black chemical on the point of my dart, gentlemen? That is a concentrated combination of a nerve paralyzing agent and a chemical known to science as scalpomine, *truth serum.*"

Moving slowly, every eye in the room on his fingers, he inserted the tiny dart into the light tube. "Then," he said softly, "it is a simple matter of marksmanship! Watch!"

He put the tube in his mouth carelessly. And suddenly he whirled and puffed. Graumann said, "Ah!" He clutched at his forehead. The little dart was firmly implanted right between his eyes. The monocle dropped from his hand, the handkerchief followed it. He sighed. Then slowly, slowly, he started collapsing in his chair, only to be caught by Jim Anthony before he hit the floor.

Now Goodloe was on his feet, his mouth open to call his men.

Jim snapped, "One moment, Goodloe! This is something I want you to hear. This man is doublecrossing both you and Rafael Guedea!"

At the sharp, whiplike snap and crack of the words, Goodloe's mouth closed, only to open again. "Double-cross?" he said and shook his head in disbelief.

Jim propped the German back into the chair. To Goodloe he said, "Listen closely, and do not forget the man has a concentrated shot of truth serum coursing through his blood stream. Either he will not answer at all, or he will tell the truth! Listen!"

Now he leaned over the sleeper. "What is your name, what is your name, what is your name?"

The answer was so low as to be scarcely audible. "Feodor Vashilov is my name."

Goodloe stiffened, his eyes went wide. "Where are you from?"

"I am from the Ukraine."

Jim looked at Goodloe, breathed, "No German at all, Goodloe, but a Russian! And he was planning to use you and Guedea. Listen."

"You were in Spain during the Civil War, were you not?"

"I was in Spain. I fought the Fascists."

Now Goodloe's face was red as fire, sparks leaped and crackled from his eyes.

"You are a Communist? A party member?"

"I belong to the OGPU!" The dreaded Russian Secret Police, whose agents were scattered throughout the world!

Never had this concentrated serum worked so perfectly for Jim. A bit at a time he drew the information from Graumann that he desired, how Graumann had come to San Carlos with the other Loyalist refugees, how one of them had discovered the cave which was a source of the richest molybdenum the world had ever known! How, seeking to market it without telling the Mexican government, Graumann had learned of Goodloe and the Boxed G.

"I knew the Fascist fool would be easy," he answered in reply to a question. "And he was!"

WHEN HE HAD finished, given the story entirely, told how at the last moment he intended turning both Goodloe and Guedea over to the government of Mexico, Goodloe greatly resembled a deflated balloon. Jim signaled Dolores with his brows.

A moment later Goodloe looked up and saw his wife at the entrance to the room. He drew back his lips in a snarl.

"Goodloe," said Jim softly, "every thirster after power, every megalomaniac that I ever encountered, absolutely had to have an audience! Because you had beaten her to her knees, because you had quirted the spirit from her, you talked and boasted and bragged to your wife, Nada. Mrs. Goodloe, will you repeat to me your husband's plans for the future? Do not be afraid."

Slowly the words came from her pale lips. "He told me that General Guedea was a fool, a bombastic fool, that after they took over Mexico, he, Warren Goodloe, would do away with Guedea and rule as dictator instead!"

"And he boasted to you of how many guns he had run across the border for his so-called 'Foreign Legion?'"

She nodded. "They are hidden in the same spot from which he gets that ore which is so valuable."

Goodloe said through his rage, "When this is over, my dear wife, I'll flog you to death for this." And to Jim, "A wife cannot testify against her husband!"

Jim smiled. "But FBI men found your cache of molybdenum in the Big Bend brush about four this afternoon. Your guards are in custody and they have admitted to whom the stuff belonged. You may be interested to know as well that Mexican Secret Police, only a few minutes ago, at eight o'clock, to be precise, entered San Carlos and the mine itself. Now, Goodloe, where are your fine plans, you great fool!"

With a roar of rage Goodloe sprang. Jim Anthony did not dodge. He let the big man crash into him, hurtle him back against the old-fashioned phone on the wall. Oddly enough, the receiver was knocked from its hook, and the bell tinkled as his crooked arm hung in the crank momentarily.

For a cripple Goodloe moved amazingly fast. Jim was still sliding sideways when he blew the dart. It caught Goodloe in the heavy jowl, and he went down as if poleaxed.

SUDDENLY A BURST of machine gun fire and a series of yelps seemed to fill the very room.

"Bandidos! Bandidos! The bandits!" The screaming came from the men in Goodloe's two cars. The firing became more intense. And the cars roared into life and roared away.

The firing stopped. Shortly a voice called, "Hello, the house." A voice that spoke with the pure language of Castile rather than with the corrupt border lingo. "Send Graumann out or we attack. Send him out at once!"

Jim whispered, "The boys from San Carlos! The Spanish Reds, the refugees!"

Tom said, "Should we fire on them? There's a Tommy gun at the window in the other room."

Jim laughed. "These are the same bandits, or mock bandits, that attacked the first night, Tommy, my boy. Get the quirt that used to belong to Goodloe and two of those hypos on the shelf above the kitchen stove!"

"Un momentito," he called in Spanish, "One moment, and Graumann speaks to you!"

Quickly he put Goodloe into a chair, hooked the quirt about his wrist again, and spread it across his lap. He leaned over Graumann, injected the contents of one hypodermic into the jugular vein. When Graumann opened his eyes, he saw Jim poised over Goodloe, the second hypo in his hand, saw the quirt across Goodloe's lap.

Swiftly Jim told him what had transpired, how he had admitted his name, and his real purpose in San Carlos. Graumann grew pale. "Outside," continued Jim, "your men, your confederates wait for you, they demand your presence! But we can stand them off until the FBI men arrive from Presidio. You, Graumann, yell out that window and tell your Red pals to get on back to Mexico and await you there!"

"And if I don't?"

"I inject this into Goodloe's jugular and let him work on you with the quirt! You've seen his quirt work, have you not?"

Graumann grew even paler. He reeled to his feet. And just then a burst from the machine gun outside shattered the glass of the window. "Quickly," snapped Jim.

Only his sharp eyes had seen Goodloe twitch.

"*Camaradas! Camaradas!*" Graumann screamed at the window. And swiftly he gave them their instructions, to get back to the border and San Carlos as hurriedly as possible, that all was well with their chief.

For long moments he stared out the window into the moonlight. At last he turned, shrugging. "Gone," he whispered. "Now—?" And he began to laugh. For Jim Anthony no longer had the hypo poised at the jugular of the man he feared. There was no need. For right between Goodloe's bushy brows was a black bullet hole, and red, viscous blood dribbled slowly from it down the bridge of his hawklike nose and onto his cheeks.

Warren Goodloe would never be dictator of Mexico. He was very, very dead.

CHAPTER XV

FINAL PROOF

LATER THE GROUP IN the living room was augmented by a half dozen new arrivals, representing the Mexican Secret Police as well as the United States FBI. Jim had finished telling the whole sordid story.

"These two agents," he said, "can bear witness to all conversation, as they were just outside the window all the time." He gestured toward the two supposed drifters who had been hired as hands that morning.

Kilowat said, "By cracky! And you boys is working for the gov'ment, too? Well, I swan."

"There's just one more thing," said Jim. "Tom, get the photos and the rest of the stuff." And when Tom had returned from the *Thunderbird*, Jim continued. "Carl Kroschel did not commit suicide, gentlemen. He was murdered!"

Dead silence greeted him.

"I think we will all agree that if I can prove the suicide note was typed by the killer, rather than by Kroschel, that we have something?"

Heads nodded gravely. He exhibited his enlarged photographs. "Note the paper itself," he said. "Note that Kroschel really rolled it into the machine himself, but pay careful attention to the queer smudge in the corner. You will see where I have divided that smudge into squares, and counted the pores or holes in each square."

They saw then that a neat figure below each square gave the number.

"Now the typewriter keys, gentlemen. Notice that Kroschel's fingerprints, a bit blurred but assuredly his, are on all the numerals as well as on five of the letters. *Those five letters did not appear in the suicide note!* Now, notice on the other twenty-one letters that the queer smudges found on the paper itself are superimposed on the prints of Kroschel. Does that suggest anything?"

Shortly one of the FBI men looked up from the photos. He nodded. "Someone with a pair of silk gloves adjusted the blank paper in the machine and typed the note. That someone would be the killer!"

"Right! Why the peculiar form of suicide? Here's why. Because Kroschel was hit on the head by the killer. His shoe was removed, his toe pressed to the rifle trigger and the gas as well as the shell literally blew off the top of his head, and thus the swelling from the blow was obliterated."

"Was it Goodloe?"

"Oh, no! Kroschel was killed for the total sum of $5000, which Tom Gentry paid him for an option on the Flying L. Tom!"

Tom laid a stack of bills on the table.

"That's the money. The killer got the money, locked up the house, using a piece of limber wire to bolt the front door. Here is a photo of the scratches left by the wire—and here is the wire!" Tom laid it on the table, beside the money.

"That was it, wasn't it, Kilowat?"

Kilowat's eyes threatened to emerge from their sockets. "How the heck would I know? How would I—"

Jim said levelly, "When we arrived to discover the suicide, yesterday, Kilowat, you were full of knockout drops, which you said had been administered by Kroschel!"

"Durned right. He gimme that there bottle, he did!"

"And on it," snapped Jim, "were the same smudgy marks as were on the typewriter keys and the suicide note. You forgot to take off your silk gloves Kilowat, when you took your first drink of the doped whiskey."

Now the man's eyes were venomous as he glared at Jim Anthony. "Maybe this will interest you! While you were out, I took some hair from that mustache of yours, and an impression of your teeth. You're not as old as you'd like us to believe, Kilowat. Your teeth are those of a man not yet middle aged; your mustache, under the black light, plainly shows dyeing. Further, the two FBI men who posed as drifters, found your cache in the cupola of the barn, my friend, your short wave radio whereby you notified your confederate, Goodloe, of all that transpired here, the money, the wire, and even the gloves!

Tom tossed a pair of black silk gloves on the table.

A strange thing happened then. Kilowat's years seemed to drop away. He straightened, his right hand snapped upward in a military salute.

"I congratulate you, sir!"

"Thank you, general. While it is hardly the proper place to say it, I must congratulate you, as well. At least you were sincere. Any man who would starve himself as you must have done, for a disguise, has a purpose in life." He turned to the Mexican Secret Police. "Gentlemen, San Carlos is well in hand?"

"San Carlos is well in hand, *Señor* Anthony. Thanks to you."

Jim nodded. An FBI man said grimly, "And the molybdenum cached in the Big Bend cave will be restored to the Mexican Government, Mr. Anthony."

Jim turned again to the police from south of the border. Oddly enough, there was sorrow in his voice. "Gentlemen, I give you General Rafael Eufemio Guedea!" He gestured toward Kilowat, who had posed as a doddering man of all work on the Flying L.

The clicking sound was Kilowat's heels as he saluted. He said, "Gentlemen, let us go."

And they went out into the silver of the moonlight.

Jim Anthony was a very tired man. He took a *serape* from the divan, spread it over the dead Goodloe. "Tom, call Presidio and tell Sheriff Dobson to bring the coroner. The Man Who Would Be King has accomplished the best act of his life—by dying!"

THE TEPEE

WHERE SUPER-DETECTIVE READERS CAN GET TOGETHER

Month by month Jim Anthony has added steadily to his host of splendid friends, friends who express their loyalty by never missing an issue as well as by their inspiring letters of criticism and approbation.

Here's what one reader says:

Editor *Super-Detective:*

Tommy and I—Tommy's the boy I run around with—have read all your stories and they were all very good and exciting. But we both thought "Bloated Death" was the best. We like woodcraft and all the tricks Jim Anthony did in the woods. We tried some of Jim's stunts and when the other boys asked what we were doing we told them to read *Super-Detective* and find out! We read other books but we like yours the best and would rather be Jim Anthony than anybody else.

We would like to hear from other boys who feel the same way. If anybody would like to write,

my address is 270 South Berkeley, Pasadena, Calif.

I always look forward to the next issue and wait for the day it comes on the newsstands. Here's to Jim Anthony—a real American!

Lyle Nelson
270 So. Berkeley
Pasadena, Calif.

Have *you* any suggestions for making *Super-Detective* a better magazine? Write us about them. We want this to be your magazine—publish the kind of story you like to read. We will pay two dollars each to the author of every letter we use in this department. It isn't necessary to praise Jim Anthony. If you like him—swell! If you don't—and can tell us why in an interesting letter—we will be glad to print what you have to say—and pay you. How about it?

www.ingramcontent.com/pod-product-compliance
Lightning Source LLC
Chambersburg PA
CBHW051133030726
47504CB00004B/848